THE AUTHO

Edward Frederic Benson was born at Wellington College, Berkshire in 1867. He was one of an extraordinary family. His father Edward White Benson – first headmaster of Wellington – later became Bishop at Lincoln, at Truro, and Archbishop of Canterbury. His mother, Mary Sidgwick, was described by Gladstone as 'the cleverest woman in Europe'. Two children died young but the other four, bachelors all, achieved distinction: Arthur Christopher as Master of Magdalene College, Cambridge and a prolific author; Maggie as an amateur egyptologist; Robert Hugh as a Catholic priest and propagandist novelist; and Fred.

Like his brothers and sisters, Fred was a precocious scribbler. He was still a student at Cambridge when he published his first book, *Sketches from Marlborough*. His first novel *Dodo* was published in 1893 to great success. Thereafter he devoted himself to writing, playing sports, watching birds, and gadding about. He mixed with the best and brightest of his day: Margot Asquith, Marie Corelli, his mother's friend Ethel Smyth and many other notables found their eccentricities exposed in the shrewd, hilarious world of his fiction.

Around 1918, E. F. Benson moved to Rye, Sussex. He was inaugurated mayor of the town in 1934. There in his garden room, the collie Taffy beside him, Benson wrote many of his comical novels, his sentimental fiction, ghost stories, informal biographies, and reminiscences like *As We Were* (1930) – almost eighty books in all. Ten days before his death on 29 February 1940, E. F. Benson delivered to his publisher a last autobiography, *Final Edition*.

The Hogarth Press also publishes *Mrs Ames. Secret Lives* and *As We Are* follow in 1985.

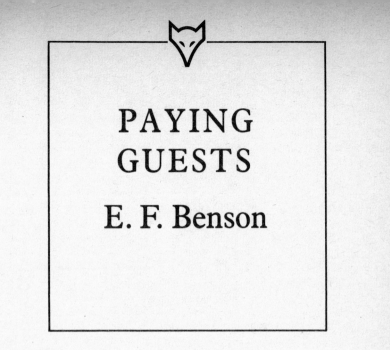

PAYING GUESTS

E. F. Benson

New Introduction by
Stephen Pile

THE HOGARTH PRESS
LONDON

Published in 1984 by
The Hogarth Press
40 William IV Street, London WC2N 4DF

First published in Great Britain by Hutchinson 1929
Hogarth edition offset from original Hutchinson edition
Fourth impression July 1985
Copyright the Executors of the Estate of the Revd K.S.P. McDowall
Introduction copyright © Stephen Pile 1984

British Library Cataloguing in Publication Data
Benson, E.F.
Paying guests.
I. Title
823'.912[F]   PR6003.E66
ISBN 0-7012-1902-5

This book has been published with subsidy from
the Arts Council of Great Britain

Printed in Great Britain by
Cox & Wyman Ltd
Reading, Berkshire

INTRODUCTION

Before we get Deep and Analytical about this book let us be clear that E. F. Benson is one of our finest humorists and *Paying Guests* is a hoot from start to finish. Why Fred (as his family called him) has been so absurdly neglected since his death in 1940 is beyond comprehension.

In the beginning Benson was a success because the facts are mildly shocking. Here was the son of Queen Victoria's stern, unsmiling Archbishop of Canterbury writing a stream of witty, camp and distinctly bitchy novels that are unepiscopal to say the least. While father wrote the life of St Cyprian and brothers Hugh and Arthur gave way to works of Victorian piety, Fred mocked all human behaviour with an eye so unforgiving that he has a strong claim to being the most cynical novelist in the English language.

His first major work was *Dodo,* in 1893, which tells of a beautiful siren who is equipped with everything except a heart. And so, early in his career, Benson found his main theme: the appalling deeds of unpleasant women who tend to rule silly men. But it was years before the comic misogynist found the right voice in which to convey it all: that English, matronly tone which only Arthur Marshall begins to inherit, although in a far, far sweeter way.

The following passage will give the flavour of things: although she is forty, Benson tells us that his heroine, Miss Alice Howard,

hardly ever walked, but tripped. She warbled little snatches of song when she thought that anyone might be within hearing in order to refresh them with her maidenly brightness, and sat on the hearth rug in front of the fire, even though there was a far more comfortable seat ready. It was not that she felt any profound passion for tripping, warbling and squatting, but from constantly telling herself that she was barely out of her teens she had got to believe in her girlishness and behaved accordingly.

We are in a world where appearance is all: the characters set themselves up as something they are not and Benson, with a delight that borders on malice, duly flattens them.

Like his Mapp and Lucia novels, *Paying Guests* shows the Benson style in its fully matured form. As ever, we are in a small English community (this time a guest house in Bolton Spa) populated with a range of the severely dotty creatures who evidently passed for normal in provincial England circa 1920. There is Mrs Bliss, who believes that all illness can be cured by Mind, despite herself having a rather serious limp that regular hypocritical visits to the health spa cannot heal. There is Colonel Chase, who prides himself on his 'magnificent robustness' and is forever cycling across the morning landscape with a pedometer attached to his foot, breaking records ('This, he felt, was a source of admiring envy to the crippled and encouraged them to regain their lost activity'). And, of course, there is Miss Howard who is 'a sort of incarnation of all the Muses. She painted, she sang and played, she danced to the strains of the gramophone with any sound pair of legs among the guests, or, if there happened to be none, she was quite willing to execute a pas seul in the lounge after dinner, which Mrs Oxney, who always said the agreeable thing, considered equal to the best Russian dancing.' The demented cast list goes on.

The plot goes hither and thither through the rural scene via art show, concert and bridge game. It is a charming world of bygone British certainty where retired majors and nosy spinsters take tea, complain about strikes, dress for dinner and bitch, bitch, bitch. For beneath this gentle, jam-making veneer of English civilization it is Benson's distinctive vision to find a seething universe of 'lies and swank', to quote the Colonel. And here we must get Deep and Analytical because, for all his frivolity, Fred is writing on a theme not unknown to Milton: the nature of truth and goodness.

Behind this apparently artless romp lies great artifice.

The first people we meet are the widowed sisters who run Wentworth, a superior guest house: the saccharine Mrs Oxney who sees the good point in absolutely everyone and Amy Bertram who does the exact opposite. And so Benson has set up his framework of good and bad behaviour into which he places variations along the scale. (Colonel Chase, for example, is 'a thoroughly good-natured fellow: people had only to make themselves pleasant to him and give him his way on every occasion and he was as jolly as possible with them.')

The central message of the novel is delivered in the vicar's sermon: ' "If, dear friends, we all invariably acted on our noble rather than our baser impulses, the world would be a very different place." There was scarcely anyone in his congregation who grasped the tremendous truth that lurked in these simple words.' (Characteristically, Benson then informs us that the vicar postpones his sick visiting to have lunch with a button millionaire.) Throughout the book everyone behaves with the basest possible motive.

All Benson's characters are totally self-centred, deluded and free from any vestige of self-criticism. Miss Howard is convinced that she is an artist of genius, even though she cannot paint fog without running the masterpiece under a tap. Mr Kemp is sicker than anyone has ever been sick before and lives only to tell you about it (and to tyrannize his downtrodden daughter, Florence, whom he 'allows' to wait on him hand and foot). Colonel Chase is always right and, of course, fitness incarnate.

In this Benson not only has an immediate comic device (in the joy of people always reacting how one expects them to), but also a moral attitude: we are all deluded about ourselves. And we all define ourselves in terms of what we fondly imagine is our most impressive feature. The concert ('Pianoforte solo – improvisations – by Miss Alice Howard') tells a sad truth about the self-obsession of us all: 'Miss Howard let them have it, very slowly and with great feeling, accentuating the melody. She gazed thoughtfully at the ceiling and all her audience gazed thoughtfully at other inappropriate spots.' But were they appreciating Miss Howard's memorised improvisation? They were not.

A perfect gale of sighs succeeded the last note and a subdued chorus of "Thank you, Miss Howard". Mrs Bertram had determined to get some more coke in at any cost, Mrs Holders had calculated that Slam (the bridge columnist) would have plenty of time to answer her enquiry in next Sunday's issue, Mrs Oxney had regretted that her late husband had sold his shares in Bolton Electric Company, and Mr Kemp had lifted his leg quite high and found that it certainly moved more easily.

It is the main task in life of a Benson character to take the mote out of his brother's eye, while polishing the beam in his own. In order to create the impression that they are better, grander, richer and generally more admirable than is actually the case, they lie at all times and in all places. It is their first and last reaction. Telling the truth would only occur to them if they had been found out. Miss Howard pretends that she has an ancestral home in Kent. And although Colonel Chase 'invariably professed never to glance at a crossword puzzle, his quiet work at it in his room before dinner often enabled him to help with some wonderful extempore solution.' He even lies about having to visit the dentist with toothache, claiming that he has a pressing engagement in London.

In this world of rampant self-love romance does not flourish. There is little passion between men and women (Benson was a realist) and Colonel Chase is classic among his lovers: 'On the whole, he was very much pleased with Miss Howard and when, in his more romantic moments, she appeared to unusual advantage against a dark wall (a rather favourite position of hers) he wondered if he might be more comfortable with an establishment of his own, and a presentable middle-aged woman to look after him and bear his name. Her occasional allusions to a place in Kent were also interesting.' But if the Colonel ever did get washed away in this tide of feeling 'it must be distinctly understood that she must not play the piano except in some remote room.'

The only hint of strong feelings in this novel (apart from the Colonel's devotion to his pedometer) occurs between two women. It is an understandable, if blushing development, since Benson himself, all his brothers and sisters, and even his venerable mother, the Archbishop's wife, were, according to their biographers, more or less homosexual when they were anything. This underlies the clearly subversive quality in Benson's attitude to marriage. Certainly, the relationship between Miss Howard and the newly-liberated Florence is the only one based upon any sort of truth-telling.

But elsewhere, far from loving, Benson's characters do not even like each other. Faced with the cycling boasts of her suitor, Colonel Chase, Miss Howard 'sometimes wished he would ride away for hundreds of miles in a straight line and never come back'. And what is more, Benson does not like them very much either. A god-like narrator, he brings them on mainly to damn, and I cannot think of an author who is consistently less charitable towards his creations: Miss Howard is 'pathetic', Colonel Chase is 'fatuous', and Mrs Oxney who sees good in everyone 'an imbecile'. He sees through every character's motive and can bitch all of them off the page.

As for the Benson plot, it is the mighty matter of unravelling that tangled web of deceit spun by his characters until everyone knows the truth about everyone else. In this book every lie is found out and every deception is uncovered, except one. It is a significant omission. Throughout Mrs Holders and Tim Bullingdon have been the mocking outsiders who see the others for what they are: smug, self-satisfied, self-deceiving bores. ('Colonel Chase had again that horrid sense of uncertainty as to whether Mrs Holders was not in some abstruse manner poking fun at him, but, as usual, the notion seemed incredible.')

In *Paying Guests* they come to represent telling the truth and that tough, unsentimental goodness which seeks neither reward nor admiration. It is 164 pages before any character faces the truth about him- or herself, and this honour eventually falls to Miss Howard, whose art exhibition has not provoked a single sale. 'I've got to face the fact that nobody wants to see my pictures or buy them.' Amidst this indifference Mrs Holders attends the exhibition: 'My word, what rubbish, isn't it, Tim? She can't paint ... What a fool the woman is to think they could sell. But rather pathetic: all that trouble, not to mention the frames. I hate middle-aged spinsters being disappointed because they've nothing to look forward to. Tim, I think we shall be obliged to buy some.' And so under assumed names they buy four and start an avalanche of copycat enthusiasm. The rest of the novel is a model of Christianity not working, in which the characters freely commit all seven deadly sins, except lust for which they have neither the energy nor the inclination since it involves touching people, which in itself is intrinsically un-English. And here suddenly is a good deed – done towards a person they don't even like – which stands out like a solitary Alp.

As the tale moves to its conclusion we begin to see why the church was eventually won round to Benson's work. By the end of his life he was no longer considered the risqué offspring of Lambeth Palace. He had an OBE for services to literature, a fellowship at Magdalene College, Cambridge. He was also mayor of Rye in Sussex, the town upon which his imaginary locations are based. The wheel came full circle when an Anglican dean, the Very Reverend H. L. R. Sheppard, wrote in his praise: 'I wonder why people who say their prayers don't thank God for aspirin, Phillip's patent soles, E. F. Benson, Jane Austen and Charlie Chaplin, and other soul-filling things ... It does seem so silly that we should be expected to thank God because three coloured lads from Wanganui have been confirmed and not for real matters for rejoicing such as I have mentioned above.'

Perhaps he realized that in his light-hearted mocking of the vanity of human wishes Fred was not that far removed from the ultimate values of his father, the Archbishop, after all.

Stephen Pile, London 1983

Paying Guests

CHAPTER I

BOLTON SPA, justly famous for the infamous savour
of the waters which so magically get rid of painful
deposits in the joints and muscles of the lame and the
halt. and for the remedial rasp of its saline baths in
which the same patients are pickled daily to their
great relief, had been crammed all the summer, and
the proprietors of its hotels and boarding houses had
been proving that for them at least rheumatism and
its kindred afflictions had a silver if not a golden lining.
Never had Wentworth and Balmoral and Blenheim and
Belvoir entertained so continuous a complement of
paying guests, and even now, though the year had
wheeled into mid-October, and the full season was
long past, Mrs. Oxney was still booking rooms for
fresh arrivals at Wentworth during the next two
months. In fact she did not know when she would get
off on her holiday, and as long as this prosperous
tide continued to flow, she cared very little whether
she got off at all. Though she did not want money,
she liked it, and though she liked a holiday, she did
not want it.

The existence, or rather the names, of Balmoral,
Blenheim and Belvoir was a slight but standing grievance with Mrs. Oxney, the sort of grievance which
occasionally kept her awake for half an hour should
it perch in her drowsy consciousness as she composed

herself to sleep and begin pecking at her mind. ' For naturally,' so she thought to herself in these infrequent vigils, ' if a lady or gentleman was thinking of coming to Bolton Spa, and wanted comfort and, I may say, luxury when they are taking their cure, they would look at the Baths Guide-book, and imagine that Balmoral and Blenheim and Belvoir and Wentworth were all much of a muchness. And then if they chose any of the others they would find themselves in a wretched little gimcrack semi-detached villa down in the hollow, with only one bathroom and that charged extra, and the enamel all off, and cold supper on Sunday and nobody dressing for dinner. Not that it's illegal to call yourself Balmoral, far from it ; for there is nothing to prevent you calling your house " Boiled Rabbit " or " Castor Oil," but those who haven't got big houses ought to have enough proper feeling not to mis-call them by big names.'

Mrs. Oxney's grievance was as well founded as most little vexations of the kind, for certainly Wentworth was a very different class of house from Balmoral and Blenheim and Belvoir, which, though it might possibly be libellous to call them gimcrack, could not be described as other than semi-detached. There could not be any divergence of opinion over that point or over the singleness of their bathrooms and the cold supper on Sunday. Wentworth, on the other hand, was so entirely and magnificently detached that nobody would dream of calling it detached at all : you might as well call a ship at sea detached. The nearest house to it was at least a hundred yards away, and on all sides but one more like a quarter of a mile, and the whole of that territory was ' grounds.' It had gardens (kitchen and flower) it had tennis courts (hard and soft) a croquet-lawn (hard or soft according to the state of the weather) and a large field in which Colonel Chase had induced Mrs. Oxney to make five widely sundered putting-greens, one in each corner and one in the middle, like the five of diamonds. The variety of holes therefore was immense, for you could play from any one hole to any other hole, and thus make a round of twenty holes, a total unrivalled by any championship course, which, so the Colonel told Mrs. Oxney, had never more than eighteen. As for bathrooms, Wentworth already had twice as many as any of the semi-detached villas with those magnificent but deceptive names, and Mrs. Oxney was intending to put in a third, while in contrast with their paltry cold supper on Sunday, the guests at Wentworth enjoyed on that day a dinner of peculiar profusion and delicacy, for there was a savoury as well as a sweet, and dessert. All these points of superiority made it a bitter thought that visitors could be so ill-informed as to class Wentworth with establishments of similar title.

But throughout this summer Mrs. Oxney had seldom brooded over this possible misconception, for, as she was saying to her sister as they sat out under the cedar by the croquet-lawn, she asked nothing more than to have Wentworth permanently full. She was a tall grey-haired woman, who, as a girl, with a mop of black hair, a quick beady eye, and a long nose had been remarkably like a crow. But now the black hair had turned a most becoming grey, the beady eye was alive with kindliness, and the long nose was rendered less beak-like by the filling out of her face. From her mouth, when she talked to her guests came a perennial stream of tactful observations, and she presented to the world a very comely and amiable appearance. Her sister, Amy Bertram, who, like herself, was a widow, and ran the house in rather subordinate partnership with her, was still crow-like, but, unlike Mrs. Oxney, had a remarkable capacity for seeing the dark side of every situation, and for suitably croaking over it.

She shook her head over Margaret's contented retrospect.

"Things may not be so bad just for the moment," she said, "and as most of the rooms are engaged up till Christmas, we may get through this year all right. But we must be prepared to be very empty from then onwards, for a good season like this is always followed by a very empty one. How we shall manage to get through the spring is more than I can tell you : don't ask me. And I do hope, Margaret, that you'll think twice before putting in that extra bathroom. It will be a great expense, and you must reckon on spending double the estimate."

"Nonsense, my dear," said Margaret. "They've contracted for a fixed sum—and high enough too— for doing everything down to a hot towel-rail, and they've got to carry it out."

Amy shook her head again.

"Then you'll find, if you keep them to the contract there'll be bad workmanship somewhere. I know what plumbers are. The taps will leak, and the towel-rail be cold. Besides I can't think what you want with a third bathroom. It seems to me that it's just to humour Colonel Chase who would like one nearer his bedroom. I'm sure the other bathrooms are hardly used at all as it is. Most of our guests don't want a bath if after breakfast they are going to soak for a quarter of an hour down at the establishment. I shouldn't dream of putting another in. And Miss Howard is sure to make a fuss if there's hammering and workmen going on all day and night next her room."

Mrs. Oxney felt this point was worth considering, for though it was worth while to please Colonel Chase, it was certainly not worth while to displease Miss Howard. These two were not guests who came for a three weeks' cure and were gone again, but practically permanent inmates of Wentworth, who had lived here

for more than a year, and when their interests con-
flicted, it was necessary to be wary.

" I'm sure I don't want to fuss Miss Howard," she
said, " though I don't know how I can get out of it
now. I've promised the Colonel, that there shall be
a new bathroom put in, and I let him choose that white
tile-paper——"

Amy gave a short hollow croak.

" That's the most expensive of all the patterns,"
she said.

" And lasts the longer," said Mrs. Oxney. " But
it might be as well to put it off till after Christmas,
for Miss Howard is sure to go down to Torquay for a
couple of weeks then, and it could be done in her
absence."

" As like as not she won't be able to get away," said
Mrs. Bertram, " for if the coal-strike goes on, the rail-
ways will all have stopped long before that. I saw a
leader in the paper about it this morning, which said
there wasn't a ray of hope on the whole horizon.
Not a ray. And the whole horizon. Indeed I don't
know what we shall do as soon as the cold weather
begins, as it's bound to do soon, for after a warm
autumn there's always a severe winter. How we shall
keep a fire going for the kitchen I can't imagine : I
could wish there weren't so many rooms booked up
till Christmas. And as for hot water for the baths——"

" Oh, that's coke," said Mrs. Oxney. " As soon
as we start the central heating, it and the bath water
are run by the same furnace. You know that quite
well, so where's the use of saying that ? There's
plenty of coke. You just try to get into the coke-
cellar, and shut the door behind you. You couldn't
do it."

Amy sighed : there was resignation more than relief
in her sigh.

" Anyhow the coal is getting low enough," she said

to console herself. " I'm sure I don't see how we shall keep the house open at all, when we have to begin fires in the rooms, unless you mean to burn coke in them. There's Miss Howard : she likes the drawing-room to be nothing else but an oven by after breakfast, and there's the Colonel as grumpy as a bear if the smoking-room isn't fit to roast an ox in after tea. I'm not sure that it wouldn't be better to shut Wentworth up altogether when the frosts begin. There's nothing that makes guests so discontented as a cold house. Once get the reputation for chilliness, and ruin stares at you. People coming here for the cure won't stand it. They'll pack up and go to the Bolton Arms or to Balmoral. Better say that we're closed. Belvoir too : I was walking along the road to the back of it yesterday, and the coal-cellar door was open. Crammed : I shouldn't like to say how many tons. Where they get it from I don't know : some underhand means, I'm sadly afraid."

Mrs. Oxney had not been attending much to her sister's familiar litanies, but the thought of those semi-detached hovels, suggested by the mention of Belvoir, put a bright idea into her head.

" I'll tell you what I shall do," she said. " I shall take a whole page in the Baths Guide-book to Bolton, and advertise Wentworth properly, so that everybody shall know that it isn't an ordinary boarding house in a row with the butcher's opposite. Golf links, twenty holes, two tennis courts, one hard, croquet-lawn, kitchen- and flower-gardens, and a tasteful view of the lounge."

" It will be very expensive," said Mrs. Bertram, who was really enthusiastic about this idea of her sister's, but was compelled by all the dominant instincts of her nature to see the objection to any course of action.

" Not a bit," said Mrs. Oxney. " It will pay for itself ten times over. Let people know they can play lawn-tennis all the winter——"

" Not if it snows," said Mrs. Bertram.

" Amy, let me finish my sentence. Tennis all the winter, and the breakfast lounge as well as the drawing-room and central heating and no extras for baths and three bathrooms, and standing in its own grounds——"

" But they all stand in their own grounds," said Mrs. Bertram.

" Stuff and nonsense, Amy. Grounds mean something spacious, not a gravel path leading round a monkey-puzzle. And no cold supper on Sundays. I shall say that too."

That point was debated : to say that there was no cold supper on Sunday night implied, so Mrs. Bertram sadly surmised, that there was cold supper all the week, and nothing at all on Sundays, and such a misconception would be lamentably alien to the effect that this sumptuous advertisement was designed to produce. Mrs. Oxney therefore agreed to word this differently or omit altogether, and hurried indoors to find the most tasteful view of the lounge for the photographer.

The morning hours between breakfast and lunch were always the least populated time of the day at Wentworth, for the majority of its guests were patients who went down to the baths in the morning to drink the abominable waters or lie pickling in tubs of brine, and returned, some in the motor-bus, and the more stalwart on their feet, in time to have an hour's prescribed rest before lunch. The two permanent inmates of the house, Colonel Chase and Miss Alice Howard were, so far from being patients, in the enjoyment of the rudest health, but they too, were never at home on fine mornings like this, for Miss Howard had left the house by ten o'clock with her satchel of painting apparatus and a small folding stool, which when properly adjusted never pinched her anywhere or collapsed.

and sketched from Nature till lunch-time. On her return she put up on the chimney-piece of the lounge the artistic fruit of her labours for the delectation and compliments of her fellow-guests. These water-colour sketches were, for the most part, suave and sentimental, and represented the church tower of St. Giles's, seen over the fields, or trees with reflections in the river, or dim effects of dusk (though painted by broad daylight, since it was impossible to get the colours right otherwise) with scattered lights gleaming from cottage windows, and possibly a crescent moon (body-colour) in the west. Garden-beds, still-life studies of petunias and Mrs. Oxney's cat were rarer subjects, but much admired.

Colonel Chase's occupations in the morning were equally regular and more physically strenuous, for either he bicycled seldom less than thirty miles, or walked not less than eight as recorded by his pedo-meter. He had two pedometers, one giddily affixed to the hub of his bicycle's hind-wheel, and the other, for pedestrian purposes, incessantly hung by a steel clip into his waistcoat pocket : this one clicked once at each alternate step of his great strong legs, and it was wonderful how far he walked every day. Thus, though his fellow-guests at Wentworth could not, as in Miss Howard's case, feast their eyes on the actual fruit of his energy since this would have implied the visualization of so many miles of road, they could always be (and were) informed of the immense dis-tances he had traversed. This he felt sure, was a source of admiring envy to the crippled and encouraged them to regain their lost activity. Mrs. Holders, for instance, who, a fortnight ago, had only just been able to hobble down to the Bath establishment on two sticks and was always driven up again in the motor-bus, and who now was able, on her good days, to walk both ways, with the assistance of only one

stick, had great jokes with him about her increasing
mobility. She used to say that when she came back
in the spring, she would go out with him for his walk
in the morning, and take her treatment in the afternoon
when he was resting. She seemed to take the greatest
interest in his athletic feats, and used to drink in all he
said with an air of reverent and rapt attention. Occasionally, however, when Colonel Chase was least
conscious of being humorous (though no one could be
more so if he wished) she gave a little mouse-like
squeak of laughter and then became intensely serious
again. This puzzled him till he thought of what was
no doubt the right explanation, namely, that Mrs.
Holders had suddenly thought of something amusing,
which had nothing to do with him and his conversation.
For the rest, she was a middle-aged, round-about little
personage, with a plain vivacious face and highly-
arched eyebrows, so that she looked in a permanent
state of surprise though nobody knew what she was
surprised about. Miss Howard thought of her as
' quaint' and Mrs. Holders did not think of Miss Howard
at all.

There had lately been a tree felled in the field where
the twenty-hole golf links lay, and when her sister
went indoors to select a tasteful view of the lounge,
Mrs. Bertram walked through the garden and out on
to the links to see what it was worth in the way of
logs for the fires in this shortage of coal. The tree
had been dead for more than a year, and she had repeatedly urged Margaret to have it cut down while it
was still sound, and had not degenerated into touchwood. But Mrs. Oxney had been very obstinate about
it, weak but obstinate, for a green woodpecker had
built in it and she said it would be such a shame to
cut it down, and completely upset the poor dickie-
bird's domestic arrangements. Then, when the woodpecker had quite finished with it, Colonel Chase said

it made a first-rate hazard for the seventeenth and nineteenth holes (the long diagonals across the field) which meant that he was the only player who could loft his ball over it without going round, and it was not till yesterday that Mrs. Oxney had steeled herself to the destruction of this magnificent bunker. Now, of course, as Mrs. Bertram had woefully anticipated, the tree was no more than a great cracknell kept together by bark, and the Colonel might just as well have been left to go on soaring over it or hitting into it as before.

As she walked back to the house from this depressing expedition she heard the hoot of the motor-bus which brought back the patients from the baths, announcing its return. There were the usual three occupants (since Mrs. Holders had taken to walking up) Mr. Kemp and his down-trodden daughter Florence, both habitual guests at Wentworth, and Mr. Bullingdon who was paying his first visit to Bolton Spa. Though he was quite a young man, Mrs. Bertram felt sure that a bath chair would soon be his only mode of locomotion, but in spite of his poor knees, which made him move as if he was performing a cake-walk with his two sticks for a partner, he was full of jokes and gaiety. He laughed at himself in the most engaging manner, and said that he really wasn't sure that he wanted to get better, since he attracted so much flattering attention, wherever he went, by reason of his antics. Apart from these flippant allusions to his own afflictions, he never talked about arthritis at all, which was a great contrast to Mr. Kemp whose idea of pleasant conversation was to pin a listener into a corner from which escape was difficult, and, beginning with the 3rd of March, 1920, which was the date on which he first felt a throbbing in his left hip, recount the progress of his rheumatisms. He had visited Harrogate, Buxton, Bath, Droitwich, Aix and Marienbad, and none of these had really done him any good, but

there was still a chance that Bolton in combination with
some of the others and Bournemouth for the winter,
might benefit him. Just as Mrs. Bertram reached the
door, he was balanced on the step of the motor-bus,
and warning Mr. Bullingdon about a certain malignant
masseur at Aix.

" Don't let him touch your knees with the tips of his
fingers." he said, " if you're thinking of going to Aix.
I was getting on nicely there, as my daughter will tell
you, when my doctor recommended me to have treatment at the hands of this villain. In a week or two he
had undone all the good I had derived from Aix, and
when I left I wasn't walking much better than you.
What was his name, Florence ? "

" Jean Cuissot," said Florence in a monotonous
voice. She knew her father would ask her that.

" Nonsense : Jean Cuissot was the masseur I went
to the year before. No, I believe you're right, it was
Jean Cuissot. Judas Iscariot would be a better name
for him. Give me your arm, please, unless you want
me to stand on this step for the rest of my life. Ah,
dear me, I've got a new pain in my ankle this morning.
I woke in the night and felt it wasn't comfortable,
and expected I should have trouble. Why, there's
Mrs. Holders already. She has walked all the way up
from the baths. I haven't been able to walk back
after my bath since I was at Harrogate two seasons
ago, and the hill there is neither so long nor so steep as
this. But I used to think nothing of it then. What
wouldn't I give to be able to walk up such a hill
now ! "

Mrs. Bertram who was lending a firm shoulder to
Mr. Kemp while his daughter disentangled his sticks
which had got muddled up in some inexplicable manner
between his legs and the door of the bus, sighed heavily,

" Yes, indeed," she said. " We so seldom appreciate
our blessings till they are taken from us, and then we

haven't got them to appreciate. But Bolton may set you up yet, Mr. Kemp, you never can tell."

Mr. Bullingdon, now that the doorway of the bus was clear, performed a sort of mystic dance down the steps and on to the ground.

"There we are," he said cheerfully. "You know they ought to engage Mrs. Holders and Mr. Kemp and me for a short turn at a music-hall. It would have an immense success : screams of laughter. There would be a glass of champagne on one side of the stage, and we three toeing the mark on the other. Then at the word ' go ', we would start off and see who could grab it first. Mrs. Holders would have to be handicapped though, you and I wouldn't stand a chance against her, Mr. Kemp."

Mr. Kemp was inclined to be offended at the suggestion of his appearing at a music-hall, and his daughter and Mrs. Bertram closed in behind him and propelled him into the house. Besides, as everybody ought to know, champagne was poison to him : you might as well expect him to race for a glass of prussic acid.

With the dispersal of the passengers by the ambulance waggon (as Mr. Bullingdon always flippantly called the bus) to their rooms to rest before lunch, the house was quiet again till the arrival of Miss Howard with her satchel and her camp-stool. The twilight scene on which she had been engaged this sunny morning had been giving her a great deal of trouble, for the dusk, even to her indulgent eye was of a strange soupy quality, as if some dark viscous fluid had been emitted from an unknown source (for she had not intended it) on to the landscape, and the lights from the cottages looked like some curious eruption of orange spots. It was very disappointing, for she had hoped great things from this sketch, but now when she put it up on the chimney-piece of the lounge, the effect was puzzling rather than pleasing. Luckily however, she found that a small flat parcel had arrived for her ; this she knew could be nothing else than 'Evening Bells', which she had sent a week ago to be framed by Mr. Bowen. That, up till now, was certainly her *chef-d'œuvre :* Mrs. Oxney had declared that she could positively hear the bells, and so Miss Howard had caused to be printed on the mount of this masterpiece, ' The mellow lin-lan-lone of evening bells '. There was the tower of St. Giles' church reflected in the river, which had caused that pretty thought to come into Mrs. Oxney's mind, and Miss Howard was sure that everybody would like to see ' Evening Bells ' again in its gilt frame. So she replaced the soupy twilight in her satchel, and determined to put it under the tap when she went upstairs to see if a thorough washing-down would not render it more translucent. There was half an hour yet before lunch-time, and she tripped into the drawing-room to get a good practise on the mellow but elderly piano.

Miss Alice Howard was a pathetic person, though she would have been very much surprised if anyone had told her so. She had been an extremely pretty girl, lively and intelligent and facile, but by some backhanded stroke of fate she had never married, and now at the age of forty, though she had parted with her youth, she had relinquished no atom of her girlishness. She hardly ever walked, but tripped, she warbled little snatches of song when she thought that anyone might be within hearing in order to refresh them with her maidenly brightness, and sat on the hearth-rug in front of the fire, even though there was a far more comfortable seat ready. It was not that she felt any profound passion for tripping, warbling and squatting, but from constantly telling herself that she was barely out of her teens she had got to believe in her girlishness and behaved accordingly. Her imagination (here was the root of the matter,) was incessantly exercised on herself, and she imagined all sorts of things about herself that had little or no foundation in fact. She could scarcely have told you how or when, for instance, she began to believe that she was closely connected with a noble house, but certainly all Wentworth believed it now. They could have had no other informant but her, and Miss Howard very nearly believed it, too, so constantly had she made rich little allusions which implied it. She had a commodious semi-detached villa of her own, conveniently close to the station at Tunbridge Wells, but it was lonely work to live there by herself, and she had let it furnished for the last year, and hoped to do so again for the next. The occupant was a gentleman on the Stock Exchange called Mr. Gradge, who lived there with his sister, but she always referred to them as " my tenants," and to the semi-detached villa as ' my little place ' in Kent. She thus contrived to produce the impression that the villa was a small ancestral manor-house, and sometimes lamented that the monstrously swollen taxes of late years had caused so many country houses to be shut up or let : she thought herself very lucky to be able to let her little place in Kent near (though it really was ' at ') Tunbridge Wells. Miss Howard, in fact, though girlish, suffered from the essentially middle-aged disease of fabrication, and whether she looked at her physical image in the tall looking-glass in her bedroom, or contemplated herself in the mirror of her mind, she now saw what she had got to believe about herself.

She was quite alone in the world without near relations or any intimate friend, and, with the little place in Kent let to her tenants, she lived at Wentworth for the greater part of the year, spent a month at a similar boarding house at Torquay which she called her Christmas holidays, and had another holiday in a

third boarding-house in South Kensington for a fortnight of the London season. From there she came back
to Wentworth quite worn out with gaiety ; everyone
had been so kind and pleased to see her, and how her
cousins had scolded her for insisting on going back to
Bolton after so short a visit. But she was much happier
at Wentworth than anywhere else, for she had come to
be, not only in her own eyes, but in Mrs. Oxney's and
those of the other guests a sort of incarnation of all the
Muses. She painted, she sang and played, she danced
to the strains of the gramophone with any sound pair
of legs among the guests, or, if there happened to be
none, she was quite willing to execute a *pas seul* in the
lounge after dinner, which Mrs. Oxney, who always said
the agreeable thing, considered equal to the best
Russian dancing. And then there was her lawn-tennis,
though she shook her head at the suggestion that she
should enter at Wimbledon next year, for that would
mean giving up so much of her sketching and her music.
And then there was her croquet and her golf . . .

She sat down at the piano after removing her hat
(shaped like an inverted waste-paper basket and
trimmed with three sorts of grapes, pink, blue and
orange) and deftly encouraged her pale brown hair to
drop in rebellious disorder over her forehead and
nearly conceal the ear that was like a pink shell. She
ran her hands over the keys : someone had told her—
or had she invented it for herself ?—that she had a
' butterfly touch,' and when the butterflies alighted
on one or two flowers where the careless things
were trespassing, Miss Howard said ' Naughty ' ! to
them, and made them do it again. She was supposed to have an amazing power of improvisation, and
these industrious little practices with the soft pedal
down, while everyone was resting upstairs, certainly
developed her gift. There were some fragments from
Chopin which were landmarks for the improvisation

when it seemed to be wandering and put it back on the
road again.   Miss Howard could scarcely tell sometimes
whether certain bits belonged to her own butterflies
or Chopin's, and if she couldn't tell she felt sure that
nobody else at Wentworth could.   Presently the gong
in the lounge announced that lunch was ready (Miss
Howard would have winced at that brazen booming
if anyone had been present) but she took no notice of
the summons, for she knew that Mrs. Oxney would
probably come tiptoeing in, and find her quite lost
in her music, sitting there with dreamy eyes fixed
on the ceiling, and a smile hovering—just that—on
her mouth.

It all happened just as she anticipated : out of the
corner of a dreamy eye she saw Mrs. Oxney enter, and
sit down with a long elaborate creak beside the door,
but she did not officially see her until she stumbled
over a chromatic run.   She gave a little start and an
exclamation of surprise.

" Oh, Mrs. Oxney," she said, " how did you steal in
without my noticing ?   And how wicked of you to
creep into the corner and listen to my bunglings !
Fingers so naughty and stiff this morning.   I could
slap the tiresome things for being so stupid.   Is it
nearly lunch-time ?   Have you come in to tell me to
run upstairs and brush my hair and wash my hands ?
Must I ? "

" Certainly you needn't, for you've given me such a
treat," said Mrs. Oxney.   " I could listen to you
playing for ever, Miss Howard.   Tiddle-iddle-iddle-
iddle-iddle !   I call it wonderful without a note to
guide you.   I wish my fingers were as naughty as that.
As for its being lunch-time, why, the gong rang five
minutes ago, but I couldn't punish myself by interrupting you."

Miss Howard was perfectly aware that Mrs. Oxney
was a musical imbecile, but in spite of that her

appreciation gave her strong satisfaction. She was also aware that the gong had sounded five minutes ago, and so she gave another little exclamation of surprise at the astonishing news.

" Fancy ! " she said. " But when I get to the piano I become so stupid and absent-minded. I came in so hungry half an hour ago, hoping it was lunch-time and I declare I've no feeling of hunger left now. Music feeds me, I think : even my feeble little strummings are meat and drink to me. Yes : little bits of Chopin. How lovely to have known Chopin ! I wish I had known Chopin."

" Well, why didn't you ever ask your mamma to get him to come down to your place in Kent ? " asked Mrs. Oxney. " He'd have liked to hear you play, I'll be bound."

Miss Howard gave her silvery little laugh.

" Dear thing ! " she said. " Chopin was a friend of great-grandmamma—let's see, which was it ?—yes, great-grandmamma Stanley. She went to see him at Majorca or Minorca."

" I have made a mistake then," said Mrs. Oxney, " but you're so good-natured, Miss Howard. And I've come to trespass on your good nature, too."

" You shan't be prosecuted," said Miss Howard gaily. " Trespass away."

" Well, it's this then," said Mrs. Oxney. " There's to be an entertainment at the Assembly Rooms next week, and the Committee deputed me to ask you if you wouldn't play at it. Such a treat it would be, and I'm sure everybody in Bolton would flock to hear you. It's for a good object too, the Children's Hospital in the town."

" How you all work me ! " said Miss Howard, immensely pleased at being asked and beginning to fix on the waste-paper basket. " It's sheer bullying, for you know I couldn't refuse to do anything for the dear mites. How I shall have to practice if I'm to be made to play in public!"

" So much the better for Wentworth," said Mrs. Oxney. " Then I may tell them that you will ? I do call that kind. And what bits will you play ? They'd like it best, I'll be bound, if you played one of your own beautiful improvisations. That would be a thing people couldn't hear at an ordinary concert, ' Improvisations by Miss Howard ' ! And then that wouldn't call for any practice at all."

" Dear thing," said Miss Howard again. " If you only knew how it takes it out of me. Such dreaming and yet such concentration. But you shall have your way."

Meals were served with military punctuality at Wentworth and the pianist and her impresario were very late to Colonel Chase's high indignation, for if people were late, the service was delayed, and the punctual suffered for the inconsiderateness of the laggard. At breakfast, which, from habits formed in India he called Chota-hazri, unpunctuality did not matter, but tiffin (lunch) was another affair. He was also soured this morning by the fact that the giddy pedometer on his bicycle had got out of order. He had felt supernormally energetic when he went out for his ride and had pedalled away in the most splendid form for nearly three hours, feeling certain that he was breaking his previous record of thirty-five miles and anticipating many congratulations on this athletic feat, which would give so much pleasure to others as well as himself. . . . But, when, on arrival at Wentworth, he had got off his bicycle with rather trembling knees and completely out of breath, to feast his eyes on the disc which would surely register thirty-six miles at least, he found its idiotic hand pointing to the ridiculous figure of nine miles and a quarter. It was most aggravating ; he would have to take the wretched instrument to be repaired

this afternoon, instead of resting after lunch, and very
likely it would not be ready by tomorrow morning
so that once more he would not know how far he had
been. That would play the deuce with his aggregate
for the month which he sedulously entered in a note-
book. At one end of it was the record of the miles
he had bicycled, and upside down at the other the
miles he had walked, and now it would appear that he
had only bicycled nine and a quarter miles on
October 17th, and perhaps none at all on
October 18th.

These depressing reflections, combined with Miss
Howard's unpunctuality, caused him to utter a mere
grunt to her salutation as she tripped by his table
with all the grapes in her hat wagging, and sat down
at her own table in the window where she could see
the church tower, and feed the sweet birdies with
crumbs when she had fed herself.

" And how many miles did you go this morning,
Colonel ? " she asked as she unfolded her napkin.
Interest in his prowess always pleased him, and of
course she did not know how wicked the pedometer
had been.

" Most aggravating ! " he said. " That wretched
instrument of mine got out of order, and after nearly
three hours of the hardest riding I've ever done, it
registered nine miles and a quarter."

There was a general murmur of sympathy with him
and of indignation with the pedometer. Unfortunately
Mrs. Holders tried to say something amusing : she
could not have done anything more dangerous. Reckless
in fact : highly culpable.

" Nine and a quarter miles in under three hours ? "
she said. " I should call that very good going. I've
often been less."

That was like an application of the bellows to Colonel
Chase's smouldering wrath. If there was one subject

which must be treated with deference and respect it
was his bicycling, and he burst into flame.

" Considerably less I should think, ma'am," he said.
" Waitress, I said bread and butter pudding half an
hour ago, and I don't see why I should be kept waiting
till tea-time because others don't come in to lunch."

" He's gone off into one of his tantrums," whispered
Mrs. Oxney to her sister. " Run into the kitchen,
Amy, and bring it yourself and a nice jug of cream
with it."

Miss Howard was grieved at this piece of rudeness.
Howards never behaved like that. Such a peppery
old thing : as if anybody cared how many miles he
went on his bicycle. Sometimes she wished he would
ride away for hundreds of miles in a straight line and
never come back. And then sometimes she thought
that if he had only a clever young wife to look after
him, she would soon cure him of his roughnesses. So
she put her nose slightly in the air, and ate curried
chicken with great elegance in a spoon, which Colonel
Chase said was the right way to eat curry.

The nice jug of cream had a mollifying effect, and
when Miss Howard came out from her lunch, Colonel
Chase was explaining to a sycophantic audience where
he had gone, and it was unanimously decided that he
must have ridden at least thirty-eight miles, which
was indeed joyful. He decided in consequence to
forgive Miss Howard for being late for lunch, and to
show the plenitude of his magnanimity, he strolled
across to the chimney-piece to admire Evening
Bells .

" I'll enter it as thirty-eight miles then in my log-
book," he said, " if you all insist on it. Why there's
another of your sketches, Miss Howard, though I
think I've seen it before. Very pretty, I'm sure.
What's that written underneath it ? The mellow
lanoline——"

Miss Howard was also ready to forgive, and gave a laughing peal of bells on her own account.

"How can you be so naughty?" she said. "The mellow lin-lan-lone, Colonel. Tennyson you know. Such a sweet poem. I shall have to find it for you."

"I declare I can hear the bells," said Miss Kemp, shamelessly plagiarising from Mrs. Oxney. "Delicious, Miss Howard. So poetical."

Her father who had been examining the sketch from a purely hygienic point of view, shook his head.

"I shouldn't like to go to evening service in that church," he said. "All among the trees, you know, with the river close by. I should wake up with a bad attack of lumbago next morning, I'm afraid. Churches are draughty places at the best of times, and if you walk there you're liable to get heated and then have to sit for an hour in the cold, while if you drive there, as like as not you've got chilly already and that's even worse. I shan't ever forget the chill I got in church at Harrogate. It was a damp morning, and I should have been wiser not to go. I declare it makes me shiver to look at that church of Miss Howard's so close to the river. I might manage morning service there, but it would be very ill-advised to go in the evening."

Colonel Chase had finished the coffee which Mrs. Oxney had sent him as a propitiation. It had arrived with her compliments, for coffee after lunch was an extra.

"Well, I must get down to the town to have my pedometer looked to," he said, "and then how about a few holes at golf, Miss Howard? I'll be back in twenty minutes. That'll make a pretty good day's exercise for me."

"Marvellous!" said Miss Howard.

"But nothing to what I used to do not so many years back in India," he said. "Military duties, parades and what not in the morning, and a polo-match

after tiffin, and perhaps a game of rackets after
tea, and a couple of hundred at billiards before I got
to my bridge. That's the way to keep fit, and get
good news from your liver if the ladies will excuse the
expression."

Mrs. Holders was not so forgiving as Miss Howard.
She waited till he had passed the window pedalling
hard with his chest well out, and then gave her mouse-
squeak of laughter.

" And it's early closing," she said. " He'll come
tiffining back and serve him right for being rude to me.
I can't stand rudeness."

Mrs. Oxney who had joined the group round Evening
Bells wrung her hands in dismay.

" Oh, what have you done, Mrs. Holders ? " she said.
" I am sorry. That beautiful hot coffee which I sent
the Colonel, why, I might as well never have sent it
at all, so vexed he'll be to find it's early closing. And
then, if he's not too much upset to play golf, he'll see
that I've had his favourite tree cut down, and it's
fallen right across the green in the middle of the
field, and that'll be another cause for vexation. I
must send the gardeners to see if they can't haul it
away before he gets back. Dear me, what a day of
misfortunes ! "

" And little better than touchwood when all's said
and done," moaned Mrs. Bertram.

So the two sisters who usually joined the guests in
the lounge after lunch for a friendly chat, cut this
short, and the one hurried away to despatch gardeners
to the scene of the disaster in hopes of clearing it before
the Colonel came back from his futile errand to the
town, and the other to order hot scones for tea, of
which he was inordinately fond. Though dirty weather
might be anticipated, Mrs. Holders was quite impen-
itent, and kept bursting into little squeals of merriment.

" Serve him right, serve him right," she repeated.

" He was rude to me, and that's what he gets for it. If those are army manners, give me the Navy."

This was a revolutionary utterance : the red flag seemed to flutter. Colonel Chase had hitherto been regarded at Wentworth as something cosmic, like a thunderstorm or a fine day. You could dislike or be frightened of the thunderstorm, and hide in a dark place till its fury was past, or you could enjoy the fine day, but you had to accept whichever it might happen to be. He was stuffy on the thunderstorm days and sunny on the others, and you must take the weather as it came.

" Here we all are," continued the rebel, " and we've got to be pleasant to each other, and not fly into passions or behave like kings and emperors, however long we've spent in India, and however many tigers and tiffins we have shot. For my part, I never believed much in his story of the tiger which charged him, and which he shot through the heart when it was two yards away. I'm sure I wish evil to nobody, but I shouldn't have minded if the tiger had given him a good nip first, to teach him manners. And why he should have jugs of cream at lunch and hot scones for tea because he lost his temper I don't know. Skim-milk and a bit of dry bread would have been more suitable."

These awful remarks were addressed to Tim Bullingdon only, for the sisters had gone to avert the wrath to come, Miss Howard had taken the soupy twilight-sketch to the tap, and Florence Kemp had gone out with her father to the chairs under the cedar, where she read aloud to him till he went to sleep.

" I wouldn't have been in his regiment for anything," said Tim, cake-walking about the lounge, for gentle exercise though painful was recommended. " I would sooner have been in hell."

" So would I," said Mrs. Holders cordially, " and thought it very agreeable in comparison. By the way, there's an envelope on the writing-table in the smoking-room addressed to his Excellency the Viceroy. That's meant for us to see. Have you seen it?"

"Good Lord, yes," said Tim. "It's been there since yesterday morning. I put it in the waste-paper basket once, but it's back again and getting quite dusty. If it's there tomorrow morning, I shall address another envelope to King George, Personal."

Mrs. Holders squeaked again.

"That would be a beauty for him," she said. "Mind you do it. Here he is back from the town coming up the drive. What a red face!"

Colonel Chase banged the front door and came puffing in to the lounge.

"Pretty state of things," he said. "It seems a perpetual holiday for the working classes. That's what makes them out of hand. Early closing to-day, and late opening tomorrow, I shouldn't wonder, and then comes Sunday, and I shouldn't be surprised if it was a Bank-holiday on Monday."

"Dear me!" said Mrs Holders. "Then you've had your ride for nothing. What a disappointment. Never mind, get a good game of golf."

Colonel Chase flung himself into a chair, and mopped his face.

"And no sign of Miss Howard," he said. "I told her I should be back in twenty minutes. Women have no idea of time. Qui-hi, Miss Howard."

"I expect that's Hindustanee," said Mrs. Holders. What a pleasure to talk so many languages. *Parlez-vous Français, monsieur?*"

Colonel Chase had again that horrid sense of uncertainty as to whether Mrs. Holders was not in some obstruse manner poking fun at him, but, as usual, the notion seemed incredible. Then snatches of song were heard from the landing at the top of the stairs, and Miss Howard came tripping along it. The tap-water had done wonders for the viscous fog, and she looked forward to making a success of her sketch after all. It was to be called ' The curfew tolls the knell of parting day '. She carried her bag of golf clubs with her and was quite ready.

The two went out together through the garden to the golf-field. A perfect swarm of gardeners and odd men and chauffeurs and boot-boys were busy hauling the touchwood tree from the middle green.

" Why, what's all this ? " said Colonel Chase, stopping short. " My tree, my hazard, my bunker, my favourite hazard. Cut down ! Upon my word now ! I wonder by whose orders that was done. Ah, there's Mrs. Oxney. What's all this, Mrs. Oxney ? "

Mrs. Oxney came forward like Esther before Ahasuerus.

" Oh, dear me, such a sad accident, Colonel," she said, " though it will be all right in a few minutes now. The tree fell right across the green. So clumsy ! But they've got it moving. I had to have it cut down : all gone at the root and so dangerous. What should I have felt if it had come crashing down when you were in the middle of one of your beautiful puttings ? "

This was an improvisation as brilliant as Miss Howard's on the piano, and far less rehearsed. But it gave little satisfaction.

" Well, you've removed the only decent hazard in the place," he said. " I'm sorry it has happened for I've been toiling all the summer to get a few sporting holes for you. I should have thought you might have had it propped up or something of the sort. No matter. Take the honour, Miss Howard, and let's be off, or it will be dark before we've played our twenty holes."

CHAPTER II

THIS inauspicious afternoon finished better than might
have been anticipated. The Colonel's favourite hazard,
it is true, was laid low, but the trunk now dragged to
the edge of the green, was discovered to be a very well-
placed bunker, when Miss Howard put the ball underneath it in an unplayable position, and thus enabled
Colonel Chase to win the match. Then it was found that
Mrs. Oxney's chauffeur who was an ingenious mechanic
could put the pedometer to rights with the greatest
ease. (He geared it a shade too high, so that for the
future when Colonel Chase had ridden seven-eights of
a mile it recorded a full mile, and so ever afterwards
when he rode thirty-two miles, as he so often did, he
could inform admiring Wentworth with indisputable
evidence to back him, that he had ridden thirty-six.
A pleasing spell of record-breaking ensued.)

After a quantity of hot scones for tea, he retired to
his bedroom according to his usual custom for a couple
of hours of solid reading before dinner. He took from
a small book-shelf above his bed, which contained for
the most part old Army lists, an antique copy of
Macaulay's Essays which he had won as a prize for
Geography at school, and before settling down to read
made himself very comfortable in a large armchair
with his pipe and tobacco handy. Then he glanced
at the news in the evening paper, which for many
months now had put him in a towering passion since
it so largely concerned the coal strike. All strikers,

according to his firm conviction, were damned lazy
skunks, who refused to do a stroke of work, because
they preferred to be supported in idle luxury by the
dole, while Mr. Cook was a Bolshevist, whom Colonel
Chase, so he repeatedly affirmed, would have rejoiced to
hang with his own hands, having heartily flogged him
first. There would soon have been an end of the strike
if the weak-kneed Government had only done what he
had recommended from the very beginning. Then,
in order to quiet and calm his mind he mused over a
cross-word puzzle, jotting down in pencil the solutions
which seemed to fit. Half an hour generally sufficed
to break the back of it, and then he leaned back in
his chair, opened Macaulay's Essays at random, and
gave himself up to meditation.

This meditation was always agreeable, for its origin,
the cave out of which it so generously gushed was his
strong and profound satisfaction with himself, and
this gave a pleasant flavour to whatever he thought
about. He had had a thoroughly creditable though un-
eventful career in the army, and on his retirement two
years ago, found himself able to contemplate the past
and await the future with British equanimity. Being
unmarried and possessed of a comfortable competence,
he could live for a couple of months in the year in
furnished rooms close to his club in London, and for
the other ten at this admirably conducted boarding-
establishment, thus escaping all the responsibilities
of house-keeping and of friendship. In London armchair acquaintances sufficed for social needs, they
afforded him rubbers of bridge in the cardroom and
ample opportunity to curse the weather and the Government in company with kindred spirits ; for the rest
of the day the perusal of the morning and the evening
papers and an hour's constitutional tramp round the
park, fulfilled the wants of mind and body. At Wentworth similarly, his bicycle rides, his excellent meals,

his comfortable bedroom supplied his physical wants
and he had the additional mental satisfaction of being
undisputed cock of the walk, whereas among the
members at his club there was a sad tendency to think
themselves as good as he.   But here his tastes and his
convenience were consulted before those of any other
guest, cream was poured forth for the mollification
of his tantrums and his wish was of the nature of law
to the economies of the establishment.   He was convinced that Mrs. Oxney had no greater pleasure in
life than to please him, no greater cross to bear than
the sense that all had not been as he would have had it ;
he regarded himself as being looked on with a pleasant
mixture of awe and respectful affection.   Every now
and then, it is true, there appeared here some outsider
who did not seem duly reverential, and at the present
moment he had occasional doubts about the true state
of Mrs. Holders's sentiments with regard to him, but
such possible exceptions were negligible and temporary.
They came for their few weeks of cure and passed
away again.   He bore them no real ill will, and hoped
they had profited by their stay.   He and Miss Howard
alone went on for ever ; on the whole he was very
much pleased with Miss Howard, and when, in his
more romantic moments she appeared to unusual
advantage as she sat in profile against a dark wall
(a rather favourite position of hers) he wondered if
he would be more comfortable with an establishment
of his own, and a presentable middle-aged woman
to look after him, and bear his name.   Her occasional
allusions to her little place in Kent were interesting.
Indeed he really asked very little of life ; only that he
should be quite well, and ride a great many miles on
his bicycle, and that Wentworth should unweariedly
admire all he did, and sun itself in his approbation.
Given that these modest requirements had been granted
when, between half-past ten and eleven at night, he

did a few energetic dumb-bell exercises before going
to bed, he claimed nothing more of the morrow than
that it should be like to-day ; sufficient unto the day
had been the good thereof. That something should
have occurred like the felling of his favourite tree, or
the unpunctuality of Miss Howard at lunch, which
had caused a tantrum, would not prove to have spoiled
the day ; he was large-minded enough to take a broader
view than that.

Plans and retrospections eddied pleasantly round
in his head, the volume of Macaulay's Essays, already
upside down, slipped from his hand, and he indulged
as usual in half an hour's nap, from which the sound of
the dressing-gong and the entry of the maid with his
hot water, roused him. Here was a fine opportunity to
linger before making his toilet, in order to demonstrate
to others what an inconvenient thing it was not to be
punctual. But, being very hungry, he scorned so
paltry a reprisal. He had not quite finished with his
evening paper for there was a leader on the coal strike
which a cursory glance had shewn him was written
in a vein which he thoroughly approved, and he took
it down with him to read it as he dined.

Colonel Chase openly used spectacles for reading
when he was alone, and furtively in company, slipping
them off if he thought they would be noticed, for they
were a little out of keeping with that standard of
perfect health and vigour of which he was so striking
an example. Still they were useful with small print
(print was not what it used to be, or the electric light,
probably owing to the coal strike, was not so luminous)
and by propping his paper against his cruet he thought
they would be unnoticed. Occasionally he glanced
over the top of it at the new arrival of the afternoon,
who sat at a table close in front of him. She was a
good-looking woman of middle age, of healthy and
attractive appearance, wearing a fixed bright smile

for no particular reason. She was evidently on the best terms with life, and until Colonel Chase saw that at the conclusion of dinner she walked out with a pronounced limp, and leaned heavily on a stick, he had felt sure that she was no patient in search of health. The dining-room had cleared before he finished his glass of port, and when he went out, the guests with Mrs. Oxney and Mrs. Bertram, were sitting in the lounge. This was the usual procedure. They all sat talking there till he joined them and proposed the pastime which he preferred. Usually he liked playing bridge and a table was formed. Sometimes he challenged Mrs. Oxney to a game of chess which always ended in the capture of all her pieces (for he ran no risks,) and a brilliant check-mate. But before that there would generally be two or three guests trying to solve the cross word puzzle in the evening paper, and though he invariably professed never to glance at a cross-word puzzle, his quiet work at it in his room before dinner often enabled him to help them with some wonderful extempore solutions. To-night, Miss Kemp, Mrs. Oxney and Mrs. Holders formed the cross-word group, and were sadly at loss for nearly everything. In a corner of the lounge, away from any possible draught, Mr. Kemp had successfully cornered the new bright smiling guest and was telling her all about Bath and Buxton and Harrogate and Aix. Mrs. Oxney, with apologies for interrupting Mr. Kemp's conversation introduced Colonel Chase to her as Mrs. Bliss, a name which seemed to suit her excellently, and then claimed his assistance in the puzzle.

"We shall get on better now that the Colonel will help us," she said. "Such a difficult one to-night, Colonel."

Colonel Chase quite forgot that he had pencilled the greater part of this arduous puzzle into his evening paper, and put it carelessly down on the table by the

particular armchair that was always reserved for
him.

" I'm sure if it's difficult I shan't be of much use to
you," he said. " I've no head for these things."

" Oh, but you're wonderful," said Mrs. Oxney,
" a town in Morocco, six letters. How is one to know
that if one's never been there ? Perhaps I'd better
get an atlas."

" No, no, wait a minute," said Colonel Chase. " Let's
do without an atlas if we can. Let me think now.
Fez ? No, that is too short. Now what is that other
place ? It's on the tip of my tongue. Six letters,
did you say ? Ha ! Tetuan ! How will that suit
you ? "

A chorus of praise went up and so did Mrs. Holders's
eyebrows.

" And it fits unicorn," cried Miss Kemp in ecstasy.
" We should never have guessed Tetuan. Then
thirteen down, the Latin for south-west wind, eight
letters, and if Tetuan's right, which it must be because
of unicorn, there's an ' n ' for the fifth."

" Latin : come, come ! I've forgotten all my
Latin," said this fatuous man. " If it was Hindustanee
now. . . . But let me try to be a boy again. There's
Boreas, but that's north wind I'm afraid, and too short
for you. You've stumped me there. Wait a moment
though : Ovid ; something in Ovid. I've got it.
Try ' Favonius '. See if Favonius will help you."

Shrill sounded the chorus of praise, because Favonius
fitted ' vampire ' and ' alpha '.

" I knew you'd make short work of it, Colonel,"
said Mrs. Oxney. " You're a positive encyclopædia ;
that's what I always say of you. And what's a trigono-
metrical term of six letters with an ' s ' for the third ?
You ought to go in for the prizes, indeed you ought,
for you'd win every one."

" Upon my word, Mrs. Oxney, you want to know a

lot to-night," said he. " I must recollect my mathe-
matics as well as my Latin, and perhaps you'll want
Hebrew next. Trigonometry now : there's equation,
no, perhaps you'd call that algebra. But there's
tangent, only that's got no 's' : there's ' sine ' . . .
oh, put down ' cosine '. Cosine's right."

" Why, I never heard of such a thing," said Mrs.
Oxney. " How can I guess what I've never heard of ?
Cosine ! Fancy ? "

A diabolical notion, worthy only of a low mind
struck Tim Bullingdon. Colonel Chase had got up
and was standing commandingly by the fire-place with
his back half-turned. So Tim drew his copy of the
evening paper from the table, and stealthily turned
to the cross-word page, where he found the entire
puzzle legibly pencilled in. Then he skilfully replaced
the paper again, and pointing to it, winked at Mrs.
Holders. That ingenious lady guessed his purport,
and gave a little squeal of laughter which she converted
into an unconvincing cough . . . So while Colonel
Chase now feigned hesitation over ' frieze ', ' cram-
pit ' and ' piston ' Mr. Bullingdon dreamily but
fluently supplied them all. These brilliant suggestions
finished the puzzle and the Colonel after magnanimously
complimenting him on his quickness, invited the three
ladies of the group to play bridge with him in the
smoking-room. Miss Howard in view of her improvisation at the entertainment next week betook herself
to the piano in the drawing-room to fix in her mind
a few fragments of extempore melody.

Mr. Kemp meantime had been enjoying a splendid
innings. He was accustomed to tell the long and tragic
history of his left hip from March 3, 1920, to listeners,
over whose eyes, as the sad epic proceeded, there often
came a sort of glazed look. That, of course, never
deterred him in any way from continuing but he told
it much more vividly to-night, for this bright smiling

Mrs. Bliss was full of attention and eager interest. She seemed intensely sympathetic, and, at the conclusion, when he had fully recounted the complete stiffening of that once mobile joint, she closed her eyes for a moment as if in prayer, and her mouth grew grave. Then her bright smile returned to it in full radiance, after this short eclipse.

"I can't tell you how sorry I am for you, dear Mr. Kemp." she said. "So sorry, truly sorry."

"Very kind of you, I'm sure," said he. "I feel that you are one of the few who realise what a martyrdom I have to go through. Most people have so little imagination. It has been a real pleasure talking to you, and to go back for a moment to that morning when first I found——"

She leaned forward, smiling more than ever.

"And shall I—may I tell you, why I am so sorry for you?" she asked.

"Please do," said Mr. Kemp. An explanation seemed rather unnecessary for it was clear that her kind and sympathetic nature accounted for that. But he was a little hoarse with talking so much, and he did not mind the interruption.

The radiance of her smile was marvellous.

"It will surprise you," she said. "But the reason I'm so sorry for you is that you think your left hip is stiffened, and that you think you suffer all these agonies. It's a huge mistake: there's nothing whatever the matter with you, and you never have any pain at all. There isn't such a thing as pain. All is harmony and you're perfectly well."

Mr. Kemp could hardly believe his ears. This declaration sounded merely like a coarse and unmerited insult. And yet when he looked at that radiant smile and those sympathetic eyes, it was hard to believe that Mrs. Bliss intended it as such. He curbed the indignant exclamation that rose to his lips.

" What do you mean ? " he said. " I've just been
telling you how I got worse and worse especially after
that miscreant at Aix had been handling the joint."

" I know, and now I tell you that it's all Error.
Sin and illness and pain and death are all Error. Omnipotent Mind couldn't have made them and therefore
they don't exist. Nothing has any real existence
except love, health, harmony and happiness."

" But when I feel a sharp pain like a red-hot knitting-
needle being thrust into my hip "—began Mr. Kemp.

" Error. Omnipotent Mind governs all. All is
mind, and there can be no sensation in matter."

" But, God bless my soul," said Mr. Kemp.

" He does," said this astonishing lady. " Hold
on to that thought and the body will utter no complaints. Dear Mr. Kemp, all belief in pain and sickness
comes from Error. Therefore there is neither pain
nor sickness : it is unreal and vanishes as soon as we
realise its unreality. Hence all healing comes from
Mind, and not from *materia medica*."

There was something challenging about so remarkable a statement. Mr. Kemp's head was whirling
slightly (but not aching) for Mrs. Bliss seemed to skip
about so, but he pulled himself together, and tried,
figuratively, to catch hold of her.

" But you yourself," he said. " Aren't you limping
very badly, and leaning on a stick ? Indeed, I was
going to ask you as soon as I had finished telling you
about my hip, what form of rheumatism you are
suffering from."

Again that radiant smile brightened.

" I'm not suffering from any at all," she said. " Error.
It is only a false claim, which I am getting rid of by right
thought. '

" But why did you come to Bolton then," he asked.
" Can't you think rightly at home ? Haven't you
come here for treatment ? "

This question did not disconcert her in the slightest.

" Yes, I'm going to have a course of baths," she said, " but entirely for my dear husband's sake, who is still in blindness. I have, out of love for him, consented to do that—bear ye one another's burdens, you know—but what is curing me, oh, so rapidly, of this false claim of rheumatoid arthritis, as I think they call it, is my own demonstrating over it. All the way down in the train, I treated myself for it, and a friend in London is going to give me absent treatment for it from ten to-night till half-past."

" Absent treatment ? " asked Mr. Kemp. " What's that ? "

" She will just sit and realise that there is nothing the matter with me, because there can't be anything the matter, since all is health and harmony."

" And will that make it any better ? " asked Mr. Kemp.

" It cannot possibly fail to do so. It is the only true healing."

" Then perhaps you won't need your bath to-morrow," said he.

She gave the gayest of laughs.

" Of course I shan't need it, dear Mr. Kemp," she said. " As I told you I am only taking the treatment for my dear husband's sake. That is not really inconsistent. It is only like telling a fairy story to amuse some dear sweet child. Though such a story is not true, it does not mean one is telling lies. What is curing me is the absolute knowledge that Omnipotent Mind never made suffering and never meant us to suffer. Hence, if we think we suffer, it is all a delusion or Error. It can't be real since Mind never made it."

" Dear me, it all sounds most interesting," said Mr. Kemp. " I wonder if it would do me any good."

Mrs. Bliss got up rather too briskly, and the smile completely faded for a moment as a pang of imaginary pain shot through her knee. But almost instantly it reasserted itself.

" There, do you see ? " she said. " Surely that will convince you. Just for a moment, I allowed myself to entertain Error, but at once I denied Error, and what I thought was pain has gone. Of course there wasn't any pain really. To-morrow I will lend you my precious, precious book, *The Manual of Mental Science*, which will prove to you that you can't have pain. What a delicious refreshing talk we've had ! Now I must be off, for my friend will be giving me absent treatment, and I must be with her in spirit."

Mrs. Bliss limped slowly but smilingly away and clinging on to the banisters which creaked beneath her solid grasp, and leaning heavily on her stick hauled herself upstairs. She paused at the top, panting a little.

" Not a single touch of pain," she said exultantly.

Mr. Kemp was delighted to hear it, for she seemed barely able to get upstairs at all, but she must know best.

Very serious and exciting bridge meantime had been proceeding in the smoking-room. The points could not be ruinous to anybody, for as usual, they were threepence a hundred, and thus anyone who lost as much as a shilling, was heartily condoled with by the resulting capitalist. The game itself, with its subtleties and intricacies, furnished the excitement, and Colonel Chase, of course, was the final authority on all points of play, and instructed partner and adversaries alike with unstinted criticism.

" A golden rule : to draw out trumps is a golden rule," he was asserting. " They always used to say of me at the mess that I never left a trump in my opponent's hands. You lost a trick or two in the last game, partner, by neglecting that, but then our opponents were indulgent to your fault, and let us off. If Mrs. Holders had led a club after you had played your king, she and Mrs. Oxney would have got a couple more tricks, and penalised us soundly.''

Mrs. Holders was still feeling Bolshevistic.

" But I hadn't got a club, Colonel," she said. (This was not true, but that made no difference.)

" Ah no : you hadn't," said he. " What I should have said was if Mrs. Oxney had led a club. That's what I meant."

" Yes, to be sure I ought to have," said Mrs. Oxney, who never had a notion what her hand contained the moment she had got rid of it.

" I think so : I think so," said Colonel Chase. " Hammer away at a suit, establish it at all costs. It pays in the end. Now let's have a look. Who dealt this ? "

" I did," said Mrs. Holders, " And I pass."

" No bid, then, is what you should say. I must consider : a difficult problem. I shall declare two hearts, partner. Two, mind : let's have no underbidding. You can trust me for having a sound reason when I say two hearts instead of one."

" Fancy ! Two hearts straight off," said Mrs. Oxney. " I should never dare to do such a thing. I can do nothing against such a declaration."

" No, I expect you'll find yourselves in the Potarge this time," said Colonel Chase. " No bid then : well, partner ? "

Now Miss Kemp had got into terrible trouble last night for taking Colonel Chase out of a major suit into a minor suit, and so though she only held two microscopic hearts, but an immense tiara of diamonds, she also passed, but Mrs. Holders without a moment's hesitation was daring enough to double. This almost amounted to an impertinence, and the Colonel drew

himself up as if insulted : he was not accustomed to
have his declaration doubled. He stared at her for
a withering moment and she saw red.

"Very well, I've nothing more to say," he said.
"I pass."

"You should say 'no bid' Colonel," remarked Mrs.
Holders.

Colonel Chase was a very fair-minded man, when it
was not reasonably possible to be otherwise.

"So I should, so I should," he said. "Peccavi!
And I trust I am not too old to learn. No bid, all
round is it ? And a club led by Mrs. Oxney. So let's
have a look at your hand, partner. Ha, six fine diamonds ! Potarge indeed. Let's get to work, and
discuss our short-comings afterwards. I find it a
little difficult to concentrate with so much agreeable
conversation going on. A club ! I'll play the queen
from your hand. Some do, some don't, but I have
always maintained it is the correct play."

A perfect whirlwind of disaster descended upon
the unfortunate man. The queen of clubs was taken
by Mrs. Holders's king, who returned it and Mrs.
Oxney took it with her ace. She then pulled out a
small diamond by mistake, and pleasantly found that
Mrs. Holders had got none. Mrs. Holders trumped it,
and led a third club. This established a very jolly
cross-ruff, for wicked Mrs. Oxney had opened clubs
from an ace and a small one.

"Never saw such luck," said Colonel Chase, as small
trumps on each side of him secured tricks with monotonous regularity. "I can't think why you didn't
take me out with two diamonds, partner."

"Because she would have required three," said Mrs.
Holders.

"Indeed ! Well, that would have been cheaper than
letting my two hearts stand. Ha ! Now we'll make
an end of this."

He trumped one of these wretched little clubs with the king : Mrs. Oxney, with many apologies over-trumped with the ace.

" I never saw such bad luck, Colonel," she said. " Everything against you. Too bad ! Of course it looked as if Mrs. Holders held the ace."

" I should think so indeed, considering she doubled me," said the Colonel. " I can't think what you doubled me on, Mrs. Holders. The rest I imagine are mine. Let's see. I declared two hearts I believe. Then we're four down. Somewhat expensive, partner, when we should have had the game if you had only declared diamonds. Well, well : we all have to pay for our experience."

" I doubled you on an excellent hand," said Mrs. Holders. " And I can't think why you declared two hearts."

Colonel Chase again stared at her. She had dared to double his declaration, she had dared to justify it, and now she dared to question his declaration. The only thing to do was to answer her quite calmly.

" Two hearts was undoubtedly the right declara-tion," he said. " I fancy that among experts there would be little difference of opinion about that, nor indeed about my view of what my partner should have done. I wager that if we sent out hands up to Slam or Pons, I should get my verdict."

" Oh, that would be interesting," said Mrs. Oxney. " Let us do that. How exciting to see our game of bridge at Wentworth all printed in the Sunday paper. I'm sure they would say that it was very bad luck on the Colonel and that he played it all quite beautifully."

The suggestion was adopted and Mrs. Holders noted down the reconstructed hands. Colonel Chase did not seem very enthusiastic about it, though he had originated the idea, and thought it very unlikely that Slam would give his opinion on so obvious a question.

This rubber came to an immediate and sensational end, for Colonel Chase naturally anxious to get back on Mrs. Holders's unjustifiable (though justified) double, returned the compliment next hand and thus gave his adversaries the rubber. There was indeed an air of defiance about that lady to-night, she was in a state of rebellion from established authority, and she made this even more painfully apparent by challenging his addition, and incontestably proving that he was wrong. This made Mrs. Oxney, though thereby she gained threepence more, quite uncomfortable ; the Colonel's arithmetic and his law-giving had both been called in question, and it was as if Moses, coming down from Sinai with the tables of commandments had been subjected to cross-examination as to their authenticity and the number of them. Moses would not have liked that, nor did Colonel Chase, and it was lucky, in Mrs. Oxney's opinion, that he opened the next rubber with a grand slam, for that smoothed down the frayed edges of his temper, and he explained very carefully the brilliance and difficulty of his achievement.

" An interesting hand," he said, " and it required a bit of playing, if I may say so. That eight of spades, partner : that might have been a nasty card for us. Lucky—at least there wasn't much luck about it, only a little calculation—that I trumped it from my dummy. Some people might have discarded a diamond but I'm too old a bird to go after will-o'-the-wisps like that. The other was the correct game : played like that there wasn't another trick to be made anywhere ! "

He was still a little dignified with Mrs. Holders for having dared to double him and to add up the sum right, and turned to her.

" Or can you suggest any plan by which I could have got another trick ? " he said.

Mrs. Holders gave a little squeal.

" Not possibly," she said. " You got all the tricks there were."

" Ah, yes. Grand slam, so it was," said he. " Amusing that I should have asked you if any more tricks were to be secured ! "

" Very," said Mrs. Holders. " Most."

Play suddenly became slightly hectic. Even Miss Kemp who never bid against no-trumps because, if anybody had got such a good hand as that it was no use fighting against it, developed unusual aggressiveness, and Mrs. Oxney was penalised again and again for supporting her partner's declarations without anything to support them with. The scores above the line went on mounting and mounting and even Colonel Chase got silent and preoccupied as he vainly tried to calculate how many threepences were involved on one side or the other.

Every now and then he broke into hectoring instruction, but somehow with the rebellious Mrs. Holders on his right, who gave little acid smiles and elevations of her eyebrows, when he told her what she ought to have played or discarded or declared, and made no reply of any sort, he felt like an autocrat in the presence of some ominously silent mob ; while the congratulations of Mrs. Oxney, who just now was his partner, if he fulfilled his contract, and her sympathy with his ill luck if he miserably failed, was only like the assurances of the old *régime*, that all was well with the Czardom. He was not at all sure that all was well ; he felt tremors pervading his throne : there was a cold devilish purpose about Mrs. Holders when she outbid him, which was much like the edge of the assassin's knife. There was a patient deadliness about her, when, having failed in her design, she ambushed herself for his further declaration, that really unnerved him. Usually she succeeded in drawing him into an impossible declaration, and when she failed, owing to his surrender, and she was penalised herself, she remained quite unmoved, and instead of finding fault with somebody else, cheerfully entered two or three hundred against her own score.

Bridge generally finished about ten o'clock, for Wentworth with its freight of invalids, was early to bed, but now half-past ten had struck and still this truculent rubber went on.

"Upon my word, most interesting," said Colonel Chase, as, with slightly trembling fingers, he shuffled the cards for the next and fifteenth hand. "You let us off there, Mrs. Holders : if you had led out trumps, as I've often advised you to do, you would have caught my queen——"

"So she would," said Mrs. Oxney admiringly. "You see everything, Colonel."

"——and then you would have cleared your diamonds, and it would have been we who were in the Potarge, instead of you. Funny how a little slip like that sticks to one through the rest of——"

"Five no trumps," said Mrs. Holders, after considering her hand for about two seconds.

Colonel Chase could not command his voice at once. But at the second attempt he mastered it.

"Come, come," he said. "You want to keep me up all night. I've never heard anybody——"

"Five no trumps," said Mrs. Holders with extraordinary distinctness.

Colonel Chase sorted his hand, and found a richness. There was a brilliant array of seven diamonds lacking the king ; there were the king and queen of hearts, there was the king of spades by himself, and he thought that with so splendid a hand, this was a wonderful opportunity to give the rebellious woman a good lesson, and establish himself for ever on his rightful throne. He doubled and Mrs. Holders redoubled.

At that, the jovial laugh to the accompaniment of
which Colonel Chase was preparing to say to his partner
that there was Potarge for two, died in his throat,
though he was far from realising that Nemesis, who
no doubt had been patiently listening to his lectures
on bridge for the last month or two, was licking her
hungry lips. He put down his cigarette, and led the
ace of diamonds. Miss Kemp displayed her hand.
It contained the ace and queen of spades, the king of
diamonds with an infinitesimal satellite, three clubs,
including the knave, and nothing else of the slightest
importance.

Mrs. Holders gave that annoying little squeal of
laughter that grated on Colonel Chase's nerves, and
discarded a small heart on his noble ace of diamonds.
Somehow that made him feel much better. Little
he knew that he was destined to be much worse. But
at present he felt better.

" That's the danger of declaring no trumps with a
suit missing, Mrs. Holders," he said. " I've fallen into
that trap before now myself. Let me see : five I
think."

He jovially slapped the trick down.

" One more trick, partner," he said, " and then the
fun begins."

" That *was* a beautiful double of yours," said Mrs.
Oxney. " Wonderful ! "

" Not so bad ; not so bad," said he. " I'm a high-
wayman this time, Mrs. Holders, exacting penalties
for your rashness in going unguarded."

" Quite," said Mrs. Holders, in a terrible voice.

" Well, I'll just clear that king of diamonds out of
the way," said Colonel Chase, " and then we'll settle
down and be comfortable."

He cleared the king out of the way, and by way of
retaliation Mrs. Holders cleared his king of spades out
of the way with dummy's ace and continued with the

queen of the same suit. Colonel Chase having no
more, and being constitutionally unable to part with
one of those winning diamonds threw out a small club.
Anything would do.

The Colonel's jaw might have been observed by any
careful bystander to drop about half an inch the moment
he had done so. He saw that he had left his queen
of clubs with only one guard. Perhaps he had settled
down to be comfortable, but nobody could possibly
have guessed that. Mrs. Holders then led the knave
of clubs from her partner's hand, Mrs. Oxney played
something of extreme insignificance, and then Mrs.
Holders sat and thought. She pulled a card out of
her hand, and held it poised. She put it back. She
pulled out another card and played the king of clubs.
The Colonel played a small one.

Colonel Chase began to perspire.

Mrs. Holders pulled out a card again and put it back.
A most annoying habit. Then she pulled it out again
and played it. It was the ace of clubs. Colonel
Chase put on the queen (it couldn't be helped), and
Mrs. Oxney discarded something pathetically unim-
portant in another suit.

" What ? No more clubs ? " said Colonel Chase in
a voice of intense indignation.

" No, I wish I had," said poor Mrs. Oxney. " Isn't
it bad luck ? And I've got such a quantity of—oh, I
suppose I mustn't say what."

" I don't mind," said Mrs. Holders, who thereupon
played out the ace of hearts, and followed it with
processions of winning clubs and winning spades.

Colonel Chase said " Pshaw ! " Cataracts of diamonds
had been spouting from his hand, and rivers of hearts
from his partner's.

" But don't we get any more ? " said Mrs. Oxney.
" All my beautiful hearts and all your beautiful diamonds ? "

"Fifty for little slam," said Mrs. Holders quite calmly, though her eyebrows had almost disappeared, "and thirty for aces. Then two hundred for my contract, doubled and redoubled, and two hundred more for the extra trick, and below six times two hundred. I think that's all. Dear me!"

This was intolerable.

"Not bridge at all," said Colonel Chase. "With not a single diamond in your hand, and spades headed by the knave. Madness! I would have doubled on my hand every time."

Mrs. Holders knew all that perfectly well. She knew also, (and knew that Colonel Chase knew) that if he had not unguarded his queen of clubs. . . . But then he had, and she went on adding up.

"And two is seven," she said, "and eight is fifteen, and six is twenty-one, and seven is twenty-eight, and seven is thirty-five, and six is forty-one and carry four, and two and three and five is fourteen and four is eighteen——"

"Yes, I make that," said Miss Kemp, licking her pencil, "and oh, just look at the hundreds!"

After they had sufficiently looked at the hundreds, the general reckoning disclosed that Colonel Chase had to pay everybody all round, and he disbursed sums varying from threepence to Mrs. Oxney up to the staggering figure of three and ninepence due to Miss Kemp. All the evenings on which everybody had paid to him were forgotten in general commiseration and nobody dreamed of consoling him with the encouragement he often administered to others, and told him that his game was improving so much that very likely he would soon win it all back again. Mrs. Oxney could scarcely be induced to accept her threepence, and she had to steel herself to the sacrifice by the glad hope that she would lose ten times that sum to him tomorrow. On other nights Colonel Chase usually stood for a long time in front of the fire-place when the rubbers were over, richly rattling coppers in his trousers' pocket, and giving them a few hints about declarations to take up to bed, but now there was no chink of bullion to endorse his wisdom, and he made as short work of his glass of whiskey and water (called ' grog ' or ' nightcap ') as he had made of the cross-word, and left the victors on the field of battle. Miss Kemp gave him time to get upstairs, in order to avoid the indelicacy of seeing a gentleman open his bedroom door, and perhaps disclose pyjamas warming by the fire, and then followed him in some haste, since her father (there was no indelicacy about that) always expected her to come and talk to him, when he had got to bed, about his evening symptoms, or read to him till he felt sleepy. She knew she was unusually late to-night, and it was possible that he had punished her by already putting out his light. This pathetic pro-ceeding, he was sure, wrung her with agonies of remorse.

No such severity had been inflicted to-night; he was sitting up in bed with a book in front of him; and a fur tippet belonging to Florence round his neck for the protection of the glands of the throat. On the table beside him was the thermos flask filled with hot milk, in case he felt un-nourished during the night, the glass jug of lemonade made with saccharine instead of sugar in case he felt thirsty, and the clock with the luminous hands.

" I am late, Papa, I'm afraid," she said. " We had a most exciting rubber which would not come to an end."

His face wore its most martyred expression : he glanced at the clock which showed the unprecedented hour of eleven.

" Surely my clock is fast," he said.

" No ; it is eleven," she said. " Shall I read to you ? "

" Far too late : far, far too late. I shall be good for nothing in the morning as it is."

" You would like to go to sleep then ? " she asked. " Shall I put out your light ? "

" Indeed, I should very much like to go to sleep," he said, " but it is already long past my usual hour for going to sleep, and as you know, if I am not asleep by eleven, I often lie awake half the night. No doubt you were absorbed in your game, and could not spare a thought to me. Very natural. Two hours bridge ! I was wrong to expect that perhaps it would occur to you—but no matter."

" Would you like me to talk to you then, if you don't feel you'll go to sleep ? " she asked.

" Perhaps a little talk might compose me," said he, " if you can spare me ten minutes. I am very tired to-night, and that makes me wakeful. I have had a great deal to do. My thermos flask was unfilled, and I had to ring. There were no rusks in my little tin and I had to get out the big tin and fill it. My clock was not wound."

Florence sat down by his bed. Her chair grated on the margin of boards as she pulled it forward, and he winced.

" You've got everything now, haven't you ? " she asked.

" Yes. I saw to everything myself. Talk to me, please. Yes ? "

" I won three and ninepence," said Florence. " Colonel Chase lost to everybody."

" I heard him thumping by just now," said her father. " I supposed he had lost, for he banged his door. I was just beginning to get sleepy. A want of consideration, perhaps. Yes ? "

At each interrogative 'yes', as Florence knew, a fresh topic of interest had to be furnished.

" Mrs. Oxney won threepence," she said.

" I am glad. Perhaps she will be able to afford me hot water in my bottle to-morrow. It was tepid to-night. I think you have told me enough about your game of bridge. Yes ? "

" Miss Howard is playing at an entertainment in the assembly rooms next week."

" I will not go," said Mr. Kemp with some heat. " I do not see why I should be expected to turn out in the evening. Yes ? "

Florence felt the swift on-coming of a sneeze. She fumbled in her bag for a handkerchief, and rattled richly among the nine coppers. Several violent explosions followed, and when the spasm subsided, she found her father spraying the air round him with his flask of disinfectant.

" Perhaps it would be wiser if you sat a little further off," he said. " Yes ? "

" I don't think anything else has happened," said Florence wheezily. " Oh yes, that new arrival, Mrs. Bliss. I saw you talking to her. How she smiles ! I wonder why ? "

Mr. Kemp shewed the first sign of withdrawing the blight he had been casting on this commandeered conversation.

" She told me strange things," he said. " I could make little of them, though I must confess they interested me. She said I was perfectly well, and that pain had no real existence. To say that to me of all people appears on the face of it to be the gibbering of a lunatic. Yet as she talked I certainly did begin to feel that there was something behind it. She told me also that she was perfectly well, though I have never seen anybody limp more heavily. I scarcely think that I was as bad as that after my terrible experiences at Aix. I thought she would hardly be able to get upstairs yet she called to me from the landing, though much out of breath, that she had not felt a

single twinge.   Her theory is that all pain is an illusion
or a delusion, I forget which, and if you only deny it, it
vanishes.   Ever since I came up to bed, which is a
long time ago now, I have been denying it and I
think—I am not sure, but I think—that I am lying a
little more easily to-night than I have done since last
Monday.   But I must not get too much interested in
it at this hour."

Mr. Kemp yawned as he spoke.

" I am beginning to get a little drowsy," he said.
" I will not talk any more.   Please go out very quietly,
and turn off my light from the switch by the door.
Don't bang it."

Florence tiptoed away to her room ; though it was
late, she felt wakeful and exhilarated.   She had
enjoyed her bridge, but it was not that alone, nor her
unusually long remission from her father, nor yet
the load of bullion that clinked in her bag which
accounted for it.   The evening had been adventurous,
for Mrs. Holders had fluttered the red flag in the face
of that formidable autocrat Colonel Chase : she had
called in question the wisdom of his declaration, she had
backed her own opinion by doubling, she had invoked
the decision of Slam.   And no retribution had followed,
no thunderbolt had split her : the Colonel had merely
paid up all round and gone to bed.

Florence wound up her watch and looked at her
plump and rather pleasing image in the glass.   Her
hair was cropped like a man's, and parted at the side :
she wore a stiff linen collar with a small black tie in a
bow, and a starched shirt with a sort of Eton jacket ;
her skirt was about the same length as the jacket.   Then
crossing her legs in an easy attitude she sat down on her
bed, and thought carefully over what had been happen-
ing this evening.   It was an application of Mrs.
Holders's defiance, rather than the defiance itself that
claimed her attention.   For Wentworth in general

dumbly travailed under the domination of the Colonel,
and if three hours ago she had been asked what she
supposed would happen if anyone questioned his rulings
and his bawlings and his tuition, her imagination would
have failed to picture so impossible a contingency.
Yet the impossible had now occurred and nothing had
happened. The application was obvious, and she found
herself wondering what would happen if she questioned
her father's right to immolate her day and night on
the altar of his aches. Daring though such a supposi-
tion was, would nothing particular happen?

Florence let the hypochondriac history of the last
seven years, from the time when her father had seriously taken up the profession of invalidism instead of
having no profession at all, spread itself panoramically
out in front of her. Her mother was alive then, and
for those first two years of this lean series, the three
of them had trodden the uneasy circle of hydropathic
establishments. Buxton, Bath, Harrogate, and Bolton
(but never Aix again) had grown to be the cardinal
points of the year, and these were followed by Torquay,
Cromer, Scarborough and Bournemouth for the after-
cure of bracing air or sunny climate. At first they
had returned to the pleasant little flat in Kensington
Square after the quarterly cure to wait for the next
cardinal point to come round, but her father who was
in his element in boarding houses with all their good
opportunities of telling relays of strangers about his
ailments, soon discovered that London did not suit
him, for it was airless in the summer, treacherous in
the autumn and spring and foggy in the winter, and
now he and Florence remained at Torquay, Cromer,
Scarborough and Bournemouth till the next cure. After
two years of this preposterous existence, her mother,
who had always been frail and anæmic, simply came to
the end of her vitality, and exhausted by her husband's
vampirism had stopped living. She had been possessed

of a considerable fortune, half of which, with the flat
in Kensington Square, she had left to Florence absolutely, the remainder to her husband for life. This
appeared to him the most ungrateful return for all the
care he had allowed her to take of him, and until his
own health had completely driven all other interests
from his mind he had sedulously nursed this grievance.
Since then, for five years, Florence had been his
enslaved companion.

She knew well that her interminable ministries to
him were not performed out of the bounty of love, but
from her own acquiescence in being crushed, and now
it struck her that she thoroughly disliked him. Though
she had not definitely stated that to herself before, the
emotion must have been habitual, for its discovery
did not in the least shock her nor did it shock her to
conjecture that he equally disliked her. Probably
all these years, he would have been happier with a
trained nurse, who was paid for being bullied and bored,
and she herself could have lived instead of merely
getting older. She might even have married, for
women did not become certified spinsters at the age
of thirty, as she was when her solitary gyrations with
him began, but the idea of marriage had hitherto seemed
very embarrassing to her virginal soul. No man alive
could justly claim to have raised the beat of her placid
blood by a single pulsation ; she had no spark of envy
for any woman however happily married, compared
with one who had her liberty. Miss Howard for
instance seemed to her to live an almost ideal existence : she went where she liked, and nobody could
claim her time or her energies, she tripped and sang
about the passages, so sunlit to her was the normal
hour : she devoted herself to her painting and her
piano, the pursuits she adored, and had no bond-slave
duties to anybody. Happy Miss Howard, gifted and
accomplished and free ! And how handsome she was :

what a charm and vivacity! Though Florence had
never experienced any sort of tenderness for a man,
she sometimes thought of Miss Howard with a sort
of shy, sentimental yearning.

There had been moments, rare and swiftly vanishing,
when Florence had seen freedom gleaming on the far
horizon, for in the sad hydropathic round, her father
sometimes made friends with suitable and sympathetic
females, especially those who had sitting-rooms and
maids and motors, and once or twice it had really looked
as if something was coming of it. He was remarkably
handsome with his fine aquiline face, his thick grey
hair and tall slim figure, and she was sure that middle-
aged spinsters and widows had given him and received
from him very promising attention. She knew well
the symptoms on his side, for when such friendship
was ripening he adopted an attitude of wistful and
tender affection towards herself; he would pat her
hand (when the lady was by) and ask her what she had
been doing, and thank her for being so devoted to
her poor old Papa. But nothing had ever come of
it, the lady who seemed within an ace of becoming
her poor old Mamma, had got some glimpse, Florence
supposed, of his unique selfishness, and had shaken
off the glamour.

She was ready for bed now, and still under the
inspiration of the revolt which Mrs. Holders had made
against the authority and omniscience of Colonel
Chase, she asked herself what would happen if she
refused to be eternally dragged about from Spa to
Spa. Naturally she could not throw off so chronic
a yoke with one comprehensive gesture of defiance;
she would have to begin gently and say, for instance,
tomorrow morning, that she was going out for a walk
instead of coming down to the baths with him in
the bus and, after doing various chemical errands for
him, sitting in the waiting-room which faintly smelt

of the awful effluvium of the waters, till he was ready
to drive up again. Perhaps, if she could summon
up nerve, she might ask Miss Howard if she might
help her to carry her satchel and stool to the scene of
her sketch. As she quenched her light, she heard
through the door which communicated with her father's
room, a sound so regular and sonorous that, if he had
not been sure he was going to lie awake for hours,
she would certainly have thought he was fast asleep.

CHAPTER III

THE warmth and clemency of October which till now
had been so pleasant, and had permitted Miss Howard
to make so many notable sketches of noon and evening
and night without the risk of catching a chill, completely
collapsed during the dark hours, and piercing blasts
from the north-east with volleys of half-frozen rain
rattled on the windows of Wentworth. Colonel Chase,
who often attributed much of his magnificent robustness to the fact that he always slept with his window
wide open, top and bottom, had a most alarming dream
that Mrs. Holders, with whom he was playing bridge
in a restaurant car on a train which was oscillating
very much, laid an odd-looking card resembling the ace
of hearts, yet somehow different from it, on the table
and said, "That card gives me the rubber doubled
and redoubled." As she spoke the oscillation increased
and the card began to give out sharp reports, and he
woke to find his blind blowing out horizontally into
the room and cracking like a whip, while the solid
walls of Wentworth trembled in the gale. He jumped
out of bed, and at the risk of undermining his health
by closing the window, shut and bolted it. Mr. Kemp
was more fortunate, for knowing that the night air
was poison to him, he always slept with his window
closed, shuttered and curtained. But even so the
driven sleet awoke him, and observing by his luminous
clock that it was a quarter past two, took a cup of hot
milk and a rusk. Warmed and comforted he turned

over in bed without a single twinge from his left hip, which was so surprising that he lay awake a long time and wondered whether it was Mind. Soot poured down Mrs. Holders's chimney, but she could not help that and instantly went to sleep again.

The gale had not abated when the guests began to assemble for breakfast, sleet still rapped at the panes, and the house was bitterly cold, for who, wailed Mrs. Oxney, could have expected so sudden and diabolical a change of weather? As soon as she got down, she ordered wood fires to be lit in lounge and drawing-room and smoking-room, for coal must be husbanded as long as the strike continued, and sent the gardener to kindle the furnace of the central-heating. But the dining-room certainly was like an ice-house at breakfast: Miss Howard's hand shook as she poured the milk over her porridge, Mr. Kemp sent Florence upstairs to get a rug for his knees, and Colonel Chase, in an appalling temper, put on a cap, which he pulled down over his ears, a long woolly muffler and a great coat. He did not really feel cold, but it was only right that Mrs. Oxney should be filled with remorse at not having foreseen the change, and having omitted to have the central-heating put on in anticipation of it. Seeing that she was looking at him, he turned up his coat collar and gave several painful coughs.

The only exception to these suffering breakfasters was Mrs. Bliss. She was limping very badly, and it took her a long time to sidle round the corner of her table, and, leaning heavily on it, to sit down, but throughout the whole of this apparently agonising process she had a bright smile and salutations right and left. She was wearing quite a thin blouse and no jacket, but when Mr. Kemp seeing that there was a reddish tinge on her nose, a bluish tinge round her mouth, and that her hands were deadly white, said that she would surely get double pneumonia, being so lightly clad on such a bitter morning, she protested she had never been so warm and comfortable.

"And what a beautiful day it is going to be!" she said, as the gusts rattled at the window. "Such a refreshing shower! The grey rain-clouds on the hills, driven along by the breeze looked so lovely as I was dressing."

Her teeth chattered slightly as she spoke, but she fixed them in a piece of hot roll.

"But it's a terrible gale," said Mr. Kemp. "I am not sure that I shall go down to the baths at all. I do not know what it is wisest to do. Perhaps if I wore my fur coat, and had a hot water bottle ready for my return I might venture. See to that, please, Florence."

"Ah, then I did hear the sound of wind during the night," said Mrs. Bliss. "That was it! A beautiful rushing noise. But I slept so well I was hardly conscious of it, and awoke so happy and glowing and fresh."

"Either the woman's mad or she's got Esquimaux blood," muttered Colonel Chase, as he listened to these remarkable views. He put his hand on the stack of so-called hot water pipes close to his chair and withdrew it hurriedly.

"Stone-cold," he observed to Miss Howard. "Disgraceful! Pipes as cold as that would keep any room cool in the height of summer."

Mrs. Oxney who had been cheered by Mrs. Bliss's impressions of the morning, overheard this, as she was indeed meant to do, and felt miserable again. She got up, her appetite completely ruined by these scathing observations, and went over to the Colonel's table, with a wretched attempt at cheerfulness.

"Oh, but the pipes will soon be hot, Colonel," she said. "My sister's gone out to see about the furnace herself, and I promise you they shan't spare the coke.

That sudden change took us all by surprise. But I've had fires lit everywhere, and we shall soon all be cosy again. . . . Good morning Mrs. Bliss ; and you slept well I heard you say ? "

Mrs. Bliss beamed on her.

" Beautifully ! So comfortable ! And so enjoying my breakfast. Delicious ! And the rain is clearing. I shall have such a refreshing walk down to the baths, and up again."

Mr. Kemp was thrilled at this astounding programme. Was she sane, he wondered, or was it Mind ? Or was she (in another sense) a mental case ? Here, anyhow, was this smiling lady, who, in spite of blue lips, said she felt warm in this refrigerating dining-room, and who, making slow sad work about traversing the smooth level of the floor, intended to walk down and up the steep hill between Wentworth and the pickling estab- lishment. It was a good half-mile each way, and he would have considered himself hale and hearty again, if he had been able to accomplish so arduous a feat. He had visions of Mrs. Bliss falling in front of the wheels of a motor as she crossed the road, or dying of exposure as she pursued her way with those minute and halting steps and frequent stoppages through this sleet-sown blizzard. That would have annoyed him, as he wanted to hear more about Mind and its method. He intervened with some agitation.

" Better not, far better not, Mrs. Bliss," he said. " The baths which can be so remedial are very fatiguing ; my doctor, and I'm sure yours, recommends the mini- mum of physical exertion, while the course is going on. I avoid all physical fatigue while I am here."

She laughed merrily.

" Dear Mr. Kemp," she said, " you still think that you are an invalid, whereas I know that I am in perfect health and harmony. Did you demonstrate last night, reminding yourself that all is Mind ? "

Mr. Kemp remembered the singular fact of his having turned over without a twinge : all those twinges
which he suffered as he dressed had expunged
it. He had finished his breakfast, and nodded to
Florence to indicate that she might go away, for he
wanted to pursue last night's subject, and though he
would have welcomed any conviction that he was well,
he did not want Florence to get hold of that idea first,
or his thermos flask might be left permanently empty,
and his smaller tin for rusks unreplenished. But
Florence, with the fumes of last night's revolutionary
debauch still lingering in her brain, paid no attention
to this familiar signal.

" If you've finished your breakfast, Florence," he
said, " you will kindly go upstairs and bring down my
hat and coat, fur coat I think, so that I shall be ready
to start. Goloshes of course. And a hot water bottle
when I get back."

Florence waved a minute red flag. This was
beginning gently.

" Presently, Papa," she said, " there is plenty of
time."

Mr. Kemp was naturally very much shocked at this
answer, for never before, to the best of his knowledge, had Florence shown such mutinous independence,
and his staring at her, with deep disfavour, which usually had so subduing an effect proved on this occasion
to have none. Instead of hurrying away she turned
to Mrs. Bliss.

" Do go on telling my father about illness being a
delusion," she said. " It would be lovely if you could
convince him of it."

Mrs. Bliss was delighted to do so ; nothing could
possibly be easier than to convince anybody of a self-
evident proposition, but owing to the apparently
piercing cold of the dining-room, they adjourned to
the lounge. The two victims of this tiresome delusion

concerning rheumatic joints were for the moment so
completely taken in by it, that they took a long
while to hobble along the slippery parquet, and
Florence certainly saved Mrs. Bliss from the delusion
of falling down. When they got there, they found that
this gale was causing the chimney to behave as if it
was upside-down, and clouds of pungent wood-smoke
came pouring out of it. Mr. Kemp then suffered
from the further delusion that wood-smoke was very
trying to the eyes, and sat with his handkerchief over
them, though Mrs. Bliss, with the tears pouring down
her cheeks asserted that she felt no inconvenience
whatever from it. Her immunity served as an excellent text for her homily, and while Florence and her
father as if overcome with emotion, held their pocket-
handkerchiefs before their eyes, she told them how
wood-smoke could not possibly have any effect on those
who realised that all was harmony in Omnipotent
Mind.

As if to endorse her words, the chimney began to
draw better, and having surreptitiously wiped away
her tears, she told them to put down their handkerchiefs and calmly but firmly deny the delusion of that
stinging sensation. Sure enough they found they
had been the victims of Error.

There was still an apparent lack of harmony in the
conditions outside, when the omnibus came round
to take the patients to the baths, for it seemed to be
pelting with rain, and Mrs. Bliss consented to be
driven down though she still said that she would much
have enjoyed the walk. But her husband, for whose
sake she was undergoing this quite unnecessary cure,
would not have liked the thought that she was exposing
herself to this odious weather (though the weather
whatever it might be, could not hurt anybody) and
with this loving thought of him in her mind, she
consented to be well wrapped-up, and hoisted into

the omnibus. As there was no chance of helping Miss Howard with her sketching things, Florence abandoned the contemplated revolt of refusing to go down to the baths with her father, and Mrs. Bliss lent her the manual of Mental Science, to read while she was waiting. She could give her father absent treatment, while he was being pickled.

The joint exertions of Mrs. Bertram and the gardener had sent rivers of hot water roaring through the central-heating apparatus, and Colonel Chase, sitting in the smoking-room found himself reluctantly compelled to discard his cap, muffler and great coat. Any idea of breaking fresh records on his bicycle was out of the question on so stormy a morning, for the roads, even if the rain stopped, would be a mere muddy liquefaction, and the hours till lunch-time had to be passed indoors. On days like these, he always felt that Nature had fixed her malignant eye on him, and was vomiting from the skies these innumerable gallons of cold water with the sole and express purpose of making the roads impossible for his bicycle. A materialist might hold that she was pursuing the miserable logic of physical laws, but he knew that did not fully account for a wet morning. And then, too, just because it was wet, the paper contained nothing of interest : even the criminal classes seemed to have joined in the conspiracy against him, for there was no news of brutal murders or other interesting crimes which might while away the hours for him. As for the coal strike he was sick of it and despaired of the Government taking the line he had always maintained they should, and sending the miners back to the pits whether they liked it or not.

He threw down the paper in disgust, and moved his chair a little further from the pyramid of logs which was roaring up the chimney, but this brought him closer to the hot water pipes which were now almost as

fervent as the fire. But there was positively nowhere
else to sit except in the smoking-room, for the lounge
was draughty, and Miss Howard was making music—
if you could call it music—in the drawing-room. Up
and down the piano she went with trills and scales
and shakes and roulades : Mrs. Oxney ought really
to ask her not to play on a wet morning, when other
people were house-bound, for there was no getting
away from that irritating tinkle. How could a man
read his paper with that going on ? It was as
distracting as when people insisted on talking while
playing bridge. If he ever decided to offer some presentable middle-aged woman the chance of looking
after him and sharing his name, it must be distinctly
understood that she must not play the piano except
in some remote room. He wondered whether there
was some such withdrawn boudoir at Miss Howard's
little place in Kent near Tunbridge Wells.

The thought of bridge suggested more disagreeable
reflections. Last night's game had been very expensive, and it had disclosed, he thought, a very ugly
spirit. Several times Mrs. Holders had made a direct
frontal attack on his most authoritative manœuvres.
She had doubled when he had declared two hearts,
openly saying that he had a very good reason for it,
she had told him (him !) that he ought to say ' no bid '
instead of ' pass ' : she had redoubled his double of
her impossible declaration, and the damned woman had
been right (if you could call it right,) every time.
Certainly he would not ask her to play with him to-
night : he would get Mrs. Bertram to take her place,
though Mrs. Bertram had an agonising habit of at once
leading out any ace she happened to hold, in order to
make sure of it ; or, if she was exhorted not to be so
insanely prodigal, of refusing to play any ace till it
was quite certain to be trumped. But no woman, so
he often thought, had any head for cards ; the finesse

and subtlety of the game was beyond them, and Miss Howard was wise in refusing to play at all. He wished her refusal to play had extended to the use of the piano.

A glint of watery sunlight gleamed on the hot water pipes ; the rain had ceased, and though bicycling was impossible Colonel Chase resolved to go out for a good tramp with the pocket pedometer. The morning was a miserable time unless you were out of doors, for without strenuous exercise then, you could not rest properly after lunch, and as for reading in the morning, what was to be done with the hour after tea, if you had read all the morning ? Only a bookworm could manage two spells of reading a day, and he thanked God he was not that. Besides that infernal tinkling from the piano was enough to put reading out of the question.

He adjusted his pedometer to zero, and shouldering his mackintosh went briskly down the hill into the town. He turned into the waiting-room at the bath establishment, though he had no right there, since it was provided for patients waiting for their baths, and friends waiting for patients, but there was no chance of Colonel Chase being challenged by the attendants. Far more likely that they would appreciate the honour he did the management by looking at the notice-board which advertised current and coming diversions. Among these was the announcement of the entertainment in aid of the Children's Hospital, and he observed with pain that Miss Howard had ' kindly consented ' to give an improvisation on the piano. Miss Kemp was sitting near, waiting for her father and absorbed in some book, but Colonel Chase gave so loud a snort of indignation at this information that she looked up with a start.

" Improvisation indeed ! " he scornfully observed. " Why Miss Howard has been practising her improvisation, so as to get it by heart, ever since breakfast !

Drove me out of the house! Kindly consented to! I wish she'd kindly consent to leave the piano alone. Humbug!"

Florence put her finger on the line she was reading, and sprang to arms at this monstrous attack on her adored.

"I think it's wonderfully kind of her," she said, "and I look forward to it as the greatest treat. And how on earth do you know that she's going to play at the entertainment what she is practising now? That's a pure invention."

Colonel Chase was considerably startled by this sudden fierceness.

"Well it's the same old tune that she's been hammering at ever since I came to Wentworth," he said.

Florence felt that her indignation was not quite in tune with the spirit of mental science which she had been studying. Poor Colonel Chase had a false claim of malice which should be treated just like a false claim of pain. Neither malice nor pain had any real existence and must be denied. She began to smile like Mrs. Bliss.

"Such lovely tunes," she said. "So sweet and harmonious and refreshing."

But Colonel Chase was clearly out of harmony.

"Make a sort of tinkling noise in my head if you mean that," he said. "Well, I'm off for a tramp. No possibility of bicycling through this mud."

Florence continued to smile.

"How you'll enjoy your walk!" she said. "And the sun is coming out gloriously."

Colonel Chase had not been far wrong in his cynical reflections, for Miss Howard was busy over what might truly be called memorising her improvisation for next week. It would be nice to begin with a few slow minor chords, all her own, (or indeed anybody else's) and an impressive pause, so that the audience would certainly think that something very tragic and funereal was to follow, and so would be pleasantly surprised when instead there came gay chromatic runs up to the very top of the piano and half-way down again, and a long butterfly shake which ushered in a few bars of a waltz by Chopin and a quantity more of her own composition. Never had her fingers been more agile and delicate, there was not a hitch or a stumble anywhere, and Mrs. Oxney, adding up the laundry book in her sitting-room next door felt sure that Miss Howard would get an encore if that was part of her improvisation. Then the waltz-rhythm ceased and something very swoony and mysterious succeeded : it was as if the dancers (so Miss Howard thought to herself) had left the gay and brilliant ball-room and were walking about moonlit glades in miserable and melancholy reverie. She had to play this section of the improvisation several times over, for there came quite unexpected effects in it, which surprised her by their beauty, and she must make sure of these. The pensive mood became more solemn yet, and the dancers seemed to sing a sort of chorale in a minor key which Miss Howard had composed last summer when suffering from toothache. She could not quite remember the last line of it, but she had written it down, and could easily perfect herself in that. A pause again followed during which the final chord of the chorale was struck four times very softly and nobody could tell what would happen next, indeed Miss Howard wished she knew herself. A long shake however must be introduced rather high up on the piano while the left hand played arpeggios up from the very bottom, crossed the shake without disturbing it, and came down again, for that was one of her most remarkable effects. She could go on playing these for ever, but since they were clearly leading up to something, they must come to an end, and make way for what they were introducing. Then she remembered that she had not put in any of those passages of octaves yet, in which the butterfly's place was taken by a powerful hammer, and she began playing octaves with both hands up and down, on black notes and white alike, with increasing speed and crescendo, and still she wondered what would happen next, and so did Mrs. Oxney who sat over the laundry book next door, openmouthed at this surpassing vigour and brilliancy. Then Miss Howard suddenly saw her way clear and swooped back into the Chopin waltz. Then Bang, Whack, Bump: three enormous chords brought the improvisation to an end. Allowing for the repetition of the swoony section, it had lasted just ten minutes, which would do nicely.

Miss Howard got up, and, hearing in her imagination rounds of enthusiastic applause, smiled and bowed to the delighted audience, just to see what it felt like. It seemed that they quite refused to be content with what she had played them and insisted on an encore. She sat down again, and pressed her fingers to her eyes (a gesture that she must remember) as if wondering what little morsel to give them next. They clearly wanted something more from the same mine, and she ran her hands delicately over the keys, still considering. Perhaps those little variations on ' Tipperary ' which she had so often played would be suitable, but there was no need to practise them for she was absolutely note-perfect in this improvisation. She just ran through them for the pleasure of hearing them again.

She went through the main improvisation four or five times more and then, putting on her rings, again went to the window. It was fine, though clearly too cold for sketching, but a short brisk walk would be pleasant after all this concentration, and she went down into the town with the intention of paying for the frame of ' Evening Bells ', but with the real object of seeing if the advertisement of the entertainment was displayed yet. As she tripped along she hummed over the more vocal parts of her piece, and visualised her hands performing octaves and arpeggios. She must get them so familiar that she would not have the slightest apprehension of not being able to produce them unerringly.

She paused opposite the bath establishment, and there was the notice prominently exhibited, and ' Pianoforte Solo (improvisation) by Miss Alice Howard ' in very gratifying type came fourth on the programme. The church choir of St. Giles's, was to open with some glees, then Mr. Graves, the amusing *masseur*, was down for ' Stories ', then the Revd. H. Banks (vicar) was to sing, and her item followed. After that the choir sang again, and Dr. Dobbs did some conjuring tricks, and the Revd. H. Banks sang again, and Mrs. Banks played a violin solo (Salut d'Amour) and the Revd. H. Banks recited, ' Curfew will not ring to-night ', and there was a performing dog and various other rich items followed by a collection and carriages at ten. Miss Howard read this through twice, pausing at the fourth item, and then her eye was caught by another advertisement. This was to say that the Green Salon at the baths, suitable for private parties or picture exhibitions, could be hired at a very reasonable sum by the evening or the week or longer periods.

Miss Howard felt very like all the Muses rolled into one accomplished incarnation that morning, and she thought of the stacks of sketches blushing unseen in her portfolios. Her improvisation still rang in her ears. Just opposite her was the façade of the baths establishment, which she had depicted in her ' Healing Springs ', and a textile company in which she had quite a number of shares had that morning announced a bonus distribution of unexpected size : thus she felt rich as well as artistic. Enquiries about the Green Salon she saw were to be made of Town Councillor Bowen, at whose shop ' Evening Bells ' had been framed, and she determined, at the least, to make them, and, at the most, to take the Green Salon (suitable for picture exhibitions) for a fortnight. She knew the room : it was close to the office where patients purchased their tickets for the baths, and was thus very conveniently placed, for many of them surely would be tempted to look in while they were waiting for their baths. Moreover, it was not too large : forty or fifty water colours, which she could easily select from her store, would be sufficient, tastefully spaced, to decorate it and to display themselves to the highest advantage. The walls, which might be supposed to be green could equally well be described as grey, and would furnish a suitably neutral background.

Town Councillor Bowen was attending to his municipal duties, and was not at home, but Mrs. Town Councillor was, and she beamed respectfully at Miss Howard as she paid a ten shilling note for the framing of ' Evening Bells ' over the counter, and waited for change.

" And I declare I oughtn't to charge you anything at all, Miss Howard," observed this most polite lady, " for it's a pleasure to frame your beautiful pictures. Mr. Bowen was touching up the gilding himself with his own hands, and though he knew his dinner was ready he stood there a-looking and a-looking at the work of art till I called out ' George, come along do, for your chop's getting cold.' ' Evening Bells ' ! I wish everybody who's fretting and worrying could have a good look at ' Evening Bells ', for it would make them all feel peaceful again, I'm sure. And half a crown and a florin make ten."

This little speech seemed to Miss Howard to be nothing less than a ' leading'. She was instantly led, after a modest cough or two.

" I see the Green Salon can be hired by the week, Mrs. Bowen," she said, " and that put it into my head that I might hold a little exhibition of my paintings. A few people, as you're so kind to suggest, might perhaps care to glance at them."

Mrs. Bowen turned up her eyes to the ceiling as if in mute thanksgiving.

" Well, that would be kind of you," she said. "As I was saying to Mr. Bowen only the other day—but never mind that ! What a treat for us all ! I'm sure I shall be walking round the Green Salon morning, noon and night. And the terms are so moderate and nothing to pay for lighting, as the establishment closes at five, while there's still sufficient daylight to see pictures. Let me see, what did Mr. Bowen say they asked ? I declare I forget, but I know you'll find it most moderate. As for the hanging of your works of art, I'll be there with a hammer and nails myself, and think it a privilege. And when would you be meaning your exhibition to commence ? Such a treat for everybody."

There was no reason why it should not open as soon as Mr. Bowen could frame the exhibits, and Miss Howard promised to select them at once. The *Bolton Gazette* of which Mr. Bowen was one of the proprietors, would advertise it on most reasonable terms, and unless Miss Howard wanted to put it in the London papers, so that her friends might run down, there would practically be no other expense beyond the wages of an attendant (and no doubt the bath-establishment would let Miss Howard employ one of the uniformed pages) and the charge of a catalogue, which could be typewritten for a song. Mrs. Bowen would see to that, and to the list of prices if Miss Howard was intending to let the public purchase her beautiful works of art. And of course, some small red stars, adhesive stars to affix to those which were sold and prevent disappointment. Such a run there would be on them, Mrs. Bowen opined.

There was no resisting such a rosy statement, and,

this agreeable conversation over, Miss Howard hurried back to the baths, in order to catch the omnibus for Wentworth, and begin making her selection without wasting a moment. Another reason for haste was that the clearing of the weather seemed only temporary, and thick fat clouds promising an imminent deluge were blowing up. The omnibus was waiting, and just as Miss Howard arrived, Mrs. Bliss came out of the ladies corridor wreathed in smiles and supported on sticks.

"Such a lovely bath, Miss Howard, so salt and refreshing and exhilarating. And how I look forward to my walk home on this breezy morning! Are you walking too? Mr. Kemp was thinking of it, but he is not quite sure. What a pleasant party we shall be if we all stroll up together."

The door of the waiting-room opened, and Mr. Kemp came out leaning on Florence's arm.

"Yes, my dear, I've been denying it as hard as ever I can," he was saying. "But I know I should never be able to get up the hill. Ah, there's Mrs. Bliss. What do you advise, Mrs. Bliss? Just now every step is agony, or, if it isn't really agony, it is something so like, that nobody could tell the difference. All the same it isn't quite so bad as it was yesterday, I'm sure of that. I walked all the way down the passage from my bath to the waiting-room without holding on to the wall. That's something you know. It's more than I've done for the last week."

Mrs. Bliss staggered towards him.

"Don't force it, dear Mr. Kemp," she said. "If you feel like that, you had better go up in the bus, but keep on telling yourself that you could walk double the distance without a single twinge of pain. Hold on to Mind, and you won't want to hold on to walls."

"Are you going to walk?" he asked.

"Oh yes. I gave myself treatment all the time I

was in my bath. It produced such a feeling of buoyancy, I'm sure I should have floated in the water, if
my attendant had not put little wooden bars across
me to keep me down."

Mr. Kemp became materialistic for a moment.

"Oh, everyone does that," he said. "It's the
brine."

Mrs. Bliss of course knew that this buoyancy was
the effect of right thought and reliance on Mind, and
assured Mr. Kemp that he would very soon get to
know that too. Then, as all the others seemed to think
they were lame, or were afraid of getting wet, though
getting wet could not possibly hurt anybody, she
grasped her sticks, and with a loving smile at the black
and menacing clouds limped slowly away. The
omnibus whizzed up the hill to Wentworth, and just
as they arrived, there burst a glacial storm of sleet,
and it was decided to send the omnibus back instantly
to pick up Mrs. Bliss, who, if she ever got to the top
of the hill at all, would be soaked and frozen. But it
had hardly started when she drove up in a taxi and came
radiantly into the lounge.

"I was having such a lovely walk," she said, "quite
free from any false claim of pain, and so much enjoying
the freshness, when a taxi drove by. The man stopped
and asked if I would not take him, as he had had no
fare all the morning. So I popped in just to please
him. A sweet little drive: so cosy."

The patients dispersed to their rooms for the prescribed hour's rest after their baths. Though Mrs. Bliss
said that she was not going to rest at all, but just lie
quiet on her bed and do an hour's strenuous work denying illness and pain, there was a superficial resemblance
between her procedure and that of the others, for they
all lay on bed or sofa, and kept quiet. . . . Mrs.
Holders rather acidly remarked that Mrs. Bliss would
soon deny having had a bath at all.

Miss Howard equally scorned the idea of rest. She ran through the improvisation again in order to fix one or two of the more elusive passages in her mind, and then began the work of selection for her exhibition. There were several fat portfolios full of sketches to choose from, and the difficulty at first seemed to be to know what to reject rather than what to choose, for they were all up to the same standard of execution. As she spread them out on her bed and her washing-stand and her table and her chimney-piece and finally, such was their profusion, on her carpet, other difficulties presented themselves, especially when she considered her catalogue. There were for instance nine pictures of St. Giles's Church, of which the famous " Evening Bells " was one : should she group them together under the collective title of " Some aspects of St. Giles's Church ? " That was prosaic, but on the other hand if she called them " Evening Bells ", and " Lengthening Shadows ", and " Morning Sunshine ", and " Reflections " (alluding to the river) and " God's Acre " (alluding to the churchyard) people might, in a carping spirit, say that they all represented the same thing. It would be better not to have so many pictures of St. Giles's Church, but it was hard to know which to reject. A similar question arose with regard to the various views of the town. They were chiefly painted from the garden at Wentworth, and in some the mist lay over the town, while the hills beyond were in sunshine, in others the hills were in mist and the town in sunshine, but ' Mist on the Hills ', and ' Mist in the Valley ' would make pretty titles for the two main types. Then there was ' Healing Springs ' which was a representation of the front of the bath-establishment, and ' Bethesda ' would be a good title for the same building from the garden at the back. A quantity of country lanes and pools of water and harvest moons must be thinned out,

and she weeded diligently among these and then found
that those she had rejected had peculiar effects of
beauty in them and that some of those she had chosen
were practically identical.   It was a relief to come to
Mrs. Oxney's cat, and the tree on the Colonel's golf
links (now prone, which gave a certain historical value
to the picture,) and a bed of geraniums, for these were
wholly unlike each other, and nobody could say that
a cat was another aspect of a geranium. . . . Then
there came the question of framing. Miss Howard
saw at once that she could not have forty or fifty
pictures framed in the style of ' Evening Bells ' at five
shillings and sixpence, for no bonuses of textile shares
would run to that. She must consult the Town
Councillor on the subject and obtain definite figures.
Something neat, something glazed, was all that was
required, without a final touching up of the gilding
by his hands. If the public appreciated her pictures
they could buy them without that.

Then there came the question of the price she was to
put on the exhibits, and instantly Miss Howard felt
as if she was dealing with problems quite unknown,
for she had not the smallest idea what to ask for them.
' Evening Bells ' was undoubtedly the gem of the
collection, but when she looked at Mrs. Oxney's cat
(which her mistress had often declared she could hear
purring) she wondered if she was not positively giving
it away, if she charged any smaller sum for it. But
what was that sum to be ?   She knew that pictures
had no absolute value, like the price of gold and silver
(and even that varied) : they were worth neither
more nor less than what anybody chose to pay for them.
But she had to start the bidding, though she also
concluded it, and since ' Evening Bells ' was clearly
not worth a hundred pounds, and just as clearly worth
more than one pound, she started the bidding by
putting it in a class by itself at three guineas.   ' Puss-

cat ' and ' Tree on golf links ', and perhaps ' Healing
Springs ' should by this standard be two guineas, and
everything else one guinea. . . . Or should she price
everything at one guinea, and hope to dispose of a
fair number of them, or should she price them all at
half a guinea, and hope to dispose of most ? So per-
plexing was the whole question that if at this moment,
anybody had offered her five shillings apiece for the
whole contents of the portfolios, she would have ecstatically accepted this meagre proposal, and have foregone
the Green Salon altogether. Yet the notion of an
exhibition was dear to her : it was not everybody who
came before the world like that, and, besides, nobody
had as yet offered her five shillings for the most accomplished of her efforts. In any case such a sum
was a derisory price to ask for the fruit of so much
trouble, for each sketch had taken her at least two
mornings' work, and many much more, and there was
such a thing as a living wage even if you had a little
place in Kent. The immediate urgency was to find
out from the Town Councillor at what figure he would
frame forty or fifty sketches neatly, but on an econo-
mical scale. She must also go into the price to be
charged for administration. The idea of season tickets
at a reduced cost was not practical if the exhibition
was to remain open for a fortnight at most, and the
idea of having a private view first could not be entertained for a moment, since Miss Howard would have
to send complimentary tickets to everyone at Wentworth, who were precisely the people whom the decencies
of friendship would compel to pay for admission.
She put the selected masterpieces into one of the portfolios, and with rather a haggard face went down to
lunch.

The storm which had burst with such violence just
as Mrs. Bliss caught the taxi, had caught Colonel Chase
a good three miles outside Bolton, on a peculiarly

bleak piece of road, and he said damn. Luckily there
was a barn standing in a field a few hundred yards
away, and finding it locked, he took shelter under its
eaves, lit a pipe, and with difficulty reminded himself
that he was an old campaigner. Half an hour's waiting
in this exiguous protection made him feel very chilly,
but the weather, no doubt accepting his challenge of
being an old campaigner, showed what it was capable
of, and continued to pour forth windy sleet with incredible violence. The eaves began to drip heavily
upon him, the wind played about his skirts in a sportive
and changeable manner, and after some more damns
the old campaigner thought it was better to get wet
quickly and then be able to change his clothes and have
a hot lunch, rather than get wet slowly and be too
late for it. He faced the blast, and with the pedometer
ticking briskly in his pocket marched homewards.
It should certainly register seven miles before he
reached Wentworth which would be a pretty sturdy
performance on so vile a day, and the congratulations
would be well earned.

Even as that vainglorious thought entered his mind
the hook of his pedometer slipped, and it slid unnoticed
through a hole in his waistcoat pocket on to the muddy
road. His mackintosh flapped, his knees became
extremely wet, the rain ran off the back of his cap
down his neck, and off its peak on to the end of his
nose, and after an hour's odious pilgrimage he came
dripping into the lounge where everyone, lunch being
over, was sitting comfortably round the fire. Cries
of admiration greeted him, but he would sooner have
felt less chilly and have foregone this enthusiastic
reception.

Mrs. Oxney hurried off to the kitchen to see if there
was still any Irish stew in existence, which could be
heated up, and be ready for him when he had changed
his clothes : the dish was snatched from the very jaws

of the parlour-maid, who was about to devour it, and
who had to be content with cold mutton instead.
Already Colonel Chase had symptoms of a cold coming
on : his throat was hot and dry, and a series of pro-
digious sneezings more than once interrupted his
discussion of the Irish stew. What made the malig-
nancy of the weather more marked was that he had no
sooner got home than the rain stopped, and there was
promise of a bright afternoon, but he thought it would
be wiser, with these ominous symptoms, not to go
out again, but sit warm in the smoking-room and allow
three guests to have a rubber of bridge with him. Of
these Mrs. Holders should certainly not be one unless
he found it absolutely impossible to get a fourth without her, for it was only right that she should be punished
for her revolutionary behaviour last night : even if
he was forced to ask her, he would be very cold and
polite to her, and not give her any advice at all, nor
explain how she might have won ever so many more
tricks.

The cheerful group he had left in the lounge had
broken up when he came back after his lunch, only
Mrs. Bliss with Mr. Kemp and Florence were left.
Mrs. Bliss had a book lying open on her lap and all
three were seated bolt upright in a row and smiling.
Their eyes were shut which looked as if they might
be enjoying a sociable nap, but their upright carriage
argued against repose. A fresh explosion of sneezing
seized him as he approached, at which they all opened
their eyes but smiled as before. This was very strange
and he could not understand what they were doing
with themselves.

" I'm afraid I've caught a fearful cold," he said.
" I got wet through in my walk and chilled to
the bone."

Mrs. Bliss looked at Mr. Kemp, then at Florence,
and finally at Colonel Chase.

"No, Colonel," she said with great sweetness of manner, "you haven't got a cold at all. Error."

"I wish it was," he said, "but there's no error about it. Shiverings, sneezings, sore throat. That spells cold."

"Error!" said Mrs. Bliss again tenderly.

This odd situation was broken in upon by warblings descending the stairs, and Miss Howard tripped lightly down, dressed for walking with a bulky portfolio under her arm and quite unconscious of the presence of other people.

"La donn 'e mobile," sang Miss Howard. "Oh, Colonel Chase! I never saw you! Not coming out again on this beautiful afternoon."

"Not I. I've got a cold coming on and I shall stop in and nurse it. Are you going into the town?"

"Yes. I've got to see about my little pickies being framed. Just fancy! I'm going to hold a little teeny picture-exhibition of some of my rubbishy sketches. So rash! But nobody would give me any peace until I promised to."

This was approximately though not precisely true : Miss Howard had told the group in the lounge that Mrs. Bowen had said that everyone was longing for her to do so, and the group in the lounge had all said "Oh, you must!" again and again and again. She had to yield.

"So frightened about it," said Miss Howard, "I shall certainly leave Bolton the day before it opens, so as not to hear all the unkind things you say about it."

"Dear girl," said Mrs. Bliss, "you know how we shall all enjoy it. Such a refreshment!"

Miss Howard kissed her fingers and dropped the portfolio of sketches. The Colonel stooped to pick it up for her, but long before he got down, the sharpest sort of pain shot through the small of his back, and he recovered the erect position with difficulty.

" Attack of lumbago, too, I'm afraid," he said, and Florence, Mr. Kemp and Mrs. Bliss all muttered ' Error '.

" Dear me, I hope not," said Miss Howard, for the social tranquilities of Wentworth were sorely disquieted when the Colonel had lumbago. " Can't I get you something for it in the town ? "

" A bottle of quinine if you'd be so good," he said, " and a packet of thermogene. Please tell the chemist to send them up at once."

Miss Howard went gaily off breaking into song again just before she closed the front door. She had every graceful gift, thought Florence, whose eyes followed her as she tripped down the drive.

" And the rest of our party ? " asked Colonel Chase.

" In the smoking-room I think," said Mr. Kemp, wishing the Colonel would not stand so close to him with that bad cold coming on. Of course it was Error, but he did not like Error in such immediate proximity. " They talked of playing bridge."

The Colonel took himself and his error off. Of course there was no reason why four people should not play bridge if they felt inclined to, but if there was bridge in the air it was usually round him that it condensed. A sound of laughter came forth from the smoking-room as he opened the door, and he knew the sort of bridge which that meant : chatty, pleasant bridge unworthy of the name. There they were, Mrs. Oxney, Mrs. Bertram and Mrs. Holders and Mr. Bullingdon all very gay, and unconscious for the moment of his entrance.

" Oh, pick it up, Mrs. Oxney," said Tim, " and put it back in your lily-white hand. We don't mind : but if you play any more cards out of turn, I shall trump them as they lie on the table."

" Most kind, I'm sure," said Mrs. Oxney. " I will take it back if no one minds. Such a beautiful

card too. Oh there's Colonel Chase. We're just
playing a rubber, Colonel, to pass the time till tea.
We'll be finished presently, and then you must cut
in and show us how."

Colonel Chase pulled up a chair between Tim Bullingdon and Mrs. Oxney. Such a position, at the utmost
possible distance from Mrs. Holders compatible with
seeing the game, was most marked. But she
being a woman of no perception and blandly ignorant
that she was in disgrace, greeted him cordially.

"Yes, do, Colonel," she said, "and win back a
bit of the fortune you lost last night. Why go to Monte
Carlo when we can play bridge at Wentworth?"

Colonel Chase from being able to see two hands,
while the third was on the table seemed to have an
almost uncanny knowledge of where the other cards
were and made useful comments to Mrs. Oxney when
she finessed or refused to finesse, or trumped or refrained.

"Yes, you should have taken the finesse then,"
he said. "Pretty certain that the king was on your
right, from the way the cards fell. . . . Ah, you ought
to have trumped that : the remaining club was sure
to be on your left."

"You always seem to know just where every card
is before anything is played at all," said Mrs. Oxney
admiringly. "I call it magic."

The magician drew his chair closer to the fire. If
only Mrs. Holders had joined Mrs. Oxney in agreeing
that he was a magician he might have forgiven her,
but she only looked very much surprised and dealt in
silence. He felt chilly and cross and grumpy.

"I hear Miss Howard's intending to open a palace
of art next week," he observed. "I call it real blackmail, as I suppose we shall all be expected to go and
buy something. Blackmail. Bless me, where's my
pedometer?"

He felt in pocket after pocket without result.

" Dear me whatever can have happened to it ? " said Mrs. Oxney. " That would be your walking pedometer would it ? "

" Naturally, as I didn't bicycle this morning," said he. " And I know I took it out with me, for I remember hearing it ticking as I started to come home."

" I warrant it was ticking pretty briskly then," said Mrs. Oxney, pleasantly but absently, for she was sorting her hand and trying to find something above an eight. " I've never seen anyone walk your pace, Colonel."

He got up without acknowledging this compliment.

" I must go and see if I've left it upstairs," he said. " Odd thing if I have, for I usually carry it about with me all day."

Mrs. Holders waited till the door was closed.

" And puts it in his pyjama pocket when he goes to bed," she remarked, " in case he turns over in the night. I pass."

" Two hearts," said Tim Bullingdon, who had heard about the sensational affair yesterday ; " and when I say two hearts I've got a reason for it, partner."

" Oh for shame ! " said Mrs. Oxney.

" Well, I have a reason for it : it means I've got a lot. I hope he's lost his pedometer : I'm sick and tired of hearing how far he's been. I shall get one I think, and tell you all if I walk more than fifty yards."

" Gracious me, I hope he hasn't lost it," said Mrs. Oxney. " He'll turn the house upside down to find it."

" I stole it," said Mrs. Holders, "and ate it for lunch. I double your two hearts, Tim. Whenever I double two hearts I've got a good reason for it."

The reason must have been that she was tired of this particular rubber, for this ill-advised manœuvre finished it.

" Cut again, quick," she said, " and then we'll begin another before he gets back. It's perfect heaven playing without him."

" Oh, pray wait a minute," said Mrs. Oxney.

" Why ? We'll pretend it's the same one. You and me, Tim. Do try to remember when the ace of trumps is played."

They had got well on in the next rubber before Colonel Chase came back with an agitated and anxious face.

" Not a sign of it in my bedroom," he said. " But I find there was a hole in the pocket where I carry it, and it may have fallen on the carpet somewhere. I trust everyone will be very careful how they walk about the house till it's found. Valuable instrument, well travelled too, all over India. Do you think you can trust your servants, Mrs. Oxney, not to have—ha—misappropriated it ? "

Now if there was one thing on which Mrs. Oxney prided herself even more than on her house-keeping it was the honesty of her staff, and she answered him with unusual sharpness.

" I'd trust them all with a bag of money and never think to count it before or after," she said. " You might as well suspect me or Mrs. Holders."

Colonel Chase could not understand why they all looked at each other and then bent their heads over the cards.

The terrible news went abroad at tea-time that the valuable instrument was missing, and everybody walked about with Agag-delicacy, peering at the places where they proposed to set their feet, for fear of trampling on this pearl. Once Tim Bullingdon's dastardly heart leaped for joy when he planted one of his sticks on a fragment of coal which cracked beneath it, much as the valuable instrument might have done, but his pleasure was short-lived ; it wasn't It. Miss Howard

had not seen it, she was sure, gleaming on the road
between Wentworth and the town. Every spot over
which Colonel Chase could have passed since he came
in this morning had been systematically searched, and
the dreadful surmise that he must have dropped it
somewhere on the other side of Bolton was probably
only too true. And all the time (what anxiety the
knowledge of this would have saved) it was safely
reposing on the fender of Mr. Amble's shop, where
Miss Howard had ordered quinine and thermogene.
His honest lad, bicycling back from an errand along
the road where the Colonel had dropped it, saw it
gleaming in the miry roadway, and picked it up. A
suspicious yellowness below the plating of the valuable
instrument had convinced him that it was not silver,
and having never seen a pedometer before, it appeared
to him to be an unusual type of watch, which was
no use for telling the time, and might possibly be traced
if he pawned it. So he gave it to Mr. Amble who put
it to dry on the parlour fender, and shortly after Miss
Howard's departure displayed a notice in his shop
window to say a pedometer had been found, apply
within. The honest lad then discounted any merit
he might have acquired by not retaining a suspicious
and useless object, by forgetting to take the quinine
and thermogene to Wentworth. Instead he put up
the shutters as dark was drawing on, spent the sixpence
that Mr. Amble had given him in cigarettes, and Mr.
Amble gave the pedometer a brush up.

Tea was always served at Wentworth in the drawing-
room. A small dinner-waggon with teapots of Indian
and China was wheeled in, solid refreshment was
arranged on a convenient table, and usually this was
a very pleasant and chatty meal, and one at which
Colonel Chase made himself most entertaining. He
had a fund of stories, which he lavishly recounted, and
often he sat there for nearly an hour before he went

upstairs to read, telling them about the Curate's egg and the little boy who took a sip of his father's whiskey and soda, and not liking the taste, put it back in the glass. Then there was the thrilling tale of the man-eating tiger which Mrs. Oxney said she could never hear without trembling, though she knew that it ended all right and the tiger did not eat this man, and the story about the ghost which the Colonel had seen in the dak-bungalow somewhere near Agra, and which was far more terrifying than anything Mr. Kipling had written. Then when he had terrified them so much that Mrs. Oxney said that she, for one, wouldn't be able to sleep a wink that night, he restored confidence and gaiety by the tale of the Dean who gargled with port wine by mistake and told his doctor he thought it would suit him very well taken internally in larger quantities. But to-night Colonel Chase had no such titbits for them ; he sneezed and scowled and was silent and made sudden excursions beneath the piano to see whether the pedometer had not secreted itself under the pedals. A great many heads were shaken over his chances of recovering it, and Mrs. Bliss alone was optimistic. She after hearing about it just closed her eyes and then said she was sure that everything would prove to be happy and harmonious. It was very pleasant to know that Mrs. Bliss had no fears about the pedometer, but it did not really help matters.

Colonel Chase roused himself from his melancholy when the parlour-maid came in to clear away tea, to question her sharply as to whether anything had been heard of It, and whether a parcel had arrived for him from the chemist's. The double negative of her answer seemed to intensify the prevailing gloom, and even the drawing of the curtains and the kindling of all the electric lights made but a hollow mockery of cheerful cosiness. Miss Howard, also sharply questioned, was quite sure she had given the order that the packet was to be sent up at once.

" That was all you asked me to do, Colonel Chase," she said with some dignity, " and I did it."

That gave Mrs. Bliss a cue.

" Dear girl," she said, " I'm going to ask you to do something nice, and oh, please do it. Won't you run your hands over the piano ? Just one of those sweet little fragments. How dear of you ! How you spoil me."

This was better than nothing, for there was a reason for silence if Miss Howard was playing, and she gave them several sweet little fragments, during one of which Colonel Chase left the room and was heard bawling down the telephone in the lounge. Everybody of course had only half an ear for the sweet fragments while this was going on, and Miss Howard very considerately played with the soft pedal down, for she was as interested as anybody. He was heard to give a number to the exchange, which Mrs. Oxney whispered was Mr. Amble's, and presently called out, " Perfectly disgraceful and if your shop's shut up and your boy's gone home, you ought to bring it up yourself now. Shameful ! " Mr. Amble, thereupon, so it was easy to make out, must have got a little heated too, and replaced the receiver at his end, for Colonel Chase after saying ' Hullo ' eight or nine times in a crescendo of fury, put his receiver back (as anybody could hear) and went upstairs. He walked with a heavy thumping tread, as if he had quite forgotten that every one else was still enjoined to step carefully, for fear of pulverising the pedometer. . . . It was all dramatic enough, but no one knew the full splendour of the situation, for even as Colonel Chase went thumping upstairs, Mr. Amble went back to his parlour and finished polishing up the Colonel's pedometer.

Miss Howard released the soft pedal and trod on

the other one : there was nothing now for which to
listen elsewhere, so they all concentrated themselves
on the long shake with the crossing arpeggios. Florence
had stolen to the chair which Colonel Chase had vacated
close to the piano and rapturously followed Miss
Howard's twinkling fingers. How nimble and slender
they were, and those same fingers had been so still
and steady when they held the brush which picked
out the reflections in the river. Life was becoming
exciting for Florence. When the arpeggio passage
came to an end, as usual in three crashing chords,
everyone felt much better, for Colonel Chase had gone
up to his room, and the eclipse for the present was
over, and there was Miss Howard at the piano. Mrs.
Oxney heaved a sign of relief and rapture.

" I wish the Colonel had heard that," she said.
" He is a little worried, isn't he, with the cold and no
quinine or pedometer. Most aggravating for him,
but please don't get up, Miss Howard. Mayn't we
have ' O rest in the Lord ', though it isn't Sunday."

Miss Howard let them have it, very slowly and with
great feeling, accentuating the melody. She gazed
thoughtfully at the ceiling, and all her audience gazed
thoughtfully at other inappropriate spots, and Florence
gazed at Miss Howard. Mrs. Oxney found herself
thinking of the late Mr. Oxney, and Mrs. Bertram
thought about coke, and Mrs. Holders thought about
the enquiry she had sent to the *Sunday Gazette* about
their bridge last night, and Mr. Kemp with closed
eyes thought about his left hip, and Mrs. Bliss thought
about Mind, and Miss Howard thought about the cost
of the frames for her pictures, but all wore precisely
the same dreamy and wistful expression. A perfect
gale of sighs succeeded the last note and a subdued
chorus of ' Thank you, Miss Howard '. Mrs. Bertram
had determined to get some more coke in at any cost,
Mrs. Holders had calculated that Slam would have

plenty of time to answer her enquiry in next Sunday's issue, Mrs. Oxney had regretted that her late husband had sold his shares in the Bolton Electric Company, and Mr. Kemp had lifted his left leg quite high and found that it certainly moved more easily. . . . But something had to be done, for this pious hour could not go on until dinner-time, and Mrs. Holders mercifully put an end to it by staggering towards the door. Tim followed suit, and as the wet and cold of the day had dismally affected them both, she groped her way along the piano and Tim cake-walked more prancingly than ever along the opposite wall. They collided at the door, for each of them tried to open it for the other, and reviled each other's clumsiness. They groped their way across the lounge, and established themselves in the smoking-room.

" That's better," she said. " Now let's be real. Don't let us rest in the Lord : let's—oh Tim, let's contemplate Colonel Chase. I would sooner have twenty colds in the head by the way, and lose a hundred pedometers than ache as I'm aching to-night. You're pretty bad my dear, aren't you ? Poke the fire."

Tim poked the fire with one of his sticks. It had an india-rubber ferule which, when he withdrew it, was fizzling and giving off a perfectly sickening smell.

" There ! " he said triumphantly. " I made that smell, and all because you told me to poke the fire. You made it, in fact. About aches : don't let us talk about such a boring subject. Nor about the Colonel; what really interests me is Mrs. Bliss. She's holding a sort of healing class. They close their eyes and smile. Did you ever see Kemp smile before ? I never did. They close their eyes and smile, I tell you, and assert that they are quite well. I wish his smile didn't make me feel so morose."

" Oh Tim, how thrilling," she said. " I hadn't grasped what they were about. I only thought they looked boiled. I hope she'll leave me and my aches alone, I should consider it great impertinence if she attempted to interfere with them."

This robust view made him laugh.

" I quite agree," he said. " I've got a strong sense of property too. My aches are my own, and they're quite real, and I should resent it very much if anybody denied it. Lord, what bosh ! And she has baths too, just like the rest of us. But here we are on the boring topic again. Much better not to think about it and play piquet."

" Come on, then. How I hate my vile body to-day."

" Loathsome, isn't it ? But you'll feel better if you rook me."

Mrs. Oxney and her sister meantime had gone back to their sitting-room. Miss Howard (after playing ' O rest in the Lord ' again, which Mrs. Bliss sang *sotto voce* in a small buzzing voice like a blue-bottle with a broad smile) went to get on with her catalogue, and the three students of Mental Science were left to their studies. Mr. Kemp refused to be interested in its larger aspects : it existed as far as he was concerned for the purpose of making him better. They all sat with eyes closed realising Omnipotent Mind for a little, and then he stretched out his left leg which was the worst. Encouraged by the absence of pain, he got up and with only one stick hobbled across the room and back again.

" I'm convinced that the joint is moving more freely," he said excitedly. " I don't believe I've walked so easily since that good week I had at Bath in the spring. At Buxton I never stirred a yard without two sticks, did I, Florence ? "

" You're walking as well as anybody else can walk, dear Mr. Kemp," said Mrs. Bliss, to whom the most atrocious lies on this subject were beautiful truths.

" If you only chose, you could jump on to that chair like a bird hopping on to a branch."

He looked at this formidable altitude, and even bent his knees as if about to spring.

" I almost believe I could," he said.

" Oh, don't, Papa," exclaimed Florence. " You know that Dr. Dobbs said that any improvement must come slowly. I mean——"

" Dear child ! " said Mrs. Bliss. " Naughty ! That's the false idea we're working to destroy."

" I know. I forgot for a moment," said Florence. " But he'd much better not try to jump, had he ? "

Mr. Kemp thought so himself, but he was much encouraged by his long walk across the room.

" Really I'm not sure that I shall have my reclining bath tomorrow," he said. " I shall only have my *masseur*. And yet, I don't know. You mean to go on with your baths, don't you, Mrs. Bliss ? "

" Yes, for the sake of my dear husband, as I told you," said she, " and there's no harm in doing it, so long as you're perfectly certain it can't possibly do you any good. All the time I was in my bath this morning, so warm and restful, I fixed all my thoughts on Mind."

Mr. Kemp's walking tour had not ended quite as felicitously as it began, and a few sharp twinges made him glad to get back to his chair.

" And what shall I do next ? " he asked. " I've had a good twenty minutes self-treatment, and you and Florence were treating me too."

Mrs. Bliss leaned forward and warmed her hands at the fire. They were not cold, of course.

" We should all spend much of our time in helping others," she said. " We get strength that way. Poor Colonel Chase now : my heart bleeds for him with all his false claims about losing his pedometer and having a bad cold and lumbago. Shall we help him ? "

Mr. Kemp did not feel any real spiritual compulsion

to help Colonel Chase, whose false claims were such petty little disturbances, but if he could get strength that way which would enable him to treat himself more powerfully, he was quite willing to help him. He would have to rest before dinner and glanced at the clock.

" Well, for ten minutes," he said.

" Dear of you," said Mrs. Bliss.   " The poor Colonel is so full of illusions this afternoon, which make him feel worried and ill and anxious.   Let us all give him absent treatment."

" Mustn't we send up and tell him ? " asked Florence. " I don't think I should like to do that."

" No, dear, it makes no difference whether he knows it or not.   Let us deny his worries and chilly feelings. Let us see him healthy and happy and full of sunshine."

This required a good deal of imaginative effort on the part of those who knew Colonel Chase, for it was no use saying that sunshine was one of his characteristic attributes.   Mr. Kemp and Florence had to close their eyes very tight on many past memories in their efforts to realise a sunny Colonel.   As for seeing him healthy and happy one glance at him when he came down to dinner that evening was enough to make that internal conception very difficult to cling to, for he had a cold of the most violent kind, he incessantly coughed and sneezed, he had a poor appetite, he was bent and stiff with lumbago and looked the picture of misery.   Luckily he was extremely hoarse, being hardly able to speak above a whisper, and so the scarifying remarks he addressed to the parlour-maid, who served him, complaining of his food and his drink, and the draught, and his napkin, and the light and the knives and forks could not be made out with any clearness, but the growling noises which accompanied poor Mabel's visits to his table, could not reasonably be interpreted as the utterances of a happy man.   There was no news

of the pedometer, the infamous Amble had not sent
his quinine and thermogene, and when, after sitting
almost on the hob of the smoking-room fire for half
an hour, he went up to bed without even suggesting a
game of bridge, it was felt by those who had tried to
see him happy and full of sunshine, that their visions
were as yet unfulfilled. Further, Mr. Kemp's hip
had suffered a bad relapse and there was no longer any
doubt in his mind that he would have his bath as usual
next day. He was much disappointed at the general
results of the evening's séance, and wondered if his
hip had ever been so bad before. Mind, in his view,
was of very doubtful value.

But none of these mutinous ideas had the smallest
effect on Mrs. Bliss's complete confidence, or diminished
the splendour of her smile. She knew, and soon everybody else would know, that all was well with Mr.
Kemp's hip and the Colonel's cold and her own arthritis
and the missing pedometer.

CHAPTER IV

IT has been said that miracles don't happen. This one did. The morning broke warm and sunny again, and Miss Howard who came downstairs, warbling the chorale of her improvisation, a few minutes before the breakfast gong sounded, observed that there was a nice parcel for Colonel Chase on the table of the lounge with perfidious Amble's label. It needed no ingenuity to surmise that this contained quinine and thermogene, and Mrs. Oxney who had been looking at the proofs of her Wentworth advertisement, thought she had better send it up to his room.

"He's sure to stop in bed all morning," she said, "and the best place too for such a nasty cold as he's got, and he can wrap himself up in that wool and dose himself at pleasure. I'll send one of the maids up with it to make sure he'll have his breakfast in bed, and light his fire for him."

At that moment the miracle manifested itself. The words were hardly out of Mrs. Oxney's mouth when a loud cheerful whistle sounded from above and Colonel Chase came tramping downstairs. His face was rosy from the cold bath, which was one of the reasons why Englishmen were stronger than anybody else, and he stronger than any other Englishman, and his whistle betokened his distinguished approval of the dealings of Providence.

"Good morning, ladies," he said standing at the salute. "You observe that Richard is himself again.

Most extraordinary thing ! When I have a cold like
that I had yesterday, I know I shall have two days
in hell, if you'll excuse the expression, and three in
purgatory. Now I was never worse in my life than I
was when I went up to bed last night. Very unwell
indeed. I went asleep at once. And I awoke this
morning as chirpy as a cricket, and not a trace of my
cold left."

"Well, isn't that wonderful ! " said Mrs. Oxney.
" I know your colds, Colonel, and I always say that
nobody I ever saw has such colds as you.
Terrific ! "

" And I took no remedies at all," said he. " That
monstrous chemist—ah, there's the parcel. I shall
send it back for I'm no more in need of his muck than
I am of prussic acid. It's a miracle, I tell you, a sheer
miracle. Such a recovery was never known before.
My colds were famous in India. ' Look out for squalls
when Colonel Chase has a cold,' was what my officers
used to say to the subs when they joined the regiment.
Lumbago gone, too : I did my dumb-bell exercises
this morning with a boy's suppleness. I declare, if
it wasn't for the loss of my pedometer, that I never
felt happier in my life."

During that recital of this adorable news Mr. Kemp
had negotiated the descent of the stairs, and now stood
staring at Colonel Chase as if he had risen from the
dead.

" You, Colonel ? " he said. " And your cold quite
gone ? Vanished in the night with no medicines ?
Miraculous."

" You may well say miraculous, sir," said the Colonel.
" Not a spoonful of Amble's rubbish, and here I am,
jolly as a sandboy, and hungry as a hunter. Ah,
here's Mrs. Bliss. Good morning, Mrs. Bliss. Delightful morning, and me quite well again. Most remarkable
thing."

Mrs. Bliss couldn't smile any more, for she always smiled to her full capacity.

"So glad, Colonel," she said. "But I'm not the least surprised. I knew for certain that you would be quite well this morning. Didn't I tell you so, Mr. Kemp?"

"I wish you'd told me too," said Colonel Chase, "and I shouldn't have felt so down and out as I did last night. Ha! Breakfast gong. There's music for a hungry man."

He headed the procession to the dining-room, leaving Mrs. Bliss and Mr. Kemp to limp after him.

"But amazing," said Mr. Kemp. "To think that we did that! There must be something in it."

"Something in it?" said Mrs. Bliss. "There's everything in it, dear Mr. Kemp. And not amazing at all. Omnipotent Mind. It couldn't be otherwise. Error gone."

"But you treated me," said he, "and I'm sure I treated myself half the night, for I slept very poorly. Why am I as bad as ever this morning? Not a sign of improvement."

This was quite easy to explain. Mr. Kemp's erroneous rheumatism was of long standing: Error was deep rooted in him. But Colonel Chase had only been in error for a few hours, and that foolish mistake of his could be annihilated at once. The explanation did not however, fully satisfy Mr. Kemp, for he argued that since rheumatism was (*ex hypothesi*) absolutely non-existent the painful illusion ought to vanish as easily as a cold, when once you turned Mind on to it. But the manifest healing of Colonel Chase had made a great impression on him and he was fully determined to persevere till his rheumatic error followed Colonel Chase's error of catarrh into its native nothingness.

Before the ambulance-waggon from the baths came round, Wentworth was buzzing with excitement and

the only person who had not been told that Colonel
Chase had been cured by Mind and Mrs. Bliss (and
possibly Mr. Kemp and Florence,) was Colonel Chase
himself, for Mrs. Oxney and Mrs. Bertram were sadly
afraid that if he was informed that his healing was
spiritual, he might fly into so savage a tantrum at
such an idea, that rage would entirely cancel the spiritual
benefit, and perhaps his cold might return again worse
than ever. It was indeed a great relief when soon
after breakfast he set off on his bicycle to see what could
be done in the way of setting up a new record, and so
everybody could have a nice gossip about it all before
going down to the baths. Mrs. Bliss assured them that
the cure was entirely the effect of Mind, and had really
nothing to do with her, but naturally nobody believed
that.

" To be sure it's most remarkable," said Mrs. Oxney,
" and if you can drive a cold away like that I don't
see what you can't do. But I shouldn't like to tell
the Colonel how it happened, for you can't be certain
how he'll take a bit of news like that. At the same
time I feel you ought to have the credit of it, for nothing
will make me believe that his cold went away of its
own accord. And neither quinine nor thermogene
did he use—lumbago too—for when he came down this
morning with his cold quite gone there was the parcel
on the table."

Mrs. Bliss gave a happy little sigh.

" Yes, I'm glad his *materia medica* didn't arrive
last night," she said, " or all you dear faithless people
would have thought that material remedies had cured
him, whereas there is no power in material at all.
Indeed,I have no doubt that if he had taken his quinine
relying on it, he would have been worse than ever."

" We have had an escape then," said Mrs. Bertram,
" But can't medicines help at all ? I should have
thought a little medicine and some Mind with it,

might do wonders.   After all, you're taking the baths yourself, and massage as well."

The idea that Mrs. Bliss was taking the baths entirely for her husband's sake, and not for their remedial qualities, somehow seemed difficult for her audience to comprehend, though it was so patently clear and logical to herself.   As for massage, that was officially called ' mere manipulation ', and even the faithful allowed broken legs to be set and put in splints, for that was ' mere manipulation ' too.   The power of Mind, she explained would undoubtedly set a broken leg, but a surgeon saved time and trouble.   Mind by itself restored everyone to perfect harmony, health and prosperity.   All went well in every way with those who relied on Mind.

Miss Howard had been running through her improvisation before this illuminating discussion began. It was most annoying to have again forgotten the passage of·octaves which led back into the few bars of Chopin's waltz and she shuddered to think what would happen if a similar lapse of memory occurred when she was on the platform.   Would everyone sit there for ever, waiting, eternally waiting for what never came ?

" But does that apply to everything ? " she asked. " If you rely on Mind, does everything go right ? "

Mrs. Bliss was getting worked up now.

" Yes, everything," she said, " for Mind is universal and omnipotent.   All is mind and mind is all.   The proposition is proved by the rule of inversion.   Invert it, and it remains equally true.   Hence Evil is nothing and nothing is evil."

" Cats eat mice, therefore mice——" began Mrs. Holders.   But the flippancy was cut short by Miss Howard, who, though a little dazed, stuck to her point.

" Quite so, I see," she said.   " But what I want to

ask is that if there was something one had undertaken to do not for oneself, but for others, would reliance on Mind make you do it beautifully ? "

" Yes, dear girl, of course," said Mrs. Bliss. " Mind denies evil, illness, failure. Whatever you want must come to you, if only you rely on Mind."

" Dear me, how comfortable it sounds," said Mrs. Oxney. " If only Colonel Chase relied on Mind, perhaps he would find his pedometer. He's gone along the road where he must have lost it, to look for it and to make it a new record. Couldn't you rely on Mind, Mrs. Bliss, and discover it for him ? "

Mrs. Bliss was observed to close her eyes for a few seconds. That was remarked afterwards. Simultaneously a series of hoots from the bus indicated that it had been waiting a long time already, and they all hurried away at their various paces. . . .

Colonel Chase had left the unopened packet from the perfidious Amble to be returned with the withering message that it had arrived too late, and Mrs. Bliss, delighted to purge Wentworth of any fragment of *materia medica*, took charge of it. She found that she had a few minutes to spare before her bath, and since, on the one hand Mind assured her that she was quite well and not at all lame, and her doctor that gentle walking was good for the supposedly affected joints, she limped away to Mr. Amble's shop, to leave the packet there. She was looking, not in scorn, but with indulgent pity at the army of futile bottles and inefficacious drugs that were deployed in his windows, when her attention was attracted to a notice that was affixed there. What met her eye was this :

Found
A plated pedometer.
Apply Within.

She opened the door and a tingling alarm-bell continuously rang in the parlour behind the shop, as if she was a thief intent on pilfering *materia medica*. It ceased as Mr. Amble emerged.

" I have brought back a packet you sent up to Colonel Chase at Wentworth," she said. " It only arrived this morning and as he is now quite well, he would be greatly obliged if you would take your goods back."

Now though Mr. Amble had felt justly incensed at Colonel Chase's very intemperate remarks through the telephone last night, he had been rather sorry that he had rivalled him with tart replies and so sudden a cutting off of his communications, for the Colonel was constantly getting sticking-plaster and soap and bicycle oil and lozenges at his shop, and Mr. Amble would regret losing his valuable patronage. Also the petitioner was a lady of smiling and benevolent address, and she limped heavily, and so was another likely customer.

" Certainly, madam," said he with great suavity. " Anything to oblige Colonel Chase and yourself."

" So good of you," said Mrs. Bliss. " And I saw something about a pedometer in your window. Colonel Chase lost his pedometer yesterday in the road. I wonder if I might take it up to Wentworth, where I am staying, and see if it is his."

Mr. Amble hastened to produce it.

" I'll wager it is the Colonel's," he said, " for if Colonel Chase lost a pedometer on the road yesterday, and my lad found one on the road yesterday, no doubt, they, so to speak, are the ones. Often have I heard it ticking as he's walked about my shop, an old instrument, but I daresay useful still. And is there anything more I can supply you with madam ? "

" Nothing thank you. So much obliged—Mr. Amble isn't it ?—and how pleased Colonel Chase will be ? "

She paused, and a playful innocent idea gleamed in her brain. She made the sweetest face at Mr. Amble, coaxing and child-like, with her head a little on one side, and her chin a little raised, and a really wonderful smile.

" And may the pedometer be a secret between you and me, Mr. Amble ? " she said. " I want to make a mysterious surprise about it. Oh, such fun, but nobody else must know."

Mr. Amble thought this was a very pleasant, though an unusual sort of lady and, completely mystified, agreed. The prospect of regaining the Colonel's custom by taking back the goods was reward enough for him, and he did not even dream of suggesting the repayment of his disbursement of sixpence on the honest lad. So Mrs. Bliss went back to the baths with the pedometer ticking jerkily in her bag as she hobbled along.

Miss Howard had not come down by the bus, but had waited up at Wentworth to have a turn at the elusive passage of octaves which had bothered her earlier. While there were so many of those who would listen in a few days to her improvisation, sitting in the lounge, she had been playing very gently with the soft pedal down, for she did not want the extempore to become too familiar before its birth. But now the patients had gone brine-wards and Mrs. Oxney had gone to the chicken-run and Mrs. Bertram to the linen-closet, and there was no reason any more for these surreptitious tinklings. She remembered that Mrs. Bliss had said that any kind deed undertaken for the sake of others would be prosperously performed, if reliance was placed on Mind, and so now, before she began, she told Mind that she was playing in aid of the Children's Hospital, and had complete confidence in its Omnipotence. Then with the freedom of the loud pedal she concentrated on her work, and lo, the stream of octaves flowed along like torrents in spring.

Of course it was easier to play when unshackled by the fear of being overheard, but never had she known so flashing an ease of execution, or so perfect a transition into the Chopin waltz. Then she tried the chorale, the last line of which had escaped her at her last attempt and now without the slightest conscious effort on her part it streamed solemnly from her finger tips. 'Most wonderful', thought Miss Howard, as, rather awe-struck at her own brilliance, she closed the lid of the piano. "I couldn't remember either of those bits just before and now, relying on Mind, I feel I can never forget them. There must be something in it."

She had to go down to the baths to measure up the Green Salon, and see how many pictures would be needed, to try genteelly to beat Mr. Bower down over the price of framing them and to arrange for the type-writing of the catalogue. She would much have preferred printing but the cost of printing was frankly prohibitive ; this seemed to have something to do with the coal strike, but the connection was difficult to understand. She tripped lightly down the hill to the imagined accompaniment of those agile octaves, and arrived at the door of the establishment at the very moment when Mrs. Bliss was entering on her return from Mr. Amble's. She came up behind her without being seen, and noticing that Mrs. Bliss ticked as she moved, wondered if this was a symptom of arthritis. Colonel Chase ticked too, but that was his pedometer, and, alas, it was sadly to be feared that his ticking days were over. Then she said 'Bo!' playfully, and Mrs. Bliss turning briskly round emitted a perfect tattoo of ticks. They seemed to come from her bag or thereabouts rather than her hip, but noises were always hard to localise.

"Sweet girl!" said Mrs. Bliss. "What a mischievous child you are to startle me like that. Have you come to see about your dear exhibition ? "

" Yes," said Miss Howard, " and oh, I must tell you . . . I could not recollect, in that passage of my improvisation—I mean I could not remember something I wanted to recollect, when I was practising earlier in the morning, and I just closed my eyes and relied on Mind, because I was going to play in aid of the Children's Hospital next week, and everything I had forgotten came back to me at once. Wasn't that extraordinary ? "

Mrs. Bliss laughed her happy laugh, but kept her bag still.

" Not in the least extraordinary," she said. " It would have been extraordinary, impossible in fact, if you hadn't recollected every note of your delicious tunes."

" But it was wonderful, wasn't it ? " asked Miss Howard.

" Yes, indeed, little one," said Miss Bliss tenderly. " All is wonderful in Mind : wonderful and loving and perfect. Dear me ; it is after eleven I see and I must hurry for my dear husband's sake or I shall have to shorten my bath. Au revoir, dear ! In a day or two I shall be climbing step-ladders and helping you arrange your sweet pictures."

The Green Salon looked quite cheerful on this sunny morning, in spite of the uncleaned skylight, the slight odour of rotten eggs which hung about the baths establishment and the bare deal floor, and these slight drawbacks would presently be remedied, for Mr. Bower had promised that the skylight should be resplendent before the day of the opening, Mrs. Oxney had promised a nice piece of carpet for the floor, and Mr. Amble could be trusted to have some sort of aromatic riband in stock which smouldered persistently and would soon overcome the less agreeable aroma. Miss Howard measured up the walls and decided that forty-five sketches properly spaced would be as many as the

Green Salon would hold without skying or earthing any of them, and having successfully reduced Mr. Bowen's estimate for framing, tripped into Mr. Amble's to consult him about the fumigatory. It was always pleasant to exchange a few words with that noted conversationalist, and Miss Howard told him that Colonel Chase's cold for which she had ordered remedies yesterday had happily disappeared.

"Yes, I was sorry to have vexed the Colonel last night about the delivery of his order," said Mr. Amble, "but I trust that's put right, Miss, for I've taken the goods back and very glad to do so. A most agreeable and affable lady called here this morning about it, and we soon settled that. Not a lady that I've seen here before, but from Wentworth, as she told me, and walking, you may say dot and go one, as I could see."

"Yes, that must have been Mrs. Bliss," said Miss Howard. "Such a favourite already with us all."

She considered whether she should tell Mr. Amble about the affable lady's treatment of Colonel Chase's cold, but decided that it would be a want of tact to do so. Mental healing was certainly in competition with Mr. Amble's business. Wiser not.

"We were all so glad that the Colonel's cold got better," she said, "for he lost his pedometer yesterday and between the two he was a good deal worried."

Mr. Amble remembered that the affair of the pedometer was a secret between him and the smiling lady, and behaved like a man of honour. He had already removed the notice about it in his window.

"Dear me, he wouldn't like that," he said. "But who knows, Miss, that it mayn't be found one of these days, and that we shall hear it ticking away again?"

There was something reserved and oracular about

this sentiment, and Miss Howard received the distinct impression that Mr. Amble knew something about the pedometer. Yet, what could he have known, for surely, he would have thrown any light that he possessed, however small and glimmering, upon the loss, now that he had been told of it? Miss Howard often had these strange sudden impressions, for she was what is called ' very intuitive '. Usually they came to nothing, and she forgot them : occasionally they came to something, and then she remembered them. Descending to business, she told Mr. Amble her errand, and he strongly recommended a fragrant riband called *Souvenir d'Orient*, which he lit and which immediately filled the shop with a swoony Arabian odour of musk, opoponax and incense, against which the rotten eggs would have no chance at all.

The bus had got back to Wentworth and the patients dispersed to their rooms to rest before Miss Howard had finished her jobs. She went out into the garden with her painting apparatus to touch up one of the sketches she had chosen for exhibition, called " Splendid Noon," which seemed to stand in need of a little more splendour, and worked away at the sharpening of the shadows till the first gong told her that lunch was imminent. Colonel Chase had come in from his bicycling in the highest spirits, and she had to guess how many miles he had been since breakfast. Remembering that his record for a morning ride (based upon the conjectural record when *that* pedometer got out of order) was thirty-five miles, and seeing his elation, she guessed thirty-six, and clapped her hands with admiration when she heard he had been thirty-seven.

" Not so bad for a man who thought he would be spending the day in bed," he said, " and I daresay I shall go out again for a short spin this afternoon."

" Oh, you mustn't overdo it," said she. " I think

I should be content if I were you. But you haven't found your pedometer ? "

His face hardly fell at all, so gratifying to himself and others was the new record.

" No, to break my record and find my pedometer would be too much of a red-letter day," he said. " I'm afraid I shall have to order another."

Mrs. Bliss had joined them in the lounge just as he said this. Mr. Kemp was there, too, and Florence, and Mrs. Oxney, and Mrs. Holders, and all were witnesses of what occurred.

Mrs. Bliss, leaning on her stick, was standing close to the Colonel with her left hand behind her back.

" No, Colonel Chase," she said, " you needn't order another. Guess what I've got in my hand : no peeping ! "

" Not my——" began the Colonel. Emotion choked his utterance. Mrs. Bliss held out her left hand to him and said, " Peep-o ! " There it lay, bright and clean, for Mr. Amble had polished it up beautifully.

" So glad : such a privilege," she said charmingly.

He grasped the beloved object and shook it. It ticked as brightly as ever.

" My dear lady, I can't thank you enough," he said. " I shall certainly go for a walk this afternoon for the pleasure of using it again. The Bliss-pedometer : may I christen it the Bliss-pedometer ? Where did you find it ? "

A dreamy absent sort of look came into Mrs. Bliss's eyes.

" Down in the town I think," she said. " Sometimes I lose myself in thought, and this morning, just before my bath, I was meditating deeply and joyfully as I strolled about in the sweet sunshine. And then there it was in my hand ! Did I pick it up ? Perhaps that was it. Or did someone give it me ? Who

knows ? But somehow I felt sure that I should find
it for you. So pleased ! "

The effect of this was immense : a sort of awe fell
on Wentworth generally, with the exception of Tim
Bullingdon, who, when Mrs. Holders told him of the
marvellous recovery of the valuable instrument
merely said, " Oh, that blasted thing has been found,
has it ? More pedometer-chat ! " But apart from
him a very profound impression was made, and the
reappearance of the pedometer was generally considered
to belong to the same class of manifestations as the
disappearance of the Colonel's cold : a notion which
Mrs. Bliss certainly did not discourage. A small
committee held in Mrs. Oxney's room after lunch
inclined to the opinion that Colonel Chase should now
be told to whom he owed (in some mysterious manner)
both these benefits. The reappearance of the pedometer, taken alone, might be held to be just a lucky
chance ; so, too, possibly might the miraculous disappearance of his cold ; but taken together with Mrs.
Bliss as direct agent (under Mind) in both, they clearly
outran any reasonable theory of coincidence. He
might have got in one tantrum if a spiritual cause had
been suggested for his convalescence only, and in another
if the same had been assigned to the recovery of his
pedometer, but when the two were presented together,
it was felt there need be no apprehension about tantrums. Mrs. Bliss took no part in this conference, for
they all knew from what source she derived these
manifestations of health and harmony, but went out
and sat under the cedar, where she pursued her mental
work.

Colonel Chase had gone off for a walk, in spite of the
morning's record on the wheel, in order to feel the
pulse of his pedometer beating again in the region of
his liver, and had given some thought to the happy
reappearance of the instrument. It was wrapped in

mystery : Mrs. Bliss apparently had found it while in a species of trance, and though he would have been naturally inclined to scoff at trances, there seemed to be something to be said for them. He already knew that she was a believer in the power of Mind and such hocus-pocus, but if hocus-pocus could find pedometers, he had no quarrel with it. In consequence, when on his vigorous return from his walk Mrs. Oxney told him that the same lady had given him mental treatment for that tornado of a cold which had fallen on him yesterday, he listened without any symptom of tantrums.

"And you know as well as I do, Colonel, if not better," said Mrs. Oxney in conclusion, " that when you have a cold it *is* a cold, not a matter of two sneezes and a drop of eucalyptus on your handkerchief. Your cold always means a day in bed, and pulls you down dreadfully, and if ever you had a cold in your life yesterday was the day. But here you are now making records in the morning and your pedometer in your pocket in the afternoon, and never looking better, though last night you were in for one of your worst."

Colonel Chase was proud of his fair-mindedness.

" Upon my word, that's all quite true," he said. " I don't wish to deny it. And then, as you say, the whole trouble vanished. Yet it must be stuff and nonsense. The woman's a crank if she thinks she cured me."

" Well, if she's a crank I'm a crank too," said Mrs. Oxney, " and that's a thing I've never been called before. It's not your cold only, there's that pedometer. I said to her, ' Couldn't you rely on Mind, Mrs. Bliss, and discover it for him ? ' Those were my very words, and no sooner had I said them than she closed her eyes and sat silent. We all noticed it. And then what does she do but find it in her hand ? "

This powerful presentment of the case impressed him.

" Yes, I'm bound to say it's most remarkable,"
said he. " I'm no bigot, I hope : I've got an open mind
on every question, and I know there are some things
I can't account for. I've seen the mango-trick in
India, but really . . . And yet one can hardly believe
it. I must look into it. How does Mrs. Bliss explain
it ? "

" She just says, with that sweet smile of hers, that
all is harmony and health, and what she did was to
realise it for you."

The Colonel's robust intellect made a final effort to
reject all it could not understand, and called his sense
of humour to its aid.

" I'm sure it's not all harmony when Miss Howard
gets to the piano," he said. " But that's flippant of
me. I'm bound to say I can't understand it at all.
Amazing ! According to all my experience, I should
have been in bed all day instead of bicycling thirty-
seven miles this morning without fatigue, and going
for a walk with my pedometer this afternoon. By all
chances, it should have been crushed to bits under
some lout's foot."

Colonel Chase, it need hardly be said, would have
pooh-poohed the whole affair if it had happened to
anybody else, calling it bunkum and piffle, and gammon
and spinach, just as he pooh-poohed every ghost story
in the world except his own psychical experiences in
the dak-bungalow, calling them liver and indigestion,
and imagination and nerves. But anything that
happened to himself was of another order of pheno-
mena, and that evening he entered into somewhat
condescending intercourse with Mrs. Bliss. He shrewdly
catechised her about the action of Mind, just as he
might have catechised a doctor about the action of
quinine, and said, " Ah ; so that's your theory, is it ? "
to her explanations. But the leaven had begun to
work, and more than once over bridge that evening,

Mrs. Oxney thought she saw him close his eyes and smile like Mr. Kemp and Florence and Mrs. Bliss. And, beyond doubt, his manner to his partner was far less hectoring. He even allowed that on one occasion he might have played a hand better.

The rest of the week passed busily but uneventfully away bringing Wentworth nearer to the momentous days which were coming. The first of the fateful series was Sunday, when there might be expected a reply from Slam to Mrs. Holder's enquiry. Most of the guests at Wentworth took in the *Sunday Telegraph* as a rule, but all those who were interested in bridge, had on this occasion ordered the *Sunday Gazette* instead. Usually it came during breakfast-time, but to-day it was annoyingly late, and most of them were in the lounge, starving for Slam, when it arrived. Every one snatched his copy, and there was a loud rustle of paper as they all simultaneously turned to the page where Slam discussed Bridge and White Knight Chess instead of to the leaf on which the cross-word puzzle for the week was set forth. It was considered certain that Mrs. Holders and Colonel Chase ran a dead heat in the perusal of the judicial paragraph, for just as she gave a little squeal of laughter, Colonel Chase said " Pshaw ! " or " Tosh ! " (opinion differed as to which), and turned with a very red face to less important items. Then a dead hush followed and everyone but he read the long paragraph through twice. It ran thus, among the " Answers to Correspondents " :

" Wentworth " (Mrs. Holders's pseudonym). " The case you submit is well worth attention, because it is an admirable example of the fatal declarations too often made by ignorant dealers. There was no possible excuse for Z declaring two hearts unless he was burdened with superfluous cash. In so doing he completely ruined his partner's fine hand of diamonds, which would easily have taken Z and Y out and given them the rubber. But, this ludicrous declaration once made, Y was perfectly right to say ' no bid ', for he naturally expected an overwhelming strength in hearts from Z, which, when once cleared, gave him six tricks in diamonds. Z's proper call, of course, was ' one heart ' (doubtful) or ' No bid ', in which case Y would have declared ' two diamonds '. B's ' double ' was perfectly sound. In fact, we can only recommend A, B, and Y to disregard any declaration of Z's, if they ever have the misfortune to play with him again, until he has learned the elements of the game. We append the hands with a diagram as a warning to those who make these imbecile declarations.''

Among the students of the *Sunday Gazette* was Florence, and she was thrilled to see her hand (Y) just as it had been dealt her with all those beautiful diamonds put in the paper with a diagram, and to be told by the oracle that she was quite right to have said no bid. Altogether forgetting Colonel Chase in the irrepressible joy of this publicity she cried out :

'' Oh, look, Papa. Here's the game we had the other night, and I'm Y. That night I was so late, do you remember ? Slam says I was quite right to say no bid. Isn't that sweet of him, and aren't my diamonds lovely ? And that's where Mrs. Oxney sat and she's A., and Mrs. Holders is B, who doubled. How it all comes back ! And Z, why——''

During the painful silence which followed these unfortunate remarks Colonel Chase was seen to close his eyes for a moment and smile, but when he opened them again, he did not seem much better. His hand which held the wretched sheet trembled with fury, and so did his voice which gradually rose to a roar.

'' I see Slam comments on the hand you sent up for his decision, Mrs. Holders,'' he said. '' I can only say that I totally disagree with him. Probably he's just a little cock of the walk at Tooting Junior Bridge Club, if all was known. I suppose he likes to play the little tin god. I shall certainly write and put my view of the case, though I expect he's too dense to understand it. I shall sign it, too, instead of cowering under a

nickname. ' Slam ' indeed ! ' Revoke ' would be a
more suitable name for him, I shouldn't wonder.
Impertinent little anonymous jackanapes."

What further ebullition would have followed is
unknown, for even as he said jackanapes, Colonel
Chase to the awe of the whole assembly was suddenly
stopped by an appalling fit of sneezing. Again and
again he sneezed, the convulsions seemed interminable.

" God bless me "—(crash), he said. " I believe
I've caught another "—(crash)—" cold. Abominable
nonsense ; enough to make a man——"

He stopped seeing Mrs. Bliss's serene and limpid
gaze smilingly fixed on him. She held up her finger
as if in tender rebuke of a naughty child.

" Harmony, peace, and health deny inharmony,
worry, sickness," she said. " All is Mind : Mind is
all. O Colonel Chase ! "

If catalepsy or sudden death had fallen on every
human being in the lounge, Wentworth could not have
been stricken into more rigid immobility. Openly
to rebuke Colonel Chase when in a tantrum was not
only impossible in fact, but incredible in theory. And
yet having done it, Mrs. Bliss smilingly closed her eyes
as if she had done nothing at all, and Mr. Kemp and
Florence followed her example, calmly demonstrating.
Mrs. Oxney tried to do the same, but curiosity as to
how the Colonel would take this was too strong, and
she had to keep a flickering eyelid open.

Colonel Chase cleared his throat ; he sniffed, he
sneezed once more and once only, and his catarrh and
his fury seemed to vanish like morning mists.

" Dear me, I thought I'd caught cold again," he
said, " but it's a false alarm. And . . . I suppose we
mustn't harbour unkind thoughts about anyone.
And bridge, too, is only a game. Ha ! Quite so !
Nearly church time, isn't it ? I shall walk there on
this beautiful morning."

The omnibus which took Wentworth to church on Sunday free of charge was unusually full after this spiritual manifestation, which brought harmony out of tantrums, and Mrs. Oxney was unable to consider it a coincidence that the first hymn was ' O happy band of Pilgrims '. All day harmony, so miraculously restored after that wild outburst, shone on Colonel Chase, he and his pedometer had a wonderful walk that afternoon and throughout the peaceful rubber of bridge in which the criminal Mrs. Holders took part, his hands dripped with trumps and kings and aces and convenient singletons. He adopted an almost reverential attitude towards Mrs. Bliss, and as he performed his dumb-bell exercises that night he beat time to his vigorous movements with denials of anger, malice and colds in the head. He was aware how rightly he had been known in India as a hard-headed fellow, but such a marvellous series of things that had happened to him personally (and therefore could not be bosh and gammon and piffle and spinach) could not be overlooked by a fair-minded man. Their attribution to coincidence must be definitely abandoned : it would not meet the case. Getting into bed he closed his eyes and battened on the conception of himself as completely happy and healthy and prosperous. Under this pleasant treatment he instantly fell fast asleep.

CHAPTER V

INDEED there seemed on the ensuing Monday morning,
no conquests which were not within the victorious
powers of Mental Science. Wentworth might almost
become an establishment in direct competition with
the baths and nauseating drinkings and general
materia medica of Bolton Spa. Mr. Kemp actually
refrained from brine that morning, and sat in the
lounge reading the Manual, demonstrating over his
hip and putting principles to the test by making short
walks between window and fire-place. Mrs. Bliss
went down to the baths as usual, but Wentworth was
now beginning to grant that this violation of right
thinking must really be for the sake of her husband,
since a woman who could cure colds and tantrums
and recover pedometers like that could not be in any
need of saline immersion. Before she left, she spoke
a few words to a gathering of students in Mrs. Oxney's
room, which was really like a regular class of instruction, and was attended by all the guests (except Mrs.
Holders and Tim Bullingdon) as well as a couple of
parlour-maids with coughs. She told them that
Mental Science filled you with health and energy for
the harmonious accomplishment of the duties of life
which must by no means be neglected, after which
Colonel Chase started blithely off on the chief duty of
his life, which was riding a bicycle, and Miss Howard
wreathed in smiles tripped down to the Green Salon
to drive into its faded walls the nails on which to hang

the pictures which were to bring joy and refreshment
to so many, and, it was hoped, profit to herself, for
the labourer, said Mrs. Bliss, was worthy, sweet girl,
of her hire. As for the improvisation which was to
take place at the entertainment next day, and not
only delight the audience, but bring in funds for the
Children's Hospital, Miss Howard scarcely gave
another thought to it, for she found that a mere closing
of the eyes, a smile and a silent lifting of the spirit to
Mind was sufficient to make her fingers reel out the most
elusive passages, and she now felt she really had them
by heart. Mrs. Bliss recommended her to give no
further thought at all to the improvisation.

The guests were enjoying a few moments quiet in
the lounge after lunch before getting to their jobs
again when the Revd. H. Banks, who was responsible
for the entertainment tomorrow, and was also himself
to sing twice and recite once, came in with 'an unique
appeal.' He was known to most of the company and
was highly popular, for his ecclesiastical duties performed at St. Giles's amid cottas and banners and
maniples and incense and genuflexions were quite a
feature at Bolton among visitors, and made you feel,
as Miss Howard said, that the Church was a living force.
He was a welcome guest also at tennis-parties and teas,
and had once said damn, quite out loud in the presence
of Colonel Chase, who thought that very broad-minded
for a clergyman. In general the Colonel had a low
opinion of parsons since they had done nothing to check
the abominable selfishness of the lower classes, in
striking for a living wage, which had caused taxation
to grow to such monstrous proportions. But Banks
was an excellent fellow : except in church you would
not know he was a padre at all. . . .

" A most calamitous thing has befallen us," said this
broad-minded padre, " for Mr. Graves the *masseur*
who was to entertain us with his most amusing stories

tomorrow night has gone to bed with influenza, and
Dr. Dobbs absolutely forbids him to take part in our
effort for the Children's Hospital tomorrow, unless he
thinks he will enjoy an attack of pneumonia."

The eyes of all the guests which had been fixed on
Mr. Banks, wheeled like a flock of plovers and settled
on Mrs. Bliss. Would Mind (such was the instinctive
though unspoken question) disperse Mr. Graves's
influenza as it had dispersed the Colonel's cold ? Mr.
Banks, of course, could not be expected to understand
what these earnest, enquiring glances meant, and
though slightly disconcerted by thus suddenly losing
everyone's attention, proceeded to make his appeal.

" Jolly rough luck just the day before our entertainment," he said, " but who knows whether there
may not be a silver lining to our cloud ? Everyone in
Bolton has heard that we have among us, present here,
a superb *raconteur*, and my Committee unanimously
deputed me to find out whether our friend Colonel
Chase would not consent to take his place. "

All eyes wheeled again to the Colonel. Wonderful
though a demonstration of Mind over the *masseur*
would have been, there was no need for it now.

" Oh, what a treat that would be," said Mrs. Oxney.
" Often and often I've felt quite selfish when Colonel
Chase has been telling his wonderful stories to just
a handful of listeners, to think how many people longed
to hear him and didn't get the chance. Do,
Colonel ! "

" Oh, do ! " said Miss Howard, " I shan't feel nearly
so nervous if I'm to follow you, for everyone will be
in such a good temper. Padre, you must persuade
him."

Florence added her appeal.

" Wouldn't that be lovely, Papa ? " she said.
" You would have to make an effort to go. Oh, do,
Colonel Chase ! "

A fugue on the subject of ' Oh, do ', followed.

" Upon my word," said Colonel Chase, highly grati-fied but tremulous, " my little twopenny stories are only fit for a friend's ear, just to pass the time. Really in public, you know, and on a platform it's a very different matter ! "

A wail of ' Oh, do ' went up in a minor key.

" Think how many more people will come," said Mrs. Oxney, " though to be sure Miss Howard's name alone would fill the hall. There won't be standing room."

" And all the poor little children in hospital."

" And helping others," said Mrs. Bliss who had been quite ready to adopt the unspoken suggestion that she would bring Mind to bear upon Mr. Graves's influenza, till this proposition was made.

" And poor Mr. Graves lying there and worrying himself over what will happen if no one can be found to take his place."

" And so much more amusing than Mr. Graves could possibly be."

" And how we shall all shudder if you tell your ghost story, and how we shall laugh if you tell us about the Dean and the port wine."

(" And what Slam said about your declaration of two hearts," whispered Tim to Mrs. Holders.).

" And the tiger ! What suspense for those who haven't heard it."

It was not in human nature to resist so universal an appeal. Colonel Chase saw himself on the platform before a tense audience.

" Indeed, I hardly like to refuse," he began.

The wailing strains of ' Oh, do ' swelled to a joyful chorus. " Well, I yield, I yield," he said. " I am not too proud to fill a gap at the last moment. But my work's cut out for me. I shall have to rehearse my little yarns over and over again to get them ship-shape by tomorrow night. Short notice, you know, padre. Miss Howard's lucky only to be improvising."

" Oh, but you know them all by heart," said Mrs. Oxney. " Tell them all just as you tell them to us after tea. Perfect ! "

Mr. Banks warmly shook the Colonel's hand and hurried back to relieve his Committee's suspense with the joyful news, while Colonel Chase abandoning all thought of a walk, retired to the smoking-room to jot down his selection of stories, and trim them into public shape. He was immensely gratified at the strong expressions of entreaty and delighted anticipation which he had heard from those who knew his stories so well, and promised to give his audience something better worth listening to than the yarns with which Mr. Graves entertained the victims of his professional manipulations. (Probably they only laughed at them because Mr. Graves was running his fingers over ticklish places in their anatomy.) So much too lay in the address and appearances of the *raconteur*, and it was pleasant to remember that Mr. Graves was a podgy little bit of a man with no presence at all and a wheezy voice. . . . " We'll begin with a good laugh," he thought : the ' Curate's Egg ' would lead off well, and he recited to himself with appropriate gestures of a man wielding an egg-spoon, the story of the Curate breakfasting with his Bishop, and being given an egg which smelt abominable ('something like the waters here,' thought the Colonel) and, on his diocesan making enquiries, how the Curate said that parts of it were excellent. Very likely that yarn had never reached Bolton yet, or, on the other hand, it might have reached Bolton so long ago that the majority of his audience would be too young to recollect its vogue. After that might come the story of the man-eating tiger which he stalked on foot through the

jungle and shot as it charged him. Then for relief
he would tell them of the Dean who gargled with port
wine by mistake, but perhaps two stories making fun
of the cloth would be injudicious, with Mr. Banks in
the chair, and he decided to tell instead the story of
the little boy who took a sip of his father's whisky and
soda, and not liking the taste put it back in the glass.
That had amused Mr. Banks before now. After that
he must make the flesh of his entire audience creep,
and the ghost story of the dak-bungalow would be the
very thing. It was rather a long story, but he had no
reason to suspect that anyone had ever found it so,
and if the lights could be turned down during it, and
Miss Howard would play a little weird music on the
piano during the most thrilling section, the effect would
be quite terrific. Then up would go the lights again,
and he would make them hold their sides over the
member of Parliament who thought he had sat down
on his neighbour's hat, and in the middle of his pro-
fuse apologies found that it was his own. How his
junior officers used to roar when he told them that
story at mess. But he must be careful to omit the
swear-words tomorrow : that was a pity.

These ought to be enough he thought, and, as an
encore, he could tell the history of the young grocer
who meaning to send a lovely rose to his young lady
sent by mistake a piece of strong Gorgonzola, enclosing
an amorous note saying ' When I smell it I think of
you.' The rose went—he might say—to a peppery
old Colonel not a hundred miles from here, as per his
esteemed order, and so the young grocer lost his
custom and his young lady. . . . He went through
them all just as he meant to tell them tomorrow night,
and found they had taken twenty-five minutes, which
would do very well : but not another yarn should they
get out of him, however much they clamoured.

Then he went to look for Miss Howard, to ask her

to play the ghost-music, but found she had gone to see about laying the carpet in the Green Salon : he followed her, for it was most important that she should make ghost-music to his recitation, but learned that the carpet had been laid, and Miss Howard had gone to the Assembly Rooms. He just looked into the Green Salon to see how her preparations progressed, but was plunged into so thick a stew of opoponax and musk and incense that it was impossible to breathe, let alone seeing anything. Violently coughing, he proceeded to the Assembly Rooms, and there was Miss Howard seeing what it felt like to improvise on a platform. She readily consented to play weird music to accompany the ghost story, and a couple of workmen, who were arranging chairs for the entertainment tomorrow, sat down in them, so as not to make a ' scraping sound ' during this rehearsal of the famous adventures in the dak-bungalow. The climax approached :

" I was just about to light my lamp," said the Colonel in a hollow voice, " when I saw, or seemed to see in the far corner a shadow forming itself into the semblance of a man. . . . No, Miss Howard, I think I should like you to come in with those chords at the word ' far corner '. And the soft pedal, please. I shall be speaking in a very low voice myself, and I fear it would hardly carry. Shall we try that again ? "

" I can't play much softer," said Miss Howard, " and the soft pedal has been on the whole time."

" Then perhaps we had better turn the piano away from the audience," said he. " Lend a hand here, one or two of you fellows, will you ? "

" But my solo follows very soon after, Colonel," she said. " The piano must be moved back again."

" Oh, that's easily done. The padre and I will see to that. Now, Miss Howard, I'll begin again at ' light my lamp ', and your cue is ' far corner '. Now please."

Once more the terrifying tale unfolded itself and when the phantom shrieked, Miss Howard produced so fearful an effect with the loud pedal and both hands violently scampering up the piano that the Colonel nearly jumped out of his skin.

"My word, how you startled me," he said. "Most effective. Just like that tomorrow please. And then dead silence till the beat of the tom-toms is heard, on one note in the bass very slow and measured. . . . Perfect. And now let us take it all through again : we must get it without a hitch. Perhaps at the beginning we might have a line or two of ' On the road to Mandalay ', just to give the local colour. Oh, much softer than that. Just a suggestion . . . fading away as I begin."

Now Miss Howard had come here on purpose to have a good practice and get used to the room and the instrument, and here she was tucked away behind the upright piano, and making ghost-music for the Colonel. Already it was growing dark, the chairs were all arranged, and the foreman was jingling his keys, wanting to lock the hall up and get home. He had heard the ghost story three times and now he could not stand it again.

"We're closing the hall for the night, sir, now," he said.

Colonel Chase forgot about Mind for the moment, and was highly indignant.

"Well, upon my soul ! " he said. "We're doing our best to give you a good entertainment for your Children's Hospital and we're told we're not wanted. It's enough to make——"

Suddenly he remembered about his cold and his pedometer.

"Just give us two minutes more, there's a good feller," he said. "And perhaps you'd be so kind as to go to the far end of the room, and tell me if you can hear. . . . That's capital of you. . . . Now Miss Howard I'm sure you don't want to keep anybody waiting, any more than I do. So let's practise the rest afterwards, and begin now at 'I was just about to light my lamp '——

The thrilling section down to the phantom's shriek was rehearsed once more, and Colonel Chase called out to know if he had been heard.

"Not a word, sir," said the foreman cheerfully. "I heard the music though. And now I must really ask you——"

"Yes, yes, at once," said the Colonel. "We can have another practice at home, Miss Howard. Let me see. I must have a table on the centre of the platform with a glass and bottle of water. It would never do if I was to get hoarse, for in the story of the little boy and his father's whisky I mean to use falsetto. And I hope there will be plenty of light ; the play of the features counts for so much. The look of tension and terror in the tiger story ; that would be quite lost if there was not enough light. But they must be turned down for the ghost story and turned up immediately after it. That must be seen to by some trustworthy man."

The next day was a succession of hectic hours for Wentworth, since Colonel Chase who had so intrepidly faced man-eaters and phantoms found the prospect of facing an audience far more formidable. He recited his stories over and over again to rows of imaginary listeners in the smoking-room, and manifested such want of control if disturbed, that Mrs. Oxney put up a notice on the door of 'Private'. Miss Howard had similarly taken possession of the drawing-room, and in spite of her confidence in Mind, found that the passage of octaves to usher in the re-entry of the Chopin waltz was fading gradually but firmly out of her memory and that constant repetition only served to hasten that distressful process. In order to fix these fugitive beauties in her mind (since Mind seemed so inconsistent an ally) she wrote down some of the most important on music paper, though as her performance was improvised, it would hardly do to play from notes when the time came. Occasionally she closed her eyes and smiled, but the smile grew very wan as its inefficacy manifested itself. Then Colonel Chase wanted to go through the music of the ghost story once or twice more, and it got muddled up with the octaves which now came out like the sun from behind a cloud when she wanted something else, and he forgot the cue he had given her of ' the far corner ', and said, ' the other end of the room '. In consequence there were no weird chords at all, for she was waiting for ' far corner '.

" Music, please," rapped out Colonel Chase.

" But my cue is ' far corner '," said Miss Howard in a strangled voice.

" Well, ' the other end of the room ' is the same thing," he said. " A little intelligence, Miss Howard. The point is that the ghost is just appearing, and you have to play. I should have thought that was clear. Let us go back to the lighting of the lamp."

Miss Howard moistened her lips with the tip of her tongue. She often did this when determined, under any provocation, to behave like a perfect lady.

" My mistake no doubt," she said. " The lighting of the lamp : yes."

This time she came in with the shriek-motif far too soon, and Colonel Chase, with his nerves worn to fiddle-strings at the prospect of this evening, stamped on the floor with his great feet.

" Good gracious me ! " he exclaimed. " It gets worse and worse. We had better have no music at all than this hash."

Miss Howard merely closed the lid of the piano.
" I think that would be far the best course," she said
and sat with her hands in her lap looking at the ceiling,
till he left the room.   Then she opened the piano again
and went on with her practice.

Colonel Chase went back to the smoking-room in
an ague of passion and nervousness. He told the
ghost story again to himself, but now he had got so
accustomed to the music that it put him out dreadfully not to have it, and a frenzied effort at reliance
on Mind had no calming effect whatever. Though
he hated to do it, he felt he must eat humble pie, and
beg Miss Howard to forgive him, for he could not get
on at all without her. Perhaps Mrs. Oxney would
carry his regrets : that would make the humble pie
less hard to swallow. She consented to do her
best.

Miss Howard had a sense of dignity, and when the
ambassadress with many compliments on the exquisite
music, sidled into the drawing-room, she met with a
cool reception.

" I am very glad that Colonel Chase feels that he
has behaved most rudely," said Miss Howard. " It
is his place to tell me so himself. Thank you, Mrs.
Oxney."

And she resumed the long shake for the right hand
which led towards the Chopin waltz. The octaves
went better now, and having given ample time for
Colonel Chase to come and apologise, she went out for
a stroll in the bright sunshine, strenuously denying
malice, nervousness and loss of memory. Naturally
she had to be unconscious of his presence at lunch,
but that was only proper. He had no existence for
Miss Howard : how then could she see him ?

Another half-hour's solitary rehearsal in the smoking-
room broke Colonel Chase down : he could not manage
the ghost story at all without those weird chords.

He apologised in person, and they went through it
twice more. After tea they sat with Mrs. Bliss in
a row and demonstrated over the entertainment.
Mr. Kemp and Florence were demonstrating too,
he over his left hip, and Florence over her need for
Miss Howard as a friend, and they all parted to dress,
calm and confident.

Dinner was early that night for the entertainment
began at a quarter to eight for eight, whatever that
meant. Colonel Chase had pinned a quantity of medals
and ribands to his evening coat, among which Mrs.
Holders swore she detected an ordinary shilling with
a hole in it. The assembly room was packed, all but
the front row where seats were reserved for the party
from Wentworth, and the four centre ones, so Mr.
Banks excitedly told them, for the Dowager Countess
of Appledore and her party. She had sent in from the
Grange that afternoon to order them, with the intima-
tion that she might be a few minutes late. As she was
patroness of the Children's Hospital Mr. Banks was
sure that this signified that the entertainment was not
to begin without her and her party. He and Town
Councillor Bowen had arranged to receive her at the
door, and he hoped that Colonel Chase would assist
them. So they all three waited for the august arrivals
in a strong draught for a quarter of an hour. Then
the glad word went about that the motor from the
Grange had arrived, and an awed silence settled on the
rest of the front row.

The reception committee bowed and smiled and an
icy blast swept Lady Appledore and party into the
hall. In number and splendour her party was
disappointing, for it consisted of two women so
wrapped up in cloaks and scarves and capes and
woollies that nothing whatever could be seen of them.
They were then partially unwound by the reception
committee and the bleak and wintry features of Lady

Appledore, whose face resembled a frost-bitten pansy
with all its marking huddled up together in the middle,
were disclosed. 'Party' was her companion, Miss
Jobson, whose life was spent in holding skeins of wool
for her, reading books to her, and sitting opposite
to her in the motor. Lady Appledore then nodded
to Mr. Banks to signify that she was ready, and the
choir of St. Giles's church sang a lullaby and a drinking
song amid indescribable apathy.

Colonel Chase's moment had arrived : Miss Howard
slipped into her place behind the piano, and Mr. Banks
introduced the gallant Colonel whose stories were so
well known to everybody by repute (and, he might
have added, to Wentworth by repetition). The
gallant Colonel like Horatio of old had thrown himself
into the breach caused by the lamented absence of
Mr. Graves and so they were going to taste what he
might call the choicest of Colonel Chase's anecdotal
vintage for themselves.

Wentworth violently led the otherwise tame applause
and Colonel Chase's ruddy face had faded to the hue
of the cheapest pink blotting paper as he told them
about the Curate's egg. Wentworth rocked with
laughter but Mrs. Oxney heard Lady Appledore say
to her companion, 'I am never amused, Miss Jobson,
at jokes about the Church,' and she remembered with
dismay that the story of the Dean was coming and that
her ladyship was the daughter of one. She whispered
her apprehensions to her sister who felt sure that
Colonel Chase would substitute the story of the little
boy and his father's whisky. That would be far
more suitable for Lady Appledore was a savage
teetotaller.

The narrator embarked on his story of " My encounter
with the Man-eater," which had so often frozen the
blood of Wentworth. But the audience, with the
curious unanimity of crowds, had made up their minds,

after the Curate's egg, that he was a comic, pure and simple, and the crack-jaw Indian names and allusions to tiffin and Chota-hazri and shikari produced little titters of delighted laughter. They became more and more certain of it as he bade them follow him (he was kidding them) into the pathless solitary jungle with the kites whistling overhead (here some dramatic boy at the back whistled piercingly between his fingers) and up the dry nullah-wallah. " All at once," said the Colonel pointing at Mrs. Oxney, " I heard a rustle in the bushes close by me, and turning I saw within a few yards of me the gleaming eyes and flashing teeth of the man-eater." He whisked round, making the movement of putting his rifle to his shoulder, and at that moment, the performing dog which had escaped from its master, leaped on to the stage and sat up and begged. So loud a roar of delighted laughter went up from the entire hall that no one ever knew whether the man killed the man-eater or the man-eater the man. As it slowly subsided amid sporadic cackles, a yelp or two from the performing dog denoted that somebody was " larning " it to be a tiger.

The story of the little boy and the whisky pleased Lady Appledore very much. " A teetotaller for life I expect," she said to Miss Jobson, " I should like some more stories of that sort."

Colonel Chase sat down for a moment after this, and drank a little water out of the glass in which he had pretended as a little boy to put back the whisky. This took the audience's fancy tremendously, and he couldn't conceive why. He was in so strange a mental state that even Mrs. Bliss, the interpreter of Mind, would have found him hard to treat. He was simmering with fury at the story of the man-eater having been received with those ribald gusts of laughter, and felt sure that he would have gripped his audience and made them catch their breath with suspense, had not that wretched mongrel bounded on to the stage at the climax. On the other hand, the roars of laughter and applause which had greeted him went to his head like wine, and he hardly knew whether to be elated or indignant. He rose to tell his ghost story, and little did they think what terrors and goose-flesh were coming : then, as the *encore*, he would restore them with the tale of the grocer.

The little boy with the whisky had rather damped the spirits of his audience, but on the announcement of ' My own ghost ' they brightened up again, and cheerfully beat time to the first few bars of ' On the road to Mandalay '.

" In the year 1895," said Colonel Chase, " I was stationed at Futipur-Sekri, and by the order of his Excellency the Viceroy——"

The quicker-witted portion of his audience began to laugh. It was like Mr. George Robey saying ' The last time I had tea with the King '. They knew the sort of thing that was coming. Colonel Chase drew himself up, and fingered his medals. So like George Robey.

" By the order of his Excellency the Viceroy," said Colonel Chase, rather severely, " I was sent into the district of Astmetagaga to make a report on the discontent among the Bizributmas. Bellialonga, the capital of the Bizributma tribe was a three-days journey from Futipur-Sekri, and I had to sleep at two dak-bungalows on the way. Just before sunset on the day of which I am speaking I came in sight of the dak-bungalow of Poona-padra, and sent my khitmagar on with a couple of coolies to cook my dinner, and deal with superfluous cobras."

" Really very good," said Lady Appledore to Miss Jobson, " a perfect parody of Mr. Kipling. I am sure something very comical is coming."

Colonel Chase could not hear what she said, but

saw that both she and Miss Jobson had their eyes fixed on him in avid attention.

"The khitmagar was in the cook-house when I arrived," said he, turning slightly towards the piano to show Miss Howard that her cue was imminent, "and night was at hand. My table was laid and I was just about to light the lamp, when I saw at the other end of the room—I mean, in the far corner—"

The piano punctually emitted a moaning wail, and Colonel Chase raised his voice a little.

"—a grey shape forming itself into the semblance of a man. As the lamp burned brighter——"

"You 'aven't lit it yet mister," said some precisian from the back.

"——burned brighter," repeated Colonel Chase, "I saw the dread form with greater distinctness, and my heart stood still. It was clothed in ragged garments, sparse elfin-locks hung over its forehead—forehead," said he, looking wildly round for the man whose duty it was at this particular moment to switch off all the lights in the hall except one close above the platform, by which the audience could see his face of horror surrounded by darkness, "and blood dripped from a jagged wound in its throat. Slowly it detached itself from the wall and advanced on me—"

Every single light went out, including that above the platform, and the man at the switches seeing his mistake, put them all on again. The laughter became general, but, as it were, expectant, holding itself in for the climax.

"—towering ever higher as it approached. Cold sweat broke out on my forehead, my throat was dry as dust——"

"'Ave a drink," said a delighted voice.

"——my knees trembled, and I knew that the powers of Hell were loose. 'Avaunt', I cried, 'In the name of God avaunt' . . . The phantom shrieked——''

Miss Howard, whose hands were poised above the keys, struck a tremendous ascending arpeggio, the end of which was drowned in a roar of laughter. The hall hooted with inextinguishable joy : never was there such a comic as the Colonel.

After this stupendous success Colonel Chase should have stopped : to tell the story of the grocer was to whitewash the lily. But it served to quiet the audience again, though when Mr. Banks in a fruity baritone melodiously bade them come fishing, since tomorrow would be Friday, there were cheerful dissentients who reminded him it would be Thursday. He most obligingly accepted the correction in the second verse, and in the third said it would be Tuesday which gave much satisfaction. He at once sang an *encore*, and then hurried to the ' artists' room ', where Dr. Dobbs was arranging top hats and canaries and handkerchiefs, and put it tactfully to the owner of the performing dog that, as that intelligent animal had already scored the success of the evening as the man-eater, and as Lady Appledore had kept them waiting so long, would it be possible to reserve dear little Toby's performance for the next entertainment at Christmas. Toby's master with some asperity, said that it would not only be possible but probable that Toby's next performance would be reserved for ever and ever, and left by the back door in high dudgeon.

Slightly crushed by this severity, Mr. Banks stole back on tiptoe to hear the piano solo. Miss Howard had begun splendidly, and with dreamy eyes fixed on the ceiling and head a little on one side to catch the messages from the harmonious spirits of the air, was improvising that charming fragment from the waltz by Chopin with delicacy and precision. Then she closed her eyes and sank her head over the pensive

section by moonlight, and made everybody feel that
tomorrow would be Monday, so Sunday-like was the
chorale that toothache had inspired. She opened her
eyes again, and was wreathed in smiles as the spirits
of the air suggested to her that pretty device of the
long shake and the crossing arpeggios, but next moment
those nearest her might have observed a slightly glazed
look coming over her face as the magnificent *fortissimo*
passage for octaves in both hands drew near. She
tried to calm herself by letting her eyes stray about
to shew her complete mastery of her task : now they
glanced at Lady Appledore, now at Florence who was
leaning forward towards her with a look of yearning
ecstasy, rather disconcerting. Now she was among
the octaves, but for the life of her once more she could
not remember how she rescued herself from this tem-
pestuous sea and slid into the calm waters of the
Chopin waltz again, and she projected anxious thoughts
into the rapidly approaching future, instead of trusting
to Mind, or at least her memory, to prompt her when
she came to that point. She wished passionately
that she had not improvised this fine passage at all :
it would have been so easy to go straight into the
Chopin waltz from the chorale. Her agitation increased, and the octaves grew faster and louder : she
missed a change of key and found herself with fingers
already aching with fatigue apparently committed
to thunder forth fortuitous octaves with both hands
till she swooned with the exertion. In vain she thought
of Mrs. Bliss, in vain she stretched her mouth in an
agonised smile and denied octaves and improvisation
and forgetfulness and fatigue and anything else that
came into her head. Her face was getting crimson,
and yet she could not stop and if she could she would now
be unable to recollect even the Chopin waltz. Finally,
in absolute despair, she took her hands off the notes,
hurled them at the piano again in three crashing chords,

and rose. The moment she was on her feet she remembered exactly what the transition should have
been, but now it was too late. . . . After the tremendous din that had been going on the applause
sounded but faint, except for Florence's indefatigable
smacks.

Long before the hour for collection and carriages
Wentworth collectively had been puzzling over what its
demeanour to Colonel Chase should be. He was sitting
a little apart from the rest, and sideway glances at
him observed that he appeared slightly morose, or
as if he was puzzling too. There was no doubt that
he had won the success of the evening, but that success
had been purchased with strange coin, for his
humorous tales had produced depression, and in others
the suspense and terror which it had been his firm
intention to evoke had roused gales of laughter. Not
even the excitement of seeing how much Dowager
Countesses gave to collections nor the pained disgust
to observe that this one considered sixpence ample,
put this difficult problem of demeanour out of Mrs.
Oxney's mind, and her sister whom she consulted in
whispers was utterly at a loss : Mrs. Bertram merely
shook her head sadly, and thought it very awkward.
Should they congratulate him on his success, or execrate
the odious light-mindedness of the audience, or ignore
the whole affair and talk lightly about the weather ?

There they all were then in a rather tense group,
waiting for Lady Appledore's motor to start and leave
the entrance clear for the Wentworth bus. The
reception committee including Colonel Chase was
bowing its thanks to her for her distinguished
patronage and her sixpence, and it was Lady Appledore
herself who solved the problem for them.

"I so much enjoyed your very amusing stories,
Colonel Chase," she said. "Did I not Miss Jobson ?
The ghost ! Quite killing ! How I laughed ! And

the man-eater ! What a clever little dog to come in just when you told it. Beautifully trained ! And the comic music for the ghost ! Most humorous."

Now two courses were open to Colonel Chase. He might either turn livid with passion and tell Lady Appledore that she was as contemptible as the rest of the yokels who had laughed when they should have shuddered, or he might adopt Lady Appledore's heresy as orthodox, and promulgate it, so to speak, as his own official Bull. The fact that he was a snob to the bottom of his appendix, and soberly considered countesses to be of a clay apart was perhaps the determining factor which settled the puzzling question of his demeanour. He bowed again and all his medals jingled.

" Delighted to have afforded you a little amusement, Lady Appledore," he said in a voice that Wentworth could hear. " We had many a laugh in the mess when I told my ghost story."

That, of course, settled the matter for Wentworth, and when he rejoined his party everybody knew exactly what line to take. That he had told the two thrilling tales of the man-eater and the ghost often and often before, and that they had been received with shudders and gasps and tremblings, and protests from Mrs. Oxney that she wouldn't dare to go to bed to-night, must now be forgotten : from henceforth, world without end, these were comic stories, and Wentworth would scream with laughter at all the points where hitherto it had frozen with horror.

" Oh, Colonel," said Mrs. Oxney, " what a treat you gave us ! You made me ache with laughing. How we all enjoyed it ! You never told them so wonderfully. Miss Howard, too ! Her comic accompaniment : how you must have practised it together. And then your lovely improvisation afterwards, Miss Howard ; all coming to you on the spur of the moment like that ! At one moment I thought the inspiration was going

to fail you, but how foolish of me to have been alarmed.
Those grand chords at the end! You two made the
whole success of the evening and Mr. and Mrs. Banks
of course as well," she hastily added at the approach
of these artists. " The violin : such a sweet instrument
And tomorrow will be Tuesday or Wednesday, I declare
I don't know what to-day is after that. And ' Curfew
shall not ring to-night ' ! What a heroine ! She
deserved the Victoria Cross at least. And your dear
little choir boys singing so beautifully and of course
—good evening, Dr. Dobbs—Dr. Dobbs's wonderful
conjuring tricks. I couldn't see how any of them
were done, and fancy the Countess of Appledore only
giving sixpence ! "

The official and orthodox view could not have been
more ably stated, and after a pleasant little refection
of sandwiches and cake in the lounge, with some hot
soup for the artists who must be exhausted with their
efforts, Colonel Chase was induced to give them the
ghost story again (new style) with piano accompaniment. Mrs. Holders had not been to the entertainment and to her unbounded astonishment she heard
the shuddering and gruesome tale received with hoots
of merriment. This was quite inexplicable and almost
more so was the evident satisfaction of Colonel Chase.

" Well, a good laugh does us no harm now and again,"
he said, " and I must say that I was pleased with the
quickness with which the audience took my points.
Nothing so depressing for the entertainer as to find
that his humour is not appreciated. Lady Appledore
—a charming woman—said she had enjoyed my little
stories immensely. Very kind of her, I'm sure. I
must bicycle over to the Grange some day soon and
leave my card."

" And Miss Howard's playing too, Mrs. Holders,"
continued Mrs. Oxney, who wanted everyone to feel
happy and appreciated. " You did miss something

there. Quite a sensation! How I should like to
hear it again! You ought to write it down, Miss
Howard, you ought indeed, so that your inspiration
shouldn't be lost, and that others might play it as well
if they had the fingers, though I'm sure only the most
superior pianists could do it. What an evening of
enjoyment! And the picture exhibition to look
forward to next week."

"But fancy the Countess of Appledore only giving
sixpence," said Mrs. Bertram, on whom this miserly
incident had made the deepest impression. "I thought
that was a very paltry sum indeed, and I could hardly
believe my eyes. Sixpence, and Miss Jobson nothing
at all."

Colonel Chase went up to bed satisfied that he had
acted for the best in taking the verdict of the audience
(especially when endorsed by a Countess) as final.
He had gone through the most poignant emotions
that evening, in which rage and disgust were the
keenest. His feelings when the house began to laugh
at the story of the tiger were indescribable, and when
that miserable little terrier came on to the platform
and begged, he would willingly have shot it, had the
imaginary rifle in his hands, suddenly materialised :
and when the house again rocked with merriment
at his ghost story, he would, had the rifle undergone
a further transmutation into a machine-gun have felt
the greatest satisfaction in mowing them down in
swathes, beginning with a Countess. Then his comic
stories had failed altogether (these rustic audiences had
the most perverted sense of humour) and probably
no more deeply-chagrined a reciter had ever stepped
down from a platform. He really could not see how
he could face Wentworth at all : it is true they had
not laughed except in the right places, and when others
laughed they had worn expressions of pain and sympathy, and throughout the remainder of the entertain-

ment he had been thinking of some very severe things
to say about being subjected to the insults of an un-
mannerly mob. Then, owing to Lady Appledore's
comments, he had seized his opportunity, and mounted
the throne of the supreme comic artist. It was like
a conjuring trick, one of Dr. Dobbs's best.

As he undressed and did his valuable exercises,
puffing out his big chest, and bending till he touched
his toes, he wondered if a more surprising success had
ever come to a man out of ruinous failure. Wentworth,
too, had caught on at once, and had laughed at the
repetition of the ghost story just now, as if they had
never known what it felt like to shudder. . . . And
then suddenly the thought of Mrs. Bliss came to him.
She had told him that if only he relied on Mind, in
his kind and unselfish efforts in aid of the poor children
in hospital, they must be crowned with brilliant success.
That had certainly happened, though as a matter
of fact the poor children in hospital had not even so
much as entered his head, since he was first approached
by Mr. Banks. And then he remembered also that
Mrs. Bliss had said that Mind was often inscrutable
in its workings : the aspirations of those who trusted
it were always fulfilled, but mortal sense could never
accurately predict the manner of it. Certainly he
had never expected that Mind would fulfil his aspirations by causing his audience to peal with laughter
at what had been designed to make their flesh creep,
and when their first giggles broke out he had determined
to have nothing to do with Mind. But now that
apparent failure wore a different aspect, one that could
only be accounted for by the theory of inscrutable
dealings, ' Upon my word,' he said to himself, as he
got into bed, ' I'll look into it all a bit further. My
cold, my pedometer, and now this ! It all seems to
hang together in the most marvellous fashion.'

Mr. Banks came up to Wentworth again next day

to see Colonel Chase, full of congratulations and with a further request to make.

" Stupendous, Colonel," he said, " you were simply stupendous last night. There were some nurses there from the Children's Hospital, and they told me on my visit there this morning that they'd never laughed so much in all their born days. ' Curfew shall not ring to-night ' seems to have pleased them too, but that's neither here nor there."

" Remarkably fine, I thought," said Colonel Chase, who could easily afford to commend minor lights.

" Very good of you to say so. I thought I gripped the audience. Well, the matron charged me to ask you if you wouldn't very kindly give the story of the tiger and the ghost in the wards. Poor little mites you know : there've got small cause for laughter in their lives, and it really would be most good of you."

Colonel Chase was highly gratified, and good-naturedly abandoned his walk, and went to the hospital that afternoon. The matron thought she could introduce her cat into the tiger story to take the place of that clever dog, while it was in course of narration, for it was a lethargic cat, usually asleep and good at staying exactly where it was put : she could put it down on one of the beds quite quietly. It was thought better to feed the cat first, for after food sleep was assured, so would the Colonel begin with the ghost story ? The children were all agog with pleasure and excitement at the prospect of hearing the funny man.

The nurses, already tittering at what was coming, preceded the funny man into the first ward, and he began his ghost story. But the effect was highly disastrous : child after child broke into shrieks of terror and dismay, nurses hurried from bed to bed to comfort the howling occupants, and assure them they shouldn't be frightened any more, and the matron had to beg the Colonel to leave the ward without delay.

So, within ten minutes of his arrival, he was on his way
back to Wentworth in a state of complete bewilderment
as to whether the ghost story was terrible or comic ;
its effect seemed to be wholly incalculable. And
surely Mind was acting again in the most inscrutable
manner.

He stalked into the lounge where Mrs. Bliss was
sitting. She hailed him with her widest smile.

" There you are, Colonel ! " she said. " How kind
and dear of you to have sacrificed your walk. How
the poor little mites must have enjoyed it ! What
brightness you have brought into lives full of Error !
I've been demonstrating over the pleasure you have
been giving ever since you started. Tell me all about
it ! "

Colonel Chase's suspicions about Mind deepened to
real distrust. But perhaps Mrs. Bliss could explain it.

" I can't make it out," he said. " I meant to give
pleasure but when I got to the ghost forming itself
in the far corner the children burst into sobs and howls.
The matron hurried in and asked me to go away at
once. Very disconcerting. What do you make of it ? "

Mrs. Bliss was not in the least disconcerted.

" Poor little mites ! " she said. " You see they are
surrounded with thoughts of illness : everything round
them suggests illness : doctors, nurses, *materia medica*,
and as you know now it is all Error. You came in,
radiating Mind, and Error boiled up to the surface,
violent for the moment, but dispersing rapidly. It
often happens like that. All is Mind. Mind is all.
Terror and evil and sickness flee before it. There is
no reality in them. There is a wonderful page or two
about it in the Manual."

She picked up the Manual and turned quickly over
the pages. " Yes, here it is," she said. " Shall I
read it ? Sweet words and so true ! ' Often when
Error is brought under the influence of Mind, there

takes place a chemicalisation. Error surges to the surface only to be instantly dispersed. An apparent relapse may occur, and this is often the first sign that the healing process is going on.' Quite convincing, is it not ? The dear little mites will be so much better in consequence of your visit. I am so glad you went."

CHAPTER VI

For the rest of the week Miss Howard had very little
time to attend to Mind, and just about as little inclination. She considered that Mind had shewn the greatest
inattention to her improvisation : she had committed
herself and it to Mind with the complete trust that a
passenger puts in the engine-driver when he makes a
journey by train, and there had been an accident.
Not only had she quite forgotten the end of the passage
for octaves, but there had been no sign whatever of an
encore, whereas Colonel Chase who had already been
cured of a cold, the tantrums and the loss of a pedometer, had been loaded with benefits. It was not
fair, and though Mrs. Bliss assured her that those last
few chords would linger for ever in her memory like
the sound of a great Mental Amen, Miss Howard would
far sooner have got back into the Chopin waltz and
finished according to plan, than have so agreeably
affected Mrs. Bliss. Besides, those chords composing
the great Mental Amen, would have come in anyhow.

Mind, too, was doing nothing for Mr. Kemp, and Mrs.
Bliss's argument that his baths and massage were a
materialistic hindrance to his recovery was met with
the deadly parry that she was having baths and massage
too, and was improving enormously.

But she only smiled unweariedly, and repeated that
she submitted to baths and massage for her husband's
sake, and that they did not hinder her progress because
she was quite sure that they had no effect whatever

on her. But the fact of submitting to them (not the baths and massage themselves) perhaps did her good for this was a sacrifice made to love, and Mind liked that. What did hinder progress was to have faith in *materia medica* and wouldn't dear Mr. Kemp give up his treatment for a week, for he was still believing it might do him good, and see how much better he would be ? It was clearly no use arguing with Mrs. Bliss for she only smiled and said it all over again with loving pity (which was so exasperating), but every night as he had a few sips of hot milk or a glass of lemonade without sugar, and a rusk, he argued the position out with Florence. Florence could not make up her mind either, and so after lengthy debate they sat with smiles and closed eyes, and since he was no better in the morning he had his reclining bath as usual. Mr. Kemp in fact served both Mind and Mammon with equal devotion and no reward from either.

But Miss Howard during the few days that remained before the opening of her exhibition of pictures in the Green Salon, worked away, relying entirely on herself and not at all on Mind : she had become, for the time being, a rank a-mentalist. The question of prices was truly difficult, for she wanted to get as much as she could for her pictures, but had not the vaguest idea what anybody would be willing to give. So instead of closing her eyes, and seeking guidance, she looked at her pictures with a critical eye, and eventually made the scale. ' Evening Bells ', with a five-and-sixpenny frame positively given away, was two guineas : Mrs. Oxney's cat under the title of ' Pussy-dear ' and ' Geraniums ' were one guinea, and everything else was half-a-guinea. This price list, to be produced on application, was entrusted to the care of one of the handsomest of the liveried pages at the Baths (who generally spent their days in playing leap-frog with each other) whom Mr. Bowen guaranteed to be the

brightest boy in Bolton.   He was also given a roll of
perforated paper, much like a roll of exceedingly narrow
toilet-paper, on each numbered section of which was
printed an advertisement of Mr. Bowen, plumber,
decorator, picture-framer and carpenter : these rolls
were supplied by Mr. Bowen free of charge, for the sake
of the publicity.   The leap-frog boy, thus made door-
keeper, cashier and bureau of information, had merely
to tear off one of these sections, and hand it on payment
of sixpence to the visitors to the Green Salon : the
device seemed fool-proof.   But he had to be tactful as
well, for if he observed a visitor looking very attentively
at the exhibits, he was to touch his cap with an insinuating smile, and ask if he would like to see a price-list.
In his left trouser pocket there was a pill box thrown
in gratis with ' *Souvenir d'Orient* ' by Mr. Amble,
containing some minute red adhesive stars, and in
case a picture was purchased, he had to write down the
name and address of the purchaser and with a genteel
application of the tip of his tongue to the adhesive
star, affix it to the corner of the picture, to indicate
that it was sold.   For these services he received a
shilling a day in addition to the salary he earned from
the establishment for playing leap-frog.

The hanging of the pictures was a task no less difficult than their pricing.   In some places the walls
were so crumbly, (owing probably to the action of the
brine) that large flakes came away under the lightest
impact of that useful little nail called the ' Small
Brad ', while in others the walls were so adamantine
(owing probably to the action of the rotten-egg water)
that the Small Brad curled up and became a minute
croquet hoop.   In the end a taut copper wire had to
be hung from corner to corner of the walls of the
Green Salon and the pictures hooked on to it.   They
had a tendency to sag towards the centre where the
wire drooped a little.   An advertisement appeared

on Friday and Saturday in the *Bolton Gazette*, and
Mr. Bowen, who was part-owner of the paper said he
was confident that Miss Howard would not regret that
little trifle of expense, when all was said and done.
This was a dark oracular saying, but Mr. Bowen
seemed quite certain about it.

By Saturday afternoon every picture was in its
place : Evening Bells, and Pussy-dear, and Geraniums
and Reflections and Lengthening Shadows and God's
Acre and Bethesda and Healing Springs and Golf
Links Wentworth, and Leafy Warwickshire and
June's Glory and Suntrap and Frosty Morning and
Dewy Eve and Harvest Moon, and Gloaming and
Beeches and Hawthorns and St. Giles's Church and
Still Life and Matins and Evensong and ' Oh, to be in
England now that April's here ', and Campions and
Sheep-feeding and Mist in the Valley and Mist on the
Hills and Swans and the ' Curfew tolls the knell of
parting Day ' and many others. Miss Howard then
went through the pantomime of being a visitor with
the custodian who pretended to tear off a section of
toilet-paper quite correctly in return for her imaginary
sixpence and looked seraphic as he sidled up to her
while she examined ' Pussy-dear ' with close attention,
and offered to show her the price-list. The light through
the scrubbed skylight was admirable and after giving
the Green Salon a final whiff of Souvenir d'Orient,
Miss Howard, in order to be on the safe side, closed
her eyes and smiled, committing the entire under-
taking, already terribly expensive, to Mind. The
Baths would be shut on Sunday, and she would not
look on her handiwork again till it was open to the
inspection and the purses of the public. She hoped
the purses would be open too.

To say that Miss Howard came down to breakfast
on Monday with either appetite or confidence or calm
would be highly misleading. She had passed a worried

and wakeful night, and her rare snatches of sleep had
been chequered by villainous dreams in which she
saw with agony that she had hung all her pictures
upside down, or that the Green Salon, crowded with
Dowager Countesses of forbidding aspect, had no pictures at all on the walls, or that they were entirely
occupied with one vast fresco representing Pussy-dear
ringing Evening Bells. . . . She was early down after an
unrefreshing night, and no one else had yet appeared,
but the papers had come in, and there on her table
was not only her usual periodical but a copy of the
Bolton Gazette. She supposed that Mr. Bowen had sent
it up as he had done on Friday and Saturday to show
that the advertisement for her exhibition had duly
appeared, but on the outside leaf he had written
in blue pencil underlined 'see page 8', and
accordingly she turned there. Big head-lines, that
seemed to dance before her enraptured gaze, instantly
shewed why she should turn to page 8. A column
was entitled 'Exhibition of Water-Colours in the
Green Salon at Bolton Baths'. She read :

" Seldom has a greater treat been afforded to the lover of
the beautiful in Bolton (and we know there are many such)
than this exhibition of Miss Alice Howard's water-colours
which opens to-day. For perfection of technique, for subtle
and exquisite observation, for radiant fancy, for that name-
less *je ne sais quoi* without which all art is as sounding brass
and tinkling cymbal, we doubt whether any modern artist
can rival this gifted lady who has at last done justice to and
conferred immortality on our lovely countryside. Nor are
Miss Howard's truly poetical interpretations of Nature con-
fined to landscape alone : all lovers of the feline species will
long to be the happy possessor of ' Pussy-dear ', and we could
have wished she had given us more animal studies. The
Green Salon at the Baths, we are sure, will be thronged all
day with eager purchasers. A veritable cabinet of gems."

The artist gave a gasp of delight. She had so lost
herself in the perusal of this masterly and sympathetic

account of her work, that she had not observed that
other guests had entered the dining-room. There
they sat at their tables, all silent, and all, oh wonder
of wonders, immersed in the *Bolton Gazette*. Admirable Mr. Bowen, whose oracular speech was now explained, must have sent copies of it to everyone at
Wentworth.

Mrs. Bliss was the first to finish this eulogy, and
catching Miss Howard's eyes, blew her a kiss (which
Florence thought a very forward proceeding) and
pointed to it.

" Not half what you deserve, dear," she said. " But
very nice as far as it goes. I told you how it would
be. Mind ! "

Murmurs of approval and applause came from other
quarters of the dining-room as the breakfasters finished
this little appreciation in the *Bolton Gazette*, and Mrs.
Oxney said she felt quite upset at the thought that
somebody else might purchase " Pussy-dear " before
she had time to go down and snap it up. It was so
tiresome that on Monday morning household affairs
always detained her till lunch-time. The simple
expedient of paying Miss Howard a guinea and thus
purchasing ' Pussy-dear ' without more ado did not
seem to occur to her, and delicacy naturally prevented
the artist from suggesting it. . . . As for Miss Howard,
now treading on air, and with her appetite fully restored, she gobbled up her breakfast and hurried
warbling away in order to get down to the Baths by
the time the Green Salon opened. She meant to go
in and out with a busy but diffident air, and everyone
who knew who she was would tell those who didn't,
and she would be a Public Character. Her one regret
at the moment after regarding the Lobgesang in the
Gazette was that she had not priced all the pictures
at double the modest sum that appeared in the list.
Such modesty just now seemed almost morbid.

Shortly after she had left the dining-room, Colonel
Chase came down to breakfast, extremely late and in a
worse temper than he had been in since Mr. Amble
had failed to send his quinine and thermogene. He
had been drinking his early morning tea and eating
his toast when a furtive and adamantine piece of crust
caused an important front tooth to part company from
its parent plate. In itself that would have been no
great inconvenience, for he had a beautiful row of
uppers left but he remembered with sad vividness how,
only last night, when Mrs. Holders mentioned that
she had to pay a visit to the dentist's, he had said in
his favourite rôle of the entirely robust and healthy
man, ' I never have any bother with my teeth, thank
goodness.' In a way that was quite true, because,
strictly speaking, he had not got any, but the inference
which he had no doubt had been drawn, was that he
had got them all. So before he came down to breakfast he spent a long time in front of his looking-glass
making the mouth-movements of speech and laughter
to see whether the loss would be apparent. He thought
that would pass undetected unless he incautiously
allowed himself to be very much amused about anything, and he would have to go up to London some day
soon. Then, being in a hurry, he cut himself
shaving, for he never condescended to the ' safety
mowing-machines ', as he contemptuously termed
the modern type of razor. ' I'm not afraid of the bare
blade ', he used to say. But he was very angry just
now with the bare blade. . . .

These untoward incidents were quite enough thoroughly to ruffle a temper that was never very equable
early in the day, and when, on sitting down to his
breakfast he demanded a couple of sausages, he was
not soothed at being told by the parlour-maid that
there were none left ; she recommended some ' beautiful ' bacon instead. He cast a glance of peculiar

annoyance at the unsolicited copy of the *Bolton Gazette* which lay by his plate, and opened it.

" What have they sent me this provincial rag for ? " he muttered. " And why page 8 ? Some local charity, I'll be bound. Children's Hospital probably. I've had enough of the Children's Hospital. Hullo, picture exhibition . . . ! "

A sideways glance told him that Miss Howard was not present, and folding the paper back he emitted frequent pshaws and faughs as he read. Then he flung it on the floor.

Mrs. Bliss observed those signs of Error (there was no mistaking them) with tender regret, and put on her brightest smile as she rose from her meal and passed, hardly limping at all, close to his table. Error must not be allowed to poison the sweet morning.

" Such a lovely little notice of Miss Howard's pictures," she said, " So appreciative. Have you seen it ? "

" Yes, indeed I have," said he, " and for myself I don't find it lovely. Ludicrous flattery I call it, laid on with a spade. I wonder who wrote it, eh ? A little suspicious."

Quite suddenly as he said the word ' suspicious ', a loud cheerful whistle sounded through the dining-room. Everybody looked up, wondering where it came from. Colonel Chase himself thought that some rude person had interrupted him (as when the kites whistled in the tiger-story) and angrily resumed.

" Our friend is indeed endowed with all the gifts," he said. "Pianist, artist, and now shall we add, art critic, Mrs. Bliss ? "

Once again came that piercing whistle, and Colonel Chase could not doubt, nor indeed could anybody else, that his own unwilling lips had produced it through the gap in the front teeth. He realised at once that he must avoid sibilants (so difficult to do) as the gouty avoided sugar, and go up to London on business without delay, for his speech betrayed him. If he hurried he would be able to catch the ten o'clock train and be back to-night. Most annoying. The only bright spot, and that a small one, was that he could not go at any rate to-day, to Miss Howard's exhibition, and if that eulogy he had just read was really by an unbiassed hand, all the pictures ought to be sold by to-morrow. He gobbled up his bacon and found an urgent call to go to London among his letters.

All that morning and all that afternoon, Miss Howard was diffidently gliding in and out of the Green Salon and welcoming friends who came in to look at her pictures with little deprecating speeches but nobly refraining from accompanying them round, for that would have made it difficult for them to avoid a purchase, and Miss Howard had a pride. But the custodian had his eye on them, and whenever anyone lingered by God's Acre or Bethesda she saw him glide up to them with his insinuating smile and politely tell them of the existence of a catalogue of prices. Unfortunately this information only seemed to have the effect of making them hurry on, and she could not help noticing that as they neared the end of the exhibition, they looked round to see if she was near and glided stealthily from the Green Salon in a way that suggested prisoners escaping. Once the custodian got as far as producing the pill box with the adhesive stars from his trousers pocket, but nothing came of it. It was all a little discouraging, and the rapture inspired by the notice in the *Bolton Gazette* gradually grew dim. Mrs. Bowen, however was a tonic, for she made Miss Howard come all the way round with her, and poured forth a continuous stream of admiring comment.

"And there's St. Giles's Church again," she said. "I should know it anywhere. No. 9—what does the catalogue say about it ? Reflections : there they are in the river. Beautiful : so clear ! And what an enthusiastic notice wasn't it, in the *Gazette*, though not a word too much. Mr. Bowen was sure you'd like that. It was written by a very clever young man on the staff, whom Mr. Bowen was kind to not so long ago. He's not here himself to-day, and so busy that he was afraid he mayn't be able to pop in before closing time, and I shall get a fine scolding if I can't tell him all about the pictures. I do think he's made a good job of the frames : so quiet and tasteful, and shewing them off, you may say, to the best advantage. Why if that isn't Mrs. Oxney's cat : I could recognise it and pick it out if there were fifty pictures of cats. What does the catalogue say about that ? ' Pussy-dear '. Not a doubt about it : so good-natured, and never scratches. And Evening Bells : perhaps that's my favourite, but with so many lovely bits, I hardly know what I like best. How sweet any of them would look above my piano in the parlour ! I must have one more look at ' Pussy-dear '—the custodian glided to her side—" but I mustn't deprive Mrs. Oxney of that, or she would be in a way about it."

The custodian ebbed sadly away.

As dusk fell and closing time for the Green Salon approached, the custodian rendered his financial statement. There had been nineteen visitors, not including a deaf old gentleman who could not for a long time be made to understand that there was an entrance fee, and then retreated in high indignation, entirely declining to pay, but the toilet-roll showed that twenty sections had been detached from it. This was accounted for by the custodian's confession that he had torn one off, not realising that each symbolised sixpence, in order to roll himself a cigarette, for which purpose it was admirably fitted. Miss Howard paid him his shilling out of the takings of the day and enjoined on him to revere the toilet-roll. With the exception of Mrs. Oxney and Colonel Chase, all Wentworth had visited the Green Salon, and Florence had been twice. Colonel Chase, so Miss Howard ascertained on her arrival there at tea-time, had gone up to London after breakfast and had not yet returned.

She was hailed with numerous congratulations, and by Mrs. Oxney with a profusion of valid excuses for her not having visited the Green Salon.

"Such a worry it has been to me all day, Miss Howard, that I haven't been able to get down. First there was the usual Monday morning settling-up, and that took all my morning and half an hour after lunch as well. And then such a fuss in the kitchen for the boot-and-knife boy, so good at his work but peppery, came late to his dinner, and Cook refused to have the cold beef back, but said he must be content with bread and cheese, if he couldn't keep time. So there were words, and Cook came to me to know if it was by my wish that the boot-and-knife boy swore at her. Fancy! As if I had ever wished anything of the sort. And then when that was over, there were the hot-water pipes in the smoking-room leaking, just when I was thinking of putting on my hat and starting, and by the time the plumber had put them to rights, it was getting dark."

"Then, oh, what a pleasure you will have tomorrow," said Mrs. Bliss. "I'm sure I could have spent all day in the Green Salon, going round and round it and seeing fresh beauties every time. Such refreshment! I went quite early, as I knew it would be crowded all day. How many visitors did you have, dear?"

"Nineteen, no twenty," said Miss Howard.

"I call that wonderful for the first day. Just wait a few days till people have had time to tell each other what a treat is in store for them! There'll be quite a *queue* outside of those waiting to get in."

"And I hope my Pussy isn't sold yet," said Mrs. Oxney. "I should be miserable if anybody else got that."

"Let me see!" said Miss Howard, pressing her finger to her forehead. "No, I don't think it is. I can't remember seeing a red star on it."

"My favourite is Evening Bells," said Mrs. Bliss. "Such peace and poetry. How they'll all be snapped up!"

Florence liked Healing Springs best; her father could not understand her preference for that over Bethesda. The discussion grew quite animated, and though it was gratifying to find them all taking such interest and pride in her work (Mrs. Bertram had cut out the notice in the *Bolton Gazette* and was meaning to paste it into her scrap-book as a compliment to Wentworth) Miss Howard could have wished that just one of them had guarded against the certainty of a favourite being snapped up, by snapping first. There seemed to be a lack of prudence in neglecting the opportunities of to-day, which might be gone to-morrow.

Next morning could scarcely rank as a morning at all, so dense and dark were the volleying clouds which swept down from the East, discharged their broadsides of rain on Bolton and hurried on to make room for fresh assailants. Colonel Chase had returned the night before, all smiles and no whistles, and it was evident that his business in town had been satisfactory. But even an old campaigner like himself, as he told Miss Howard at breakfast, could not face the wrath of such weather, and, after the cold that had threatened him last week, he felt it wiser to postpone the pleasure of seeing her delightful pictures. Mrs. Oxney was full of similar lamentations, and though distraught at the notion of Pussy's picture being snapped up by somebody else, it still did not occur to her to telephone to the Baths and bid the custodian affix the adhesive star to the treasure. Even Mr. Kemp preferred to miss a morning of Bethesda, and see whether Mind would not do something striking for him as he sat close to the log fire in the lounge and the bus went down with only two passengers in it, Mrs. Bliss who for the sake of her husband was willing to brave any erroneous inclemency, particularly as it could not possibly hurt her, and Miss Howard.

The Green Salon was absolutely empty of art lovers, and the skylight was leaking a little on to Mrs. Oxney's nice carpet. Patients from neighbouring hotels and from Belvoir, Blenheim and Balmoral came through the vestibule in dripping mackintoshes, and how much nicer it would be, thought Miss Howard, if it was they who were dripping on to Mrs. Oxney's carpet instead of the skylight. In fact the only focus of cheerfulness about the Green Salon was its custodian who felt certain everyone would come flocking in as soon as the weather cleared : no one in his opinion could ' have the heart to look at pictures, miss ', on such a day. Miss Howard paid him his shilling before lunch, not meaning to return if the down-pour continued, and inspected the sad integrity of the toilet-roll. But it would never do to present the appearance of a down-hearted exhibitor and after lunch she established herself in the lounge to make an indoor sketch. The perspective of the staircase was a most intricate problem, and no amount of sympathetic colour would make it look other than unscaleable.

Though the old campaigner could not face the weather for the ten minutes walk to the Baths to see the pictures he faced it that afternoon for a solid six miles by his pedometer, leaving and returning to Wentworth by the back door, so that Miss Howard, sketching in the lounge close to the front door should be ignorant of his perfidy. A good deal of diplomacy was needed in these manœuvres, for he had to get his mackintosh from the hall, and take it up to his bedroom for the purpose of sewing a button on, and on his return from his walk, convey it by a round-about route to the hot-water pipes outside the dining-room in order to dry it. This done, he came thumping down to tea, flushed and rosy with exercise and successful trickery.

" I'm not one to complain of an occasional wet day," he said, " for I've got through some arrears, and had a good spell of reading in my room—wonderful author, Macaulay : he gives you something solid to think about. And if anyone asked if I'd had a snooze as well, I should change the subject."

" Nothing to be ashamed of, Colonel," said Mr. Kemp. " A nap during the afternoon has often been recommended to me. After the wear and tear of the morning nature needs a restorative. I get sounder sleep sometimes in half an hour after lunch, than I do in the whole course of the night. At Buxton it was part of my *régime*."

" Well, it freshens one up," said Colonel Chase, who always interrupted Mr. Kemp's experiences at Spas, " I feel brisk enough for anything now. We might have a rubber perhaps before dinner now the day's work is over. The evenings are drawing in now : we can play with a good conscience, and not feel we're wasting the daylight. Cards and candles, I always say."

Mrs. Oxney had entered as he spoke. She had just come along from the dining-room, where she had been distributing the menu cards for dinner, and had seen Colonel Chase's mackintosh spread over the radiator and sending up clouds of steam.

" Well, that would be very comfortable," she said,

" and if you want me to take a hand, I'm ready.
But to think of your having gone out on this miserable
afternoon, Colonel. I'll be bound you had to make
your pedometer tick briskly to keep yourself warm.
And your mackintosh, why, you might have thrown
it into the river : a button off, too, letting the wet in."

Mrs. Holders caught Tim's eye, who, trying to
strangle a laugh, swallowed a crumb of cake by an
unusual route and violently choked. This happily
changed the subject, which Colonel Chase would
certainly have had to do for Mr. Kemp who was an
authority on false passages of all sorts begged everybody not to pat Tim on the back, for such a well-
meant treatment only made matters worse. He
ought to sit bolt upright, breathe deeply in through
the nose and expel the air vigorously through the
mouth. Everyone's attention was therefore diverted
to Tim, and they watched him recover by degrees.
Mrs. Bliss had clearly been demonstrating during his
fit, so it was uncertain whether Mind or Mr. Kemp was
responsible.

But though there was then no definite further exposure of Colonel Chase's rank duplicity, everyone
was aware of it, for no one could possibly forget that
he had told Miss Howard that the weather was too
bad for even so old a campaigner to venture out.
It was no wonder that she moistened her lips several
times and determined that nothing should drag from
her the smallest comment on his most deceitful behaviour. What made his falsehoods more revolting
to the feelings of a lady was the hearty and rollicking
manner in which he said he had been reading in his
bedroom and perhaps snoozed. But she scorned to
return to the subject and ask how many miles he had
walked.

Morning brought a renewal of tranquil and sunny

weather, and had it not been for her exhibition, Miss
Howard would certainly have returned to lunch at
Wentworth with a veritable ' Ode to Autumn' in water-
colour to display on the chimney-piece of the lounge.
But she could not bear in these critical days to absent
herself so long from the Green Salon, and she longed
to know whether her custodian's optimism was justified
in expecting an influx of visitors now that the improved
weather conditions would give them the heart to look
at pictures. At present, when she arrived there soon
after breakfast, there was only one visitor, a rather
odious looking young man, who, so the custodian
secretly informed her, had refused to pay for admission
on the grounds that he was the press. Instantly she
was divided between high hopes and low suspicions.
Was he (rapturous thought !) ' our own correspondent ' of some influential London paper, sent down to
study the contents of the Green Salon, which the
Bolton Gazette had found so exquisite, or was he some
clever thief who intended, when the custodian's small
back was turned to cut out from their frames some of
the choicest gems and dispose of them to shady dealers ?
He did not look like her idea of our own correspondent :
on the other hand it would have been unlike a clever
thief to have called attention to himself by saying
that he was the press. In either case, he had better
know who she was, for if he was the press he might
like to have an interview, while if he was a thief he
would know that the artist had taken note of him.
So she tripped up to him, and gave him the benefit
of the doubt.

" The press, I believe," she said. " I am Miss
Howard. These little things of mine—— "

The press had not very good manners : it did not
remove from the corner of its mouth a cigarette whose
fumes mingled strangely with the odour of the waters,
perceptible this morning, and that of Souvenir d'Orient.

" Pleased to meet you, miss," he said, " and pleased to have given you a leg up in our organ the *Bolton Gazette*. I laid it on thick, didn't I ? Just looked in to see what sort of a show you'd got. Very pretty, I'm sure."

" I thought your article was most sympathetic," she said. " And so pleased you've paid my little exhibition a second visit, after studying it so closely."

He looked much surprised.

" No, I've not been here before," he said. " I just had a look at the catalogue, and wrote my stuff on that."

Poor Miss Howard felt her last support slip from her. Hitherto she had clung to the comforting knowledge that though visitors might be few and purchasers completely non-existent, the trained eye of the professional critic had appreciated and admired. Now that consolation was gone.

" You don't seem to have had any purchasers as yet," went on this dreadful young man, " but I'll give you a tip about that, miss. You tell that young buttons who wanted me to pay sixpence, to fix labels on to half of them to say they're sold, see ? You bet other people will begin buying them then, for fear they should be too late. Just make them think that if they're not slippy everything'll be gone, see ? I must be off though : wish you luck."

For some time after the departure of this dreadful young man there were no other visitors, and the optimism of the leap-frog boy had to exert its ingenuity, and he supposed that on such a fine morning gents would want to be out of doors. It seemed in fact as if gents required very unusual weather to make them feel drawn to picture exhibitions ; neither fine nor wet suited them. Miss Howard had one or two bill-paying errands in the town, and on her return she found that Mrs. Oxney had been in, though there was no token of her visit on the glass of Pussy-dear, but only a message of ardent appreciation. Colonel Chase evidently was one of the gents who wanted to be out of doors, for the custodian had seen him riding by on his bicycle, as if for a wager, and Miss Howard supposed she would be asked to guess at lunch-time what the new record was. Though she had no malice (or very little) in her spiritual outfit, she determined to guess either that he had been eighty miles, which would make his actual accomplishment appear a very paltry feat, or ten miles, which would show that she had a very poor idea of his powers.

Meanwhile the diabolical tip given her by the press, continued to leaven her thoughts. She had rejected the notion at first with scorn as being a dishonest trick, but soon she began to wonder whether there was any harm in it. As long as no one bought her pictures, she might be considered to have bought them herself for they *were* hers, and certainly she had bought and paid for the frames. She did not know what the custodian would think of her if she suddenly told him to put little red stars on half the pictures, but after all, it mattered very little what the custodian thought of her. On the other hand it would be a great chagrin if after having starred ' Oh, to be in England now that April's here ' some visitor took a violent fancy to it and found it was sold. She hated deceit, at least she had felt that Colonel Chase had made himself truly contemptible, when he had said yesterday that the inclement weather prevented his going to see her pictures, and was detected in having gone out for a walk instead, but was it deceit to put red stars on pictures ? She did not actually state that they were sold, though the custodian, if asked what this decoration meant, would doubtless tell enquirers that such was its significance. But again if nobody further came to see the pictures (a contingency which was

beginning to look lamentably likely) nobody would be
deceived. Her fingers itched for the pill box, but she
could not quite face asking the boy for it. She would
wait one day more, and if by that time there were still
no purchasers, she would buy five or six herself. . . .

It was getting on for lunch-time : all the morning
patients at the Baths had passed and repassed the open
door of the Green Salon, but only one of them, an
elderly lady like a horse had even paused there.
Instantly the custodian, who was beginning to wonder
whether a shilling a day compensated him for so much
inactivity, sprang to attention with the toilet-roll,
but the horse only tossed its head with a sort of neigh,
and muttered, ' Only pictures ', in a tone of deep disgust. Miss Howard felt she could not stand the
kindly and cheerful enquiries that would be put to her,
if she drove up with the Wentworth bathers in the bus,
and she started to walk. Outside on the wall of the
porch was a type-written advertisement of the exhibition which the rain yesterday had partly detached,
so that the upper half of it drooped over the lower and
the print had run : she had hardly the spirit to fix
it up again. She was thoroughly depressed, for apart
from the expense, and from the approaching difficulty
of knowing what to do with a stack of nearly fifty
framed pictures there was the far more bitter loss of
prestige. As long as she had not tempted Fate in this
manner, she had been the accredited fount of artistic
authority at Wentworth : she could shake her head
over Sargent's slap-dash methods, and say that of
course he was marvellously clever, but she personally
admired a more detailed and highly finished technique :
careful work was what lived. No doubt if she had the
heart to continue putting her sketches on the chimney-
piece of the lounge, Wentworth would still say that they
were exquisite, but at the back of everybody's mind
would be the knowledge that a roomful of such gems

had been on view, and had attracted but few visitors and not a single purchaser, even at prices immeasurably below Sargent's. She had piped, but nobody had danced : the Muse felt her insignia slipping from her.

These gloomy reflections so occupied her that she had not seen that she was catching up a woman walking ahead of her up the hill, and it was not till she had got quite close that she saw it was Mrs. Bliss, limping slightly and leaning on her stick, but able to proceed at a very respectable pace. In the ten days that she had been at Bolton she had indeed made the most marvellous progress. " But however much she calls it Mind," thought Miss Howard in a spasm of revolt, " I call it brine."

Mrs. Bliss turned round when she was quite close. It struck Miss Howard that the smile was whisked on when she saw who it was.

" Sweet one ! " said Mrs. Bliss. " How fortunate I am to have such a dear companion for the rest of my walk. I'll be bound that your lovely picture-show was crowded with visitors this morning and probably most of them sold. How I demonstrated about it in my bath this morning ! How Mind looks after us all ! See how I'm flitting along to-day."

That certainly was wonderful, though ' flit ' was still slightly on the optimistic side of accuracy. And it wasn't Mind : it was brine.

" No ; there wasn't any crowd at all," said the sweet one firmly. " In fact there was no one there at all. And I haven't sold a single picture yet."

A wave of bitter illumination swept over her, calling for her protest.

" In fact I don't think much of Mind," she added.

Mrs. Bliss remained quite unshocked by this blasphemy. That was one of the truly annoying things about her, thought Miss Howard : you couldn't stop

her smiling any more than you could stop an express
train by defying it, nor could you cool her exasperating
certainty that everything was perfect, and that everybody was a skipping lamb in green pastures. She
laughed merrily.

"You darling rebel!" she said. "What joy it
will be when your dear blind eyes are opened."

"I intend to keep them shut," said Miss Howard
in the vain attempt to shake this fearful confidence.
"I've got to face the fact that nobody wants to see my
pictures or to buy them. So it's no use saying that
Mind is looking after my exhibition. I give up Mind."

Even this did not dim Mrs. Bliss's radiance.

"Dear thing!" she said. "But Mind won't give
you up. Think of all the wonderful things Mind has
done for us quite lately at our pretty Wentworth.
Colonel Chase's cold, his pedometer, his success at the
entertainment. All Mind! Look at me, too, in spite
of the baths and the massage."

"And look at Mr. Kemp," said Miss Howard.
"He's no better. If anything, he's worse."

Mrs. Bliss laughed again.

"But, dear, he's well," she said. "He doesn't
know it yet but he is. It often happens that Error
still blinds people even when they are cured, and they
still think they are suffering. But soon that passes.
You're just the same about your pictures. Only
wait a little: abide patiently."

It was a relief to Miss Howard when they got to
Wentworth, and Mrs. Bliss went to lie down on her
bed not to rest but to work, for she found such optimism
harder to bear than her own pessimism. She felt that
after this solitary morning in the Green Salon, a similar
afternoon would be intolerable, and determined not to
go down again that day. It would be time enough
to-morrow morning to learn that not a sixpence had
been recorded on the toilet-roll, or a red star appeared

on the walls. She occupied herself till lunch-time with the sketch of the lounge.

Now while she was trying to make the staircase appear scaleable, two very important scenes took place in the hollow where the town lay. The first of these began with Mrs. Holders and Tim coming simultaneously out of the ladies' and gentlemen's sections of the establishment after their baths, and meeting in front of the Green Salon. The door was open, and the custodian had gone to eat his dinner and have a little exercise with his friends. They looked in.

"My word, what rubbish, isn't it, Tim?" she said. "She can't paint. I think I shall give a vocal recital, or act Ophelia."

"Do: may I be Hamlet?" said he. "Look at Bethesda falling down, and Healing Springs. I wish they would heal me. And not a picture sold yet, or they would have labels."

"And God's Acre: it's not nearly an acre," said Mrs. Holders. "What a fool the woman is to think they could sell. But rather pathetic: all that trouble, not to mention the frames. I hate middle-aged spinsters being disappointed because they've nothing to look forward to. Tim, I think we shall be obliged to buy some."

"I'm damned if I do," said Tim.

"You'll be damned if you don't, dear, because you'll have been a brute. And I said 'some'. It's no use our buying just one each. We're both rich, thank God. And she hasn't warbled all to-day and all yesterday. Not a note."

"Well, don't set her off again," said Tim.

"And the improvisation wasn't a success. And she's feeling terribly down. Now be a man."

The custodian at this moment returned from dinner and leap-frog, and seeing somebody in the Green Salon rushed gleefully in and pulled out the toilet-roll.

" Sixpence each, please, sir," he said.

" How many people have been in to-day ? " asked Tim.

" Only one and he didn't pay. Said he was the press. Sixpence—— "

" And yesterday ? " asked Mrs. Holders.

" We didn't have any visitors yesterday, ma'am. Catalogue free, and there's a price catalogue, too."

They hobbled round together with it.

" What's that squirrel ? " asked Tim.

" Pussy-dear," said she. " One guinea. Oh, it's the Wentworth cat. Mrs. Oxney ought to buy that of course. . . . Tim, I think you and I must have five each. That'll make a start. Half-guinea ones will do. No, we can't do that quite."

' ' I'm glad," said he.

' ' I don't mean what you mean. What I mean is that if you and I each buy five, there'll be a sort of indelicacy about it. Compassion you know, which is always objectionable. We must think of another plan. I know. Bring me a chair, you boy, or I shall fall down."

" Two," said Tim.

The conspirators seated themselves.

" Now attend, Tim," she said, " for I'm being very bright. This morning, just now in fact, quite a lot of people came in to the show. You and I, that's two and four more."

" Then they had to pay for admission," said Tim.

" I'm glad you thought of that. Of course they had. Four more tickets, boy. You pay, Tim. I haven't got a sou."

" You're running me into a great deal of expense," said Tim.

" I'm going to run you into more. Give this gentle-man four more tickets, boy, and he gives you two

shillings. That's right, isn't it ? Now go away till
we call you again."

Mrs. Holders sat silent a moment, arranging the
conspiracy.

"What has happened, Tim, is this," she said at
length. "These four people whose tickets you have
just so kindly paid for each bought two of Miss Howard's
pictures. You must think of two friends of yours
and I'll think of two friends of mine, and we'll give
their names and addresses and money to the boy, and
write to them to say that they will shortly receive
two sad little water-colours each. They'll get them,
of course, when the exhibition closes. You can tell
your friends to send the pictures back to you,
if you like. That will be eight pictures, and you and
I each buy one on our own account, and that makes
ten. Now you've got to think of the names and addresses of two friends : after that all you have to do,
is to pay and look just as unpleasant as you choose.
I don't mind. I'll give you a cheque for my share."

"Good old thing," said Tim. "Now we'll get the
boy and din it into his head."

Leap-frog showed himself very intelligent, and after
two minutes coaching, he repeated without flaw the
following remarkable occurrences. Mrs. Holders and Mr.
Bullingdon (address Wentworth) he rehearsed, had
come in, and paid their sixpences, and each had bought
a picture (numbers 2 and 11). They hadn't been gone
more than a minute, when two ladies came in, and
after paying for admittance (toilet-roll as before)
called for the price catalogue. They each bought
two pictures (numbers 7, 13, 24 and 31) which they
paid for, and gave their names and addresses which he
duly entered. Just before (or after) they left two
gentlemen came in, paid their sixpences and went
round. They too called for the price-list—seeming to
admire the pictures very much—and bought two each

(numbers 20, 35, 39 and 40).   They paid their money
and gave names and addresses. . . . The custodian then
went to the bar to get change, and put into his breast
pocket five pound notes and five shillings.   A half-
crown, the reward of intelligence he put into the
pocket where was the pill box.   The conspirators
waited to see him lick ten adhesive red stars, and fix
them to the corners of pictures, 2, 7, 11, 13, 20, 24, 31,
35, 39 and 40.   There seemed no possible risk of de-
tection.   Then they found they had missed the Wentworth bus, and took a taxi, arriving late for lunch and
rather cross with each other.

The other important event was concerned with the
spiritual life of Colonel Chase, and was therefore of
deeper significance than these mere financial benefits
to Miss Howard.   He had started that morning
meaning to pay a visit to the exhibition at the cost
of sixpence, though of course he would not dream of
buying one of her faint little daubs.   But her pleasure
and gratification at his visit would efface from her
mind that impression of paltry fibbing which might
possibly be rankling there owing to Mrs. Oxney's
silly chatter about his mackintosh.   Having thus
re-established the candour of his character, he would
go for a fine ride to make up for having missed one
yesterday. . . . But as he went quietly down the hill
(it was not worth while getting up speed if he was to
dismount so soon) the thought of Miss Howard's exhibition began to arouse acute annoyance in his mind ;
it was a barefaced levying of blackmail on her friends,
they could not in decency refuse to put at least sixpence into Miss Howard's pocket.   The thought of
this moral compulsion revolted him, and he determined
to strike a blow for English freedom, and not go at
all.   He therefore put on speed and was seen by the
custodian pedalling, as if for a wager, past the Baths,
feeling that he was a champion of liberty.   He did not

mind giving Miss Howard sixpence, but he refused to be obliged to . . .

The roads had dried up wonderfully after the deluge of yesterday, he drew in long breaths of the cool fresh air, and his great fat legs revolved as if nothing could ever tire them. It was impossible (and so he did not attempt it) not to reflect with strong satisfaction on his own health and vigour and heartiness. His Indian contemporaries were mostly wizened and yellow little men suffering from liver, or obese waddlers who sat all day in arm-chairs, and perhaps occasionally played a couple of rounds of golf, six or seven miles all told, and were very tired after it, whereas here was he active in mind and body, ready to cover mile after mile on foot or saddle without fatigue, and be fit afterwards for strong brain-work over reading or cross-word puzzles or bridge.

These gratifying thoughts put him in a better temper, and forgiving Miss Howard for her exhibition he registered the fact that he had never felt so well as he had done during the last fortnight. His superb vitality had thrown off in a single night the most undoubted symptoms of a crashing cold and his mind shifted to Mrs. Bliss and that extraordinary gospel of hers. Was it perhaps she who had called down on him this amazing access of health and prosperity? There was his cold, there was his pedometer, there was his huge success (though not quite in the manner he had anticipated) at the entertainment, and as for that small distressing incident in the Children's Hospital, she had assured him, though in terms he did not attempt to fathom, that Mind was acting just as beneficently there as in its more obvious manifestations. He had never completely determined whether he seriously ascribed all this benefit to her agency : his cold might possibly have disappeared through natural causes, but the reappearance of the pedometer fairly puzzled him.

She had no account to give of it : it had just come to
her, like manna, miraculously. But to her it was not
miraculous at all : it was a perfectly normal result of
relying on Omnipotent Mind, and being full of loving
and trusting thoughts.   After all he was a thoroughly
good-natured fellow : people had only to make themselves pleasant to him, and give him his way on every
occasion, and he was as jolly as possible with them.
He must keep that up, and with the hope of obtaining
further benefits from Mind, he resolved to go to Miss
Howard's exhibition.   Mind would like that : it would
be a good-natured act towards poor Miss Howard
who had not got an *encore* at the entertainment nor
roused the smallest enthusiasm, and who had not sold
a picture.   To be sure the whole thing was blackmail
but he felt that, in view of Mind, he was big enough to
overlook that, and give pleasure to Miss Howard.
Her little place in Kent too : he wondered . . .

Though a swift bicyclist, Colonel Chase was not a
rapid thinker, and by the time he had arrived at this
conclusion, he saw that he had been riding for over an
hour.   Absorbed in these spiritual problems, he had
been paying little attention to the passage of the landscape, and now, looking about him again, he saw
that the country was wholly new to him.   He had
certainly started by the Denton road, and had followed
its familiar windings, but here he was at the end of an
hour quite beyond his usual beat.   Never had an
hour or a bicycle sped so swiftly : he could not believe
that so much time had passed or so much ground been
covered.   Behind him lay a long stretch of upward
incline, which had flowed under his wheel as if it had
been level, and he was neither out of breath nor
conscious of any fatigue : he had climbed as if on eagles'
wings.   " It must be Mind," he said to himself, " it
can't possibly be anything else. I shall go to poor
Miss Howard's show this very afternoon, and I'm not

sure that I shan't buy one of her well-meaning little
sketches. I was wrong to think of her as a blackmailer.
All is health, kindliness and prosperity ! "

A sign post confirmed his immense distance from
home, making him exult in the splendour of his powers,
and after a round which he had not previously believed
was traversible by a leg-driven wheel he found himself
back in Bolton again. There had been a slight abrasion
on his ankle yesterday and not wanting to bother
Mind over so small a matter, he stopped at Mr. Amble's
to purchase a phial of New Skin. You painted it on
the place and it smarted, but, relying on Mind, very
likely he wouldn't feel it. Mr. Amble was delighted
to see him in his shop again, for this visit was a token
of reconciliation after those choleric speeches on the
telephone, and he entirely forgot the existence of the
' little secret ' between him and that odd though affable
lady. . . .

" New Skin, sir ? " he said. " Yes, I can supply
you with that. And I was very pleased, Colonel, to
have been the means of restoring your pedometer to
you. My lad picked it up——- "

" Eh, what's that ? " said Colonel Chase.

" Your pedometer, Colonel, which you lost last
week. My lad picked it up on the Denton road ; let
me see it would be ten days ago now and I gave it a
clean and sent it—Good Lord, why I quite forgot that
the lady I gave it to, asked me not to mention it. But
there's no harm done, I hope, and anyhow she's not
been in here since, nor bought anything then. She
saw the notice in my window that a pedometer had
been found, and since she looked respectable and said
she came from Wentworth, I let her take it to return
to you. I hope there's been no—no mistake, and that
she did give it you."

Mind's greatest miracle of all had collapsed, as if a
flood of corrosive light from some devilish Higher

Criticism had been poured on it. Colonel Chase's
faith in Mind trembled, tottered and crashed : it was
an infidel who stood there holding a bottle of New Skin
in his shaking hand. What liars women were ! To
think that this abandoned wretch distinctly said that
she had no notion how she got the pedometer. She
said that she was lost in meditation, and, lo, it was in
her hand. He felt positively sick.

" No, there was no mistake," he said—the irony of
that !—" she gave it me."

He went out of the shop, and pedalled up the hill
with a mind reeling with atheism. If this was the true
history (and it certainly was) of the most inexplicable
of all Mind's miracles it was not any longer possible to
credit Mind with his restoration from his cold, or with
his success at the entertainment. And if Mind had
not showered these benefits upon him, why propitiate
it by going to Miss Howard's Green Salon, let alone
buying anything therein ? Even the joy of having
certainly beaten all records this morning almost faded,
when he dismounted at Wentworth and when he looked
at his pedometer it was completely extinguished, for
once more the pedometer had stopped. The hands
sarcastically affirmed that he had gone six miles.

Lunch had begun, and he entered the dining-room
in the manner of Hyperion " full of wrath." He stopped
opposite Mrs. Bliss's table, who, unconscious of what
was coming, smiled gaily up at him.

" What a lovely morning you've had for your ride,
Colonel," she said. " I expect you've been ever so
far away over the blue, blue hills."

He raised his voice. It was right that what he had
to say to her should be known to all.

" I have to thank you, Mrs. Bliss," he said, " for restoring to me the pedometer I lost, which Amble the chemist
gave you. He tells me that his shop-boy found it."

She did not sink into the earth or behave like

Sapphira. She laughed delightedly and clapped her hands.

" That was it ! " she said. " I could not recollect how I got it. I only knew I had to give it back to you. But it comes back to me now."

Dead silence had fallen on the lunchers and had it not been for Colonel Chase's heavy tread, as, leaving her without a word, he went to his place, anyone might have heard a pin drop. Then hurried conversation broke out, and Miss Howard so far forgot her malicious design of guessing that he had gone eighty miles as to say to him, " And how far have you been this morning, Colonel ? "

" I haven't the slightest idea," he said. " Once more the pedometer on my bicycle (pedometer, he repeated) got out of order and stopped. Odd things happen to my pedometer."

This withering remark had no effect whatever on Mrs. Bliss. She finished her fish and sat gazing out of the window in happy reverie, till the parlour-maid brought her the next dish.

CHAPTER VII

MR. BANKS in his sermon last Sunday had made a very profound observation. It must not be supposed from this statement that profound observations coming from his pulpit were of rare occurrence. They were on the contrary so common that they often passed unnoticed or at any rate not fully appreciated. For instance, when in this same sermon he said, 'If, dear friends, we all invariably acted on our noble rather than our baser impulses, the world would be a very different place,' there was scarcely anyone in his congregation who grasped the whole of the tremendous truth that lurked in these simple words. Shortly afterwards he uttered another truth, which likewise attracted no particular attention at the time but was soon seen to be not only profound but, as regards the affairs of Miss Howard, prophetical.

" People," said this subtle observer, " are like sheep. If one leads, in things great and small, the rest will follow. Let each of us therefore lead in all high thought and selfless deeds, and we shall speedily find that we are not alone as we tread the upward path of Christian endeavour. And now—— "

Mrs. Banks had been much struck by this analogy between people and sheep : it seemed to her ' very teaching ', and at lunch afterwards she thanked her husband for the enlightenment it had brought her. She was of a quaintly humorous disposition and she knew that a playful application of his words would not displease him, for he often said that what we learn in church we should use in daily life.

" It is true in all sorts of ways, Hildebrand," she said. " For instance at the entertainment the other night, it only needed that one rude boy should laugh at Colonel Chase's ghost story to set the whole room off. I wonder if it was meant to be funny or meant to thrill us."

" Oh, meant to thrill without a doubt," said Hildebrand, " but it just turned out different from what he expected. Like puddings. I only hope Miss Howard's exhibition will turn out different to what I expect, for if it doesn't she won't sell a single picture. But we must both go to it."

" Of course. Poor Miss Howard. But perhaps somebody will buy one, and other people follow as you said."

This duty of going to the Green Salon had escaped their memories (or was inconvenient to fulfil) for the first three days that it was open, and thus, when on Wednesday Mrs. Holders and Tim made their amiable conspiracy, neither the Vicar nor his wife had seen the numerous pictures of his church. But on Thursday morning it so happened that she had to go to the post office, and he to visit a sick parishioner. Their ways lay in the same direction, and they set off together; the sight of the Baths put the forgotten duty into Mrs. Banks's head.

" Let us pop in for a moment and see poor Miss Howard's pictures," said she. " She may not be there yet, which would be a good thing, for if she comes round with us and looks sad, we shall find it difficult not to buy one."

Miss Howard was there, going through some list with the custodian. But so far from looking sad, her face expressed high elation, and she came tripping towards them with the greatest cheerfulness.

" How de-do Mrs. Banks ? " she said. " So good of you and the padre to look in. Very little worth seeing, I'm afraid."

" Ah, you mustn't think this is our first visit," said Mrs. Banks, who had a perfect genius for just not telling lies. "And as for there being very little worth seeing, well I can't agree. Oh look, Hildebrand, there's a lovely, lovely picture of St. Giles's. Why it has a little red star on it. Does that mean it is sold Miss Howard ? What a disappointment ! "

" Yes, I'm afraid that's gone," said Miss Howard. " But you'll find one somewhere from nearly the same point of view, but in the evening. There it is. Ah, that's sold too. I can't keep pace with them."

Somehow this put a very different aspect on poor Miss Howard and her exhibition, and when she went back to the task of verifying the purchased pictures with the custodian, looking the very reverse of sad, and not showing the slightest inclination to go round with them, the two, who had not been near the Green Salon before, began at the very beginning on an attentive and respectful scrutiny. The padre's sermon was assuming the prophetical aspect.

" What a lot she's sold," said Mrs. Banks in discreet tones. " And really they are very charming. Look at No. 7, Hildebrand. ' The curfew tolls the knell of parting Day ', with the spire of St. Giles's among the trees. Sweet ! But I see that's sold."

" I think I like No. 6 even better," said Mr. Banks. " Number 6, God's Acre. Very feeling. Tombstones. Really I should immensely like to possess that. A truly religious touch about it. God's Acre, too, a beautiful description."

While he stood there with his head on one side, quite lost in admiration, the custodian who had finished the agreeable task with Miss Howard, sidled up to his wife.

" There is a price-list, madam," he softly insinuated.

" Yes, let me look," she whispered, and found it was only ten-and-sixpence.

" I'll take it," she said. " Mrs. Banks, the Vicarage. Put a star on it at once and get me change."

Miss Howard, seeing that business was going on delicately left the Green Salon, and Mrs. Banks joined her husband who was still basking in God's Acre.

" Hildebrand, dear. God's Acre is yours. My Christmas present to you. I had been wondering what to give you."

He gave a start of pleasure and surprise.

" My dear," said he, " what a delicious present. I can't tell you what joy——"

" But you must forget all about it again," she said, " till I give it you on Christmas morning."

After that it was only fair that Mrs. Banks should have her turn to be lost in admiration of another picture, and the one she happened to select for that purpose was Evening Bells . When it was quite clear that she liked this more than any, Hildebrand wandered quietly away to the custodian who was busy at the moment detaching a strip of toilet-paper for Colonel Chase, and asked for the price-list. Two guineas was rather a staggerer, and it was distinctly bad luck that his wife had so firmly set her affections on Evening Bells, when almost anything else might have been had for a quarter of that sum, but he could not be blind to her clear choice. He produced two pound notes, a shilling and two sixpences.

" The Vicar," he said rather sadly. " Put a label on Number 27 as sold."

" Hurroi ! " said the custodian, and went out to find Miss Howard and tell her of this huge accession to the treasury.

Colonel Chase was in a rather lofty mood that morning. Kind but lofty.

" Well, padre," he said. " We meet on a charitable
errand. Wouldn't do to have nobody coming to our
friend's little effort. What ? You've been buying
one, have you ? Well, I call that kind. I'll be bound
it's the first that's been sold, and, I shouldn't wonder
if it was the last. I suppose I must get a catalogue.
What ! Is there nothing but that type-written thing ?
Nothing printed ? Oh, they don't charge for it.
I dare say it will do very well."

He began reading the catalogue glancing hastily
at the pictures to verify the titles.

" Golf links, Wentworth," he said. " Yes, that's
right, and a lot of trouble I spent over them too.
But that tree has gone now. Quite changed the look
of the place, as well as spoiling one of the best holes.
Number 5 now.   Bethesda . Ah yes, I see, a cat.
I suppose Bethesda is the name of the cat. No, no :
my mistake. Number 5 is ' Pussy-dear '. That's
Mrs. Oxney's cat : I hear enough of it at night without
wanting to see a picture of it, and ' Pussy-dear ' doesn't
quite interpret my feelings about it. Still, the picture
has a sort of look of the animal. Good morning,
Mrs. Padre : how's the violin ? It was a pretty piece
you played us the other night. Fully deserved an
encore, I thought."

" No time for the violin to-day, Colonel Chase,"
she said. " Every minute that I can spare this
morning I shall give to these pictures. Impossible to tear oneself away. And just think, my
husband has given me Evening Bells , the loveliest
of all, as a Christmas present. Isn't it too dear
of him ? "

" Very kind I'm sure," said Colonel Chase, " now
let's see. Number 6. God's Acre. What are those
white things ? Ah, tombstones : yes, God's Acre.
That's got a little star on it, which I suppose means
it's sold. And Number 7 is sold too, and 13. Why,

there seems to be a regular run on Miss Howard's pictures. I am surprised."

" I'm sure I'm not," said Mrs. Banks, who being the owner of one picture and the purchaser of another was bound to spur everyone else to buy too. " Such feeling! Such beautiful technique. And the critics think the world of them. There was an article in the *Bolton Gazette*, and the writer couldn't have said more of them if they had been by Mr. Sargent. I think I am indeed fortunate to have Evening Bells before anybody else snapped it up."

All this was beginning to work a subtle change in Colonel Chase : he was looking at these little efforts with quite a different eye. He had come in Baalam's first mood, inclined to curse the expenditure of six-pence as the payment of blackmail, but this public eagerness to secure an example of Miss Howard's skill, made him wonder whether he should not be blessing a blackmail which seemed to offer an opportunity of securing something worth having at a most reasonable outlay. He had hazarded the cynical conjecture that Miss Howard had written that laudatory notice herself, but, however that might be, purchasers were rife, for he saw, looking enquiringly round, that a dozen of the little efforts had already been snapped up, and were twinkling with little red stars. The priced catalogue, into which at this moment the custodian, that fine psychological observer, suggested he might like to glance, told him that almost any of the remaining pearls could be acquired for half-a-guinea, and what if they turned out to be of the true Orient destined to be eagerly sought for by the *cognoscenti* ? A bargain always appealed to him if it did not entail much outlay, and the fact that Florence, who had just come in, was looking fixedly at Golf-links, Wentworth made him hate the notion that anyone but he should possess a work which in addition to its artistic merit should surely be owned by the creator of the golf links. 'A pretty sketch,' he could imagine himself saying, 'I laid the links out myself.' He hurriedly produced a ten shilling note and six coppers and entered his name on the lengthening list as its purchaser. Out came the pill box and the custodian's tongue and he shot forward with a red star on the tip of it, and in his eagerness affixed it to the centre of the picture.

"Snapped up, I'm afraid, Miss Kemp," said Colonel Chase jovially. "One has to make up one's mind quickly if one wants one of Miss Howard's sketches. I couldn't let anyone else have that picture of my golf links with the dear old tree still standing by the centre green. Very beautiful effect is it not?"

Colonel Chase had now enrolled himself in the ranks of those who, having bought pictures, were all agog that others should buy as well, thus endorsing their own wisdom and artistic taste, and presently he and the padre and Mrs. Banks were all strongly advising Florence to secure 'Oh, to be in England now that April's here', before it was too late. She had only just put it out of the reach of other aspirants, when there arose a perfect hubbub at the door, and the custodian's voice was heard respectfully but shrilly demanding an entrance fee.

"No, my lady," he said "the exhibition isn't free to nobody. Admission sixpence each," and there was Lady Appledore and Miss Jobson, the former in a state of dignified resentment.

"Pay it then, Miss Jobson," she said, "though after all I've done for the town, I should have thought my admittance was a matter of course. Let me see: Colonel Chase is it not; who told us those amusing ghost stories. And Mr. Banks. And Mrs. Banks: the violin. Quite a crowd. I cannot understand why I have received no notice of Miss Howard's exhibition before, as it is well known that I make a point of encouraging local industries. An odd omission. It was quite by accident that I saw a small placard outside the Baths as I was driving by. 'Miss Jobson,' I said, 'kindly go and see what that placard is.'"

They all three assailed her with laudatory remarks.

"A lucky accident indeed," said Mrs. Banks. "You will be charmed with Miss Howard's work."

"We all are, Lady Appledore," said Colonel Chase. "The art critic in the *Bolton Gazette* was most enthusiastic."

"My wife has given me God's Acre for a Christmas present, Lady Appledore," said Mr. Banks.

"And I have got ' Oh, to be in England now that April's here," said Florence, who, not having been introduced, stated the fact to nobody in particular.

"And my husband has given me Evening Bells, which I think you will agree is the gem of them all, Lady Appledore," said Mrs. Banks.

"A catalogue," said Lady Appledore, putting out her hand. Four catalogues were thrust into it.

"I will look round and judge for myself," said she. "Dear me, do all those red stars on the pictures mean that they are sold ? "

"Yes " said everybody.

"I am sorry not to have heard about this earlier," said she, "for I have always been a great judge of water-colours. Miss Howard must have made quite a fortune. It was Miss Howard, I think, who played us little pieces of Chopin the other night, but I do not know her, do I, Miss Jobson ? I hope I shall like her pictures better than her playing. Number 6 is pretty : a good middle distance. What is Number 6 called, Miss Jobson. Oh, God's Acre, I see to be sure. But it is bought."

"Yes, am I not fortunate ? That is mine," said Mr. Banks.

"You have not chosen badly. Full of feeling. Number 9 Miss Jobson."

"'The Curfew tolls the knell of parting day', " said Miss Jobson.

"That is not bad either. It is evening, Miss Jobson. Curfew is invariably in the evening. About eight o'clock. That is not sold, I see. Put a mark against it till I have seen the rest. Somebody will lend you a pencil if you have not got one."

The majestic procession moved slowly on.

"A cat," said Lady Appledore. "I do not like cats. Miss Howard should not have painted a cat. Mist in the Valley represents Bolton Spa, Miss Jobson, but you cannot see it because of the mist. Put a smaller mark opposite Mist in the Valley. Mist on the Hills is Bolton Spa also, but now you can see Bolton Spa because there is no mist in the valley. Put nothing opposite Mist on the Hills. Geraniums that is better. They are red : I should say that they are decidedly geraniums. Let somebody give me the catalogue of prices. . . . Geraniums, one guinea : that is a great deal of money. Still Life : I should call it Still Death because there is no animation about it."

Mr. Banks who was holding the price catalogue in front of Lady Appledore like the Book of the Gospels gave a sycophantic laugh.

"Excellent ! " he said. "How you hit it off, Lady Appledore. Still Death ! I must remember that. Did you hear that, Colonel ? My lady says that Still Life should be called Still Death. I did not care for the picture myself and now I know the reason. No animation : an admirable criticism."

"Very true, very true indeed," said Colonel Chase. "I hope you like the little picture I have bought Lady Appledore. Golf links, Wentworth. I took a lot of trouble in laying them out."

Lady Appledore kindly retraced her steps to Number 6.

"A matter of taste," she said. "It does not appeal to mine. If I were you I should instantly purchase Geraniums , Colonel Chase. Geraniums is well worth a guinea. I should not let Geraniums slip through my fingers. But I would not buy Still Life . You may trust my judgment, Colonel Chase, and have nothing to do with Still Life, but buy Geraniums before it is snapped up. You will never regret it."

She fixed him with an implacable eye which was not removed till he had told the custodian to put the fatal red star on Geraniums.

"Make a rule, Colonel Chase," she said, "always to buy the best work, and then you will know—well, that you have the best. Geraniums and The Curfew are undoubtedly Miss Howard's master-pieces. (This was agonising for Mr. Banks, who might have bought both masterpieces for less than he had paid for Evening Bells). Of the two I prefer The Curfew which I shall now purchase. Miss Jobson see to a star on Curfew, and say the remittance will follow."

Miss Howard meantime had been hovering about outside the Green Salon, torn between the desire not to appear supplicant for purchase, and the longing to make Lady Appledore's acquaintance, for she had not been introduced to her on the evening of the enter-tainment. Her curiosity also to see how many more pictures had been bought (for the custodian had been flitting about all this time with the price catalogue) was becoming unbearable. So she tripped in quite unconscious of Lady Appledore's presence, and of the unusual number of visitors in the Green Salon and felt the temperature of the hot-water pipes. She withdrew her fingers with a little exclamation of dismay at their intense fervour and turned off the tap.

"I can't have you all roasted, Mr. Banks," she said.

" That would be too bad after your kindness in coming to see my little pictures."

That was sufficient indication of her identity, and Lady Appledore held out her hand.

" I am pleased to have seen your pictures, Miss Howard," she said. " That is not any empty compliment, for I have bought your Curfew. A very creditable effort. Nice tone. Should you ever be in the neighbourhood of the Grange, you will find some fine subjects in the Park. You may tell them at any of the lodges that I have given you leave to paint in the Park. Miss Jobson, kindly tell the motor that I am ready."

Miss Jobson hurried out to inform the intelligent machine, which thereupon ousted the bus for Wentworth that was standing at the entrance, forcing it to drive out of ' Out ', and came in again behind it at ' In '. Miss Howard saw Lady Appledore off, leaving Colonel Chase trying to revoke the purchase of Golf links on the grounds of having chosen Geraniums instead. The custodian was contesting the point with great firmness. . . .

It was now so near lunch-time that Mr. Banks who was engaged to take this meal at the Warwickshire Hotel with a button king from Manchester decided to postpone his visit to the sick parishioner till afternoon. As was natural he told his host about the honour Lady Appledore had done to the exquisite exhibition in the Green Salon, and about her purchase of Miss Howard's finest example. The best of the pictures (as well as far the most expensive he was afraid) had already been secured, but there were some very charming pieces left.

" The art critics are wild about them," he said, " it is a great opportunity for any collector."

The button king had most artistic tastes, and owned a gallery of pictures.

" 'Oward ? " he said. " Never 'eard of ' Oward.
Have we got a 'Oward, missus ? Don't think we've
got a 'Oward. Better 'ave a look at them after lunch
before my bath. Glass of champagne for you, Mr.
Banks. Wish I could drink champagne, but it's
poison to me. And the Countess of Appledore bought
one, did she ? Pleased to know about them."

This promised well but ended in a fiasco. The
button king hobbled into the Green Salon before his
bath, but was vexed at being charged sixpence for
admission : this was paltry. Paltrier yet was the
price-catalogue, for nothing for which you were charged
only half-a-guinea could possibly be worth purchase.
He had hoped that the least price would be fifty-guineas
or a hundred : that might have been worth considering.
But who wanted a ten-and-sixpenny picture ? Paltry
he called it, and went to be pickled instead. Missus,
however, took a different view : she thought them
sweetly pretty, and bought two for her boudoir.

Colonel Chase mounted his bicycle when he came
out having been unable to induce the custodian to
refund anything, and went off for his ride. He did
not intend to return to Wentworth for lunch, and had
taken with him what he called ' a snack ', which caused
the pockets of his Norfolk jacket to bulge with light
refreshment. In one there were some rolls stuffed
with ham, and a large lump of cheese, in another a
couple of hard-boiled eggs, an apple and a stick of
chocolate, in a third a flask of whiskey, a cold sausage
and a small thermos flask containing coffee. His
regard for Miss Howard had soared since breakfast,
and his contemptuous compassion for her unpatronised
wares and unpurchased walls had given place to a
strong feeling of respect for one whose work was so
eminently marketable and had won the admiration
of a Dowager Countess. She could go warbling out
in the morning with a paint-box and a bit of paper,

just for her own amusement, and bring back the best part of half-a-guinea. That was a gift, a solid asset, and as he selected a convenient fallen tree-trunk by the wayside on which he could sit and spread out his little snack, where the sun was warm on his back, and his folded mackintosh kept him safe from damp, he began to consider, as he was periodically wont to do, whether on the whole he would be more comfortable if he was married, and whether he was likely to find anyone more suitable than Miss Howard to make him so. She was not young, she was not, though neat and presentable, pretty any longer, but that was all to the good, for the excited, hysterical element which entered, he believed, into alliance between boys and girls, must have no place in this union. Wentworth, with a few weeks of lodgings in London and meals at his club, was a very easy sort of existence, but the worry and trouble of a house and household would, of course, if he married, be borne by his wife : his part in it would only be to mention if the bath water was not hot, or the food not to his liking, much as he did now. She, in fact, would be a sort of Mrs. Oxney, though honoured with his name. Then there was the question of expense, but since Miss Howard could afford to live at Wentworth, and go off once or twice a year to Torquay, it looked as if she ought to be able to bear half the charge of a small household. Besides, she had her little place in Kent, near Tunbridge Wells ; when the lease of her present tenants came to an end, they could live there, rent free. He figured it, on the impression he had got from her allusions to it, as a pleasant manorial house of stone or old brick, with a stable and a garden and ' grounds ', too small perhaps to call a Park, but with room no doubt for a miniature golflinks, and an air of landed dignity. There was sure to be a club at Tunbridge Wells, fre quented by business men, who went up to the City

by early trains, and by local gentry, and he could drop
into the club for a cup of tea and a rubber of bridge
before getting back to his little place and Mrs. Colonel,
who would scold him if he was late. The days would
pass very pleasantly : he would bicycle as usual all
the morning, and she, after seeing to her household
duties, would turn sheets of drawing-paper into half-
guineas : he would potter about his garden or golf
links in the afternoon, and, perhaps he would have a
small car. ' Squire Chase ' he thought to himself.

The snack had almost completely disappeared
during these reflections, and Colonel Chase, nourished
now and well-warmed by the sun felt very benevolent
towards the whole world. There was just one egg
still uneaten, and this he peeled and chipped into
small pieces with his pocket-knife generously strewing
them on the trunk of the tree where he sat, so that the
birds might eat and be filled, and bless him in their
pretty twitterings. He mounted his bicycle again
and wondered how he could find out more concerning
Miss Howard's little place in Kent. She let it, as she
had said, because she could not afford to live in it,
but with Squire Chase to share expenses, which he
would be quite willing to do if the little place was a
nice little place, it might be manageable. The more
he thought about Miss Howard in connection with
her little place the brighter grew Miss Howard's prospect
in connection with him. This marriage would be a
sensible contract for mutual advantage : she
would get a husband who would look after her
place for her, and he a wife who would look after his
comfort.

Unconscious of these plans for her advantage, Miss
Howard meantime had flown rather than walked up
to Wentworth for lunch, with all this wonderful news
to give of the Green Salon, and positively eager to
recant her blasphemy against Mind. Yesterday at

this time when no picture had been sold and not a
visitor had demanded toilet-paper, she had firmly announced that she gave up Mind, and that fell determination had been confirmed by the subsequent
revelation that Colonel Chase's pedometer had not been
miraculously wafted into Mrs. Bliss's possession by
Mind's mysterious agency but had been placed there
in answer to her simple request by an ordinary chemist.
But now she thought no more about pedometers :
a cataract of purchasers had descended on the Green
Salon, and she unhesitatingly accepted the benevolent
power which had guided them there and opened their
hearts and their purses, as identical with that which
had removed the Colonel's cold in a single night.   And
there was Mrs. Bliss in the lounge smiling and joyful,
though as yet she knew nothing of what had occurred.

" Dear one ! " she said.   " And how have things
gone to-day ?   Have you less of that despondency
which keeps you in Error, and of the Error which
keeps you in despondency ?   Sweet one, how lovely !
I see it has gone from you.   You have been denying it,
and Mind has shown you its nothingness.   Evil is
nothing, nothing is Evil.   Love, Mind, Omnipotence
deny hate, Error—Tell me all about it.   I could jump
for joy."

Miss Howard could have jumped too.

" Oh, Mrs. Bliss, it's too wonderful," she said.   " It
has turned out just as you said it would. I went down
to the Green Salon this morning, still in Error, and
expecting to find that nobody had been in, or bought
anything, and instead there was the most wonderful
news.   Kind dear Mr. Bullingdon whom I had thought
rather unappreciative of my pictures—and oh, how
wrong I was—I suppose that was Error too—and
dear kind Mrs. Holders, who, I thought, didn't care
about them either, each bought a picture yesterday
morning, and they had hardly gone when two ladies

came in, and would you believe it, each of them bought two pictures, which made six——"

She broke off a moment, as Mrs. Holders hobbled downstairs from her rest.

" Oh, Mrs. Holders," she said, " how good it was of you and Mr. Bullingdon to buy those pictures yesterday ! That started everything : I mean Mind began then, I was just telling Mrs. Bliss. Do you know that you and Mr. Bullingdon had scarcely gone when two ladies came in, and each of them bought two more. I can't think who they can have been, for their names were quite unknown to me. I suppose they came from one of the hotels : they were just two ladies, the boy at the door told me, and he couldn't describe them at all. And then they had hardly gone when two gentlemen came in and they each bought two, and I didn't know their names either, and that made ten pictures all in one morning. Wasn't it wonderful ? Just when I was beginning to feel so dreadfully low about it, and to wish that I had never thought of having an exhibition at all."

Mrs. Holders looked very much surprised : up went the eyebrows.

" That looks like Mind, doesn't it ? " she said, in a rather cold sarcastic tone, and she hobbled off without another word in the direction of the dining-room.

Miss Howard thought it very kind of her to have bought a picture, but her manner was far from sympathetic. She turned to ecstatic Mrs. Bliss again.

" And that wasn't all, not nearly," she resumed, " for soon after I went down this morning, and was hearing about all this, in came the dear padre and Mrs. Banks, and not their first visit either, and though I made myself busy with checking the names and that sort of thing, so as not to look as if I wanted them to buy anything——"

" Quite right, dear one," said Mrs. Bliss. " We have

to trust to Mind completely, when we have done our best, and make no interference. Yes?"

"——they asked for the catalogue of prices," said Miss Howard who had held her mouth open during this interruption, so as to go on again at once, "and first she bought God's Acre, and then he bought Evening Bells, which was the highest priced of all. And they had hardly bought theirs, when Colonel Chase came in—dear Colonel Chase, what wrong thoughts I have had about him too, for I thought he was not meaning to come to my exhibition at all, and as for buying anything! But it was all Error. Let me see, where was I? I had gone out, but I kept just peeping in, as I walked about outside. . . . So Colonel Chase came in and he bought Golf Links, Wentworth, and then dear Florence Kemp (I'm getting so much drawn to her) bought 'Oh, to be in England now that April's here', and looked at me so lovingly and sympathetically."

"Mind again!" crowed Mrs. Bliss.

"Yes, and then who do you think? Lady Appledore and Miss Jobson. She thought so highly of them— I was introduced to her afterwards, and she implored me almost to go and sketch in the Park at the Grange— and bought Curfew tolls the knell, and told Colonel Chase, so the boy informed me, that he should certainly buy Geraniums, which was a guinea. I think perhaps he only meant to buy one——"

"But Mind took him by the hand and led him up to Geraniums," said Mrs. Bliss.

"Yes, it really looks like it," said Miss Howard, "or anyhow Lady Appledore did. Oh, Mrs. Bliss, how untrustful I was yesterday, thinking that nobody cared. I shall go down again after lunch, and I shan't be a bit surprised to find that somebody else has come in and bought some more. Sixteen sold already within twenty-four hours: nearly one an hour! Or do you

think I ought not to go down this afternoon but leave
it all to Mind ? Which would Mind like best ? "

Mrs. Bliss uttered a peal of musical laughter.

" Sweet one, Mind loves you to do whatever gives
you most joy and happiness," she said. " Just deny
evil, depression, unhappiness, which don't exist.
Didn't I tell you that all would be harmony and prosperity at your lovely exhibition if only you trusted
Mind ? "

" But I didn't," said Miss Howard, contrite but
still joyful. " I gave Mind up yesterday. I remember
telling you so."

" No, you only thought you did, and that was Error,
as is now proved. I worked away at your Error
yesterday, and I knew it would be removed. And the
pretty gong—such a beautiful sonorous note—has
sounded, and here's Mrs. Oxney come to scold us for
not going in to lunch, and to hear your good news."

Mrs. Oxney was seriously alarmed to hear that so
many pictures had been sold, and that Miss Howard
apparently was not certain whether ' Pussy-dear ' was
among them. Miss Howard, as a matter of strict
fact, was quite sure ' Pussy-dear ' was still in the market,
but it would be good for Mrs. Oxney to have a little
fright owing to her remissness.

" There was such a crowd of purchasers," she said,
" and really those little red stars to show that pictures
were sold, were being put up here, there and everywhere.
I should not wonder if I had to get another supply of
them. But ' Pussy-dear ' may be unsold still. I don't
think Lady Appledore bought it."

" And has the Countess of Appledore been among
your visitors ? " said the awe-struck Mrs. Oxney.
" Dear me, what I've missed by not going down this
morning ! I must put on my hat directly I've had
a bite of lunch. . . . Oh, Mrs. Bliss, but you're walking
without a stick, and moving along so that I can scarcely

keep up with you ! I never saw such an improvement.
Dr. Dobbs will be pleased with you. I declare it's
like one of his own conjuring tricks. You've got
reason to be thankful to Bolton Spa."

Colonel Chase came back with a sound appetite
for tea, after the mere snack by the wayside shared
with the birds, and heard the new and gratifying
intelligence that the button queen staying at the
"Warwickshire" had bought two more pictures, and
that Mrs. Oxney had secured Pussy-dear, a thing she
would never have done had she not seen the button
queen regarding it with an admiring eye. Owing to Mrs.
Bliss's deceitful conduct with regard to his pedometer
he addressed no conversation whatever to her, and had
only the shortest and coldest replies for her when she
spoke to him, for if there was one thing he disapproved
of (and indeed there were many) it was anything that
savoured of deception. But his displeasure seemed to
have no effect on one who basked in the effulgence of
Mind, and, though his attitude was most marked,
(for he was full of agreeable conversation for everyone else, including Mrs. Holders) it may be considered
doubtful if she ever noticed it. As he had been unable
to get out of his purchase of Golflinks, Wentworth,
for the leap-frog boy refused to refund a penny of
his takings, it was best to be congratulatory to Miss
Howard, and console himslf with the fact that there
were now many financial victims of the Green Salon.
Another reason for being pleasant to her was that
he wanted to learn more about her little place in Kent.

"My Geraniums ! " he said, (grasping the nettle,
so to speak, for it was the guinea that smarted most,)
" I was delighted to secure Geraniums, and much
gratified to find that Lady Appledore, with her fine
taste, approved my choice. One of your master-
pieces, she said, Miss Howard. Where did you paint
that ? I cannot remember seeing a bed of geraniums

of such wonderful brightness here. Perhaps it was at
your little place in Kent."

Miss Howard, secure beneath the aegis of Mind, was
rather daring.

" Was it there ? " she said, pressing her finger to
her forehead in the effort of recollection. " Perhaps
it was. Let me see : the herbaceous border and then
the little sunk rose-garden. No : I think I painted
it here last summer long after my tenants were in
possession of my old home. Or did I paint it from
memory ? Somehow I seem to feel——"

Mrs. Oxney felt she had to claim Geraniums for a
product of Wentworth : Pussy-dear and Geraniums
and ever so many more were inspired by Wentworth.

" Oh no, Miss Howard," Mrs. Oxney said. " You
painted Geraniums from the bed below the dining-
room windows. Such a show there was of them. I
saw you doing it, and I said to myself, ' Now Miss
Howard's got a beautiful subject. That'll be one of
her best sketches.' And I was right, for it and Pussy-
dear were a guinea each. So here am I with Pussy-
dear, and the Colonel with Geraniums, and the Reverend
Banks with Evening Bells, which was the choicest of
all. How things move about, don't they and what a
pleasure they give ! "

" And were there no sketches of your old home in
the exhibition ? " asked Colonel Chase.

Again Miss Howard had to press her finger to her
forehead.

" Now did I put Chrysanthemums into it ? " she
asked. " Or Hearts of Oak ? I remember painting
Hearts of Oak just before I was obliged to let my little
place. Two such wonderful trees, ever so many hundreds of years old, and quite hollow inside. The dear
old place ! How I long to see it again ! Such a lovely
view over the valley, and the sweet little old-world
town once so fashionable. The Pantiles."

" But a very charming little town still, I believe,"
said Colonel Chase. " A golf links, isn't there, and a
country club ? "

" Yes, oh yes," said Miss Howard. " Papa used
to like his round of golf and his rubber before dinner.
He thought it his duty to take part in the social life
of the little town. I have such sweet memories of
the Croft—my little place, you know—and it is dreadful to think of it in the hands of strangers. But what
was I to do ? We're all so hard hit by these monstrous
taxes. And my tenants are very good, nice people,
and they promised to take great care of my little bits
of things."

Miss Howard was enjoying this immensely : without
being guilty of downright fabrication, she was building
up a most interesting fabric.

" Beautiful furniture, I suppose," said Colonel
Chase.

" Just some little family things," said she with a
sigh. " But after all what does it matter ? If one cannot
afford to live in the family place, one has to live somewhere else. It has happened to so many of us."

Miss Howard's chance of matrimony, had she only
known it was soaring upwards as on eagle's wings.
She had said nothing really definite but a great deal
that was truly impressive in a vague and sumptuous
manner. Colonel Chase allowed his imagination to
run riot and it flowered into a paved courtyard with
a sundial, and a gallery-room with Queen Anne furniture
and portraits. His regiment, on his retiring had
presented him with one of himself, one hand holding
a rifle and one foot in a beautifully polished boot on
the famous man-eater. It hung at present in the dining
room at Wentworth just opposite his table, but Mrs.
Oxney could put ' Pussy-dear ' there when it was removed
to the gallery-room at the Croft. He felt that he might
even change his name to Howard-Chase.

Miss Howard was certainly the heroine of the day and to none was she more worshipful than to Florence Kemp. For a couple of weeks now Florence's admiration of her had been ripening into a shy and silent adoration, and this afternoon, as the drawing-room emptied, she felt that it could be stifled in silence no longer, but must be allowed to begin expressing itself. Miss Howard must know in what tender esteem she was held, and how Florence longed to dedicate her affection by open avowal. She aspired to intimate friendship, and if that was out of reach, she wanted definite and indulgent permission to cherish and serve. Miss Howard (who surely would permit herself to be Alice for the future : that would be something) seemed to her the incarnation of brilliant existence. She could improvise, she could paint and sell those beautiful little sketches she dashed off so easily ; she was gay and independent and self-reliant. Then again how picturesque was the background she had several times indicated of an ancestral home to which she was evidently so much attached, though she accepted without unavailing regrets the penury which debarred her from living there. But all these gifts and qualities and conditions were but little decorations and fineries fitly adorning the surface ; admirable accessories and attributes of the adorable. Florence felt moreover with the infallible certainty of instinct that the other was not one who cared much or indeed at all for the companionship or affection of men, and in this she recognised a secret kinship of nature with herself. Yet at present Miss Howard had no devoted friend or she would not be living at Wentworth in this unattached manner, and Florence longed to take a place that was clearly vacant.

The drawing-room was empty now, but for these two. Mrs. Bliss had been the last to go, smiling herself away, and Florence's virginal heart rose into her

throat, as she took the first step, and moved across
to an empty chair by Miss Howard, at the thought that
a place next and close to her might possibly become
hers by right.

"Oh, Miss Howard," she said, "I must tell you how
I love your pictures. And I want you to do me a
great favour. I want you to let me come down with
you to-morrow, and to advise me one to buy. I did
get one, such a precious one, this morning, but I must
have another, and I should like to have the one you
recommend. Is it very bold and forward of me to
ask for your advice?"

Miss Howard was by no means surfeited with success : she was quite capable of assimilating more.

"Of course you shall have my advice," she said,
"and it's sweet of you to want any of my little daubs."

"Little daubs !" said Florence in a sudden ecstasy
of irony. "Aren't they horrid little daubs? How I
envy your gift, it must be too lovely to sit down and
make beautiful things like you !"

Miss Howard had already observed a little diffident
signalling going on from Florence, but this vigorous
waving of the flag rather astonished her, for she had
looked on Florence as too deeply consecrated to the
service of an entirely selfish father to have any vivid
emotional interests of her own. But as her 'beautiful
things' witnessed, sentimentality was a magnet to
her, and now she jumped to it like iron filings.

"Oh, but how dear of you to think of me like that,"
she said. "And in a way you're right. It is lovely,
anyhow, to want to make beautiful things."

The firelight shining encouragingly as the dusk
deepened outside made admirable conditions for the
growth of intimacy. Florence was naturally reserved,
but like most reserved women, when once the cork
came out, it made an explosive exit, and a stream of
bottled-up effervescence followed.

" And it's not your painting only," she said, " or
your music which make you so wonderful, but you,
yourself, and your self-reliance and independence.
Oh, but I should envy all your gifts if they weren't
yours. How I've watched and admired you all this
last fortnight since we came here ! And this evening
I simply could not help myself : I had to tell you.
You may laugh at me if you like, but please don't."

Florence gave a gasp of astonishment at her own
boldness, wondering whether she had only made the
most dreadful fool of herself. If she had, well, there
it was, and she would just have to search for the cork
which had popped so magnificently, and bottle herself
up again. But instead of so lamentable an end to this
burst of self-expression, Miss Howard's cork showed
signs of popping too : it did not fly forth with the
vigour of Florence's explosion, but there was a little
fizzing at its edges.

" Indeed I shan't laugh," she said. " I think it's
delightful of you to like me, and to tell me so. As for
self-reliance and independence, I've got no one to de-
pend on, so I must rely on myself. You've got your
father —— "

" Would you rely on him if he was yours ? "
asked Florence.

" But you're so devoted to him. I often have
admired the way you give yourself to him."

" I don't," said Florence, with all the candour of
devotion. " I don't give, he takes. We thoroughly
dislike each other —— "

" My dear," began Miss Howard.

" But it's true and it's such a relief to be able to tell
anybody that. I don't think anyone was ever so
lonely as I am ! I long to get away from him : he
surrounds me, he cuts me off. He wouldn't miss me :
anyone who would read to him, and fill his thermos
flask and tuck in his rug would do just as well. I have

thought sometimes of trying to get a nurse for him, and having a life of my own. It's you with your lovely independence that put it into my head. I could do something of my own then. It isn't as if he liked me : that would be different. In ten days now I suppose we shall go to Bournemouth, and stop there till we go to Buxton about Easter."

"But he may get better, and then you would settle down. Didn't you say you had a flat in Kensington Square ? "

"Yes : but it has been shut up all these years. Besides, he wouldn't know what to do with himself if he got better. And all the time we're at Bournemouth I shall be wishing I was back here."

Something in this touched Miss Howard with a sense of need. Her cork began to fizz a little more.

"So shall I," she said.

"No! But how perfectly wonderful!" said Florence. "Will you really? And will you say ' Florence ' ? "

"Yes, if you'll say Alice."

"Oh, Alice ! " said Florence.

They kissed and then neither of them knew what to say next in a situation which was new to them both. In slight embarrassment Alice, still holding Florence's hand, began out of habit to warble something.

"Oh, sing something or play me something," said Florence. "Sit down at the piano and make something beautiful. Improvise."

It was a relief to do something, and Alice went to the piano.

"Shall I ? " she said. "Just anything that comes into my head ? "

"Please, and may I sit where I can see you as well as hear you ? "

Alice made her light butterfly excursions up and down the keys and from the lounge outside Colonel

Chase heard these familiar noises. His mind was now made up to begin his romantic wooing, and the sooner he took it in hand the better. He softly opened the door and stole in : there was Miss Howard with her eyes dreamily fixed on the ceiling, looking really quite attractive, and there was that tiresome Miss Kemp gazing at her as if she was some beautiful vision, and herself, so thought Colonel Chase, as if she was some large swooning frog. He sat himself where he could look at Miss Howard too, and put on the sort of face which concert-goers wear when they listen to slow movements by Beethoven, an expression of remorse and reverie. So there they all sat till the stream of inspiration ran dry, and ended in a minor chord. Miss Howard sighed, they all sighed.

" Beautiful ! " said Colonel Chase. " Very fine. Dear me ! A great treat."

Miss Howard raised her eyes from the contemplation of the minor chord, and smiled at Florence, quite ignoring the Colonel.

" Did you like it, dear ? " she said.

" Don't stop ! " said Florence.

So Miss Howard went on again in another key, while her two lovers settled down to see each other out. In the middle of the next improvisation a maid came in to tell Florence that her father wanted her, but she did not move and only whispered ' Hush : presently.' Then the evening paper was brought in for Colonel Chase, and he let it lie unread, and gazed at various points of the ceiling, and strangled a yawn. At the end, which did not come off for a long time, for a perfect flood of half-forgotten fragments poured into Miss Howard's mind, she closed the piano and got up with a gay laugh.

" Florence, darling, you shan't work me and bully me any more," she said, and perched herself airily on the arm of Florence's chair.

" Too lovely, darling," said Florence. " Thank you."

" Thank you indeed," said Colonel Chase with an air of correcting Florence. " Exquisite. What a gift. Never shall I forget your accompaniment to my ghost story."

This was a pretty direct hint that he should be asked for his ghost story, but nobody expressed the slightest desire to hear it.

" What a delicious frock you've got on," said Florence, as if Colonel Chase was non-existent.

" Do you like it, dear ? So glad," said Alice. " But gracious me, look at the time ! I believe the dressing-bell must have gone, and we never heard it."

" Something better to listen to," said Colonel Chase, very handsomely.

" Dearest, we must fly then," said Florence, and away they flew, arm in arm, leaving the baffled Colonel, alone with his evening paper. He searched his memory in vain for an occasion on which his compliments and attentions had met with so indifferent a reception.

CHAPTER VIII

THE tonic of this declared devotion proved itself to be a wonderful stimulant to Florence in her revolt against parental tyranny : it was as if she was taking a course of psychical strychnine, and every hour almost saw some fresh insubordination. She told her father that she had not been able to come to him when he had sent for her just now because Miss Howard was playing to her and that when she had finished, it was time to dress for dinner : and she paid him the briefest of bedside visits that night, leaving him to drink lemonade or eat rusks, or concentrate on the power of Mind, or go to sleep or lie awake just as he pleased, and off she went for a long talk till after midnight with Alice. She flowed into confidences, she babbled and expanded in new found freedom of speech after these sealed up and suppressed years : it was the richest joy to reveal to Alice all the little flutterings of her soul which hitherto had groped in dusk and silence.

Next morning she did not wait to accompany Mr. Kemp in the bus down to the bath, but started off earlier to walk down with Alice to the Green Salon. There a very pleasing tussle took place for Alice after selecting Dewy Eve for her, as the most creditable Howard that still remained unsold, absolutely refused to be paid for it. She would really be very much hurt if Florence (obstinate Flo !) would not accept it, and so with a squeezing of Alice's hand obstinate Flo did accept it, and instantly bought Gloaming (which made a

beautiful ' pair ') on her own account. Alice said
this was a very shabby trick, but Flo was firm, and so
two more red stars were needed. A third was presently
required, for Alice determined to give June's Glory to
Mrs. Bliss as a slight recognition of the services rendered
by Mind. After lunch Florence gave the leap-frog
boy the daily wage, and sent him off to amuse himself
as he liked, while she enjoyed the office of custodian,
sitting on his high stool with the nearly exhausted
toilet-roll and the pill box of the few red remaining stars
(slightly sticky) in order to be doing something for her
new friend. There was not much to do, for visitors
were few, but, as compensation, they had the Green
Salon almost entirely to themselves.

Mr. Kemp, all that day, naturally felt himself the
victim of a series of atrocities, for he had to get in and
out of the bus without Florence's aid, in the afternoon
he had to read to himself instead of being read to, and
fall asleep alone, and personally to ring the bell before
doing so, to ask a maid to bring him his second thickest
rug. Then again the move to Bournemouth was to
take place in only nine short days from now, and it
was high time to begin looking up the journey, and
settling whether it would be more comfortable to leave
Bolton in the morning and lunch in the train, thus
arriving at Bournemouth in time to have tea and
rest before dinner, or leave Bolton directly after an
early lunch and only get into Bournemouth at a
quarter to eight at night. Then there was the further
alternative of sending Florence on in the morning with
the luggage, while he followed later. This would
save him waiting about at draughty stations while she
got luggage labelled and collected, and she would
have time to unpack for him at Bournemouth before
he arrived. True, he would be obliged to open and shut
windows in the railway carriage for himself, and personally take a taxi for crossing London, but if he

provided himself with plenty of small change, he believed he could manage it. These studies in comparative fatigue were very puzzling to pursue alone ; it was scandalous of Florence not to be at hand, for she knew so well what sort of thing tired him most.

As he turned over the pages of his Bradshaw, the small print of which, he was sadly afraid, would very likely give him a headache from eye-strain later on, he lit upon a series of stations printed in rather larger type : these were Bolton Spa, Reading, Basingstoke, Southampton, Bournemouth. He gazed at this revelation in astonishment, for there appeared to be trains from here to Bournemouth by these lines and junctions, which would convey him there without a single change. He had for several years now gone at the end of his Bolton-cure to Bournemouth, but Florence looked up the trains, and they had always travelled up to London and changed stations there. At the moment of this dazzling discovery she and Miss Howard came prattling into the lounge, having closed the Green Salon for the day.

"Florence," he said excitedly. "Please verify this for me at once. There seems to be a train which goes from here to Bournemouth without change, and all these years you have taken me up to London. Look : 11.35 a.m. from Bolton."

Florence held out a casual hand for the Bradshaw, and continued speaking to Alice.

"Let's have tea at once, dear," she said, "and then we can have a stroll afterwards : you must have a little more walk, so good for you. What is it, Papa ? "

"I beg you will attend," said he shrilly. "At the top of the page there."

Florence, not attending, dropped the Bradshaw and the page of the epoch-making discovery was lost.

"How careless you are," said Mr. Kemp. "Now we shall have to search for it all over again. And I don't know where you've been this afternoon, not near me, anyhow. I've had to forage for myself whenever I wanted anything."

"You've foraged very successfully if you've really found such a wonderful train," she said. "Whereabouts was it ? "

Mr. Kemp's excitement was very excusable : even his ill-temper might be pardoned, for it was a long time since so important a railway discovery had been made.

"Pick up the Bradshaw and give it me," he said. "Very stupid of you. And I don't know the page : it wasn't on the ordinary Bolton page."

"Try the index," said Florence, "if you want to look it up yourself. Won't you bring it into the drawing-room ? Tea is ready, and we'll find it there."

"Certainly not," said he. "I could not touch my tea, till I've found it again."

"Very well : bring it in when you've got it," she said, "and I'll see if it's right."

She joined Miss Howard in the drawing-room, where others were assembling, while Mr. Kemp in the lounge fruitlessly searched the innumerable pages, and it was not till daylight began to grow dim and tea cold, that his tragic face appeared at the door.

"And here's Mr. Kemp at last," said Mrs. Oxney pleasantly. "Why how late you are, Mr. Kemp, and whatever's happened ? You look so worried."

He explained the nature of the catastrophe.

"Most disastrous," he said. "I distinctly saw the train, and I've searched and searched but can't find it again."

"Well, I'm no use," said Mrs. Oxney. "Bradshaw's a sealed book to me, and always has been. How anybody can make it out, I don't know. Send away that tea, Mr. Kemp, and have a cup of fresh."

"I don't really want any," he said. "11.35 a.m.

from Bolton. I saw it, and then my daughter dropped
the Bradshaw."

"Things do fly out of the hand sometimes," said
Mrs. Oxney. "And what's the Colonel been doing?"

The Colonel had been walking, and the record on the
pedometer (he glanced darkly at Mrs. Bliss who only
smiled in return) was satisfactory. Florence and Miss
Howard, seated in a remote window-seat took no notice
of anybody, and presently they got up and moved
to the door.

"We're going for a little stroll, Papa," she said.
"Miss Howard is taking me to the place where she
painted Gloaming. Do you want anything done for
you in the town?"

"I beg you will not go out till you have found the
train," said he. "My eyes are getting very tired:
I feel I shall have a headache soon. Go on looking for
me, Florence; read every page carefully."

"I'll find it when I come in," said Florence. "Don't
fuss, Papa."

He could only gasp in sheer astonishment at the idea
that he could be thought fussy.

The two friends went down across the garden and
the fields below it, to the site of Gloaming. It was
gloaming already: they would see the spot just as it
had looked when it inspired Alice, though she had
painted it in the morning. There was a nail-paring
of a moon in the West, and they duly curtsied to it
and sometimes Alice sang staves of song, and sometimes they walked arm-in-arm and then exuberantly
chasséed for a few steps. This dawn of emotional
attraction, rendered and responded to, excited and
rejuvenated Florence the repressed and unconsidered:
she suddenly found the drab of her dull and
monotonous existence shot with colour: she
expanded and blossomed with the warm sense of
giving herself to someone who wanted her not

for service, but for free comradeship. Her virginal
heart seemed to sprout with fresh growth under these
fruitful showers. She skipped and *chasséed* beneath
the sickle moon, rather out of breath but enraptured.

" It's a new life, darling," she panted, as, quite exhausted they dropped to a more sober pace, " and it
has gone to my head : I'm tipsy with it. Obstinate,
tipsy Flo ! And I've got, oh, such a delicious plan in
my head, but I shan't tell you a single word about it
for fear it shouldn't come off."

" Oh, you must tell me, Flo," said Alice. " I must
share it with you. Please ! "

" Not if you said please a hundred times."

" Obstinate Flo ! " said Alice, pretending to pout.
" I don't like you any more. You shall be Miss Kemp
again. Good evening, Miss Kemp."

" Good evening, Miss Howard. So pleasant just to
have met you before I go away to Bournemouth next
week."

" The same to you. . . . But do tell me the plan.
Please, please, please, please. . . . Oh, here's the place
where I painted the trumpery little sketch you were so
obstinate about. Obstinate Flo : O.F."

" Which stands equally well for Old Fool," said
Florence.

" Well, it's not my fault if it does. The stream,
do you see, and the woods beyond, and just the top
of the steeple of St. Giles's. It was just a month ago,
at the time of the last new moon. Dear slim girlie of
a moon, little did I think that when next you came
round, I should be here again, but not alone ! "

Florence replied with a hug first.

" But I think your sketch is far more beautiful than
the original," she said. " You've left out that ugly
siding, with the roof of the station, and filled it with
poetry instead ! "

Alice put her head a little on one side and half closed her eyes.

" Have I made it poetical ? " she said. " How dear of you to think that ! I painted it as I *felt* it was. And I didn't feel the station, so I left it out."

" You made a perfect poem of it," said Florence. " You always put yourself into your sketches. Oh, the station. May we pop in for a moment, as we're so close and then I can find out about poor Papa's train. How I hate trains that go away from Bolton while you are here. But perhaps, who knows——"

She broke off.

" Why do you stop ? " said Alice. " Oh I guess ! What you were going to say concerns the plan. Doesn't it now ? "

But Flo was just as obstinate as ever, and Alice again pretended to be cross, and wouldn't let O. F. take her arm, and was very cold and polite. Indeed there was quite a quarrel for exactly two minutes, at the end of which obstinate Flo admitted that she had stopped because what she was going to say did concern the plan in a sort of a way, but that it would be very mean of Alice to try to guess it. So Alice relented, and said she would not bully her any more, and they skipped and sang again. Then, going into the station they found that a portion of the 11.35 train went to Bournemouth every day, without any changing just as it had done for the last ten or twelve years, so that Mr. Kemp need never have gone up to London at all. They tripped back to Wentworth, where Colonel Chase was getting quite anxious about Miss Howard being out so late, but appeared not to care at all how late Miss Kemp was out.

Her father had gone to his room where he was resting after the visit of his *masseur*. He gave her one glance, and then in dead silence continued his search in Bradshaw. The silence, rightly considered, was a chorus of reproaches.

" You need not bother about that train any more," she said. " I went to the station and found out about it. It leaves here at 11.35 and there's a through carriage to Bournemouth."

His sombre face brightened.

" That is good news," he said. " But are you quite certain ? Who told you ? "

" The station-master."

He handed her the open Bradshaw.

" He ought to be reliable," he said. " But my mind would be easier if I saw it confirmed in Bradshaw."

" But you found it there yourself," said she.

" I certainly thought I did. But it is very mysterious that I could not find it again. Take the book carefully and don't drop it this time, and go on, please from the page at which it is open. My eyes are aching sadly, and I had no tea to speak of. Is it a new train ? "

" No ; it's been running for years."

" You mean to say that we might have gone by it last year and the year before, and have saved me all the agitation and fatigue of crossing London ? "

" Yes," said Florence.

Mr. Kemp felt justly indignant.

" I do not expect much from you, Florence," he said, " and if I did, I shouldn't get it. But considering my condition, my utter helplessness, I do think you might have taken the trouble to find this out before. You would have saved me much. Last year I remember, it was a full week before I recovered from the fatigue of the journey. But I make no complaints. And is there a luncheon car on the train, or shall I have to take my lunch with me ? "

" I didn't ask," said Florence. " There is plenty of time to find out. You are not going till the day after tomorrow week."

" A rusk, please," he said. " I had no tea. I am
surprised you did not think of ascertaining that.
These rusks are not quite fresh. No crispness . . .
Florence, I am not sure, but I think my knee is moving
a shade more easily. Do you consider that is the
effect, if I am right about it, of Mind or massage ? "

" Perhaps a little of both," said Florence cautiously.
" Mind may be doing it, and massage helping you to
believe it, or it may be the other way round. They
seem to go together in Mrs. Bliss's case."

Mr. Kemp closed his eyes for a moment. His
masseur had already been treating him, so now it
was Mind's turn.

" Yes, I think they do," he said, " so why shouldn't
they go together in my case ? Let me see : Mind
denies evil, pain : there is no pain in Mind, there is
no Mind in pain. Mind is all, all is Mind. Hence there
is no pain. . . . Certainly Mrs. Bliss's improvement
has been marvellous. I am not sure that I should like
to progress quite so quickly as that, for I should be
afraid that something else was developing. But I feel
sure that I have been on the up-grade this last week,
though it would be more satisfactory if I knew exactly
what caused it. I could then have more Mind or more
massage accordingly. I think that at Bournemouth
I shall have no massage at all for a week but work at
Mind, and note very carefully if any change takes
place."

He thought over this, still muttering incantations,
then he shook his head.

" Even then it will be very difficult to be certain,"
he said. " If there is improvement, it may only be the
after effect of Bolton. Or indeed, if I seem to be worse,
that may be after effect. The first week after the
cure is over is sometimes very discouraging. I do
not know what to do."

Florence had been turning over the pages of

Bradshaw. At this moment she found the long-sought train.

"I've got it," she said. "And there's an asterisk opposite it which means luncheon car."

Mr. Kemp gave a sigh of relief.

"That's a great weight off my mind," he said. "I was almost beginning to fear I had had a hallucination and that the train did not exist. I ought to have trusted Mrs. Bliss who told us she knew all would be well. You had better go to the station again tomorrow and see about engaging a place in the luncheon car. It would never do to leave that to chance, for if the luncheon car happened to be full when we joined the train, it would be no better than if there was none at all. Get one of those tables for two. They give more room than two places at a table for four. And you never know who may be next you."

Florence turned down the corner of the page, for her father would certainly want to verify this all over again for himself, and, reinforcing her courage with the thought of Alice, divulged the plan.

"I'm going to make a proposal to you, Papa," she said, "which I think may surprise you a good deal."

"Then I beg you will not," said Mr. Kemp nervously. "A surprise always means something unpleasant and agitating."

"It needn't agitate you at all," said Florence, "if you just keep calm, and talk it over quietly. I don't believe you will find it unpleasant."

He clenched his hands tightly.

"Make haste then," he said hoarsely. "Suspense as you ought to know, wears me out more than anything."

"I don't want to come to Bournemouth with you," said Florence. "I want you to take a nurse instead. A nice one who would be a companion to you as well."

Mr. Kemp shut his eyes. Some idea of invoking

Mind occurred to him, but he knew he could not manage it.

" Quite impossible," he said.

" No, not at all impossible," said Florence. " She would look after you. much more skilfully than I can and she would have nothing else to do."

" But you have nothing else to do," said he.

" We won't argue about that," she said. " But I really believe a good nurse would suit you much better than I do. I think you would soon find yourself much more comfortable."

He opened his eyes again : Florence was speaking in a calm confident voice which impressed him.

" Do you really think I should ? " he asked.

" I think it is quite worth trying."

He felt he could now summon Mind to his aid. Naturally, if he would really be more comfortable, Florence's idea was not impossible at all : it was, on the contrary highly likely. And if the nurse did not suit him, Florence could come back at once. But there were other things to be considered too.

" But then there is the expense," he said. " I should have to pay her wages, should I not, and there's her keep as well. That will be a great drain. You have your own money to pay for your keep, as your poor dear mother left you half her fortune. I should be very poor indeed if I had to pay for a nurse : indeed I don't think I could do it. Of course, if you think that I should be more comfortable with a nurse, we must consider it very carefully, but we must not let the idea run away with us, and not consider the expense."

" I will help you with that," said Florence.

" Well, that is very generous of you, though perhaps it is no more than fair, considering how your poor mother left her fortune. By the way, what will you do with yourself ? "

" I should stop on here for a little," said she, " and

then very likely I should go to live in my flat in Kensington Square. There are a couple of servants there all the time and we've not been there for more than a few weeks during this last year. Let us try my plan. I don't mean to cut myself off from you at all : I will come down to Bournemouth when you are there, and often pay you visits in your hotels. But I want to have some sort of life of my own."

Mr. Kemp suddenly remembered he had not been pathetic, for his brain had been entirely occupied in trying to picture all that this change would mean. Of course a trained nurse would listen to the recital of his symptoms with much more perception and insight than poor Florence : if he felt that tiresome numbness in his right arm she would be able to reassure with real authority that it was not the approach of general paralysis, whereas Florence could only recommend him to think about something else. And she had no true understanding of his endless symptoms : her robust uninteresting health did not realise the many possible significances of a pain in his left side or a throbbing in his throat. But she must not imagine that he was not deeply hurt at her proposed desertion of him. Desertion : that was the keynote.

" You have wounded me," he said. " I had thought that you and I were so happy together, and that you felt it to be a privilege to minister to the needs of your crippled old father. It would not have been for long : I know that my life hangs by a thread. But I was wrong : you want to be quit of me, before my death releases you."

Florence got up. She knew quite well what she was about.

" If you feel like that, Papa," she said, " I give up the idea altogether. We go to Bournemouth together the day after to-morrow week by the luncheon car train. I will see to the seats."

Mr. Kemp saw he had gone too far.   The notion of a
pleasant nurse, to whose maintenance Florence con-
tributed had begun to assume attractive colours in his
mind.   He visualised a comprehending woman, who
entered into his sufferings and who would bring novelty
into Buxton and Bath.   Dear Florence often bored
him : she listened in a most perfunctory manner to
the recital of ailments that were familiar to her, and
could not guess from her ignorance of medical knowledge
what new complication they might foreshadow.   He
must push in that bleating *Vox Humana :* it had been
too loud.

" I beg you not to be so hasty, dear," he said "Anything in the nature of hurry always unsettles me.
Take the two seats in the luncheon car of course : we
shall want two seats for me and another however we
settle this.   You have told me that you think a trained
nurse will be able to look after me better than you
can do, and we must not reject your idea in that off-hand
manner.   We will think it over quietly to-night, and
tomorrow morning while I am having my reclining
bath, you must talk it over with Dr. Dobbs and get
his view.   You had better ring him up at once and
make an appointment with him for tomorrow.   Tell
him it is very urgent, for indeed we have not got too
much time, if this all has to be settled in nine days :
and say you will come at whatever hour suits him.   You
could slip across after dinner to-night, if he is booked
up all morning tomorrow.   Indeed that might be the
best plan : you had better telephone to him at once.
Very urgent.   I will try to get a little rest now, but
my hour for resting after massage has been sadly
encroached on.   At dinner you shall tell me what you
have arranged."

Florence was at the door when her father called her
back.

" My rusks," he said.   " They have quite lost their

crispness. The tin should be placed open for half an hour in front of a good fire, but not too close."

There was much suppressed excitement and sense of unrest at Wentworth after dinner when it was known on what errand Florence was going to see Dr. Dobbs that very evening : Mrs. Oxney said that the atmosphere reminded her of that of the three days before the beginning of the Great War, for momentous decisions were being made which might alter the whole course of people's lives and nobody could be certain what would happen next. Mr. Kemp felt strongly that Mind should be consulted as well as Dr. Dobbs, and accordingly went into the pros and cons of the scheme very carefully with Mrs. Bliss, and then asked her whether she could obtain any guidance from Mind. It was clear from the way he put the case that so far from thinking it impossible any longer, his personal inclination was all for it : the idea of having a trained listener always at hand whom he could regale with his symptoms, and who was paid (by Florence) to listen to them now strongly attracted him. It was equally clear that Florence was eager to resign these privileges which had been hers for so long. Father and daughter Mrs. Bliss had also observed, were bored to death with each other, and this state of Error no doubt was an impediment to the clear shining forth of Mind. So when she retired to a quiet corner of the lounge, where she closed her eyes and realised that all was harmonious, it took very little time for her to be convinced that Mind was in favour of the scheme. Mr. Kemp was delighted to know that, and by the time Florence came back from her consultation with Dr. Dobbs, it would have needed strong disapproval on his part to have put him off the idea. But as she brought the glad tidings that Dr. Dobbs thought the scheme well worth trying, there was no struggle or antagonism between *materia medica* and Mind. All, as Mrs. Bliss had known, was indeed harmonious.

Mind, in fact, during the last few days had been going strong at Wentworth, and Mrs. Bliss had emerged brilliantly from the slight cloud that hung over her on the discovery of how she had got hold of Colonel Chase's pedometer. For since then, during those black days when from morning till night neither visitor nor purchaser came near the Green Salon, Mrs. Bliss had continued serenely confident that Mind was turning a special smile on the unpopulated exhibition, and was preparing a peculiarly rich harmony with regard to it. That had triumphantly proved to be the case, and now purchasers had come forward in such number that instead of the Green Salon closing at the end of this week, Miss Howard had determined to keep it open for another similar period. Then again, there was Mrs. Bliss's own amazing recovery as a further witness of Mind's beneficent functioning, and so her repeated assurance that Mr. Kemp, though apparently as lame as ever, was quite well, must be received with respect. Truth was nibbling away hard at his Error, and he would very soon find that it was so. This added to the general excitement.

But more thrilling even than the news that Mr. Kemp was quite well, and was therefore going to take a trained nurse with him to Bournemouth and that Florence was to remain here for the present, was the conjectured state of Colonel Chase's heart with reference to Miss Howard. Mrs. Oxney had long felt certain that from time to time he had ' had his eye ' on her, and had been ' considering it ', but nothing as yet had come of it and indeed a week ago she had almost given up the notion when he called her exhibition a black-mailing project, and had thrown doubt on the *extempore* character of her improvisations.

" I'm afraid he has settled against it, Amy," she

had said to her sister on the occasion of his using that unlover-like expression, " for a gentleman doesn't talk like that about the lady of his choice. It would have been a treat to have had a courtship at Wentworth, and perhaps a marriage too."

" We should have lost two of our permanent guests," Amy had said, for she saw the gloomier side of all situations however romantic. " They'd both have gone away."

" Don't be too sure of that," had been Mrs. Oxney's reply. " They might have taken the end of that wing, and made a little flat of it, seeing that Miss Howard's country seat is let, and she couldn't have gone to live in the Colonel's club. That new bath-room would have come in convenient then. But now I'm afraid it's all over. He asked me only just now whether there was no means of stopping Miss Howard chirping all over the house like a canary."

Then suddenly the whole attitude of the Colonel towards the lady had changed. Not only had he paid a visit to the exhibition, in which, as a protest against blackmail, he had sworn he would never set foot, but he had bought two of the blackmailer's pictures, and had asked no end of respectful questions about her little place.

" And if there's as much as a note sounded on the piano," said Mrs. Oxney to-night, as she and her sister had their usual chat when the guests had gone to their rooms, " you'll hear a door opening somewhere, if the Colonel is within hearing, and he'll tiptoe into the drawing-room. Why, this morning I was just dusting the keys, and made a scale up and down with my duster, like one of Miss Howard's commencements, and he came peeping in. What disappointment there was in his face when he saw it was only me, and out he went again in a jiffy ! He's after her now and no mistake."

Mrs. Bertram finished her patience : there had been

no bridge to-night, for the Colonel had sat the whole evening in the lounge talking to Miss Howard and snubbing Florence.

"You may be right, Margaret," Mrs. Bertram said, "and I'm sure it would be pleasant to let the end of that wing for ever, as you may say, and I should be the last to want you not to put in the new bathroom if that was the way of it. But he can't get a word alone with her these days. There's always Miss Kemp sticking to her like plaster. I call it want of tact not to see that she'd be better away. She won't give him a chance."

"Such faces as he makes at her too," said Mrs. Oxney, "when he finds them together, as they always are now. They would scare me out of the room quick enough, not to mention the snubbings. And now Miss Kemp is settling to leave her Papa to go to Bournemouth with a nurse, and is stopping on here. I can't but be glad she's staying, for a guest is a guest, but I do wish she'd have the sense to let the Colonel have a turn without her. Such friends as she's become lately with Miss Howard, I never saw the like. They go skipping about together like two school-girls and if it isn't 'Alice this' it's 'Flo that'. It would be only friendly if she made herself scarce sometimes. But I wager the Colonel's in earnest now, and 'Love will find out the way' as Mr. Oxney used to whistle when he was after me. Why, if it isn't close on midnight ! Just crush the fire down, while I put the burglar alarm on the shutters. You mark my words : Cupid will be busy in Wentworth yet. Such a fine man as the Colonel is too. I wouldn't hesitate long if I was Miss Howard. She's not likely to get such a chance again."

It was not likely that Cupid's elegant flutterings which were so manifest to Mrs. Oxney should have escaped the notice of Miss Howard or obstinate Flo, and to Miss Howard they were both gratifying and embarrassing. Gratifying they could not fail to be (for there was no doubt that Colonel Chase was after her) whether she intended to be caught or not. Obstinate Flo and she made a great joke of the strenuous attentions of her swain, as they sat over their usual midnight cocoa, in the bedroom of one or the other, after Mr. Kemp had summarily been made comfortable with his rusks and milk and hot-water bottle and lemonade, and Flo who had a rough rude gift of mimicry would affix a cotton-wool moustache to her upper lip and reproduce the imaginary wooings of the suitor, and his respectful kiss when accepted and Alice would giggle and slap her and say she was a silly girl, and ask her how she herself *could*, but in her heart of hearts she was not absolutely sure that she couldn't. Herein lay the embarrassment, for Flo took it for granted that their friendship satisfied all Alice's emotional needs for ever, and it was already settled that after Mr. Kemp's departure they were going off together to spend a fortnight alone at the flat in Kensington Square. Alice rightly interpreted this sojourn as being, in Flo's mind, a sort of honeymoon, a symbol of eternal and exclusive friendship, but now, with Colonel Chase so obviously in earnest, she was not sure whether she looked forward to the adventure with quite the rapture of her partner. Flo was a sweet thing, and the Colonel could not possibly be called a sweet thing, and it rather surprised Alice to find that she, who had never seriously felt the need of a man, could be weighing in her mind, as she certainly was doing, the comparative merits of the permanent companionship of a friend and of a husband. Though she found it difficult to imagine herself saying ' yes ' to the offer that she felt sure Colonel Chase was ready to make her, whenever obstinate Flo gave him a chance, she found it nearly as difficult to imagine herself saying ' no '.

She put all this to herself as she sat to-night waiting for Florence to come in for cocoa and a chat over her

fire. Florence was late, as she thought would most
probably be the case, for Mr. Kemp had engaged a
sympathetic nurse, and was to leave next morning
by the luncheon-car train for Bournemouth : it was
therefore certain that a particular suitcase would have
to be packed overnight, which must contain all that
he could possibly require (with an imaginative margin)
on the arduous journey . . . Alice really could not
come to any decision, for Florence looked down a
much longer perspective than that of this little honeymoon in London, and anticipated that, at the end of
it, they would settle to live together in devoted spinster-
hood, as so many women did to whom either the desire
or the opportunity for matrimony had not come.
It was quite an agreeable prospect, and one which,
a few weeks ago Alice would have welcomed. But
now that the other opportunity was certainly about
to offer itself, she saw that though matrimony might
not be more permanent, it afforded a certain dignity
and completeness which the other lacked. Then too,
Colonel Chase seemed really to care for her, he bought
her pictures, he listened with a rapt face to her improvisations, and more than once he had preferred to
spend the evening talking to her, and trying to get
rid of obstinate Flo rather than play bridge. He had
even asked her to accompany him on one of his bicycle
rides, and what more solid token of esteem could he
give ? In his judgment they would be very comfortable
together, and she could not but respect the opinion
of a man who so clearly was an adept in the art of
comfort.

There was another embarrassment entirely private
to herself : neither of her suitors had any notion of
it and as this topic came into Alice's mind, she drew
back a little from the fire feeling a sudden flush of heat
invade her. This embarrassment was concerned with
the ancestral home at Tunbridge Wells. Of late

Colonel Chase, keenly interested in all that pertained to her, had often mentioned her little place, asking her gratifying questions about it, and making gratifying assumptions which were very difficult to contradict. Beyond any doubt the answers she had given to his questions and her own allusions to it, now and previously, had made it dreadfully clear to Alice that the little place as it really was, differed considerably from the little place as he imagined it to be. It was quite true that it was mildly ancestral, since her grandfather, a most respectable auctioneer, had built it (and anyone is at liberty to reckon a grandfather among his ancestors) but it was not quite what Colonel Chase and Mrs. Oxney and anybody who had heard her sigh over the cruel necessity of letting her old home, pictured it. It was quite true also that it had a rose-garden—for who, when all was said and done could deny that a bed of roses was a rose-garden?— and that there were some fine trees just outside the garden, for there were some remarkable old oaks on the common, of which so near a view was visible, and that the dining-room where the family portraits hung, looked out on to the lawn. The family portraits did hang there : there was one of her grandfather, and another of her mother, and, though the artists were not known to fame, these were portraits, for in the English language that word was invariably used for pictures of people. Besides she had distinctly said that there were no Sir Joshua Reynolds' among them . . .

Similarly the little square of plantains, daisies, wormcasts and grass in front of the dining-room, separating ' The Croft ' from the Station Road, could not be more accurately described than by calling it the lawn. Alice had not measured it and so could not give the actual dimensions even if anyone had asked for them. In the same way it was perfectly

true that, Mr. Gradge (such was his amazing name)
who had taken 'The Croft' on a year's lease
at a most moderate quarterly rent, and lived there
with his sister were 'my tenants'. Alice had
every right to call them her tenants : while the gardener (three mornings a week) and the boy who 'did'
the knives and coals and boots, and spent the rest of
his time in the potato-patch could not, without long
and tedious explanations have been alluded to otherwise than as 'my gardeners'. Even the two cucumber
frames were in a manner of speaking, a couple of glass
houses. All these allusions, casually dropped here and
there were strictly founded on fact ; indeed they were
facts, but it was also a fact, though unknown to Colonel
Chase and Mrs. Oxney and all those who had rever-
entially heard Miss Howard allude to her sober little
ancestral splendours, that 'The Croft' was not a
Queen Anne house, but a semi-detached villa standing
in the Station Road.

It was all rather awkward, and for the life of her,
Miss Howard could not imagine how she had got into
such a position. She had told no lies, she had hardly
been guilty of any infamous exaggeration (except
perhaps in the matter of the two cucumber frames),
and yet she knew that all Wentworth believed her to
have a beautiful little country seat near Tunbridge
Wells, the glories of which she had probably dimmed
rather than polished. It was like a Saga or the poems
of Homer, which by untraceable processess had grown
from small oral beginnings into epics. No one could
analyse the psychology of such a growth any more
than they could analyse the physiological growth of
the grain of mustard seed into a bird-haunted tree :
it grew and that was all that could be said about it.
In the same way she had alluded quite casually and infre-
quently to the lawn and the fine timber and the rose-
garden and her tenants and her gardeners, and she was

credited now with a mansion and a park and a pleasaunce and a host of old family retainers. She could no doubt have instantly nipped this sumptuous growth in the bud by stating the plain fact that ' The Croft ' was a semi-detached villa, but instead of that she had enjoyed seeing it sprout, and had watered it and tilled the ground. Now, at the thought of Colonel Chase's wooing, the little place had become almost like an angel with a fiery sword preventing her entering that possible Paradise. For if she consented to marry him, it would not be unreasonable in her husband to want to know more of the little place : he might, still not unreasonably, suggest living there on their combined resources, when the lease of ' my tenants ', which was only a yearly one, came to an end. Sooner or later, and probably very soon, the truth about the little place must come out, and though she had never told any real lies about it, the aggregate of information amounted to a falsehood that was appalling to contemplate. Obstinate Flo, no doubt, had gleaned the same impression as the Colonel but that was a situation easier to deal with. If the worst came to the worst, and exposure was certain, she could contemplate without intolerable dismay actually telling her that she had got a perfectly wrong idea about ' The Croft ' and had oddly exaggerated to herself its splendours, just as she (dear thing !) attributed all sorts of talents and graces to the character of her poor friend. " I think I could tell Flo that," said Miss Howard to herself, " but I feel almost sure that I couldn't tell Colonel Chase."

These disagreeable reflections were interrupted by the arrival of Florence in a blue dressing-gown and slippers.

" Darling, what ages I have been," she said, " and I thought that I would get ready for bed first, so that when I left you I could just hop there, and lie thinking

of you and our talk without the interruption of un-
dressing. Dear me! Have you been impatient
because I was so long? Do say you have : do
tell me that you were furious with me for not coming
sooner. But I couldn't help it : Papa has been too
tiresome for anything."

" How naughty you are about your father," said
Alice. " But tell me about him : I want to be naughty
too."

Florence gave her a loud kiss, and assumed her
father's voice.

" Mind you put in a pair of old gloves at the top of
the suitcase, Florence," she said, " for I shall have to
go from my carriage to the luncheon car, and anything
I touch on the way will be grimy. And my cachets :
the ones I take in water after a meal. You had better
pack the bottle of them in my portmanteau and give
me a couple of them, done up in a screw of paper,
which I can put in my waistcoat pocket. And remember
to give me a telegraph form addressed to yourself,
for in the bustle of departure you may have forgotten
something, so it would be well to have a telegraph form
handy. I regret that Nurse Babbit only joins me at
the station : it would have been wiser if she had slept
at Wentworth to-night. My thermos flask with some
hot coffee in it must be seen to in the morning, and
do not forget to give me some small change for tips . . .
Darling, what a duck he is, and how glad I am that he's
going to Bournemouth tomorrow. Now for a happy
talk. How sweet of you to have made some cocoa
for me! And how weird Colonel Chase-Alice—is
not that a good name for him ?—was this evening.
He can't see that you and I only want to be left to
ourselves. You were delicious with him when you
said you knew he wanted to go and play bridge :
O.F. knew that you meant that you wanted him to.
What do you bet he doesn't buy another picture of

your's tomorrow?   He's crazy about you, and who
wouldn't be."

Alice would have let all the Colonels in the British
Army go crazy about her and remain unrequited for
ever, if she could only have felt towards Florence as
Florence felt towards her, for she had the perception
to see that the worshipper has a far more exciting time
than the image that he worships. She felt no atom
of condescension or graciousness towards her worshipper
but rather envy at her potentiality for rapture. How
amazingly Florence had expanded in the warmth of
her own emotion! A fortnight ago, in spite of her
sturdy and manly appearance, she had owned a squashed
and middle-aged soul; now though she was still
essentially the same, all that had been repressed and
nipped in her had opened like a flower. Self-expression
had vivified her . . .

"I'll bet you any picture in the Green Salon that
isn't sold," said Alice, "that Colonel Chase-Alice (how
wicked of us!) doesn't buy another. He hasn't got
much longer: we close the day after tomorrow."

"Oh, how I love you saying 'we close'," said
Florence. "But I shan't love the closing: no more
sitting surrounded by your pictures and hoping
that no visitors will come in and interrupt."

Alice did not feel that she had ever quite shared
this hope, for after all she had not taken the Green
Salon only for the purpose of uninterrupted conversation with Florence.

"Dear little Green Salon!" she said. "I have
become so much attached to it. Then what a day's
work there will be: we shall have to pack up all the
pictures that have been sold and send them to the
purchasers."

"Miles of string, reams of corrugated paper like
Colonel Chase's forehead, oceans of ink, books
of labels," said Florence appreciatively. "How I

shall enjoy it, simply because we shall be doing it together. Everything that we do together is so lovely, just for that reason. . . . And then we go off alone with no one to bother us for a month in London."

" I thought you said a fortnight," said Alice.

" I shall say a year if you're so tiresome," observed Florence, who had said a week originally and then had lengthened it into a fortnight, and now for the first time mentioned a month. " And then I must go to Bournemouth for Christmas. Papa insists on that, for he says that he and I have always spent Christmas together, though for that matter we have always spent every other day together. Christmas means as little to Papa as I do : all there is to it, is that he doesn't feel even as well as usual on Boxing Day, because he cannot resist two helpings of rich plum-pudding. But I know that by that time Nurse Babbit will be suiting him so well, that afterwards I shall be free. So you must come back to me in London again, and we will settle what we do next."

Florence's complete confidence that Colonel Chase hadn't a chance still seemed rather premature to Alice, and this complete ignoring of this possibility made his prospects appear brighter. Certainly Alice had not determined she would not marry him . . . . And then she thought of the revelation which must be made to him about the ancestral home, and his prospects grew dark again.

" Yes, we've got to talk about that," she said rather vaguely.

" Oh, and I've got such a delicious plan for us to do one day when we're in London next week," said Florence. " I know you'll love it. I will give you one hint, and then you shall guess. It will mean a day in the country at a place you adore."

A rather sickening sense came over Alice that she could make a pretty good guess, but she hoped she was wrong.

"Darling, how can I guess just from that?" she said. "Is it Epping Forest where I did that picture of the trees reflected in the lake, which you liked?"

"No, but there are trees," said Florence, "and pictures too, and roses, only I suppose they won't be out now. I'll give you another hint: Alice's Wonderland. There! Now you can guess."

This made Florence's plan absolutely certain, and so Alice said she hadn't the slightest idea what it was, while she cudgelled her brains to think of any decent excuse for not going with obstinate Flo to the ancestral home.

"Darling, aren't you a little slow?" asked Florence. "Where else could it be but 'The Croft'? How I long to see the Park ("Has it come to that?" thought Alice) and the lovely rose-garden and the dining-room with the portraits, and your old nursery from which you used to see the sunsets, and learn to love them."

Though Alice had felt that she could perhaps tell Florence the truth about the ancestral home, whereas she could not tell Colonel Chase, the idea of going there with her was a nightmare.

"Oh, that would be fun," she said wretchedly. "But the house is occupied you see; my tenants are there, and I don't even know them. All arrangements between them and me were made by my—my agents."

"Oh, but they will surely love you to come and look round," said Florence. "Or—oh—what a selfish little beast I am: would it be painful to you to see your lovely home in the hands of strangers? I never thought of that."

Alice was delighted that she had thought of it now, for it made an admirable excuse. She had only to admit to Florence this tearing of heart-strings for her to be overwhelmed with compunction at having suggested so cruel an ordeal.

"I'm quite silly about 'The Croft'," she said. "I know how stupid it is of me, but it would hurt just a teeny little bit. But what does that matter. Of course we'll go."

Florence slid to the ground by her side, and clasped her knees.

"What a pig I am not to have thought of that," she said. "I've got no sensitiveness, no perception: oh, what a lot you've got to teach me! Of course we won't go! But someday I must go alone: you won't mind that, will you darling? I must see your kinderscenen—that lovely Reverie by Schumann (or was it Schubert?) you played me—I must see your scenes of childhood—I love everything that tells me more about you."

The prospect opened up by these pretty sentiments was hideous. If obstinate Flo intended to show a touch of her quality in this passion for seeing 'The Croft', what would happen to all those pretty sentiments when some taxi-driver at Tunbridge Wells whom she directed to take her to 'The Croft,' set her down after a career of about fifty yards at the third house on the left in Station Road? That was too ghastly to contemplate: it would be better, thought Alice, if this fell determination persisted, to tell her straight out that 'The Croft' was not what it seemed, and would not repay a sentimental journey. . . . She thought it all over after Florence had said an affectionate good night some half-dozen times, and had come back after each to tell her something she had forgotten about, and resolved to make this odious disclosure when it could no longer be avoided. She had an uneasy dream in which she and Florence and Colonel Chase all went together hand in hand to stay at 'The Croft', and found it to be a cottage in a brickfield with only one bedroom. She woke in agonies of embarrassment.

There was little time next morning, until the 11.35

had irrevocably left Bolton Spa station for embarrassment or anything else except the concerns of Mr. Kemp.
Excitement had caused him to pass a night not less
troubled than Alice's, and it was not till he had taken
his temperature for the second time with encouraging
results, that he decided he could undertake the journey.
But during these dark watches he had made a further
list of memoranda in faint pencillings, and having
finished his breakfast by nine, he sat in the lounge and
tried to decipher them, with the travelling suitcase
open by him on the floor, and Florence ready to per-
form these last offices.

" Umbrella," he read out. " Yes, as it's fine I want
you to take charge of my umbrella, and hand it to me
when I am in the train. I will have my two sticks,
the pair with crutch handles. Aspirin : I must take
ten grains half-an-hour before I start, and then sit
quiet till the bus comes. Otherwise all these movings
about and going up and down steps into buses and
trains will be agony. Really I ought to have insisted
that Nurse Babbit should come here : I do not know
how we shall get through without her. Ten grains
will be two tablets, Florence ; you had better make a
note of that. Umbrella, Aspirin : I will cross those
out. Monkey . . . It can't be Monkey : I should
not dream of taking a monkey in my suitcase.
What can that be ? And it is a very dark
morning. I wonder if it will rain before I am safe
in the train. Or is it that my eyes are worse this
morning ? "

In this very natural agitation about monkey, he got
up from his chair and walked straight across to the
window without using his sticks.

" Ah, I see now," he said. " It is not monkey, it is
Mrs. Oxney. I want you, Florence, to get Mrs. Oxney
to have my room thoroughly searched after I have
gone, to see if you have forgotten to pack anything :

last year it was a flannel belt. Now let us get on :
we have not too much time."

Mrs. Bliss who was sitting by the fire, suddenly
jumped up with a cry of rapture.

"Oh, Mr. Kemp!" she said, "I knew it would
come. You have walked to the window and half-way
back again to your chair without your sticks. Mind
has conquered Error. Didn't I tell you that you were
perfectly well ? Now you know it."

Mr. Kemp immediately clutched at the back
of a sofa, and heavily leaning on it got back to
his chair.

"Dear me, I did walk there without my sticks," he
said, "and felt no twinge at all. But then why did
I begin to hobble again ? "

"Error's last effort to deny health and harmony,"
chanted Mrs. Bliss. "Oh, how pleased I am that you
know you are well. But I must say good-bye as I am
to have one more bath for my dear husband's sake.
When next we meet, I know I shall see you running
about like a boy."

Mr. Kemp shook hands.

"Indeed it was most remarkable, most gratifying,"
he said. "I must have my manual of Mental Science
to read in the train, Florence. Please get it out of the
green portmanteau, and put it in the suitcase. . . .
Now let us get on : Mrs. Oxney, we've done that.
Carpet slippers. You can put them in one of the port-
manteaux instead of in the suitcase, for I have decided not to change into them in the train. Daily
paper : that explains itself. Pencil : ah, yes, I shall
partly occupy my time with a cross-word puzzle. If
I get through it, I can ink it in at Bournemouth. . . .
Florence, do you realise that I walked to the window
without a twinge ? Shall I trust to Mind and not have
my aspirin ? "

"I think I should have the aspirin, Papa," **said**

Florence. "You can trust to Mind just the same, and tell yourself that the aspirin can't have any effect. Mrs. Bliss has her baths and massage for her husband's sake."

"True," said Mr. Kemp, much relieved to be excused from this great trial of faith. "So as you wish me to take my aspirin, I will do so for your sake."

"Thank you, Papa," said Florence, and went to get a wine-glass and some newly-decanted water.

The list of agenda and addenda was finished in time to enable Mr. Kemp to sit quiet for a full half-hour before the bus came round, and then once more he walked right across the lounge without assistance.

"It was a mistake to have had any aspirin," he said reproachfully to Florence, "for I am convinced that I am walking so well entirely owing to Mind. But I took it for your sake: remember to tell Mrs. Bliss."

The bus had been ordered in time to give the traveller a full quarter of an hour at the station: this would not be a moment too much to enable Mr. Kemp to confer with Nurse Babbit, to settle finally and irrevocably what baggage was to come into the carriage with him and what to travel in the van, and rest for a little after these decisions. Florence meanwhile would see the heavier pieces labelled, and after a pause make sure that all the labels were duly adhering. Then she had to put a second porter in charge of suitcase, rugs, coats, air-cushions, hot-water bottle, daily paper, and all else that was to be handed in to the travellers after Mr. Kemp had taken his seat. Mrs. Oxney, who had also come to the station, made herself very useful, as soon as the train came in, by ascertaining that the conductor of the luncheon car had reserved a table for two. Though all went off without a hitch, as far as could at present be ascertained, Mr. Kemp's face looked drawn and anxious as Nurse Babbit adjusted the window precisely to his liking, and he shook his head sadly at them through the glass, as the train moved out of the station.

CHAPTER IX

THE full and glorious noon of the Green Salon had evidently passed : collectors who were anxious to secure Howards for their galleries must have satisfied themselves, and when, on the morning of the day preceding its closing, neither visitors nor purchasers had entered its pictured walls the friends decided to occupy the remainder of the hours in beginning the packing of the works with little red stars on them. The pill box with these brevets inside was now found to be unaccountably empty, and the custodian when pressed acknowledged that, despairing of employing them for their ordained purpose, he had used them up (so that they should not be wasted) by affixing to the wall behind the door his own initials executed in red stars. There indeed his initials were, and Alice and Florence had to spend a considerable time in soaking them off. That was a matter of difficulty for they proved to be of first rate adhesive quality. But it was done now, and Florence in her homespun Norfolk jacket with no hat had hurried off into the town to purchase strong corrugated cardboard and brown paper.

Alice was feeling on edge : she had spent a sticky hour in detaching the custodian's odious initials, she was disappointed that the last few days of the Green Salon had been fruitless and she was worried over the deception she had been driven to practise on Florence about the ancestral home. That figured itself to her as a black hole in the fabric of life out of

which at any moment might pop out something sur-
prisingly unpleasant. So while her friend had gone
on her useful errand, she had nagged at the custodian
(on the lines of a wage-earning man behaving like a
child) for giving them so much trouble and the custodian
had grown sulky and sat perched on his stool like a
ruffled bird in livery with the pip, instead of the brightest
boy in Bolton. Yet after all the exhibition had been
a great success, and she thought with fortitude how
narrowly she had escaped acting on the diabolical
counsel of the young man from the *Bolton Gazette*, who
had criticised her pictures without ever seeing them,
and had advised her to put a quantity of stars on
virgin frames in order to encourage purchasers. She
had nearly done so : had it not been for Tim and Mrs.
Holders and those mysterious ladies and gentlemen
about whom the custodian could remember nothing,
she would surely have fallen. Nowadays she knew
something of the tangled web of deceit over her fabulous
ancestral home, and she was thankful to have been
spared further complications over the Green Salon.
If she had succumbed, she would now be in the power
of the sulky custodian.

This Pharisaical reflection had hardly entered her
head when there strolled into the Green Salon just as
if he had been the proprietor of the place the odious
young man to whom Miss Howard had in effect said
' Get thee behind me, Satan '. But here was Satan
in front of her again, and as he looked round at the
walls, on which twinkled this red milky way, he broke
into a broad grin and quite distinctly winked at the
artist in a most familiar manner. The moulting
bird slipped off his stool and produced the roll of
toilet-paper.

" Sixpence," he said sullenly.

" Press," said the critic.

He turned to Miss Howard.

" Well miss, you've had a rare success," he said,
" I see you took that tip I gave you. I remember
telling you to make believe to have sold half a dozen
pictures and you'd bring the buyers in all right. Very
pleased to have been of assistance, for that tip and my
little article did the trick for you. I'm not too proud,
I may add, to accept any little recognition you might
care to make me."

Miss Howard gasped with indignation. It was
really no use attempting, as Mrs. Bliss had recommended
her to do, to broadcast thoughts of love in every direction, for Mrs. Bliss had clearly no idea how some
situations could play the deuce with atmospherics.
But though powerless to broadcast loving thoughts,
she could still remember she was a Howard, and
moistened her lips with the tip of her tongue.

" I do remember your advising me to commit that
most dishonourable action," she said, " but I am glad
to say that your suggestion only appalled me."

This appeared to nettle Satan.

" Oh, come ! " he said. " I gave you a friendly
tip which I'm sure you took, and now you call me
dishonourable. Nasty of you, miss."

Trembling in every limb with the effort of being a
Howard, she turned to the custodian.

" Give me the list of the names and addresses of
purchasers," she said. " I want to show it to that
(she did not pause at all) gentleman."

A situation of peculiar psychological intensity had
arisen. There was Miss Howard in the consciousness
of virgin innocence, tempted but unfallen, there was
Satan blandly certain that she had fallen, and was a
liar too, there was the brightest boy in Bolton sulky
from his scolding who knew that there had been some
amazing hocus-pocus about the cataract of sales on
the first day when purchasers appeared, and had been
bribed to silence by half-a-crown. As he produced

the list of purchasers he began to think about
revenge.

Miss Howard spread this register in front of Satan.
All the entries were in order, number of pictures sold,
purchasers, addresses, and ' paid '.

Satan sniffed.

" Well, some do it direct, and some by deputy,"
he jeeringly observed.

At that, as the custodian thought of the two invisible ladies who had bought two pictures each, and
the two invisible gentlemen who had done the same,
the whole case became clear to his powerful intellect :
he no longer entertained the slightest doubt that Miss
Howard had bought the pictures herself by deputy.

" Will you kindly tell this gentleman," said Miss
Howard, " how you personally sold all these pictures
to different ladies and gentlemen and that I made no
private arrangements of any sort with you."

He hesitated : vengeance was sweet. It was on
the tip of his tongue to say what had actually happened.
But some of that half-crown was still in his pocket,
for his daily shillings nearly sufficed for his simple
needs.

" That's so," he said.   " Ladies and gents came in
here one after the other and made their buys, and
Miss Howard never said a word to me."

At the moment Miss Howard saw through the open
door, the approaching figure of Florence carrying the
contents of a stationer's shop. She turned her back
on Satan, and gave a little silvery laugh.

" Such fun, dear," she said. " This gentleman
once advised me to buy some of the pictures myself
in order to encourage others, and now he tells me that
I took his dishonest advice and wants me to give him
something for his suggestion.   A little like blackmail."

She turned to Satan again.

" Miss Kemp is one of the purchasers," she said.

" You will find her name there. I'm afraid that without
notice I cannot produce more of them. So if this is
all now quite clear, perhaps you would pay sixpence
for admission, if you want to look at my pictures
again. Please do not offer me your apologies which no
doubt you are anxious to do, because I could not
accept them. Good morning."

" Lor, that's a knock-out," said the brightest boy
in Bolton, in enthusiastic admiration of this superb
effrontery. (Of course Miss Howard had bought her
pictures herself.).

" A little off his head poor fellow," said Alice, as
soon as Satan had gone back presumably to his own
place. " Now let us begin our packing, dearest."

" What a monster," said Florence. " I wish I had
been here to tackle him."

" Quite unnecessary, darling," said Alice, still
trembling with passion. " Oh, what lovely corrugated
cardboard. I always feel it is a shame to use it."

The work of packing so many purchases and making
them safe for travel was lengthy, and conduced to
meditation except when Alice sat on the scissors or
Florence lost the pen for the direction of labels, when
it conduced merely to frenzied search. Florence
meditated about Alice, and said ' Liebster ' to her now
and then, when she could not repress her feelings, so
that the custodian should not understand. Alice
occasionally warbled a phrase of song but the undercurrent of her mind was occupied with the perfidy of
men in general as exemplified by her late visitor.
Above that ran a stream of thought concerned with
the eternal and infernal subject of the ancestral home,
which was daily getting more embarrassing. Only
last night she had been practically compelled, in answer
to a most inquisitive question of Colonel Chase's, to
say that the stables were at some little distance from
the house, for short of saying there were no stables

at all (which would have been incredible in a spacious
Queen Anne mansion) there was nothing else to be
said. Then too, Mrs. Oxney hoped before long to
spend a day or two with a cousin close to Tunbridge
Wells, and she wanted to know if the public were
admitted to the Park on any particular day of the
week, and whether ' The Croft ' was visible from the
line. Miss Howard had to give a guarded answer
to that ; she said that her tenants made their own
arrangements about admission, and that she did not
know what they were. She added (which was absolutely true) that you could see ' The Croft ' on the left
of the line as you approached Tunbridge Wells, and
in answer to a further pestering from the Colonel
(how she used to enjoy such pestering once !) that
there was no pheasant-shooting. It was really a
detestable situation for anyone who was not a professional liar, and it seemed to her thoroughly unde-
served. She had just let slip a few hints (all founded
on fact) about her little place, and it was her audience,
not she, who had distorted them into these monstrous
splendours. Colonel Chase was much the worst
offender : poor Alice would have been ready to take
her oath that she had never mentioned stables at all
till he asked about them, or alluded to the shooting,
and now her little place had stables at some distance
from the house, and though she had flatly denied that
there was any pheasant-shooting, she felt that she had
given the impression that there was plenty of room for
it. All the good that had come out of the growth
of her little place was that it had enabled her to make
up her mind that, with the Colonel's present conception
of it, it was quite impossible to marry him. Below
these uncomfortable meditations there continued to
flow the undercurrent of thought about the perfidy
of men, and suddenly it burst up like a geyser on to
the surface of her mind, startling her so much that the

ball of string with which she was tying up Lady Appledore's Curfew leapt from her lap and rolled away across the floor. She saw it all . . . this violent interest of the Colonel's in her little place was contemporary with his industrious wooing of her affections. The base wretch wanted to find out what (as well as whom) he would be marrying.

She gave a hoarse cry.

"Oh, the wickedness of him," she exclaimed. "I will never speak to him again."

Florence thought she was speaking of Satan, and laughed as she retrieved the ball of string.

"I ought to have been here to settle him," she said. "But you did it pretty well, liebster."

"No, I don't mean him," said Alice gasping. "I mean that base wicked Colonel. You know how he's been questioning me about my dear little home. I see it all. He wanted to find out about it before asking me to marry him. I couldn't have believed it of him, as I hate thinking evil of anybody, but I feel sure it's true. I am never wrong about the sudden intuitions which sometimes come to me."

Though Florence had repeatedly asserted that Colonel Chase was crazy about Alice for her own sake, she soon began to share this intuition, and the wooing which had been to her up till now a huge joke, assumed a sinister aspect. She had intuitions too, and now she remembered that she had never trusted the Colonel from the first moment that she set eyes on him, and she was never wrong about her first impressions. She would not quite give up her belief that he was crazy about Alice, but he was certainly crazy to live in her lovely house, and shoot over—no there weren't any pheasant-covers—and be the Squire of the countryside. He deserved—what did he not deserve—as punishment for his baseness ?

"Punished, punished, he must be punished," said

Florence, fiercely folding corrugated cardboard round
Geraniums. And look darling, at this very moment
I'm packing his picture for him. I do call that a
coincidence ! You mustn't mind about him : he isn't
worth it. Punished."

" But it hurts me," said Alice.

" Only because you're so good, and it hurts you that
a man can have been so wicked," said Florence.
" They're like that you know, I've often heard of men
wanting to marry girls because of their money. Base
creatures ! But it isn't as if you had ever cared about
him : you never dreamed of marrying the fat old
bicyclist. What are we to do to punish him ? That's
the point. For myself I shall simply cut him, though
I'm afraid he won't think that much of a punishment.
In fact he'll prefer it. We must think of something
better than that."

Alice again remembered, but with difficulty, that
she was a Howard. She moistened her lips.

" I beg you to drop any such idea altogether," she
said. " Because he has behaved like—well, like a
cad, that is all the more reason that we should behave
like ladies. It will mark the distance between us.
If he actually tells me he wants to marry me, I shall
permit myself a little scorn in refusing him, but that
will be all."

" But you would have done that in any case," said
obstinate Flo. " That's not punishment as I mean it,
I want something extra. He must be brought to feel
that he's not lost you only, for he never would have
got you, but all the wonderful things of yours he would
have got, if he had got you."

This seemed a very refined and complicated sort of
punishment, but as they proceeded with their packings
in the gradually fading light of the November day, the
shape of it outlined itself to Florence's vindictive
imagination. She disliked men, as such, to begin with,

she adored her Alice, and what she wanted (as she
whittled her idea to a sharp point) was to humble
Colonel Chase and exalt her well-beloved by one fell
stroke. She had for years suffered dumbly under the
yoke of paternal tyranny, and, now, emancipated,
she longed in the manner of a suffragette to damage a
man. Her emotional awakening had quickened her
keenness for the combats of life in which she used
mutely to surrender, and the design, yet vague, was
that Alice should not only win, but in the hour of
victory humiliate her adversary. Florence's chivalry
only existed for her own sex, men, as typified by the
Colonel, had to be beaten, and then rubbed in the dirt.
Simultaneously Alice, though she had told Florence
that they must behave like ladies, was following up
the same train of thought. Vengeance was surely
compatible, if she could only see how, with perfect
gentility. But for the life of her she could not see how.
She was startled from her gentle vindictive reverie
by a hoarse crowing sound from her friend. Only
extreme exaltation, she had already learned, made
Florence crow like that.

"I've got it," she cried. "Oh, darling, it's too
lovely ! He wants to know about your little place,
so tell him no end of lies about it. Make it bigger and
grander and splendider and magnificenter. A lake :
a lot of box hedges : a moat. Oh, don't you see ? Make
it a palace with a family vault and a village of tenants
and no entail. And then he'll propose to you, and
you'll say no, and he'll be in hell because of what he
has lost."

Now it might have been supposed that Miss Howard's
own uneasiness about the grandeurs of her ancestral
home would have made her recoil in horror from such
a suggestion. So for the first moment it did, and she
only just checked the exclamation of disdain that rose
to her lips. But immediately she saw like the gleam

of a lighthouse over stormy seas, a beam that heralded salvation. If she continued, now voluntarily, to ply the mercenary Colonel with visions of splendour and sumptuousness, she could save her face with regard to Florence. All her previous hints about the magnificence of ' The Croft ' which had been causing her such serious agitation, would be merged with all future lies as having been punishment for him. Florence no doubt, at this moment, shared Colonel Chase's illusions about her little place, but it would be much easier to muddle her up about them, if now, at her suggestion, Alice deliberately magnified its splendours.

" Darling, that would serve him right," she said thoughtfully. " But it wouldn't be truthful. ' The Croft ' is really quite a modest little place."

" You *must* do it," said Florence. " He must be punished, and I'm sure there's no better way of degrading him. How lucky he hasn't proposed to you already when he only knows the truth about ' The Croft ' ! "

Any impulse that Alice ever had to confess to her friend that the truth about ' The Croft ' was not known to anyone at Wentworth except herself, vanished. The far better chance was to adopt Florence's suggestion and go on making ' The Croft ' more and more manorial, until as might happen, it was necessary to demolish the exquisite old home, and reveal it to her in its true character as a semi-detached villa. Florence would be confused by that time : she would not know what magnificence, lawn or lake or park, ante-dated the Colonel's punishment which she had suggested. But there was Mrs. Oxney to think about as well, for she was one of the greediest imbibers of ancestral grandeur.

" And how about Mrs. Oxney ? " she asked. " She will hear it too, and get such a false idea about my little home. And if she goes to Tunbridge Wells as

she threatened—I mean, as she thought she might
be doing soon—she would be very much perplexed."

" Then wait till you get the Colonel alone," said
Florence brilliantly.   " You and me and the Colonel
I mean, for I'm in the plot, and of course I shan't
believe a word you say.   I shall egg you on.   I shall
make you tell lies."

" It will make me very uncomfortable having to
exaggerate so," said Alice with a sigh.   But she had
been very uncomfortable as it was.

Wentworth was emptying, as was usual in late
November, but there were fresh paying guests coming
in next week, and Mrs. Oxney, though she saw no
prospect of getting to Tunbridge Wells yet awhile,
oberved with strong satisfaction that Balmoral and
Blenheim and Belvoir were already closed for the
winter.   Mrs. Bliss having finished the cure she had
undertaken for the love she bore her husband, and
miraculously better in spite of it, owing to her per-
sistent denial that anything had ever been wrong
with her joints, since all was Harmony, left on the day
the Green Salon was closed, in the happy belief that
Mind and not Mrs. Holders and Tim had started purchasers.   So full of Harmony was she on the morning
of her departure that she refused to go to the station
in the bus, but set off to walk there (leaving plenty
of time in order to enjoy the sweet air) while her luggage
was to follow in a hand-cart.   It was well that it did
so, for Harmony most unaccountably became Discord
in the middle of this pedestrian effort, and produced
so realistic a similitude of shooting pains in her hip
that she was quite unable to proceed, but stood like a
statue, though still smiling, by the side of the road
waiting for deliverance.   The hand-cart overtook her,
and she was with difficulty hoisted on to it.   Pre-
cariously balanced on the edge of it, and holding on

to her dress-basket, she was trundled into the station, protesting that she had never enjoyed herself more. A comfortable seat in the train and rest soon brought Harmony back again.

Discussion over her and her gospel raged at Wentworth after she had gone : *pro*, there was the Colonel's cold, the success of his ghost story, her own improvement (or was that brine ?) and the miraculous sale of pictures; *contra*, her failure to walk to the station, and the fact that Mr. Kemp had not really improved at all : it was thought that his walking to the window had been a flash in the mental pan. The affair of the pedometer was not mentioned at all, because it always excited Colonel Chase. Tim Bullingdon, supported by Mrs. Holders, said that the whole thing was utter rubbish, and that he would sooner be completely crippled than cured by such charlatanry, and Mrs. Oxney ever pleasant, said, well, what an interesting talk they had all enjoyed.

An even more interesting talk, more stupendous, more imaginative, was held in the lounge that day after tea. Mrs. Holders and Tim had engagements with *masseurs*, Mrs. Oxney and her sister retired to their sitting-room, where their joint efforts over the cross-word puzzle were to compete with the solitary genius of Colonel Chase, who had consented for once to try his hand, and in consequence the three conversationalists were the two devoted friends and he. He had settled down with the paper and a sharp pencil in order to sit Florence out, and proposed to occupy the interval with the defeat of Mrs. Oxney and Mrs. Bertram. 'Small Scotch farmers' (undoubtedly beginning with *c*) was puzzling and Florence's account of the letter she had just received from her father distracted him.

"He's ever so much pleased, darling, with Nurse Babbit," she said to Alice. "Such bright conversation and so much interested in his case. She feels sure that within a week he will get the good effect of Bolton, but she doesn't think anything of Mind, and says that massage is far more reliable. A most comfortable journey, and quite a good lunch. He thinks he has left the small tin that held his night rusks behind, but there are rusks in Bournemouth. . . ."

Colonel Chase made an impatient movement in his chair. Who could concentrate on small Scotch farmers beginning with *c*, with such imbecile drivel going on ? She ought to have gone with her father. . .

Florence was silent a moment.

" Now do tell me more about the garden at ' The Croft '," she said. " I'm beginning to picture it."

Colonel Chase rapidly pencilled in the required word.

" Ha, I've got you to thank for that, Miss Kemp," he said, with unusual amiability. " Your saying the word ' croft ' put ' crofters ' into my mind. A remarkable coincidence."

" Quite extraordinary," said Florence.

" We don't disturb you by our chatter ? " asked Alice.

" Indeed no. Charming conversation, I'm sure," said he, laying down his pencil.

" My dear little house ! " said Alice. " I insist on your coming down to see it, Flo, when we are in London next week, for indeed I cannot do it justice. The dining-room windows open on to the lawn, or rather on to a raised terrace wall that runs the length of the house. Then you turn round the corner to the right, and there's the shrubbery with the winding walk through it. All beautiful flowering shrubs, some rare, I believe, but I'm so ignorant. It wants thinning out, my gardeners tell me."

" It sounds delicious," said Florence.

" Charming," said Colonel Chase. " Not half enough flowering shrubs in most old English gardens,

Pardon for interrupting you, Miss Howard, pray go on."

"Then you come into the bit of the garden which I love most," said Alice. "Another lawn with a little marble fountain and basin in the middle of it. The sweet cool drip of water on a hot day ! What a naughty little girl I must have been, for I bathed in it once. Papa only laughed, but Mamma sent me to bed. . . . On each side are the two long borders, very deep you know, as borders ought to be, with hollyhocks and sunflowers at the back. But sad ravage from the hollyhock disease this summer, I hear. I'm afraid it must be replanted. Then at the end the steps leading down into the rose-garden with the box hedges round it. Clumps cut into fantastic shapes, peacocks, and things like that."

" And are there any real peacocks ? " asked Florence.

Alice felt she could not manage peacocks.

" Ah, don't talk of them," she said, " for I've no peacocks now. How lovely they used to look sitting on the terrace wall. But they do make such a dreadful screaming, and they used to wake Mamma up in the early summer dawn, and she couldn't go to sleep again. They damage the flowers terribly too, so disappointing for the gardeners. And one day Papa said to me, ' Alice, do you vote for peacocks or gardens ? ' I felt like a murderer, though we gave them to friends and they got quite happy homes."

Florence cast a reproachful eye on her friend, for not saying that there were flocks of peacocks. But Alice's elaborate explanation almost made amends.

" I'm picturing it all," Florence said. " I am beginning to see it as if I was there. Take me behind the box hedges ; isn't the kitchen garden there ? "

" Yes : nice, old red-brick walls, and the glass-houses at the end."

" How many ? " asked Florence.

Alice sighed.

"Papa was always very particular about the glass," she said. "He liked to eat his own grapes, for then he knew they hadn't been covered with dust in a shop, and picked by goodness knows whom. . . . Let me see. There was the peach-house with the pots of strawberries for forcing ; we always had strawberries on Easter Day. Then there was the grape-house, black Hamburgs and Muscats, and a third for flowers. Bougainvillia and plumbago climbing up the walls and regiments of carnations."

Colonel Chase, greedily listening, began to wonder whether all this would not be beyond their joint means. The cross-word puzzle had long lain unregarded on his knee.

"Terribly expensive, was it not ? " he asked. "The garden must have cost a fortune to keep up."

Both the conspirators were at once on their guard against discouraging the Colonel : there was really no need for Florence to break in.

"Oh no," she said. "You told me, dearest Alice, that the gardens were self-supporting."

"Papa used always to say so," said Alice, "for after the house was supplied with flowers, the carnations used to be sent up to Covent Garden in great boxes, and they fetched an immense price. Grapes too and peaches. Papa used to say he should have been a fruit and flower merchant."

Colonel Chase was visibly relieved.

"Now take us inside the house," said greedy Florence. "I can't hear enough of it. Oh, it's cruel that you don't live there."

"No use making a fuss," said Alice, "and the same thing has happened to so many of us. Perhaps if I save up for a year, or two more, I might be able to live in a corner of it. But for the present it's let and I don't think about it at all bitterly. Indoors, did you say, Flo ? Is there a little summer shower which drives us indoors·? Let's come in then at the door opening into the rose-garden from the library. That will be the nearest way."

This voluptuous improvisation was as brilliant as anything that Alice could have executed with a great deal of practice on the piano, but it must be remembered that she had already practised diligently on her little place in Kent. The effect on Colonel Chase was admirable : the evening paper had fallen to the ground, and it was evident that if Miss Howard went on much longer Mrs. Oxney and her sister would easily win the cross-word race, for he had as yet got no further than ' Crofters ' and one other word along the top. It had also, as the astute Alice had anticipated a curiously confusing effect on Florence : Florence was already beginning to mix up what she thought was true about ' The Croft ' with what she knew was imaginary. Had Alice said there was a rose-garden before to-day, or told her about the shrubbery of flowering rarities ? ' Glass ' had certainly been mentioned before but without specification : there was only the impression of glass.

" Yes, come indoors quick, darling," said Florence, playing up admirably, " or you'll get wet, and I shall be obstinate and make you change before you show me round."

Colonel Chase said ' pshaw ' under his breath : he hated this silly playfulness and wanted to get to work indoors.

" Take care you don't slip on the parquet floor in the library," said Alice, pursuing these pretty fancies. " But just glance at it : cedar-wood parquet, and smells so good. That was Grandpapa Howard's addition : so stravvy of him ! But he loved his little library : not large, you see, but such a pleasant room. The chimney-piece looks empty now, but my tenants wouldn't take the responsibility of having the Chelsea figures out. Beauties they were——"

" Quite right of them," said the Colonel. " Fine
Chelsea is irreplaceable. I should put them in a cupboard myself. How many, Miss Howard ? "

" Only four," said Alice. " Poor little shepherds
and shepherdesses all in the dark in the strong room
at the Bank ! But they've got the Queen Anne silver
and a few little odds and ends to keep them company
and talk over the dear old times. And then we go
out across the hall, a pretty staircase, Flo ; there is
nothing like it at the Victoria and Albert Museum
(this was absolutely true) and into the drawing-room.
Rather long, rather narrow, like a gallery."

This was just what Colonel Chase had imagined :
telepathic almost.

" And I seem to see Queen Anne furniture again,"
he interpolated.

" Just a few choice little pieces. But such a ragged
carpet, is it not, though it was once a good Aubusson.
But Papa would have it used. At the far end is the
door into the smoking-room."

Mrs. Oxney and her sister came hurrying out of
their room at this rich moment.

" We've finished it all but the top right-hand corner,
Colonel," she said. " How far have you got ? Don't
say you've done it."

Had not four ladies been present, Colonel Chase
would certainly have damned two of them for their
interruption. He wanted terribly to hear about the
smoking-room which would probably be his ' den '.

" What can the small Scotch farmers be ? " asked
Mrs. Bertram. " That would give us the clue to the
difficult corner."

" Aha ! " said he. " I'm not going to tell you that.
And the time limit for our competition was dinner.
I've been lazy, listening to Miss Howard telling us
about her charming little place. Now I shall go up
to my room, and have a spell at the puzzle."

He picked up Mrs. Oxney's paper which she had carelessly laid down on the table, and saw a word or two which might be useful as starting-points. He put it down again hurriedly.

"God bless me," he said. "I thought that was my paper. Lucky I didn't see any of your words. And may I remind you, Miss Howard, that I put you on your honour not to betray the small Scotch farmers."

It was no use stopping any longer in the lounge, for the ladies would certainly sit chatting and chattering till the dressing-bell sounded, and there would be no chance of getting Miss Howard alone, but he took upstairs with him besides the evening paper, the fixed determination to propose to and be accepted by her, on the first possible opportunity. He had once harboured doubts about the size and quality of the little place in Kent, but it was evident now that instead of its being less imposing than he had cynically supposed, it was far more splendid than he had hitherto allowed himself to imagine. In her talk just now with that podgy masculine friend of hers, it was impossible that Miss Howard should have exaggerated its charms, for she was intending to take her down to see it and, as she had said, she could not do it justice in description ; and he was sure it would suit Squire Chase admirably. But he did not care for this friendship which had blazed into such flaming intimacy, and when he was married he would have to make it clear to his wife, firmly and if she was reasonable, kindly, that though ' Kemp ' (so he thought of her) had apparently renounced all girlish duties to her father for Alice's sake, there must be no question at all of her living with them or of paying more than brief and occasional visits. A man —the husband's friend—making long visits to the house was a different matter, for men effaced themselves all day on the golf links, and hobnobbed together in the host's ' den ' in the evening : besides a man required a little society of his own sex.

About the result of his suit he had no real doubt, for that would imply an absurd lack of self-respect, and, thank God, he had plenty of that. In the early days at Wentworth, before he had contemplated matrimony or had heard about the little place in Kent, he had been obliged several times to take no notice of Miss Howard's hints that she could ride a bicycle too with great speed, for he had not wanted to encourage false hopes. Now he regretted not having encouraged this, for they had ceased to be false, and the great plunge would have been easier to take : he would have slid into the water. Then that matter of the tenants must be looked into : he did not at present know what lease they held : a short one, he hoped, but if not it might be possible to get a clever lawyer to find a hole somewhere in it. Lawyers were all rascals : that was why you paid them so high : the convenient fellows did dirty work for a clean man.

He took a turn at the cross-word puzzle : the glimpse he had got at Mrs. Oxney's paper supplied some useful clues, and before the dressing-bell sounded he had finished with it, and sat down in front of his fire to think over the new life that was soon to open for him. He could not imagine why he had delayed to get married for so long, for, now that he was absolutely face to face with it, matrimony presented great attractions. Comfortable as he was at Wentworth, really remarkably comfortable, a home of his own would suit him better especially such a home as was waiting for him. He had debated at one time whether he should not give Mrs. Oxney the opportunity of providing one for him, but pleasant though that might be, he had never steadily regarded that prospect, and had shied away from matrimony in vague apprehension that it would entail loss of liberty and alarming obligations. But on approaching it now in a business-like manner, these terrors quite faded : he saw that instead of being bound to take care of a wife, it was her duty to take care of him. The idea of marrying a girl who had romantic notions and expected ecstasies of conjugal tenderness would have been a positive nightmare, but this was quite a different business. He felt himself indeed in luck, and Miss Howard was in luck too. To capture a fine upstanding honourable man like himself, with no blot on his scutcheon but several medals on his coat and a comfortable competence was more than any woman could expect at her age. She need be under no apprehension of frailties and infidelities on his part, which so often wrecked matrimony, nor need he, for they were both well past the skittish age.

With the closing of the Green Salon and the despatch of the purchased pictures to their owners, Miss Howard was now at liberty to paint more, or do anything else that presented itself as an agreeable pastime. She had still to settle what disposition to make of those pieces that remained unsold : of these there were some twenty-five. Christmas presents would absorb some ; her bedroom walls would absorb more, or Florence would ecstatically absorb them all. But next morning was warm and tranquil, and instead of tackling the heap of frames that were piled up in her bedroom, she decided to get hand and eye in touch again (for she had not taken up a paint-brush at all for a fortnight) and from the felled tree on the Colonel's golf links, of which a substantial trunk still remained, to make a little picture of Wentworth which, under the title of ' Home, Sweet Home ', she would present to Mrs. Oxney as a reward for having bought ' Pussy-dear.' But though this kind scheme was sufficient excuse for her spending the morning in so wonted a manner, it was not the reason for it. The reason she had talked over with Florence, and they had settled that the Colonel was ripe.

They were right about that, for he came down to breakfast, strung up and resolute, and had dreamed he dwelt in marble halls. Alice had moved over to Florence's table after Mr. Kemp's departure and when he appeared they were both demurely eating eggs. He ignored Kemp, but asked Alice what she was going to do on this lovely morning which was quite like spring. She thought she would do a sketch of the house from the links, and he figured her sitting there with Kemp holding her hand or her brushes. For his part, he was going to have a spin on his bicycle : wouldn't she join him ? Regretfully she wouldn't : she was going to be very industrious. The girls finished their breakfast first, and as they went out with waists and arms entwined, Alice certainly gave him a little sweet smile. Not a great joyous grimace like Mrs. Bliss ; that would have meant nothing, but something secret with a quiver at the corner of her mouth and a quiet glance, which seemed highly propitious. When he had finished his breakfast he found the lounge empty and the smoking-room empty, and the drawing-room empty, and supposed that they had gone out together. He damned Kemp and sat down to look through the illustrated *Morning Standard* which he had been taking in lately. After that he would start for a stupendous pedalling and bring home fresh laurels. Miss Howard reverenced these records. He felt quite up to proposing to her this minute, but he made sure that Kemp was with her. There were advertisements in the paper showing entrancing young ladies in corsets and knickerbockers and of fine stalwart men in plus fours. He thought the plus fours would suit him, and imagined seeing his wife in just such an elegant corset.

Along the landing upstairs came familiar warbling

noises and tripping feet. He scarcely looked up from his paper because he felt so certain that he would see the ubiquitous Kemp following Alice with her painting-satchel. Instead there was Alice alone carrying the implements of her craft herself. Alone— was it with a heightened colour that she perceived him ? —she went out of the front door, and of Kemp there was no sign. He stole to the window and observed her figure—really a very neat figure for her age— flitting in and out of the shadows of the trees in the garden. She went out of the gate into the golf field, and an obstructing shrub hid her further progress. She had said she was going to sketch there.

Mrs. Oxney, who had been very late that morning came out of the dining-room.

" What a lovely morning you've got for your bicycle ride, Colonel," she said. " Like April, isn't it ? I remember your saying that we often got April mornings in November, and November nights in April. So true. Will you be taking your lunch with you ? A sandwich or two of that capital cold turkey now."

" No, I shan't be out for lunch," said he. " Just a good spin and home again."

" And a fresh record, please, or I shall be sadly disappointed," said Mrs. Oxney going through to her sitting-room.

The sitting-room looked out the same way as the lounge : they both looked out on to the golf field. Mrs. Oxney was fond of birds and as she stood for a moment in the pale but genial sunshine, that poured in at the window, before ordering the bus that was to take Mr. Bullingdon to the station, she thought she saw a green woodpecker fussing about on the grass near one of the holes. It proved to be only a starling which was less interesting, but the same glance shewed her bits of Miss Howard through the edge of the shrub that had hid her movements from the Colonel in the lounge, seated on the trunk of the felled tree. She was facing the house and was evidently going to sketch.

She heard the front door bang (that would be the Colonel going out) and waited a moment more for the pleasure of seeing him set forth on his bicycle. Such vigour, such legs, such a mastery of the vehicle. There he was, but not on his bicycle whirling down the drive, but crossing it in the direction of the garden and the golf field. But he had not got his golf sticks with him : he was not meaning to play golf instead of going for his ride. Then in a flash the solution struck her. " I believe he's going to do it," she said to herself.

But though a woman, she was still a house-keeper, and she hurried to the bell, and ordered the bus to come round at 10.45 sharp for the London train. When she returned to the window Colonel Chase had vanished behind that tiresome shrub, and she wished she had had it cut down. But specks of him appeared at its edge, and they ranged themselves by those of Miss Howard, and Mrs. Oxney felt certain what his business was. Florence in her bedroom directly overhead knew it too and she had the advantage of being able to see over the tiresome shrub.

Miss Howard seated on her tree-trunk of course saw his approach but quite unaware of it, measured the height of a Wentworth chimney against her pencil. When his advancing presence was too large to disregard, she looked up brightly.

" Not gone for your ride, Colonel ? " she asked. " I call that lazy. Not like you."

A suitor's knees, he reflected, ought to tremble. His knees did not : they were as firm as oak-posts.

" No one can accuse you of laziness," said he. " Doing one of your charming sketches I see. A sketch of Wentworth is it ? Dear old Wentworth. Ha ! Dreams of happiness I've had here."

That was an excellent gambit: an improvisation
worthy of Miss Howard.

"Oh, how pleasant," said she. "Tell me about
them."

Any suitor would have considered that promising:
it sounded like an invitation, like an assured welcome.
She appeared quite calm too, though surely she must
have known that as he had abandoned his bicycle ride
and had come to the golf field, without his clubs, he
must have had some special and unusual mission.
He thought it would have been more like a lady of
true delicacy and refined instincts to have bent her
head over her drawing, unable to check the trembling
of her fingers, but her hand was as steady as his knees.
Or could it be that she had no idea that she was
presently to promise to be his wife ? Or did she guess
his mind more subtly yet, and know that in the approaching alliance, regard and respect were to fill the
place of tumultuous passion ? In any case she went
on drawing the cowl of the chimney with calm precision.

This direct invitation to tell her about his happy
dreams encouraged him to sit down on the trunk beside
her. Perhaps it was better, in case she was still unaware of her destiny, to make a few more remarks that
would lead up to the revelation.

"Somehow I don't seem to have had the opportunity of getting any quiet talk with you of late," he
said. "Your friend Miss Kemp——"

"Sweet Florence !" said Miss Howard very un-
expectedly. "She never knows when she's not
wanted, does she ? Such a dear, and such a crashing
bore."

That was splendid: he felt they understood each
other.

"I've found her so," he said, "I've often wished
she was at Bournemouth. Or I should have, if I had

not thought she was a friend of yours whose presence always gave you pleasure."

Miss Howard held up her sketch at arm's length and looked at the chimney : she had got it much too large. She looked at Wentworth, and saw the crashing bore at her bedroom window, peeping out from a half-drawn curtain.

" Tell me about your happy dreams, Colonel Chase," she said.

The moment had come. There could not be a better opportunity, nor one more obviously meant for him. He cleared his throat.

" Happy dreams about my future," he said. " I'm getting to be a lonely man, Miss Howard, and though I'm not old yet, the years are passing. I want a companion, a dear companion with whom I can share my joys and my sorrows. One who will make me happy, and whom, I trust I shall make happy. I shall do my best. I've long wanted to tell you this, and ask you, in fact I do so now, to be that companion. Will you marry me, Miss Howard ? "

" Certainly not," said Miss Howard.

He jumped to his feet as if he had been pinched, and now he found his knees were trembling. He could hardly believe what he had heard, but there seemed no doubt as to what she had said.

" You don't mean that ? " he asked.

" Yes, I do," said Miss Howard.

The little place in Kent seemed to explode into a million fragments with Colonel Chase among them : he fell giddily through the air and found himself again in the golf field at Wentworth, where Miss Howard seated on a tree-trunk was just opening her paint-box. As the incredible truth branded itself on his brain, he found that next to his disappointment, his keenest emotion was the desire that nobody should know of his awful, his astounding humiliation.

" I hope you will regard my proposal of marriage to you," he said, " as absolutely private. I made it out of my regard for you and of affection—— "

Miss Howard put down her paint-box in a great hurry : her hand was trembling now as much as Colonel Chase's knees.

" That's the finishing touch," she said. " Are you ashamed of having wanted to marry me ? Oh, Colonel Chase, you cut a very poor figure."

Three seconds later, Mrs. Oxney from her sitting-room window to which she had been glued, saw the Colonel reappearing on the left of the tiresome shrub, and her first mental ejaculation was ' Well, he has been quick.' Then, as he completely emerged, she saw he was alone and it looked as if Miss Howard had been quick. " I do believe she's gone and refused him," was her second ejaculation. " Well, I never ! What will he be like ? "

As he came closer, she fled from the window and busied herself in household affairs, for she had seen enough to know what he would be like. His foot crunched the gravel and she heard the front door bang. Then came the sound of an electric bell ringing, and after a pause in which no parlour-maid, though winged like Mercury, could have answered it, a repeated and a longer summons. At the third peal she reinforced her courage with her curiosity, and went out into the lounge to see what he wanted.

His hand was still on the bell-push.

" My sandwiches, Mrs. Oxney," he roared at her. " It's half-past ten and there's no sign of my sandwiches. Everything is disgracefully late this morning. Wentworth isn't what it used to be."

" But you told me you wouldn't take your lunch out, Colonel," she faltered. " I'll get it ready for you in a jiffy : turkey. But you did tell me—— "

" And am I not allowed to change my mind if I

choose ? " he interrupted. Off she flew to the kitchen, colliding with a parlour-maid who was running to answer the bell, for only Colonel Chase ever rang like that, and when the Colonel rang like that, O Lord !

Mrs. Oxney sliced off the choicest morsels of turkey, the cook cut the most delicate slices of bread, the kitchen-maid tore the heart out of a lettuce, the scullery-maid polished up an apple, and in an incredibly short space of time Mrs. Oxney was hurrying back with a pile of these propitiatory offerings neatly tied up. She could not, being a woman, help glancing at his furious face with eager sympathy as he stored them in his pockets, and the awful conviction came over him that it mattered very little whether Miss Howard behaved like a woman of honour or not, since nothing could be more evident than that Mrs. Oxney, by some infernal feminine instinct, knew all about it. He scowled back at her sympathetic looks, and she saw him from the window recklessly careering down the drive.

" Well, he is taking it like a man," she thought, and went to tell her sister.

It was impossible not to be thrilled, but it was difficult not to be a little anxious about the social atmosphere when Colonel Chase returned. The company of paying guests at Wentworth was now diminished, and out of the four left in the house, one was a rejected swain, the second a rejecting mistress, and the third the mistress's bosom friend. Wentworth prided itself on its harmonious existence for, given that the Colonel was in a good temper, they were all, as Mrs. Oxney often said, more like a happy family party than a collection of promiscuous guests. But it was stretching optimism to breaking point to suppose that he could possibly be in a good temper, and the prospect of a happy family party that evening was indeed small.

Mrs. Bertram (though thrilled) shook her head sadly over the outlook.

" I could almost wish the Colonel would catch one
of his worst colds," she said, " such as would keep him
in his room till Miss Howard and Miss Kemp leave us,
but that's not till the day after to-morrow.   Yet I'm
afraid there's little chance of that on such a mild day.
I can see she's sketching still, and Miss Kemp with her.
I didn't see the Colonel after his disappointment.
Was he much cut up, Margaret ? "

" More as if he'd like to cut somebody else up, and
I'm sure I don't wonder," said Mrs. Oxney.   " The
Colonel refused !   It hardly bears thinking of.   An
awful tantrum I should call it.   Such a ringing of
bells and such scowls at me when I brought him ever
so tasty a lunch."

" More angry than love-sick then ? " asked Mrs.
Bertram.

" I never thought he was love-sick, Amy," said Mrs.
Oxney.   " But when he expected a happy future in
store for him in that beautiful place of Miss Howard's,
it must have been a slap in the face.   Enough to
make any man in a tantrum, if he'd counted on it.
And such a pleasant arrangement for them both !   I'm
sorry."

" And then at dinner to-night," said Mrs. Bertram.
" Very awkward for Miss Howard sitting just opposite
the man she's refused.   Luckily you can always
count on her behaving like a perfect lady.   I only
hope that she and Miss Kemp won't sit and whisper
and giggle in a corner as they do sometimes, for the
Colonel's sure to think they're whispering about him,
and that'll make him mad.   I declare I shall be glad
to see the two ladies' backs when they leave us, and
never yet have I been glad when a guest has gone from
Wentworth."

An after-thought slowly struck her.

" And yet we don't know that the Colonel has proposed to Miss Howard," she said, " or that she's refused

him. You only saw him go out into the golf field, and come back quick and alone in a tantrum."

Such a suggestion was not, of course, worth answering.

Meanwhile the bright nickel-plated bicycle had been flashing along up hill and down dale with a speed unequalled in the establishment of any previous record, and its rider's state of mind may be faintly indicated by the fact that he had forgotten to put the pedometer back to zero. Rage and humiliation spurred him on, and it was not till he had left familiar country far behind, and his ankles ached with pedalling, that he dismounted and, sitting on a convenient gate, that he attempted coherently to review the repulsive situation. Love-sick he certainly was not : in a tantrum, yes. He had paid Miss Howard the highest compliment a respectable man can pay a respectable woman, and in refusing to take him, she had not expressed the smallest regret : it was idle to suppose that she felt any. And then there was ' The Croft ' : in losing Miss Howard he had lost ' The Croft ', and all the leisurely dignity of his imagined life there. He had vividly seen himself installed there, looking after his wife's agreeable property and he could scarcely yet believe that there was no more chance of his becoming Squire Chase of ' The Croft ', than there was of his being Archbishop of Canterbury. More than that, he had decided that matrimony in the abstract was preferable to bachelor life in the concrete, and now nobody, as far as he knew, was going to marry him at all. More than that, there was the return to Wentworth facing him, and just now he would almost sooner have faced the man-eater again. Wentworth, he unerringly divined, had been expecting him to honour Miss Howard, and in spite of his request to her that she should not mention her disdain of the honour, he already gathered that Mrs. Oxney knew. If Mrs. Oxney knew,

Mrs. Bertram would know, and as Miss Howard certainly knew, Kemp would know. He might just as well not have asked her to keep silence on this painful subject, and have been spared the information that he cut a very poor figure. Thinking it over, he was afraid he saw what she meant and, unaccustomed as he was to find fault with himself, it was rather a pity to have said that. . . .

He ate his lunch, and unable to go further, turned his bicycle homewards. Anyhow he would show Wentworth how gallant gentlemen behave in heart-breaking situations.

CHAPTER X

In spite of this manly resolution, Mrs. Bertram's gloomy forebodings were fulfilled, and the evening was ghastly in the extreme. Colonel Chase was rather late for dinner (unlike him) but his soup was being kept warm, and he marched into the dining-room with the evening paper under his arm and a fund of unnaturally cheerful observations. He could not notice Miss Howard, for that would have rendered magnanimity ridiculous, but never had he been otherwise so affable.

" Ha, Mrs. Holders," he said. " I crave your partnership at the bridge table after dinner. Mrs. Oxney and Mrs. Bertram? Yes? How you spoil me! I shall hope to wipe off the memory of the adverse fate—— "

From that moment everything went wrong. The news of his ' adverse fate ' with Miss Howard that morning instantly occurred to everybody and there was a general exchange of stealthy glances, and a feeling of great unease before the Colonel could indicate that he only alluded to the adverse fate which lost him one and ninepence last night.

" And there looks to be a tough cross-word puzzle this evening," he said to Mrs. Oxney. " I took a glance at it, and I think we shall find a worse crux than crofters."

This time he paused : he felt he must really take care of such pitfalls. Mrs. Oxney gallantly plunged into the silence.

" And you had a good ride I hope, Colonel," she said, skilfully changing the subject. " Where did you go ? "

" Out beyond Denton : a considerable way beyond Denton."

" Well, I do call that wonderful ! And you starting so much later than usual."

Mrs. Bertram trod heavily on her sister's foot under the table, to remind her what was the cause of the late start, and Mrs. Oxney's voice ceased as if the Telephone Exchange had cut her off. She gave a thin faint cry of dismay at what she had said, and of pain at what her sister had done, and Mrs. Bertram tried her hand at tactful conversation.

" It grows a little chilly," she said, " and we'd better have our game of bridge in the smoking-room. There's a beautiful fire of logs there : that trunk of the tree in the golf field had some sound wood in it— "

So Mrs. Oxney trod on her foot, and again there was silence. It was broken by Florence giving a sudden shriek of laughter for no apparent reason. So Miss Howard tried to account for that by implying that she had said something very droll.

" I thought that would amuse you, dear," she said loudly. " I saved that up to tell you. I was wondering, do you know, as I sketched this morning . . ."

Everybody joined in to cover up *that*. Mrs. Oxney called across to Mrs. Holders to know if she liked sea-kale cooked like this, and Florence put some eager questions to Mrs. Bertram on the subject of Pekinese dogs. Then it was seen that such pairings of conversationalists would never do, for they left Colonel Chase and Miss Howard sitting as dumb as sphinxes. In this diminished company all the occupied tables had been moved up near the fire for warmth and intimacy and Mrs. Oxney wished she had scattered them to the remotest corners of the room instead. Nervousness gripped them all for it seemed as if every topic of normal conversation had a live bomb entangled in its innocent meshes and no one knew exactly in what trivial subject it might not hide. Even the parlourmaids were becoming jumpy and losing their deft precision, and presently the hapless Mabel who served the Colonel let a perfect avalanche of walnuts fall on to his lap and the table-cloth and his plate and into his finger-bowl. The appalling explosion that followed drowned the rattlings and splashings of the nuts.

Mrs. Oxney hoped that when they settled down to bridge, the awful effort to behave naturally would be less of a strain. But Colonel Chase's resolve to conduct himself like a gallant gentleman produced the most embarrassing effect, for instead of hectoring and instructing and swanking as usual, he was polite and courtly and altogether unreal. Decorous silence reigned since conversation was so dangerous, interspersed with little compliments between partners on each other's sound declarations and skilful play and bad luck. Mrs. Oxney made a few attempts to be natural. She told her sister that she ought to have taken out trumps, and appealed to Colonel Chase to know whether that should not have been the correct course, but instead of lecturing about it, and repeating that he was famous throughout India for the observance of this excellent principle, he only said " I have no doubt you are right," which made Mrs. Holders look more surprised than she had ever been. They all knew that Miss Howard and Miss Kemp were together in the drawing-room, from which there proceeded occasional bursts of laughter, which sounded very merry, and it was impossible not to conjecture what caused them. It could only be one subject, and who could pretend to be interested in bridge, while the exact details of what had occurred that morning were

probably being humorously discussed ? Certainly Mrs.
Oxney could not. At half-past ten precisely, Colonel
Chase revoked and, instead of blaming Mrs. Holders for
not having asked him if he had any more clubs, had
apologised. This finished the rubber : he paid, said
good night to the stupefied company and went upstairs.

Tongues were loosed, for the strain was over. All
three ladies talked simultaneously, and when the
first torrent was spent, they agreed that they had
never seen a man so changed.

" Greatly improved," said Mrs. Holders severely.
" It would do him good to be refused every day."

" Oh, Mrs. Holders, how unkind ! " said Mrs. Oxney.
" Just think how affable he'd have been if Miss Howard
had accepted him."

" Affable ? Intolerable ! " said Mrs. Holders.
" But I doubt if the improvement's real. Did you
hear him when the nuts were spilt ? "

" Yes, he seemed more natural then," said Mrs.
Bertram. " But what a difficult thing it's been to
avoid dangerous ground. I shall go to bed, for it's
tired me out."

They were all tired out.

Florence was the first to come down next morning.
Papers and letters had arrived, and by her place was
the *Morning Standard*, which Colonel Chase also took
in, a chatty sheet with many pictures and thrilling
stories of how a Marchioness had swallowed a thimble,
and a child had rescued a Newfoundland dog from a
watery grave, and a golfer had taken a hole of pro-
digious length in one stroke which was an Eagle or a
Dodo, or some picturesque fowl. Alice took in *The
Times*, so also did Mrs. Oxney, though she never read it,
and Mrs. Holders had no paper at all.

Just as Florence sat down she saw a telegraph boy ride
past the window on a red bicycle. She wondered if

the telegram was for her, but when a couple of minutes had passed without its being brought her, she came to the very shrewd conclusion that it must be for somebody else. With a pleased anticipation of attractive little tit-bits she opened her paper. And then she opened her eyes and her mouth as well in horrified amazement. Though the letters seemed to dance before her eyes, she read :

FIRE AT TUNBRIDGE WELLS.

" A fire happily unattended with loss of life broke out about midnight at a semi-detached villa called ' The Croft ', in the Station Road at Tunbridge Wells. The house was tenanted by Mr. Algernon Gradge and his sister who with the two servants had a narrow escape. The flames mounted so quickly that they could not descend the only staircase but had to get through a trap door in the roof, and thus made their way into the adjoining house. ' The Croft ' itself was entirely burned out with all its contents and a mere shell of the outer walls remains."

For a moment, so wildly dissimilar was ' The Croft ' of the paragraph from the ancestral home of the Howards, Florence thought how odd it was that there should be two Crofts at Tunbridge Wells tenanted by four Gradges, but instantly she swept the notion aside as puerile. Then all that was finest and most loyal in her nature rallied from the shock, and thanking God that she was the earliest breakfaster and alone in the dining-room, she scudded across to Colonel Chase's table, plucked from it his copy of the *Morning Standard*, folded it up and sat on it. Hardly had she effected this noble larceny, when the door opened and he came in. Florence felt faint at the thought of what would have happened if he had been half a minute earlier, or if she had not pulled her wits together so quickly. That he should know that ' The Croft ' was a semi-detached villa was so appalling a thought that she felt as if her hair had turned grey. Even as it was, she might not have averted the catastrophe, for there might be some mention of the fire in *The Times*. She opened Alice's copy and skimmed the pages : to her unutterable relief there was no record of it.

" Mabel," said Colonel Chase in an awful voice. " The papers have come in, haven't they ? Why isn't my *Morning Standard* here ? "

Mabel couldn't say. It was not her job to distribute the papers.

" Then get me another copy," said the Colonel.

Florence's heart sank like lead in an unplumbed sea. It rose again like a balloon when Mabel came back to say that the paper boy had gone. All might yet be saved.

" Pshaw ! " said Colonel Chase, whose gallantry seemed to have evaporated during the night. " Boiled egg and bacon, not cut in cubes, but in slices."

" Beg your pardon, sir ? " said Mabel.

" Thin," said Colonel Chase.

Mabel hurried out and Alice hurried in. She held a telegram in her hand and spread it before Florence.

" The most terrible shock," she began. " All my beautiful——"

" Hush," said Florence in a low voice. " I know all about it. There was a paragraph in the *Morning Standard*. Station Road, semi-detached villa."

She sank her voice lower yet.

" He doesn't know," she said. " I was down first. As soon as I saw it I stole his *Morning Standard*. A narrow squeak. I'm sitting on it."

The immense relief of that took precedence of everything else in Alice's mind.

" You angel ! " she said.

" I know. It was smart of me. Now we can't talk here, so finish your breakfast quickly and join me."

By a marvellous piece of legerdemain Florence

managed with much rustling to fold the stolen copy
of the *Morning Standard* inside Alice's *Times*, and
having appointed her own bedroom as a rendezvous
where they would be certainly safe from Colonel
Chase, she left Alice to follow her. Alice had acknowledged the identity of the ancestral home with a semi-
detached villa in the Station Road, and Florence felt
rather puzzled.

Alice lingered rather than hurried over her breakfast,
for a little quiet meditation would not be amiss before
she talked things over with Florence. The more she
considered her loss, the less shocking did it appear,
for the family seat was an odious little house when
shorn of the trailing clouds of glory with which she had
decked it, and it was fully insured. She had been
anxious also about the disclosure she would have to
make to Florence before her projected pilgrimage to
visit the shrine ; it would have been an unpleasant job,
but this convenient conflagration had removed the
necessity of telling Florence, for now Florence knew.
It was as if she had been dreading the extraction of a
tooth, and now awoke (as from an anæsthetic) to find
that the agony was over without her having perceived
it : the family seat, which had been causing her pangs
was gone. Exactly how Florence would take the loss
was another question, but she had no very grave
apprehensions about that, for Florence had herself
suggested that she should tell the Colonel all sorts of
lies about the little place, and after that these greater
splendours which she knew to be false would eclipse
such lesser glories as she might believe to be true.
There was therefore not more than a shade of nervousness about her tripping step or her warblings as she
went upstairs to Florence's bedroom. The moment
she opened the door her friend began to speak : she
had been thinking things over too.

" The evening paper is the next danger," she said,

" but I daresay there'll be nothing about it. Only a semi-detached villa, you see, and no lives lost, and even if there had been, it would only have been Gradges. Oh, darling, I am so glad that 'The Croft' wasn't what I thought it."

Alice did not much like that last remark : Florence was not as muddled up as she hoped. She pressed her hand to her forehead.

" I feel so confused," she said. " It was only two days ago that you insisted on punishing Colonel Chase— that was what you called it—by making me tell all sorts of fibs about 'The Croft'. But you knew they were fibs."

" Oh, but what I meant was before that," said Florence. " What makes me so glad was that it wasn't a big place as—as I thought it, with rose-garden and a Park and peaches."

" But, I don't understand," said Alice. " I never mentioned a Park or peaches till you insisted on my doing so, in order to encourage Colonel Chase and then make him writhe over what he had lost."

Florence did not understand either.

" But the lawn," she said, " and your gardeners, and all those other beautiful things."

" There was a lawn," said Alice, " not large, I never said large, but a lawn."

" And the greenhouses——" said Florence.

" You made me invent the greenhouses," said Alice, " and the box hedge. That was two nights ago."

" But the general sense," said Florence. " Ask Mrs. Oxney what she thought 'The Croft' was like. And you said it would hurt you to go down there with me. A semi-detached villa wouldn't hurt anybody."

There was a dreadful truth in that which it was impossible to combat. But all the wise men in the world in consultation with all the wise women in the world could not have suggested a sounder manœuvre than that which Alice instantly executed. She burst into tears.

"You are very cruel," she sobbed. "To please you I invented a lot of lies, and now you tell me I'm a liar. Whose fault is it that I am?"

"No, but before that, before that," repeated Florence.

"Before or after makes little difference," said Alice, continuing to sob, "if that's what you think of me. If you feel like that, I can't imagine why you took away Colonel Chase's *Morning Standard*. I can't think why you didn't shew it him and laugh over it together. If you believe I've been telling you lies it's your duty to expose me. Tell Mrs. Oxney, tell Mrs. Holders, and particularly tell Colonel Chase."

Reason and affection battled together in Florence's rather male mind. She knew she was right and she knew that Alice knew she was right. It was not just that she should have to give up her point. Meantime the friend of her heart, the brilliant, the accomplished Alice was sobbing.

"Darling, don't suggest such absurd things," she said. "Don't you see that my whole object is to keep this secret? I should hate anybody to know what 'The Croft' was really like. But how—oh, what is there to cry about?—how could I have got the idea that it was an old country-house with lovely gardens except from you? Nobody else ever told me about it or—or I should have known what it really was. And I daresay it was a very nice little house."

Alice took not the smallest notice of this admirable logic. She continued sobbing and sticking to her point. "And now just because you've got a wrong idea about it," she wailed, "owing to what you yourself insisted I should tell Colonel Chase you say I've been deceiving you. First my house is burnt down and all my things, and on the top of that the only person in the world whom I thought trusted and loved me turns against me."

This was heart-breaking.

" But I don't turn against you," said the agonised Florence. " And I do love you."

Alice held out the copy of the *Morning Standard* in the hand that was not engaged with her handkerchief.

" Please take it to Colonel Chase," she said. " I think it's your duty."

" It isn't my duty, and if it was I shouldn't do it." cried Florence.

Alice made a master-stroke. Quite improvised.

" Then I shall," she said. " I shall say my best friend tells me I have been deceiving everybody. I shall not dream of saying that you suggested it. I shall take the whole blame."

" But you can't," said Florence bouncing to the door, and standing in front of it. " Besides I am responsible for all the worst things. Telling anybody is the one thing out of the question. I couldn't bear anybody knowing. You shan't go ! Oh, do sit down, darling, and let me think a minute."

Alice sat down again and with tear-dimmed eyes, gazed out of the window over the golf field, while Florence's heart made furious attacks on her brain. She thought over the larger splendours of ' The Croft ', the shrubbery of flowering rarities, the sweet rose-garden, the fountain where naughty Alice had bathed, the greenhouses of Muscat grapes, the stables, the pheasant-shooting (no, not the pheasant-shooting ; Alice had distinctly stated that there was no pheasant-shooting) and all these, it was true, had been inventions made at her instigation. Indoors there was the library and the cedar-wood parquet, and the gallery-room, and at the bank the Chelsea figures and the Queen Anne silver and all these too, had sprung into being at her behest. She began to wonder on what her earlier impressions (though still distinct) of 'The Croft' were based : she tried to recollect a single definite statement of Alice's made previously, she began to grow confused and vague. Had all the splendours which she knew to be inventions stained her previous memories and rendered them more highly-coloured ? She knew that it was not so, but now her heart had got a strangle-hold on her mind, and was forcing it to make admissions under torture, for there was Alice, whom she adored, blowing her nose and wiping her eyes and being miserable. Every now and then reason gasped out to her. ' But Alice *did* lie about ' The Croft.' Ask Mrs. Oxney,' but these rational gaspings were growing fainter as her pain at Alice's distress grew stronger, and the need for her affection more insistent. Florence believed that Alice, too, was fond of her, and it was wretched for her to lose her house and her friend before lunch-time. And she herself could not face the loss of Alice.

" Perhaps I'm altogether wrong," she said. " Perhaps it was only the inventions which I insisted on that made me think you had said the same sort of things before, only less so, about ' The Croft '."

" Far better ask Mrs. Oxney, if you're not sure about it," said Alice, repeating the master-stroke, " or best of all ask Colonel Chase. Tell him all about it."

" How could I do anything of the kind ? " asked Florence. " How can you think me so disloyal ? "

" It isn't very loyal to think those things of me at all," said Alice.

Florence's heart gave a crow of triumph, for her reason gave one convulsive struggle and expired.

" I must have been entirely mistaken," she said. " Oh, how dreadful of me. And I've hurt you : that's worst of all."

" A little," said Alice huskily. " Not much. It doesn't matter."

" But it does matter. It matters terribly. Oh, do forgive me."

The reconciliation, though now certain, was not fully accomplished. Florence, in contrition, had to abase herself further, and Alice to concede that perhaps, unthinkingly, she had said things about The Croft which might lead imaginative minds to think that it was something of larger scale than a semi-detached villa in the Station Road. She could not think what they were, but there might have been something. . . . Then they turned with kisses and caresses to consider the dangers and exposures that still threatened.

" There's nothing in *The Times*," said Florence, " and I don't think it is likely to have anything to-morrow."

" But there are the evening papers, that *Evening Gazette* which the Colonel takes in," said Alice. " It has columns of little paragraphs."

" That's true. But he's usually out when it comes, and I will lie in wait and glance through it."

" And if there is ? " asked Alice.

" Steal it, darling," said Florence, " like his morning paper."

" How brave you are ! But won't he think it odd if both his papers go wrong to-day ? "

" I shouldn't wonder if he did," said Florence. " But he would think it odder if he saw about ' The Croft '. And after to-day, there won't really be any risk, and to-morrow we go. Oh, what a lovely time we shall have in London now that we're at one again."

" You dear ! " said Alice. " By the way, ' The Croft ' is fully insured. And what shall we do now ? Shan't we go out ? "

" Let's ! And may I come and sit with you in the

golf field while you finish your sketch ? I shall sit just where the Colonel sat and make love to you."

Alice pressed her hand.

" And when my sketch is finished," she said, " it shall be your's. I thought of calling it ' Home Sweet Home ', and giving it to Mrs. Oxney. But now it shall be ' Blessings on the falling-out '. No one will understand that but you and I."

They went out together in a stiff gale of renewed tenderness, with linked skippings and gambollings, Florence carrying the satchel with the painting utensils for the falling-out picture, and Alice gaily warbling. Careful though they had been in providing against future perils by the plot of stealing Colonel Chase's evening paper, they forgot, like most criminals, the most obvious precaution of destroying the two copies of the incriminating *Morning Standard*. The consequences might have been dire, for Mabel, hurrying in with duster and slop-pail to ' do ' Florence's room, found them there, and bethought herself to take one to the Colonel. Then, luckily, she remembered how odiously disagreeable he had been about the cataracts of walnuts last night, and decided not to gratify him. Instead, she took them away, and tossed them on to the store of paper used for kindling in the kitchen cupboard. There for the present they lay innocuous, but like mines charged with deadly matter, they needed only a touch of blundering circumstance to cause a devastating explosion.

The thieves spent a tuneful, artistic and affectionate morning. Now that the catastrophe had happened, Alice felt greatly relieved, for all anxiety over Florence's discovering the truth about ' The Croft ' was over, and so well and pathetically had she herself managed that the crisis had only brought them closer together. The sketch promised to be one of the artist's most successful pieces, and the paint-brush dripped with sentiment, for the window of Florence's room, where the endearing falling out had occurred was visible above the shrub, and Alice attempted to portray her figure standing there. But her face would not look otherwise than like the globe of a lamp, and so she drew a blue curtain over it, and obstinate Flo was now behind the blue curtain just as she had been yesterday morning, when Colonel Chase made his declaration. Then there were plans to be made for the future : the fortnight in London became a firm month, after which Florence must spend Christmas with her father, and Alice would go to Torquay for sea-air and marine material for artistry.

" You must join me there for a bit," said she. " Red sandstone cliffs, the blue, blue sea. Anstey's Cove. Such lovely serpentine rocks."

Florence did not reply for a moment, and Alice having made a blue, blue curtain, nudged her.

" Won't you ? " she said.

Florence drew a long breath. She felt her moment had come.

" Yes, of course I will," she said, " but those are only little temporary plans. I want a permanent one. Mayn't we make a permanent plan, darling ? I mean, won't you come to live with me altogether in London ? The flat is mine, Mamma left it me, and I believe we should be so happy. Don't say ' Certainly not ', as you said yesterday to that absurd man. I would do all the housekeeping, or, if it amused you, you should. I think you'd like it better than Wentworth, and as for me, bliss. You shall subscribe to expenses or not just as you like. And Papa won't want me again, for Nurse Babbit exactly suits him. I shall be quite alone otherwise, but that mustn't influence you : I don't appeal to you, though I should be miserable without you."

The sketch, with Florence supposedly behind the

blue curtain, slipped unregarded from Alice's hand, for Florence had come out from behind all curtains.

" Oh, Florence, are you sure ? " she asked.

" Positive," said Florence.

" So am I, then," said Alice.

The moment had grown quite solemn. They looked at each other in silence, they gravely kissed. Then Alice said :

" I told a heap of lies about that villa, I made it out to be grand and it was a horrible little place, and the shunting at the station used to keep me awake. The rent was fifty pounds a year."

Florence appreciated that at its full value.

" Oh, I am glad you told me," she said hurriedly, " and now it's quite over. Darling, just think ; yesterday the Colonel sat just where I'm sitting, when you said ' Certainly not ', and now, bless you, you say ' Certainly so '. I long to tell him you're going to live with me instead of him. How he would hate me ! Delicious ! But then you'll have to tell Mrs. Oxney that you're not coming back here, so it will get round."

The two went off next day on their honeymoon, but as their rooms were to be filled up at once, Mrs. Oxney resigned herself to their departure. She felt, too, that the Colonel would never settle down to his old ways while the constant reminder of his disappointment was there. Indeed the news that Wentworth would never again ring with Miss Howard's bright little snatches of song was compensated for by the consideration that Colonel Chase would very likely have gone away if she had stopped, and of the two she vastly preferred him. A man, and such a fine big man, was a much more valuable social nucleus in the house, for in his robust hectoring way he kept things up to the mark, and told his grim or amusing stories, and laid down the law at bridge, and made it seem an honour to play with him. Of course he lost

his temper, and had tantrums, but then he recovered
it again and made a fresh record on his bicycle. He was
an asset, a distinction, a Colonel was better than a
plain Miss to rally round. She quite made up her mind
to put in the extra bathroom when he went away for a
fortnight at Christmas. It would be ready for his
return, and that would be a nice surprise for him.

Colonel Chase made a remarkable recovery after
Miss Howard's departure, and in the week or two that
remained before his Christmas holiday, so well earned
by his busy life at Wentworth, he established himself
with the new paying guests, elderly and hobbling
ladies, as an athlete and an authority on most subjects.
There was some very pleasant bridge the night before
he left, but he broke the table up at ten o'clock, as
he was off quite early in the morning and had yet his
packing to do.

"I never trust anybody to do my packing for me,"
he said, "and if I had fifty valets I would still do it.
In India, whatever the thermometer stood at, I invariably packed for myself. Give me plenty of paper
to wrap my kit up in, and there'll be no shaking about
or breakages."

"Nobody can pack like you, Colonel," said Mrs.
Oxney, "I always used to pride myself on my packing,
till once I saw you doing it. Like a mosaic : everything fitting so that there wasn't a chink anywhere.
And the amount you get in, astonishing ! "

Colonel Chase's bed was piled up high with his
clothes and other effects, waiting for his mosaic touch,
but he had made very little progress in his astonishing
art, when he saw that there was not nearly enough
paper. Up came Mabel in answer to his summons,
and down went Mabel, and up she came again with a
pile of newspapers.

"Thankye," said Colonel Chase, feeling in his pocket

for some small change as Christmas was approaching. Three of the larger coins would be a generous tip, but then he remembered the cataract of nuts, and let one of them slip back into his pocket again.

His manual dexterity did not entirely occupy his mind : he could ruminate while he made his mosaic, and as he wrapped up boots and fitted Macaulay's essays among them to keep them tight, he thought over his disappointment. It was still a bitter reflection that owing to a woman's perverseness he could not now look forward to being the master of a fine Queen Anne Manor House with gardens and greenhouses and galleries, for he still felt that he was absolutely cut out to fill that post. Instead the misguided lady had gone off to live in frumpy spinster partnership with one of the most tiresome creatures he had ever come across. Together perhaps, for he understood that Kemp was well off, they would settle into ' The Croft ', when Miss Howard's tenants came to the end of their lease, and get cheated by the gardeners and never have a peach or a bunch of grapes for their own table. A woman could manage a house (he had fully intended his wife to manage her's) but with an estate like that a man's grasp and authority were required, or everything ran to seed. The county club, the comfortable little parties, the position of Squire Howard-Chase ! Well, it was no use thinking about it, and after all Wentworth was very comfortable, and the newcomers seemed reverential women, and he hoped they would stop on.

He picked up one of the papers that had been brought him by Mabel, and his eye was arrested by a remarkable picture of a baboon on the first page, which was unfamiliar to him. Yet the paper was the *Morning Standard* which he saw every day, and he could not imagine how he had forgotten this grimacing ape. He turned the leaf, and found another picture he was sure he had not seen before, and at that fateful moment he remembered that some few mornings ago his *Standard* had not arrived. Then his eye fell on a headline: "Fire at Tunbridge Wells", and in the ensuing paragraph on the words, "a semi-detached villa called 'The Croft'." He gave one loud raucous exclamation, and next moment, without pausing to put on his coat, which he had shed for his mosaic-work, he was bounding downstairs, with the pedometer clicking madly in his pocket. The smoking-room where they had played bridge, was empty and he hurried to Mrs. Oxney's sitting-room, and entered without knocking. There she was with her skirt turned back over her knees, warming her shins at the fire and eating seed-cake.

"Why, whatever's the matter, Colonel?" she cried, hastily putting down her skirt and her seed-cake. "Nothing wrong, I hope?"

"Wrong?" he echoed, brandishing the *Morning Standard*. "Listen to this. Fire at Tunbridge Wells, Mrs. Oxney."

"Gracious me, how dangerous! Not . . . not Miss Howard's beautiful place?" she cried.

"You've guessed! You're right! But there's something you've not guessed. 'The Croft' was burned out, but what do you suppose 'The Croft' was? A semi-detached villa, Mrs. Oxney, a semi-detached villa in the Station Road!"

"It must be another one," said Mrs. Oxney faintly.

"Not a bit of it. Tenants were occupying it: the Gradges. Don't you remember the name? I do. Station Road: semi-detached villa. What a liar the woman is with her manor house and her shrubberies and her rose-gardens, and her gallery-room. Family portraits too: a couple of photographs I expect. I'll tell you what I think: the descendant of the noble house made up all that swaggering nonsense just to entrap me into——"

On second thoughts that wouldn't do, but the Colonel continued with no pause at all.

"—she wanted to make us all think she was of the landed gentry. Swank! Lies! The painful necessity of letting her beautiful place, but no repining, brave girl, because it's happened to so many of her class! But what's the class, I ask you? The semi-detached class. Curates and apothecaries and chimney sweeps! Why my tailor's name is Howard, though I never taxed Miss Howard with that. But to think of the escape I've had! 'The Croft', a semi-detached villa!"

This was a mistake. Mrs. Oxney, horrified as she was (for she had been talking only this evening to some of the new guests, with regret that Miss Howard, who had that lovely place in Kent, had just gone) could not think so ill of the Colonel as to imagine that he had been "after" the exploded and now burned-out 'Croft', instead of its mistress. Yet his words did lend themselves to such an interpretation.

"Why, you speak as if it was The Croft that had enticed you, Colonel," she said. "To be sure, it does look as if Miss Howard had made it out a bit grander than it was, but surely it was she you wanted. I should hate to believe otherwise of you, though to be sure it was disappointing to think that you'd lost all that beautiful property as well as your young lady."

Colonel Chase thought for the moment that he was in a hole. But his excitement had sharpened his wits to an extraordinary acuteness, and he saw a loophole.

"I repeat that I've had an escape," he said weightily. "When I proposed, as I did, to the lady you designate as young, I thought her an accomplished woman within limits, and not without charm, but above all an honourable and truthful woman. This information, which I stumbled on by accident, shows me that her

idea of truth is different from mine, and long may it
remain so. That's what I mean by an escape. Sooner
or later, it would have turned out that she had grossly
lied about 'The Croft'. I could never have trusted her
again, and misery would have followed on marriage.
And when I think of all I have done for her, the pictures
I have bought, the offer of a name which though no
doubt obscure is yet honourable : then I repeat, as
often as you like, that I have had an escape. Ha ! "

Mrs. Oxney, pored over the fatal paragraph, sadly
clicking her tongue against her teeth.

" It does look as if she had deceived us," she said.
" I wouldn't have thought it of her."

" Then I would, Mrs. Oxney," said Colonel Chase.
" I never really trusted her. That improvisation at
which she had been practising for days ! I could
have whistled it before she played it at the entertainment. It's all of a piece."

Mrs. Oxney felt that Miss Howard could not be so
black as the Colonel was painting her. She had to
stand up for her sex.

" But you knew that before you proposed to her,"
she said. " Besides, where's the harm ? "

" I did know it : you are right," said Colonel Chase.
" I hoped that these little superficial fibs were no part
of her real nature. But now ! Instead of the Queen
Anne manor house, and the grape-house and the
peach-house and the bathing-pool —— "

" No ! Not bathing-pool ? " asked Mrs. Oxney.

" Bathing-pool. She bathed there when a girl—
and the shrubberies and ancestralcies, we have a semi-
detached villa in the Station Road. Ha, ha, ha !
Stupendous I repeat. Enough. Dear me, I am
talking to you in my shirt-sleeves. Very remiss of
me ; I hope I have a better idea of what is due to the
other sex than Miss Howard has. The peaches and
the Muscat grapes ! If a peach or a grape ever found

its way into 'The Croft', it came from a barrow in the
Station Road. We should have had a banana-grove
next. However, I wish Miss Howard well, and I shall
certainly send her a sympathetic note, condoling with
her on the loss of her semi-detached villa, and hoping
that its treasures are amply insured."

So happy a mixture of essential spite and apparent
magnanimity could hardly be believed, and, hoarse
with rhetoric Colonel Chase ceased foaming at the
mouth and straddling in front of the fire-place, and sat
down as calm as the centre of a cyclone. Mrs. Oxney
he supposed, had got used to the informality of his
shirt-sleeves by now, and if she hadn't, she never would.

" Well, I'm sure you're very forgiving, Colonel," she
said, " after the way Miss Howard has treated you.
I've often noticed how large-minded soldiers are. Mr.
Oxney was, though, to be sure, he was only in the
Militia. And I quite misunderstood you, I see. I
thought at first that you meant that you'd had an escape
because ' The Croft ' wasn't quite what you thought
it, now I see you weren't such a mercenary. Poor
Miss Howard, what she's lost when you gave her the
chance. It all comes of not being quite truthful."

It occurred to Colonel Chase that Miss Howard's
painful untruthfulness had been the cause not of her
losing him, but of her having the opportunity to win
him, if she had been disposed. But to correct Mrs.
Oxney (as they were not playing bridge, but having
a heart-to-heart talk), would be the act of a pedant,
and he let her faulty logic pass. . . . There she sat in
her rich evening silk, very sympathetic and very
comely, and quite void of deceit. He knew all about
her, the solidity of her connexion, the excellence of
her table, the admirable house-keeping qualities which
made Wentworth so comfortable. After this turmoil
of emotion these were peaceful thoughts.

" I have been deceived in Miss Howard," he said,

" but I dismiss it from my mind, and will not suffer it
to sully the respect in which I have always held her
sex. My experience of it has been far otherwise,
and I have no doubt that it will continue to be so."

He was astonished at the perfect phrasing of his
magnanimous sentiments : Macaulay's Essays could
contain nothing more simple and dignified. The
clock on the mantel-piece struck, and with scarcely
less astonishment he heard it announce midnight.

" God bless my soul," he cried, springing actively
up from his low chair. " I had no idea it was so late.
My packing still only half-finished, and you—ha, your
beauty-sleep. Time for little boys and girls to be in
bed, Mrs. Oxney. But this little boy has still to finish
his packing. He will be glad when the day comes for
him to pack again, and return to charming Wentworth."

Mrs. Oxney was almost daring enough to offer to
help in the mosaic-making. But perhaps that was
a little too modern, and she contented herself with
reciprocating his wish.

" Come back soon, Colonel," she said. " Your
room will always be ready for you, and I hope I shall
have a little surprise in store for your return. It won't
be Wentworth without you."

EPILOGUE

Florence and Alice happened to go to the Zoological Gardens on the afternoon of the day when Colonel Chase's letter of condolence on the loss of the semi-detached villa had arrived. There they visited the monkey-house, and observing the antics of a most indelicate and ill-favoured ape exclaimed simultaneously :

" The Colonel ! "

" So like, and just that swaggering manner," said Alice.

" And look at him chattering with rage," said Florence. " Just like his face when there came that avalanche of walnuts. Poor Mabel."

" But this one chatters because there are no nuts," said Alice. " Otherwise there's no difference at all."

" Let's get him some nuts," said Florence, " and we'll see how he behaves when he eats. That'll be a test if he's really the Colonel."

This was done : they burst into shrieks of laughter.

" So it *is* the Colonel," said Alice. " No one else eats like that : no one could. What a sad change for him ! No pedometer and bicycle rides. But I daresay that swinging on that rope does as well, and he tells them all how many times he has swung."

They laughed again, and the keeper asked them not to irritate the animals.

The month's honeymoon had gone in a sunny flash, and now after Florence's Christmas visit to Bournemouth they were back in the flat again and had settled down.   Alice was terribly busy over the most important picture of her career :   Winter Sunset in Kensington Gardens,   a very large sketch.   She painted chiefly in the morning, because it was warmer then, but often came back towards dark for colour notes.   Florence always sat on a camp-stool to her right, in order to keep the admiring connoisseurs of London from encroaching too near her painting-arm.

To-day at breakfast Florence was urging her friend to take a morning off, for she thought she had been working too hard.

" Besides, darling," she said, " the sun's so very bright.   You can't paint dusk in very strong sunlight, you've often said so.   There'll be plenty of grey days. And you do look a little tired.   Stay quiet this morning :   you may play the piano."

" Are those Doctor Florence's orders ? " asked Alice picking up *The Times*.

" Yes, and she's very firm.   This afternoon we'll go to the Zoo again, and see how the Colonel is getting on.   We haven't seen him for an age."

Alice's eye had been travelling down the first column of the outside sheet :   her answer to Doctor Florence was a shrill scream.

" Flo, darling," she cried.   " Talk of the Colonel and he'll appear.   Here, the very first thing I saw. Guess ! "

" Oh, is he dead ? " asked Florence.

" No, guess again."

" Not married ? " she asked.

" Yes.   Listen !   ' On Jan. 4, 1927, at St. Giles's Church, Bolton Spa, by the Reverend Hildebrand Banks, M.A., assisted by the Reverend Eustace Toogood '—yes, it's coming presently—' Colonel Albert Chase late of the Indian Army to Margaret Oxney, widow of the late Septimus Oxney, of Wentworth, Bolton Spa.' "

"My dear, let me look!" cried Florence. "Well, I never! Did you?"

"That settles it," said Alice. "We must go to the Zoo, not this afternoon, but at once, and congratulate him."

They bought a bag of wedding nuts. The Colonel was swinging madly on his rope.

"Probably doing a record," said Alice. "Come, Colonel! Such delicious nuts."

The Colonel paid not the least attention to them, but when he had broken his record, sat and cuddled up to a stout and rather comely lady-ape, who received a few trivial connubialities with marked favour.

"And Mrs. Oxney!" said Alice.

THE END